FAUST

VOLUME ONE

FAUST

VOLUME ONE

BALLANTINE BOOKS
NEW YORK

Faust, Volume 1 is a work of fiction. Names, characters, places, and incidents are the products of the authors' imagination or are used fictitiously. Any resemblance to actual events, locales, or persons, living or dead, is entirely coincidental.

A Del Rey Manga / Kodansha Trade Paperback Original

Faust, Volume 1 copyright © 2003 Kodansha Ltd. All rights reserved.
English translation © 2008 Kodansha Ltd. All rights reserved.

First published in Japan in 2003 by Kodansha Ltd., Tokyo
Publication rights for this English edition arranged through Kodansha Ltd.

All rights reserved.

Published in the United States by Del Rey Books,
an imprint of The Random House Publishing Group,
a division of Random House, Inc., New York.

DEL REY is a registered trademark and the Del Rey colophon is
a trademark of Random House, Inc.

ISBN 978-0-345-50061-8

Printed in the United States of America

www.delreymanga.com

2 4 6 8 9 7 5 3 1

Cover illustration: take

CONTENTS
▲▼▲▼▲

Introduction by Katsushi Ota vii

FICTION AND ESSAYS

xxxHOLiC: ANOTHERHOLiC an excerpt 3
NISIOISIN *original story and illustrations by CLAMP*

Outlandos d'Amour 64
Kouhei Kadono *illustrations by Ueda Hajime*

Drill Hole in My Brain 111
Otaro Maijo *illustrations by the author*

F-sensei's Pocket 181
Otsuichi *illustrations by Takeshi Obata*

The Garden of Sinners: A View from Above an excerpt 246
Kinoku Nasu *illustrations by Takashi Takeuchi (TYPE-MOON)*

H People: An Evolving World 295
Kozy Watanabe *illustrations by TAGRO*

Yabai de Show 301
Ryusui Seiryôin

Yûya Satô's Counseling Session 304
Yûya Satô *illustrations by Icco Sasai*

Tatsuhiko Takimoto's Guru Guru Counseling Session 314
Tatsuhiko Takimoto *illustrations by Chizu Hashii*

Approaching Twenty Years of *Otaku*   325
Kaichiroō Morikawa *illustration by the author*

BONUS FEATURES

The Garden of Sinners: An Interview with Kinoku Nasu and Takashi Takeuchi   331
interview by Katsushi Ota

From Japan to the World, From the World to Japan   347
Yukari Shiina

WELCOME TO FAUST!

▲▽▲▽

Faust: a legendary literary journal that's swept like a fever through the young readers coming of age in the new millennium, changing the face of Japan's literary scene in the blink of an eye. I'm overjoyed to be able to cross the barriers of nation and language to meet with you this very moment. Thank you from the bottom of my heart!

If there's one major problem that everyone has to tackle once in their life, it's that feeling of self-consciousness in early adolescence. *Faust* is a leading-edge publication where you'll see radical portrayals of this theme exploding one after another—an avant-garde crossover in which Japan's manga, anime, and video game–based pop culture collide, tempestlike, with the hottest young writers on the Japanese literary scene.

I've been dealing head-on with many of the shining talents who represent Japan's modern culture since the first issue of *Faust* as well as single-handedly editing it from day one. That makes this anthology everything to me. On every page of *Faust*, you'll find nothing less than 100 percent of the artists'—and my—sincerity, passion, and soul.

The word *Faust* has a special ring to it, and I'm convinced that the feverish excitement it gives off will reach you, too.

KATSUSHI OTA, editor of *Faust*
Translated by Paul Johnson

A NOTE ON READING THIS VOLUME
▲▼▲▼▲

Faust collects the best in cutting-edge Japanese fiction—whether the author's chosen medium is prose or manga.

Japanese books customarily read from right to left. Of necessity, the prose fiction and essays that follow are laid out left to right. However, the manga selections in this volume present a different challenge—to preserve the artist's original vision for his or her artwork. Therefore, in order to respect the creators' vision, the manga selections are presented on the other side of this volume, in their original right-to-left orientation. Please turn the book over to read the manga selections.

FICTION
AND
ESSAYS

▲▽▲▽

xxxHOLiC: ANOTHERHOLiC
Landolt-Ring Aerosol
an excerpt

NISIOISIN
Original story and illustrations by CLAMP

No, ghosts are real. You can see them, touch them, and hear them. But they do not exist. Which is why science ignores them. But to claim they are a fabrication and do not exist because science ignores them is a mistake. Because ghosts are real.

—NATSUHIKO KYŌGOKU, UBUME NO NATSU

This excerpt from the novel, *xxxHOLiC: ANOTHERHOLiC*, represents a collaboration between two creative powerhouses: CLAMP, an internationally renowned collective of four manga artists; and NISIOISIN, one of the most prominent young authors in Japan. The novel will be published in its entirety by Del Rey Manga in October 2008.

xxxHOLiC: ANOTHERHOLiC contains three all-new episodes set in the world originally introduced to readers in

---

*Natsuhiko Kyōgoku Extremely successful author of supernatural mysteries. *Ubume no Natsu* (Summer of the Ubume, Kodansha Ltd., 2003) was his first novel. He is known for very long books containing elaborate philosophical and psychological reinterpretations of Japanese folklore and for a very methodical and exacting approach to writing. He hates it when a sentence runs onto the next page and lays out all his works himself to make sure that never happens, revising the works extensively for each new edition.

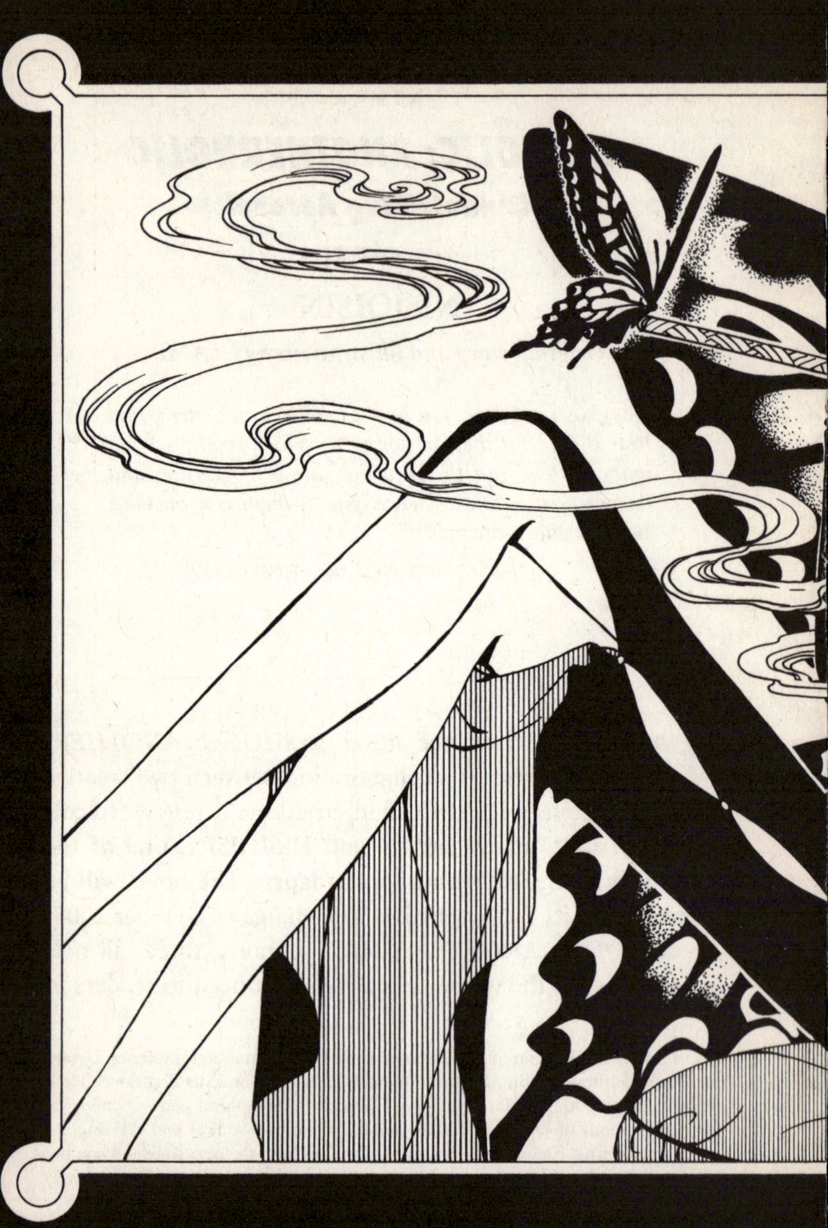

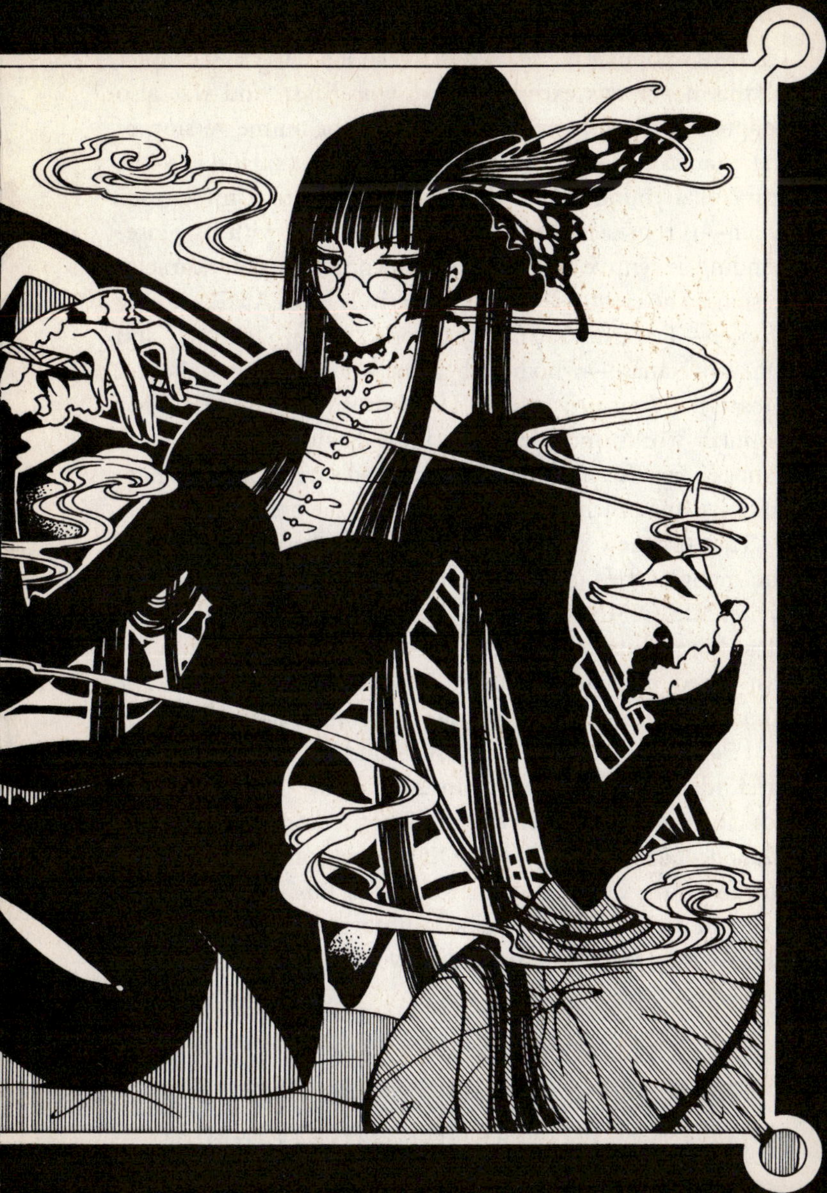

CLAMP's popular manga series, xxxHOLiC. The first chapter of this novel was excerpted in *Comic Faust,* and was also adapted as the seventeenth episode of the anime version of the manga series. The elegantly morbid xxxHOLiC—the story of a young man bound in servitude to a mysterious witch—is representative of the CLAMP style, with its genre-bending, inventive storytelling, and iconic, graceful character designs. The creators, known collectively as CLAMP, are four women—Igarashi Satsuki, Mokona, Nekoi Tsubaki, and Ohkawa Nanase—who have become world famous while still preserving their privacy and a certain mystique. Their other popular works include Cardcaptor Sakura, Chobits, and Tsubasa. For this novel, CLAMP created several all-new illustrations, one of which is reproduced on the preceding pages.

That this new story is more than a mere novelization of the manga series is owed to the outstanding talents of the writer NISIOISIN. Born in 1981, the prolific NISIOISIN has already revolutionized the Japanese literary world with his fast-paced, pop-culture-fueled novels. He debuted with *The Kubikiri Cycle* in 2002, beginning his seminal Zaregoto series, and *Bakemonogatari* was published under Kodansha's popular Kodansha Box imprint. In 2007 came the magnificent conclusion to his twelve-month consecutive serial novel *Katanagatari*—for which NISIOISIN wrote one novel a month for an entire year—also for Kodansha Box. In addition to xxxHOLiC, NISIOISIN tackled another major manga franchise with *Death Note: Another Note: The Los Angeles BB*

An Ubume, according to folklore, is a bird with a woman's head that steals newborn babies. This particular quote posed a bit of a translation problem: the first and last sentences use the word *iru,* which means "to be," while the third and fifth sentences use the noun *exist.* To keep the distinction, I was unable to translate *iru* as "exist." It took quite a while to figure out another way of saying the same thing that kept the connotation and remained true to the context of this quote in the original novel.

Murder Cases, based on Tsugumi Ohba and Takeshi Obata's blockbuster series. *Zaregoto, Book One: The Kubikiri Cycle* will be published in the United States by Del Rey Manga in 2008.

▲▼▲▼▲

——heartless eyes.

My first impression of the black-haired woman, Yûko Ichihara, settled on that phrase.

——frightening eyes.

——cruel eyes.

——bewitching eyes.

——hard eyes.

——eyes that looked at you as though you were less than human.

——eyes that looked at you from the other side.

——eyes that looked right through you.

——eyes that appraised you.

——eyes that measured the world in reverse.

——eyes that denied the way of the world.

That sort of eyes.

Unable to stand having those eyes focused on me, and unable to continue staring back at them, I consciously dropped my gaze.

It settled on the cup of coffee in front of me.

That boy, Kimihiro Watanuki, had made it for me; he had asked if I wanted coffee or tea the moment I sat down, and I had said coffee.

Even though I wanted tea.

I refused milk and sugar.

Even though bitter coffee is undrinkable.

The same coffee sat in front of her. She had said nothing except to give me her name, just sat there staring at me. But I was sure that Ichihara-san had wanted to drink coffee and did not require either milk or sugar.

Steam rose from the black liquid.

Pitch-black liquid.

Ooh . . .

If I flung this liquid at her, how would her expression change? What kind of eyes would look at me then?

I knew I should not do that.

She would be angry—and I had only just met her.

I was here only because Watanuki-kun had been nice enough to bring me. I wasn't sure if she could provide counseling or what, but there was absolutely no connection between me and Ichihara-san. . . .

"Call me Yûko," she said.

Just as my fingers had touched the cup's handle, absently seeking a way to fill the silence, Ichihara-san corrected me, even though I had never said her name aloud.

"And—that thing you were about to do? Don't," she snapped.

I looked up, surprised.

Her eyes were the same.

Still staring fixedly at me.

Then Yûko Ichihara smiled faintly. "Or perhaps . . . this way of putting things would work better with you, Nurie Kushimura-san.

"Go ahead. I dare you."

▼▲▼

There are are a great many strange things in the world.

But no matter how odd . . .

How incredible something may be . . .

If a human does not touch it...
If a human does not see it...
If a human is not involved with it...

It is simply something that happened.
Simply a matter that will fade with time.

Humans.
Mankind.
Homo sapiens.

Humans are the most profoundly mysterious living things in the world!

Kimihiro Watanuki was perceptive.
Not in the sense that he possessed any superhuman penetrative insight. He did not have a knack for reading personality and character and never said anything along the lines of "He might act thuggish, but he'll grow into a strong leader eventually. But that may well mean he becomes a powerful enemy." Or "You can trust her. The rough way she talks is just a pose, and deep down she's really very docile. It would help if she could learn to forgive herself."
He was not insightful, merely perceptive.
He did not see people but spirits.
Spirits: things that are always around but cannot normally be seen.
Things not of this world.
Things that, perhaps, were not meant to be seen.
But Kimihiro Watanuki could see them clearly.
This was a problem for him.
It was not an ability, simply a faculty, innate and not acquired, resulting not from conscious thought but from the flow of blood through his body. It was a vision that was al-

ways with him—a problem that nothing he did would ever solve. Seeing alone was bad enough, but there were also spirits that came to him, drawn by his blood, which always caused an unholy mess.

A mess he had to clean up.

He had done everything he could, but there had never been anything he could do in the first place. It would have made sense just to give up, and that might well have been the best thing he could do. But even so, even in full knowledge of that, there was not a day when he didn't wish.

If only he couldn't see.

That wish went through his head every day.

But it was less a wish than a prayer.

———

A few months ago, someone had promised to grant his wish.

———

"This has got to be a joke," Kimihiro Watanuki muttered. No, the way he spit out the words was closer to a snarl, and his shoulders were shaking with rage. He was standing in front of the coin lockers outside the gates of JR Glass Station, about ten minutes' train ride east of the station closest to his high school, Cross Private School. The people around him had collectively decided to go out of their way to avoid his vicinity.

He was holding a letter in his hand.

A very short letter.

Fake glasses (not an eyepatch).

Perhaps more of a memo than a letter.

---

*JR Glass Station Not a real station. NISIOISIN actually uses the kanji for *glass* (or *Gurasu—glass* being a word imported back when they were still creating kanji readings for foreign words). In Japan, the *xxxHOLiC* novel and NISIOISIN's *Death Note* novel were published at the same time, and there is also a mention of a Glass Station in Los Angeles in the *Death Note* novel.

Watanuki glanced up again at the locker in front of him: number 45.

The memo had been inside the locker.

"She could have just said this! Why does she always have to be so roundabout—and what the hell does 'Fake glasses (not an eyepatch)' mean? Nobody in the universe would mix those two things up! Oh, wait, she's talking about Date Masamune, who founded that place where they make the zunda mochi ... Sendai. Aggh! That's such a reach I can't even think of a comeback!"

It was evening, rush hour.

Kimihiro Watanuki's very audible fury directed at someone who was not even there sent people moving swiftly away from him like an ebb tide, but he was in no mood to notice or care.

The day before, his employer had given him a key. The number 45 was inscribed on the key—the key to this locker. His employer—although besides Watanuki she oversaw only a pair of girls who may or may not have qualified as employees and a sort of pet thing like a black yukimi daifuku—had given him no details or instructions beyond, "Go open that door for me."

"All that work I put into figuring out that this key came from the lockers outside Glass Station, and all I find is another order!? I'm too old to think this crap is fun!"

No amount of screaming in rage could heal the frustration.

---

*Date Masamune Samurai, founder of the city of Sendai. Sendai—capital of Miyabe Prefecture—is famous for a snack called zunda mochi, which appears to consist of beaten rice (mochi) and green soybeans. Date was a skilled tactician who had only one eye; he was called the one-eyed dragon because of this. The rather tenuous connection to fake glasses comes from the word *Date,* which means "dandy" but when combined with the word for glasses (*megane*) becomes fake glasses. Date Megane and Date Masamune are not very easy to confuse, but the Date part does have the same kanji.

*Yukimi daifuku Ice cream wrapped in mochi.

All of his effort boiled down to his employer ordering him to find a pair of fake glasses. He did not venture to dream that things would end with the acquisition of said phony spectacles; that quest would soon be followed by some new order, which would in turn be followed by another and another....

"She's just toying with me.... This has absolutely nothing to do with my actual job."

His shoulders stopped shaking, and he slumped.

He appeared to have come to terms with it.

Indeed, no matter how absurd, no matter how obviously the request served her own amusement, as long as the orders came from his employer—Yûko Ichihara—Watanuki had no choice but to obey.

Absolute obedience.

Why? Because it was a fair price.

The price he had to pay before his eyes would stop seeing.

"Hahhh..."

Yûko Ichihara's shop, where Kimihiro Watanuki worked, was a shop that could make wishes come true. As long as one paid a reasonable price, no matter how extravagant or fantastic the wish—even if you wished to not see spirits, to not have blood that attracted spirits—this shop could fulfill your request.

A shop that granted wishes.

"Except the way she's working me, it might just be faster to go out collecting dragonballs. Does she actually mean to grant my wish?"

Watanuki had worked for Yûko for several months now and was quite sure that she had the ability to grant wishes in return for that fair price. He was well aware of the extent of her power.

But he had his doubts about her intentions.

"As much as she goes on about fair prices, she can't possibly expect me to work for free . . . but what does she want with fake glasses? She gonna wear them? Yûko-san in fake glasses? Or is there some massive Warashibe Chôja–style success lurking in my future? Will I end up rich? Gosh, what an exciting prospect. Damn it. Anyway . . ."

He could not stand here fuming forever.

With that in mind, Watanuki forced himself to think. He had never bought a pair of fake glasses before, or even entertained a fleeting desire to do so, and literally had no idea where he could purchase such a thing. "Fake" meant that the lenses were just glass, so they could hardly be as expensive as functional spectacles. If she wanted sunglasses, he was sure the message would have said as much, so he should avoid tinted lenses. Which meant, in short—

"I don't know this area well, but surely there's one around. They would have it."

—the obvious first stop.

A hundred-yen shop.

There was one in every area with a certain level of population, and they generally carried quite a wide selection of products, all of which cost only a hundred yen. Since he had no idea where Yûko's demands would take him next, it seemed prudent to keep expenses to an absolute minimum, which a hundred yen certainly was.

He left Glass Station, looking for a hundred-yen shop.

Luckily, he found one just across the street. He entered the shop and looked around. There were any number of frames so bizarre Watanuki was sure no one in the country would ever dream of wearing them, but among them he found what he was looking for.

"They've got glasses for old people, too. . . . Quite a time we live in. Well . . . Should probably get one that doesn't look too cheap. . . . Hmm, guess there are limits to what you can get for a hundred yen. Red feels right, somehow. . . ."

The purchase, with tax, came to 105 yen. He was out of change and had to pay with a thousand-yen bill, which left him carrying around a fistful of coins. Watanuki always felt slightly foolish whenever he got a lot of change.

He left the shop and waited. For his next orders.

He had the fake glasses, completing the mission provided by the locker. Watanuki waited to see just how his next orders would arrive, uncharacteristically excited.

From behind? From the sky? From underground? Or directly into his head, supersonically . . . ?

Nothing.

Apparently, the fake glasses completed Yûko's requests for the day.

"Is that it? I'm never gonna be rich? Such a shame," he said softly, well aware of how selfish a line of thought that was. Watanuki sighed deeply. It was already late, and he had to deliver the fake glasses to Yûko and then make her dinner before he could get off work. How much had he earned toward his wish that day? He felt like an RPG character wandering aimlessly around the dungeon, trying to raise his level from 98 to 99. A living example of the phrase "getting nowhere."

"Wonder if she'd make me a stamp card. . . . Then at least I'd have some idea of how much progress I'm making."

Or was his goal so far off that seeing it was more depressing than not seeing it? It was said that even the longest journey begins with a single step, but if you counted each of those steps, nearly everyone would give up long before they completed the journey.

What he needed to think about right now was the possibility that this had all been an elaborate practical joke on Yûko-san's part, and that he had fallen for it and then slid quite some distance. He needed to decide just what kind of reaction he should display once he was back at the shop. The joke was a bad one and the timing of it so off that this was a task rather more difficult than tracking down "Date Masamune's eyepatch."

He headed for the crosswalk.

The light was red.

Cars were zipping by, so, naturally, Watanuki stopped. Four or five other people were waiting for the light to change as well.

"Mm?"

One of them caught his attention.

She was biting her lower lip . . .

. . . looking very, very desperate.

But that was not what drew Watanuki's eye. Not that at all.

She was a rather petite woman, and on her thin shoulder . . .

———

. . . something.

———

By the time he noticed, it was too late.

Too late to do anything.

The woman flung herself out into traffic.

▼▲▼

Oh.

I did it again.

When I woke up in the hospital bed, I plunged instantly into a torturous well of self-loathing. Tomorrow was a very important day— No, I'd been out too long. Today.

Today was a very important day.

What was I doing in a hospital bed?

I looked out the window.

I couldn't see from here.

But right now, at work, Hyôdô-kun must be doing the new project presentation, the one I was supposed to do, the one I should have been doing. That was what we had planned in case of an emergency, an emergency that should never have come to pass.

I'd caused problems for them all again.

We had all worked so hard to get that plan ready.... I knew Hyôdô-kun would do a good job covering for me, but that wasn't the point.

I had done it again.

Let myself do it—do what I knew I should not do.

Just as I had ever since I was a child.

I longed to violate taboos.

According to the nurse, I had been waiting at a crosswalk, then suddenly jumped out into traffic. I had no memories of the accident—but even without those memories, I knew myself.

I had jumped out into traffic at a red light. I had done the same thing, or other very similar things, over and over, my whole life.

Fortunately, this time I had got off with a fracture of my left arm. Probably because I'd been hit by a scooter.

But if it had not been a scooter, I would have died.

Maybe that would have been better. Frankly, the fact that I had survived this long was miraculous. The world's most pointless miracle.

When I was in elementary school, I jumped out the classroom window. Like the main character in that famous novel. For that matter, I had touched blades to my fingers more than a few times. As an adolescent, I'd tried my hand at cutting my wrist, though only once.

But that once might have been enough.

---

*Famous novel Soseki Natsume's classic *Botchan*. The main character jumped out of the classroom window at the beginning of the story.

I might have died.

People asked me, "Why did you do that?"

They scolded me. "You shouldn't do things like that!"

But were they right?

Everyone had feelings like mine occasionally. Like the urge to pull the fire alarm in the school hallway (I had done so countless times before graduating high school) or the urge to leap in front of the train as it pulled into the station, wind gusting, buzzer sounding (I always had to fight myself). If you climb up somewhere high, do you never wonder what it would be like to jump off? (I'm battling those feelings before I even start to climb.)

Everyone felt like that sometimes, some more than others.

No exceptions.

I just felt like that more than most.

My urges were abundant and vast.

I knew that—I was very, very aware of that—but even knowing that, even aware of that, there was nothing I could do about it, which was exactly why I called such feelings urges.

Urges.

Urges, destructive urges.

To put it simply, it was the commonplace idea of the button that says Don't Push taken to extremes. How many people could honestly say they would not push that button?

As for me . . .

I promise I would push it.

Junior high entrance exams.

The day of the test for a famous private school I'd been assured I would be able to pass—I feigned illness and spent the day lying in bed at home. High school entrance exams were the same. I ended up at ordinary public schools for both junior and senior high. If someone had asked me why I needed to pretend I was sick, the only thing I could have said was that

I wanted to see what would happen if you got sick on such an important day.

When it came time to go to college, I deliberately didn't write my name on the application for my first-choice school.... No, maybe I did write it, but either way, I ended up at my safety school.

For the same reason.

Yes. Yes, I know.

The fact that I have managed to survive to the age of twenty-seven cannot be described by any word except *miraculous*. Presumably my reason barely managed to restrain my emotions—but that reason is starting to get a little threadbare. The conflict between the two is swiftly reaching its limit.

While I'd caused a lot of problems for myself, I had managed to avoid any massive failures at work so far. And while it will sound like I'm bragging, if this presentation had been a success, it would undoubtedly have opened the door to a promotion.

Instead, I had given that chance to my subordinate. That interpretation of my behavior makes it a lot easier for me to take. It always felt comfortable to coddle myself. It was my left arm I'd fractured, so my injury wouldn't be that big a problem at work; it was Friday, and I'd probably be back at work next week.

But that thought brought them back again.

Brought back the urges.

What if?

What if next week I did not go back to work, if I never went to work again?

Oh, that would be awful.

That plan involved things that only I could do. Even if Hyôdô-kun nailed the presentation, the plan itself would probably be squashed. And the other members of my group would pay the price; no one would be talking about promotion anymore.

Did I care?

It's not as though this company had been my first choice.

It was my second.

At the interview for my first choice, I had tripped and fallen down—I can still remember the disgusted looks the interviewers gave me. But they had never suspected that I had fallen over deliberately.

So . . .

. . . could I just stop going to work?

Oh no.

No, stop thinking about it.

I didn't want to do that.

I didn't.

I didn't. I didn't. I didn't. I didn't. I didn't. I didn't. I didn't. I didn't. I didn't. I didn't. I didn't. I didn't. I didn't. I didn't. I didn't. I didn't. I didn't.

I didn't—so I couldn't let myself.

I hadn't let myself screw up at work—that much was true.

But then I remembered. . . .

When was that? Just after I started?

I put an important document through the shredder.

Deliberately, of course.

Disguised as a coincidence, so no one would know.

Because of that, everyone in the department had barely slept for a week—but we had managed to pull through.

It had been an important document but not a critical one.

So it didn't count.

Neither did this event.

I would recover. I could make it up to everyone.

I could.

But then the second wave hit me.

What if?

When it was time for me to apologize, I insisted I'd done nothing wrong and berated them all . . . what would they do then?

They were so nice.

How would they look at me?

Oh, I wanted to do that.

Urges like that possessed me.

They always had.

But no more.

Let me be clear: I was neither self-destructive nor suicidal. That much I was sure of. I could deny that with confidence. I had as much reason to crave death or danger as anyone else—a love for roller coasters, nothing more than ordinary curiosity.

I just had these urges.

To violate taboos.

To do things I really shouldn't do.

There were all kinds of things that should matter more to me than those feelings—relationships, work, so many other things I should care about more—but here I was wondering what would happen if I jumped out the window of my hospital room.

They'd be mad at me.

I might even die.

But.

But that's why I wanted to.

I wanted to push the button marked Don't Push.

"Why did you do that?"

"You shouldn't do things like that!"

That's why I wanted to.

Why? Because I wanted to.

That's all.

It had been a scooter, so I was still alive, and it was no big deal, but if it had been a dump truck, there was no way I could have survived.

It was a miracle that I was alive.

So I thought . . .

Maybe things would be better if I was dead.

But if I died, what would everyone do?

I managed to trample down the urge to jump out the window and took a deep breath, preparing myself to fight the next urge.

There was a knock on the door, and a voice called out, "Kushimura-san! Can I come in?"

Must be the nurse.

I said sure.

A moment later, the door opened and the nurse came in, in her pink uniform . . . but she was not alone.

There was someone with her.

A boy in a school uniform, with glasses on.

I had seen him before.

But where?

He said his name was Kimihiro Watanuki.

▼▲▼

"Uh-huh. I see," the black-haired woman said ominously. "So that's why you skipped out on work without permission or even a phone call, and that's why you came to work late today without permission or even a phone call." Wreaths of smoke curled from her pipe, and her left hand toyed with the fake glasses Watanuki had purchased the day before for 105 yen (tax included).

Yûko Ichihara.

The owner of the shop that could grant any wish.

Owner, operator, whatever you wanted to call her, she was the one who employed Kimihiro Watanuki and who would, in the future, be his salvation. If she wasn't, he was in trouble.

Some people called her the Dimension Witch, but he wasn't sure why. Her age and history were a mystery, and she would not even tell him her blood type, let alone her birthday. Even her name, Yûko Ichihara, was fake. Watanuki knew it was fake because she had told him as much when they first met, no more than five seconds after giving her name. The most brazen fake name around. Presumably her real name was something much more obviously sinister.

Yûko smirked. "Such a lot of bother."

"Nah. It was nothing. But did you need those glasses for something?"

"Not really," she said.

Innocently.

It really had been just a joke. . . .

"Think of it as a scavenger hunt."

"So it was a scavenger hunt instead of a treasure hunt? Not a whole lot of difference. And I would greatly prefer if you would not waste my time on either. Just leads to trouble, frankly."

"But you can hardly say it was boring. For all your complaints, you enjoyed it. The moment you opened the locker, you must have thought, 'Seriously? Can this possibly be true?' "

"I did."

But probably not in the sense she meant it.

"That kind of thing might be the next big trend."

"Except I am not a high school girl."

"Oh, how boring of you," she said, sounding disappointed.

She would have preferred him as a girl?

"Personally, I'd welcome an apology for being forced to participate in your pointless little game."

"Quite an attitude. You want an apology? There is nothing more pathetic than asking for an apology. Watanuki, I thought better of you."

"Petulantly trying to change the subject seems equally pathetic. . . ."

"Nothing in this world is devoid of meaning, Watanuki. Even games," Yûko said decisively. She pointed her pipe at Watanuki. "How was she?"

"Who? You mean the girl I saw at the hospital?"

Yesterday.

While he stood at the crosswalk, on his way home after successfully purchasing the fake spectacles in the hundred-yen shop near JR Glass Station, a woman had suddenly thrown herself into traffic.

Watanuki had called the ambulance.

He had also gone with her to the hospital and contacted her family.

And today, after school, before coming to work at the shop that granted wishes, he had bought flowers and gone to see Nurie Kushimura in the hospital.

As a result of which . . .

He had earned black marks for skipping work and arriving late.

But Yûko Ichihara did not seem the type to be particularly put out by something like that. Indeed, she seemed more likely to use the fact that Watanuki had not even bothered thinking up a good excuse for his behavior as leverage.

But now?

She asked about the woman.

"Of course, the girl at the hospital. Watanuki, you said there was something on her shoulder."

"Yeah . . . but I might just have been seeing things. I mean, I was looking out of the corner of my eye—"

"But," Yûko interrupted, "you thought you 'saw' it."

He had.

"Uh, but . . . it was just a glimpse, that's all. It might have been something sewn on her shoulder bag that reflected the streetlights into my eye. . . ."

"But," Yûko said again, "you don't think it was."

He did not.

"That's why you went to see her today. That's why you talked to her."

That was true, but how she could be so sure was beyond him.

Watanuki was extremely undecided about whether he should relate the contents of that conversation to Yûko. If this were the kind of mystery novel found in every home—"A chance encounter involves Watson in a most troubling affair. Whereupon gallant Holmes arrives to cut through all complications and solve the matter with alacrity"—consulting Yûko would be faster, but this was precisely the kind of problem he did not want to bring to her attention.

Putting aside the comparison to Holmes, Yûko Ichihara was fundamentally not reliable.

And even if you chose to rely on her . . . you needed to pay a fair price.

And Yûko could be outright mean when it came to that.

The word *volunteer* was not in her dictionary.

Over the last few months Watanuki had not once borne witness to the sight of Yûko doing anything without payment. Nothing available in this shop was ever for free.

She always exacted payment, to the point of heartlessness.

That went for Watanuki . . .

. . . and it would go for the woman as well.

Watanuki was currently carrying out his own payment,

and occasionally, very occasionally, he wondered: even if his wish was granted, what she took in return was of equal value, and in the end . . . did it really make a difference whether the wish was granted or not?

His eyes.

The eyes that saw spirits.

When he had paid the price, and his eyes could no longer see . . . how much would he have lost in return?

The idea scared him.

So he always pushed it away.

Tried not to think about it.

But when it came to other people—that was different. Kimihiro Watanuki's feeling was that introducing people with wishes to Yûko Ichihara was something he absolutely should not do.

Not ever.

"Tell me about it, Watanuki. If this were Doraemon, I would be Doraemon, see?"

"If you're Doraemon, then mentioning the name of the show is redundant."

"And you, Watanuki, are Sewashi-kun."

"Not Nobita-kun!?"

"Are you Nobita-kun?"

"No . . . no, I'm not, but—"

"Then you must be Sewashi-kun."

"I have to be one or the other?"

An extremely limited selection.

He couldn't even remember what kind of character Sewashi-kun was.

**Doraemon* A very famous children's manga and anime. The title character is a robot cat from the future, with items that can do almost anything hidden in his fourth-dimensional pocket. The main character, Nobita, is a rather helpless boy, prone to crying. Sewashi is Nobita's great-great-grandson, the man who sends Doraemon into the past. He appears only in the first few stories.

And hijacking the analogy—Yûko Ichihara was about as far from a character that had become a national icon as it was possible to be. Her position was much closer to that of the salesman wearing a funereal suit in another work by the same author. But as Yûko's employee, he could hardly point this out. To his frequent regret, it was vividly clear which of them controlled the other, and beyond that, the situation he found himself in now was entirely the result of his own careless failure to call the shop before going to the hospital earlier that day. "You smell like flowers, Watanuki," Yûko said, driving him even further into the corner. "You should know better than to bring such heavily scented flowers to a hospital."

"Nah, that's not . . ."

"Oh? Not what?" Yûko purred, looking extremely confident. As if she hardly needed Watanuki to explain.

As if she already knew everything.

But if he pointed that out, she would inevitably say something frustratingly Zen. Such as, "If you believe I know, then I probably do, but if not, I don't." She might not be deliberately attempting to cover the issue in smoke, but Watanuki would be coughing anyway.

Not a pleasant sensation.

So he just answered her question.

"Um, so . . . this woman's name was Nurie Kushimura. In her late twenties, I think. *Kushi* is comb," he said, idly wondering whether Yûko actually needed him to explain the kanji but deciding that it was the normal thing to do. "*Mura* is village, and her first name is paint and picture."

---

*Salesman in a suit Fukuzo Moguro, the main character of *Warau Salesman* (Smiling Salesman) by Fujiko Fujio, who always wears a black suit. The story is famous for its cynicism and black humor and would never have been suitable for children. Watanuki associates Moguro's mean and dark character with Yûko's.

*Nurie Kushimura NISIOISIN is famous for creating extremely odd names, and "Nurie Kushimura" is no exception.

"Hmm . . . Is that her real name?"

"That's what was written on her hospital bed, so I assume so. Those charts are based on your proof of insurance."

"I see. Nurie Kushimura. What's her birthday?"

"I don't know."

"I see." Watanuki had been prepared for a scathing remark, but Yûko just nodded. "So, why is it that you smell of flowers? Were you randomly embraced by a woman wearing far too much perfume?"

"Of course not."

"I guessed as much. Then I shall assume that you have just begun wearing perfume."

"Please don't."

"Then why?"

"Um . . . well, when I gave her the flowers . . . Kushimura-san, um . . . hit me with them," Watanuki admitted reluctantly.

"My!" Yûko exclaimed, as if she could not be happier. Her target acquired.

"Not many people have the privilege of being beaten with a bouquet when they come for a hospital visit. Only someone as hapless as you, Watanuki."

"Hapless? Since when am I hapless?"

"You always were. I'm amazed you can even ask without blushing. If we removed the haplessness from you, what would remain? A Watanuki who is not hapless is like a Watanuki who was not born on April first."

"Like the vast majority of people named Watanuki?"

"I didn't mean them."

"Sigh . . . okay."

He knew she hadn't.

"In that case, Watanuki, why did she do that to you? Did you do something to make her mad? Make a silly joke, like 'Since this hospital was founded, not one patient has ever left alive?'"

"My life has not become so devoid of meaning that I would find such bizarre black humor amusing."

"Hmm. Then why?"

"Well . . . that is the weird part. Apparently . . . there was no reason."

"No reason."

Hit a visitor with flowers.

For no reason.

"Yes. After she hit me with the flowers, Kushimura-san apologized profusely. She said she didn't mean to do it, that she knew it was wrong."

A meaningful silence from Yûko.

She did not smile.

He'd seen that look before. It never failed to make him feel small.

Trying to shake off that feeling, he cleared his throat. "So I talked to her a little more, and it sounds like she's been that way for a while. Habitually doing things she knows she shouldn't do. She insists it isn't self-destructive, but I found that hard to believe."

A button marked Don't Push.

If she saw one . . . she would absolutely push it.

That was why she had jumped out into traffic the day before. It had meant that she would miss a major event at work, one that could lead to a promotion. That knowledge had led her to it.

Kimihiro Watanuki related everything Nurie Kushimura had told him. But she had been very flustered after smacking him with the flowers, and he was forced to summarize for coherency's sake. He was getting pretty good at that sort of thing.

Essentially . . .

. . . she violated taboos.

"It felt kind of like she is deliberately, intentionally wrecking her own life. Ever since she was a child. She calls it her 'urges'—which is at least the extent to which she is aware of herself. I couldn't begin to imagine how strong they really are. What do you make of it, Yûko-san? Are there any spirits that can do that to people?"

Just before she jumped into traffic.

The thing he'd seen on her shoulder.

What . . . was it?

"There are," Yûko said. "There are, or should I say, there is such a thing. But that said . . ."

"That said?"

"Mm . . . no, well . . . I see."

She almost never hesitated like that.

What could it mean?

"Watanuki."

"What?"

"I'd like some flowing somen."

". . . Huh?" He blinked.

"I want some flowing somen. Prepare it."

"Uh, um . . . now?"

"Yes. For dinner."

"Dinner . . . If you eat that for dinner at this time of year, it'll make the heat worse."

Which wasn't the point.

Kimihiro Watanuki was remarkably skilled at cooking and all kinds of housework. But flowing somen required an incredible amount of preparation. It was hardly the sort of thing that could be whipped up on short notice—out of the question.

"It shouldn't take that long. Just go cut a few stalks of bamboo grass on a nearby mountain."

**Flowing somen* See the notes for manga volume 7. Bamboo grass (*sasa*) is simply a young bamboo tree (*take*).

"Or I could get a bamboo tree, so we could use it for Tanabata."

"My, my, Watanuki. So uneducated. Bamboo grass and bamboo have no clear difference, scientifically speaking. Much like eagles and hawks."

"Eagles and hawks aren't different?"

"Eagles are bigger than hawks. The names were given based on appearance, but they are actually the same thing."

"But even so, you couldn't use bamboo grass for flowing somen."

"You could if you tried."

"You couldn't, even if you tried." You could only send a couple of noodles at a time, making the entire process even more involved.

"But I want to eat flowing somen. I want to eat it so, so bad! My body demands it!"

"Who are you, Yang Guifei? If you really insist, I might be able to get it ready for lunch tomorrow, Yûko-san. It's a Saturday, and that should be enough time for me to borrow some tools from friends."

"Knowing exactly what to do, despite all your complaints, is what makes Watanuki Watanuki."

This proof of identity he found particularly ominous. If a shape-changing enemy appeared, they would have to prove which of them was the real Kimihiro Watanuki based on each one's ability to acquire the implements for preparing flowing somen. . . .

Tanabata is a summer festival during which people often write wishes on pieces of paper before tying them to trees.

Yang Guifei Known in Japan as Youkihi. One of the four beauties of ancient China, she was the concubine of Tang dynasty emperor Xuanzong. She was known for outrageous culinary demands and had an entire network of horsemen set up for no other reason than to bring her lychee. She apparently hung herself after her family was blamed for a rebellion, but there are legends in Japan that she escaped there instead.

Which would suck.

"Lunch tomorrow... That will try my patience. If I am forced to eat something besides flowing somen today, I may well die."

"Glad to hear it.... Pretend I didn't say that."

"Mm-hmm."

"Anyway, tonight's menu is already set. We're having curry soup. You told me to make that, so I picked up the ingredients on the way here from the hospital—"

"Watanuki."

Then...

... Yûko asked the question.

"Can you understand the feelings of people who are unable to accept everyday happiness?"

"Huh?"

"For example... if someone won three hundred million yen in the lottery but never claimed the prize... could you understand their feelings?"

"Umm... no, not really."

If you win the lottery, you take the money.

Stands to reason.

"I mean... that's what you would call a 'fair price,' isn't it?" he said.

"It is. The airs you give yourself are most unpleasant, but you are absolutely correct. Let me try another example. Imagine Himawari-chan tells Watanuki she loves him. What would you do?"

"Wh-what would I...?"

Himawari-chan was Himawari Kunogi, Kimihiro Watanuki's classmate at Cross Private School.

A very, very cute girl.

"No, I mean... Yûko-san, that would... Out of the blue like that I just can't..."

"Oh? You'd turn her down?"

"God no! O-obviously, I'd be thrilled!"

"Mm." Yûko nodded, narrowing her eyes. "That is because you are capable of accepting happiness."

"Happiness?"

"That's why you don't understand how she feels."

". . . . ."

"How Nurie Kushimura feels."

That . . . was true.

Watanuki had been able to understand the facts of what Nurie Kushimura had told him, but . . . if he were honest, none of it made any sense to him.

He did not understand her.

He even found her unsettling.

Self-destruction, self-destructive tendencies, self-inflicted injuries.

For no reason at all—or simply to violate taboos.

"She can't . . . accept happiness."

Was that feeling even human?

He wasn't completely immune to the impulse to do things that were forbidden; as she said, everyone could understand the desire to push the button marked Don't Push.

But . . . rejecting happiness was different.

Put another way, it was like deliberately throwing yourself into unhappiness.

Flinging yourself into oncoming traffic.

Telling someone you love that you hate them.

Telling someone you hate that you love them.

Behaving in such a way . . .

. . . was not normal.

It was not what humans did.

Which meant . . . spirits.

At this point, Yûko-san peeled herself away from the sofa,

where she had been sprawled regally, and placed her pipe aside.

And . . .

Brushed her long hair back so she could put the fake glasses on.

They were cheap things, only 105 yen, but . . .

When Yûko Ichihara wore them, they were incredibly becoming.

"Very well. Watanuki, bring her to me."

"Huh? Who?"

"That woman. Bring her here."

Here.

To the shop that granted wishes.

"Er . . . no, but she's still in the hospital. . . ."

"But she's not seriously injured. Just a fracture in one arm. There shouldn't be a problem with her slipping out for an hour."

"Well . . ."

She was right.

Still, he wasn't sure.

After all . . . it would require a payment.

"Whether you bring her or not, the results will be the same. My shop is everywhere and nowhere. If there is a thread leading here, anyone can enter from anywhere, and if they have entered, then they have sufficient hitsuzen to have done so."

". . . Hitsuzen."

"Hitsuzen," she said again. "If this one succumbed to her 'urges' in front of you, then that is a thread, that is hitsuzen. If you don't bring her here, I will simply have to go to her."

"More pushy sales?"

"Hitsuzen!" Yûko answered smoothly. "If you ever say that again, I will halve your wages. Do you hear me?"

"Yes, but if you did that, I would definitely quit."

"Oh dear. If you quit, I will have no idea what to eat anymore. Let me withdraw it. If you press the point any further, I will turn you into a pressed flower."

A pressed flower?

Would she flatten him between the pages of a book?

"I'd rather you halved my wages."

"Oh? I shall remember that. At any rate, this case should be a good experience for you."

"A good experience?"

"Yes."

"You mean . . ."

A case like this?

What kind of case was it?

"Watanuki, surely you haven't forgotten why you're working here?" she said, taking off the glasses. She came over to Watanuki and put them in his hand.

He wondered why.

"Put them away somewhere," she said airily.

Done playing with them already?

He'd spent more on train fare than on the glasses. This just drove home what a waste of effort it had been.

What was he working here for?

"Right. Let's have that curry soup," Yûko said.

With an innocent grin.

▼▲▼

I couldn't accept happiness?

Watanuki had hesitantly asked me whether this was so.

"Happiness?" The question flustered me.

Not because I didn't know what he meant but because those words had gone right to the source of me.

---

*Pressed flower Not as much a non sequitur as it might seem. The term for "pushy sales" is *oshi-uri,* while "pressed flower" is *oshibana.* The first character is the same in both phrases.

They were . . .

. . . too accurate.

"Th-that's just . . . so sudden. I . . ." I found myself babbling, trying to cover.

"Yeah . . ." Watanuki didn't seem very confident in what he himself had said. He scratched his head awkwardly, nodding.

Watching me.

Or, no . . .

. . . watching my shoulder.

Weird. It was as if . . . he could see something.

Like he was trying to see something.

Was something there?

I glanced down at my shoulder . . . but, of course, there was nothing there. How could there be? How could there be anything on my shoulder without me knowing?

On my shoulder . . .

Was it the left or the right shoulder that ghosts attached themselves to?

Yeah, right.

"I just meant . . . a normal life, normal happiness. . . . Can you accept that as it comes to you?"

Watanuki-kun tried explaining it a different way. But he was saying the same thing—like a junior high school student whose class presentation consisted only of repeating the contents of a book he'd borrowed from the library. He said the words without knowing what they meant.

Words he'd been given by someone else.

I thought.

". . . Yes," I said, nodding.

The day before . . .

This boy, Kimihiro Watanuki, had come to visit. Apparently he had been standing behind me when I jumped out into traffic. He was there for shopping or work or both.

That's probably why he looked familiar. Such an adorable face that it had stayed with me. I remembered hardly anything leading up to the accident, but I did remember him; human memory is the strangest thing.

But he was quite a busybody.

He had called an ambulance . . . which was, well, normal enough; doing that was increasingly rare these days but not out of the question. But for a complete stranger, a random passerby, to be concerned enough to come visit with flowers in hand was sort of alarming.

Was he just being nice?

Or was he born that way?

I would never have done anything like that. At most, after being hit by a car, I might have taken a picture of myself with my cell phone camera and sent it around to my friends.

Mean as that would be.

After all, I would have deserved it.

I was the one who had jumped out into traffic.

Even though I knew I would get run over.

I knew that perfectly well.

Which meant he was nice.

Alarmingly nice.

What drove Watanuki-kun to involve himself, of his own free will, with someone who was obviously bad news? With someone like me? When he had visited yesterday, I had merely thought he was unusually nice, but . . . here he was again. Despite the way I had treated him, he had come a second time.

Sure, I had apologized, and Watanuki-kun had forgiven me.

Was he a masochist?

He did appear to be a rather unfortunate boy. Unlucky in love, very few friends, bullied by his boss . . . If all that were true, it might explain the look in his eyes.

"Weird... I feel like someone is thinking very rude thoughts about me. Must be Yûko-san," Watanuki muttered, looking around.

Good instincts.

But who was Yûko-san?

"Or maybe Dômeki? Curse you, Dômeki! Ahem... Anyway. Kushimura-san, yesterday you told me quite a lot of things that made me think, and the more I thought about it... it all just seems very odd."

Odd.

She knew that. Without him pointing it out.

"So... don't you want to do something about it?" He looked at me.

"Do...?"

"I mean, it's not good for you. This time you were lucky enough to get off with a fracture, but if you keep doing this sort of thing..."

"Keep doing like I've been doing? Walking hand in hand with those inexplicable, inarguable urges? It baffles me, too. A complete mystery. Do I have no interest in my own happiness? That might well be true. I've never... been very aggressive in the pursuit of happiness."

Apparently the pursuit of happiness was a right everyone in Japan possessed, guaranteed to us in the constitution. Which meant I was waiving that right. And not only waiving it—trampling it.

Even denying my own right to life.

Even though I didn't want to die.

"Wanting to do things you're told not to do... a very childish way of putting it, but that very childishness makes it easy to understand. It's the simplest way I can explain it. Watanuki-kun, haven't you felt like that yourself? Even at your age?"

"Well... I guess I understand, but when I hear you

talk . . . I find it hard to believe what you feel is just an extension of what I do. To me it feels like you jumped the tracks ages back."

Jumped the tracks.

This time it was his own words; there was a real confidence to them. And once again . . . he was right.

Getting right to the root of the matter.

"I must seem so ugly," I said.

". . . Ugly?"

"I'm so different from . . . normal people. It must make them sick to look at me."

". . . Sick."

"Yes. Just like you said, Watanuki-kun. I was trying to generalize the problem by saying that everyone has the urges I do . . . but that's not really true."

I knew that.

I'd insisted I was normal, perfectly normal, to the point of genuine weirdness—which had just made my condition worse. I had been so reluctant to let go of that connection to normal, to what was ordinary.

No matter how far from the tracks I got, I wanted to believe our roots were the same.

Finally I said, "Not being able to accept happiness . . . That is odd, isn't it? But I'll just go on like this, I'll just keep making trouble for people around me, and then . . . do something like the other day, and this time I'll hit my head; this time I'll finally die."

"N-no, you won't!" Watanuki-kun roared, suddenly furious.

His appearance had been so gentle that I had never dreamed my attitude would enrage him like this. I bit back the next words.

I didn't say it would be better if I was dead.

"P-probably . . . none of this is your fault, Kushimura-san! Something bad has taken hold of you, and it is causing you to make the wrong decisions where it matters most! I'm told there are things that can do that! Which means none of it is your fault!"

"Taken . . . hold of me?" A dramatic way of putting things.

Despite myself, I glanced at my shoulder again.

Which shoulder was it where the ghosts took hold of you?

"Wrong decisions . . . wrong choices . . . I mean, trying to be happy is just normal! Pushing happiness away . . . that just doesn't make sense!"

"Y-yeah . . ."

Honestly, I nodded here not because I agreed with him but because I was bowled over by his force, his earnestness. My head bobbed before I could think to stop it.

But.

I knew this boy was happy.

People who pushed happiness away didn't make sense to him. He couldn't believe that anyone could be like that; it had no connection with the world as he knew it. Which meant the world he lived in must be overflowing with happiness.

So much for him being unfortunate.

I was actually a little jealous.

Oh.

I could feel another urge coming on.

Watanuki-kun had said all this for me, yet I found myself wondering what would happen if I got mad at him—I couldn't think of any logical reasons to refute what he said, so I would just have to reject his goodwill as forcefully as possible.

Maybe even slap him.

What would he do then?

Someone this nice—what would he do?

Someone this happy.

I wrapped my free arm tightly around myself. Watanuki-kun noticed that immediately and must have assumed my condition had taken a turn for the worse, because he asked if I was feeling all right.

Oh no—I didn't think I could resist this urge.

Watanuki-kun reached for the nurse call button.

The nurse call . . .

Since I woke up, I had pushed it for no reason so many times, all day, all night. Because it was a button I should not be pushing. A button I should be pushing only in emergencies. Which meant I wanted to push it all the time. The nurses had been very angry with me, and if Watanuki-kun pushed the button, I was sure they would assume it was nothing again and ignore it.

Even if it was real.

Even though it was real!

If I slapped this boy hard enough to knock his glasses off . . .

I didn't want to do that.

I didn't.

I didn't. I didn't. I didn't. I didn't. I didn't. I didn't. I didn't. I didn't. I didn't. I didn't. I didn't. I didn't. I didn't. I didn't. I didn't. I didn't. I didn't.

I didn't, but I couldn't—

"Look at me!" Watanuki-kun said quite loudly.

That was just enough to bring me back to myself.

But it was not enough.

He had to leave. I couldn't stop myself a second time.

"Uh, um . . . Kushimura-san," Watanuki-kun said, before I could work out how to ask him to leave without being breathtakingly rude, "there's someone I think you should meet. . . ."

And an hour later . . .

I was in that shop.

The shop that could grant any wish.

▼▲▼

Describing the situation with such a clichéd expression may fail to communicate the exact nature of the tension in the air, but allow me to use it anyway—it was like a snake and a frog staring each other down. No matter how grimly both parties were glaring, to the independent observer the eventual victor was a foregone conclusion.

Yûko Ichihara and Nurie Kushimura.

Yûko Ichihara sprawled languidly like arrogance given clothes, while the tiny Nurie Kushimura failed to project anything like confidence and was unable even to meet her opponent's gaze. They were opposites, images reflected in a mirror.

Kimihiro Watanuki observed their interaction from the next room, peering through the crack in the screens. He had brought Kushimura to the shop that could grant any wish, prepared coffee for her and Yûko, and had left the room since his presence did not seem particularly welcome. But he had been unable to restrain his curiosity, which was why he was hunched over like a Peeping Tom.

His role was completed.

If hitsuzen had been at work, then it had ended where Watanuki was concerned the moment he brought Kushimura here.

Which had been difficult enough.

But today she had not hit him with flowers—largely because he had known she would overreact if he brought anything with him and so had gone empty-handed, rude as that might seem—or done anything else out of the ordinary, so his difficulties had resided entirely in the effort it took to persuade her to see Yûko Ichihara.

But it had not been all that difficult.

He had done as Yûko instructed—explained the proposal with reluctance, hinted strongly that he did not personally recommend it and that the risk involved was fairly high—and indeed, before he knew it, Kushimura was demanding that he take her to the shop.

When Yûko had told him to present things in that way, Watanuki had had no idea what she meant, but once he saw it in action, it was obvious. Her instructions had played on Kushimura's urges to violate taboo to get her to do exactly what Yûko wanted.

This was not the first time he'd seen her pull off something similar. Yûko Ichihara was as cunning as they came.

But . . .

When he had been hinting that he did not recommend it, and that there was risk involved, Watanuki had not been lying. He had not tricked Kushimura.

Both those things were true, in his opinion.

Just how great a "fair price" would Yûko Ichihara demand from Nurie Kushimura? To solve her worries, to grant her wish, how much would Kushimura give up?

Concern getting the better of curiosity—indeed, throwing it right through the saloon doors of his mind—Watanuki gulped as he watched Yûko and Kushimura interact, although all they had done so far was give their respective names (and Kushimura had been forced to give her birthday). Neither one seemed inclined to say anything further. Nor did either of them show any signs of drinking the coffee Watanuki had prepared. He had even gone to the trouble of warming up the cups, so he would definitely have preferred them to drink it hot.

Then at last Kushimura reached for her coffee.

"Call me Yûko," Yûko abruptly said. "And—that thing you were about to do? Don't."

Kushimura looked up, surprised.

Yûko smiled faintly. "Or perhaps . . . this way of putting things would work better with you, Nurie Kushimura-san.

"Go ahead. I dare you."

"Eh? Uh, um..." Kushimura spluttered, obviously taken aback by what must have made little sense to her. Already Yûko had taken control of the conversation, Watanuki thought. He waited breathlessly, wondering if Kushimura would be able to keep up. "I-I don't know—"

"What I mean? Sure," Yûko spit.

Maintaining superiority.

Watanuki had explained Yûko to Kushimura as a sort of counselor, which seemed the most easily acceptable way of describing what went on in Yûko's shop. Her haughty manner must have come as a bit of a surprise.

"So, what exactly do you want from me?" his employer continued.

"Eh... um, I just..." Followed Watanuki here, Kushimura explained, in a very small voice. The end of each sentence trailed off so quietly that Watanuki was unable to overhear.

"This is the shop where wishes are granted. Where all wishes come true. If you have entered this shop, if you have been led to this shop, then you must have a wish you long to have granted. Whether you are consciously aware of it or not."

"... Any wish?"

"Of course. Any wish at all."

"Um... I'm not... exactly normal. Is that a problem?"

"Absolutely not."

If a fair price was paid, Yûko added.

To Kimihiro Watanuki's eyes and senses, Nurie Kushimura's wish had grown quite desperate—her life depended on it. Which meant the price she would have to pay... might well involve her soul.

That would square things.

But even so, even with that in mind...

Yûko had called this case a good experience.

"I . . . ," Kushimura said, after a long silence. "I want . . . to stop myself."

"Stop yourself?" Yûko echoed deliberately.

"Yes. I want . . . to stop myself."

Stop herself . . . from doing what she did not want to do. That was her wish.

"I believe you already are."

"Huh?"

"Never mind. So, if that is your wish, what is it, specifically, that you wish to stop yourself from doing?"

Kushimura started to answer, then hung her head. She seemed to be choosing her words carefully, but what eventually came out was exactly what she'd said to Watanuki.

"My urges," she said. "I have these urges that make me want to violate taboos."

"To push buttons marked Don't Push?"

"Y-yes. Exactly."

"You can't accept happiness," Yûko said, looking directly at Watanuki.

She was well aware that he was watching. But she soon turned her gaze back to Kushimura.

"For example, if you bought a lottery ticket and won three hundred million yen . . . what would you do?"

"What would I . . . ?"

"Would you claim the prize?"

"Well . . ." Kushimura hesitated, made a show of mulling it over, and then answered with what she had most probably known instantly. "No, I don't think I would."

Watanuki had known how she would answer.

But he could not accept it.

He thought Yûko would ask why not, follow up on the question, but instead, she just nodded.

"I see" was all she said.

She seemed oddly uninterested in Kushimura, to the point where Watanuki longed to say something.

Putting aside issues of customer service—even putting aside the fact that Yûko herself had ordered Watanuki to bring Kushimura here—this was hardly a way to treat an injured woman, a woman with her arm in a sling. Not that Yûko was the type to care about any of that.

"I-I've been like this since I was a child. Every time I saw the right way to do things, the better path to follow . . . I found myself doing something else, messing everything up . . . just like I knew I would."

Since Yûko refused to say anything, Kushimura seemed to be forcing herself to talk, trying to cover the awkward silence.

"I don't have any real reason to wish I was dead, but I've done things that look suicidal. It's like when something good happens, I want to die; when I'm happy, I want to be unhappy. Um, Ichiha . . . Yûko-san, do you know what I mean? Do you ever feel like I do?"

"No and never," Yûko snapped. "Those feelings belong to you."

Kushimura said nothing.

"I don't know how you feel about them, but they are your feelings and your thoughts," Yûko went on. "If you agree with them, if you believe them to be the right thing, then that is what they are."

There's no reason to stop yourself, Yûko said.

"Every human being thinks different things are right and different things are wrong. Whether something is normal or not, it is still different for every person. Happiness is the same—everyone has their own definitions of it. Do you still want to stop yourself? Stop those feelings you call your urges?"

"O-of course. This is all . . . all so odd. I'm causing problems for everyone, and . . . these injuries . . ."

"I heard about that from my Watanuki."

My Watanuki?

"You heard . . . ?"

"That boy loves to gossip."

Now she was spreading rumors about him.

"But how much is true? You say you're causing problems for everyone, but to what degree are you including yourself in 'everyone'?"

"M-myself?"

"Everyone finds happiness differently, but ultimately, happiness is a bargain with yourself," Yûko said.

"A b-bargain?"

"A promise to yourself."

This . . .

. . . Watanuki had heard before.

And he knew what followed.

"You need two things: action and sincerity. Effort must be rewarded. If you pile hardship upon hardship, overcome difficulty after difficulty and give yourself nothing in return, you violate your contract."

"Violate . . . my contract."

"And how can that be anything but insincere?"

Yûko seemed to be enjoying herself immensely, inappropriately.

"You are betraying yourself. And not only betraying but cutting the thread."

The thread.

Hitsuzen.

"I'm sure our boy told you there are no people who reject happiness . . . or something similarly naïve."

He had.

But how did she know?

"But calling him naïve hardly covers it. Being happy is not

a right but a duty. A duty to yourself. Waiving rights is one thing, but failing in your duty is downright irresponsible."

Insincere—and irresponsible.

Which meant that behavior also was taboo.

"If you win the lottery, you should claim the prize. That is what I call fair price. You should pay ten thousand yen for something worth ten thousand yen, and you should be paid three hundred million yen for something worth three hundred million yen. Discounts and bargains simply upset the balance."

As she said the word *balance,* Yûko inclined her head upward and clapped twice. Watanuki could not work out what this gesture meant and did nothing. Yûko clapped again. Twice.

"Where are you?" she snapped, clapping a third time.

Is she calling me? What am I, some sort of ninja? She wants me to appear from the rafters? These and many other angry questions flooded through Watanuki's mind as he silently opened the screen. "At your service."

Responding appropriately, despite himself.

Yûko had been well aware that he was watching, but apparently Kushimura had not been, and she gave a sigh of relief when she saw him. Being alone with Yûko must have been extremely stressful for her.

"Watanuki, bring the item," Yûko said haughtily.

As if addressing one of her minions.

"The item?"

"The item you obtained the other day at the shop where items of little value gather."

". . . . . ?"

---

*Ninja Cheesy samurai dramas often had ninja hiding in the rafters, waiting to be summoned by a clap of their employer's hands.

He almost insisted that he had never been to such a fantastic-sounding place, but before he did, it occurred to him that she must mean the hundred-yen shop.

Such a poetic description.

"Hurry!" Yûko said, in a tone that did not allow for argument.

Watanuki nodded awkwardly and left the room.

If the shop where items of little value gather meant the hundred-yen shop, then the item must mean the fake glasses. He had been told to put them away somewhere, so he had . . . but where? Oh, right, certain they would never be used again, he had put them in the storage shed out back. The shed . . . which Yûko called the treasury.

Her mountain of treasure.

When he first heard this, Watanuki had secretly pitied her inability to distinguish between treasures and junk, but certain events since then had caused him to reconsider. He had his doubts about how much of it qualified as treasure, but it did seem to be true that much of what lay inside was decidedly not normal.

He found the fake glasses quickly, then went back to the room and gave them to Yûko.

Without so much as a glance in his direction, let alone a word of thanks, Yûko showed them to Kushimura. "These glasses have quite a distinguished history."

Yeah, a very distinguished hundred-yen shop.

"If you wear these regularly, a mysterious power will lead you down the right path. They will prevent you from making wrong choices. They will show you how to select the behavior that will help you become as you see yourself, to do what is best for you."

"Th-they will?" Kushimura was dubious but unable to take her eyes off the glasses. Was she really going to buy all that? "Those are . . . some very impressive glasses."

"They have been linked to Date Masamune."

For some reason, Yûko was adding extra unneeded lies. It made Watanuki's knees tremble just to listen.

"I now give them to you," Yûko said, reverently handing to Kushimura the distinguished item that had been linked to Date Masamune. Kushimura did not seem at all sure she should be taking them, but she did anyway, bringing them up to her eyes.

"But I have good eyes...."

"The lenses aren't curved at all; don't worry."

"Oh, I see... but I don't have much money...."

"They're free," Yûko said. "That's what *give* implies."

Kushimura nodded. Watanuki, however, was flabbergasted. "Give?" Yûko-san? "Free?" No fair price at all?

"You are 'free' to do with them what you like. Use them, throw them away, as you like. Decide however action and sincerity dictate. Now, shouldn't you be getting back to the hospital? You slipped out without permission, didn't you? You can find your own way back, I'm sure. I would love to have our boy walk you back, but he has important work to do."

"Ah... right, yes, I'll be fine. I can get back, I'm sure. Umm... thank you."

A very uncertain expression of gratitude.

As well it should be; if she left here, she would only wonder why she had come. There was not one single reason why she should be thanking anybody. Nothing had been done for her, and she had done nothing. At the very end, she had been given a highly dubious pair of fake glasses. Given? More like, forced to accept. And then sent packing.

But once Yûko had wrapped things up, there was nothing more to say.

That much was perfectly clear.

Without a drop of the coffee Watanuki had prepared passing her lips.

Kushimura left the shop where wishes were granted.

Watanuki did walk her to the gate, considering it the least he could do.

When he returned to Yûko, she was puffing on her pipe.

Had she refrained from doing so as some small consideration for her injured guest?

That did not seem likely.

"What was that all about?"

"What was what about?" Yûko said blankly.

"Where do I even start? Um . . . first of all, the fake glasses?"

"What about them? They are undoubtedly an item of distinguishment, and they are undoubtedly linked to Date Masamune."

"Date Masamune has nothing to do with them."

"You cannot deny the possibility exists."

"I believe I can," Watanuki insisted. "And the rest of what you said to her, about how they would help her choose the right path . . . That was all nonsense, right?"

"Oh? You noticed?"

"Fake glasses that cost 105 yen the other day do not simply acquire such properties overnight."

"That is not necessarily true, but in this case, yes, those glasses are perfectly ordinary glasses."

Without so much as batting an eye, Yûko admitted that they had no effect at all.

"I thought as much. You would never hand over something that impressive without demanding a fair price."

"I don't much like your tone, but for the moment I'll agree. Nevertheless, Watanuki, that perception of yours is not quite accurate."

"Oh?"

"I did receive a fair price from her," Yûko said. "And her wish was granted."

". . . How so?"

But Yûko just smiled.

Regally.

"To further the example from yesterday: If an English gentleman came up to you on your way home from school and said, 'I'd like to give you one hundred trillion yen.' Perhaps he says this in Japanese, perhaps in English, it does not really matter—if that happened, Watanuki, what would you do?"

"I-I'm not—"

"Would you take it or not?"

"Well . . ." He couldn't answer.

But this was the sort of question that not being able to answer instantly was in itself the answer.

"Well, no. I wouldn't."

"Why not?"

"I mean, that just sounds so suspicious. He must be up to something."

"I see." Yûko nodded. "Exactly my point."

"Said point being?"

"That is the best way to explain people who can't accept happiness. I gave no indication that this English gentleman was up to anything—and English gentlemen are the most honorable gentlemen in the world. They would never be up to anything suspicious."

"I have no idea what inspired such deep-seated trust in you, but a figure like a hundred trillion yen would make anyone suspicious."

"That's a comment I would have liked to hear in the 'Himawari-chan tells you she loves you' hypothetical. But essentially, the opposite of what I said to her."

The opposite.

Looked at from the other direction.

Yûko went on. "To become happy, you need to pay a fair price. Which means that excessive fortune can only be viewed as a threat. You need to earn that fortune through an appropriate amount of work and struggle."

"A contract with yourself?"

A promise to yourself.

Action and sincerity.

"You know the expression 'It all works out in the end'? Human lives ultimately run on a balanced budget. If there is good, there is bad, and when bad things happen, there must be good things as well."

"That . . ."

That would square things.

". . . I have heard that."

"But the expression is not strictly accurate. Fundamentally, to be happy, you have to bear the burden of an equal amount of misery. See? To get something good, you have to put up with something bad. Nothing as carefree as 'taking the good with the bad' makes it sound. That doesn't fulfill the promise."

Watanuki thought about it. Yûko went on:

"To put it another way, the higher your position at a job, the more you have to work. Not being able to do so is insincere and irresponsible. Still another way: if where you are is a step lower than normal, if you are in an unfortunate position, then you must allow yourself to not expend as much effort, to abandon your stubborn pride. All part of the promise."

"But . . . um . . ."

Was this true?

He could comprehend the gist of what she was saying, but . . .

"B-but she—Kushimura-san, Nurie Kushimura-san, in her case—she didn't have excessive happiness, she was abandoning normal happiness."

Waiving her rights and abandoning her duties.

"She was not, Watanuki," Yûko said. "She was maintaining her balance."

"Balance?"

"All humans have a certain level of fascination with forbidden behavior, but Kushimura's urges have little to do with her situation. You must not mingle or confuse the two. All that I have just explained ought to have been enough for you to understand that happiness, excessive or otherwise, carries with it a degree of pressure. Happiness is not entirely a good thing—not as long as you have to pay a fair price for it. And not as long as you are unable to pay that price."

"Huh . . ."

If you accepted the hundred trillion yen from the English gentleman, you would have to work off a hundred trillion yen's worth of debt to yourself.

The debt would be hitsuzen.

Not to the English gentleman—but to yourself.

"When she was with me, the only thought in her mind was that she wanted to go home. Talking with me was a source of pressure. That's why she was so relieved when you came in."

"Yeah, I did notice that. . . ."

"In return for abandoning happiness, she can escape that pressure. She made that choice. Just as she said, this is not self-destructive or suicidal; it was all carefully calculated."

"C-calculated?"

Calculated, measured, weighed.

Not the hallmarks of impulsive behavior.

"In other words, she was an immense coward about getting what she wanted most."

"B-but . . . you don't think she was simply throwing herself at unhappiness? Even if that was less stressful."

"Throwing herself into unhappiness . . . or into traffic?"

"Yeah, like that."

"But she was hit by a scooter," Yûko said dismissively. "She chose when to jump. And jumping out in front of a dump truck is a much bigger taboo."

If she was hit by a scooter . . . she would not die. Especially if she blocked it with her arm. It made sense; Kushimura had chosen when to jump out in traffic and chosen to jump in front of the scooter.

"As a result of which, she did not have to give a major presentation at work. She was able to avoid such a stressful situation, to avoid that pressure."

"Yeah, but—"

"And while she claimed she caused trouble for everyone, it wasn't actually that big a deal. Someone filled in for her. . . . What was his name? Hyôdô-kun? He did her job for her, and whether she was there or not, she was still part of the group that had made the plan, and no matter what she might say, the road to promotion is not as firmly closed as she claims."

"Well . . . I guess not."

No guess about it.

That was it, plain and simple.

"Or maybe she simply didn't want that promotion. Truly meek, she fears success more than failure. That promotion brings with it greater responsibility, and there are any number of people who would prefer to avoid that. For all her concerns about causing trouble for her group, she also admitted that they were all really nice people. And she knew that better than anyone."

"But . . . she hit me with those flowers. . . ."

"A visitor so Sewashi-kun-ish—abnormally nice and so eager to be helpful that he calls an ambulance for a total stranger—is hardly likely to be particularly enraged when the injured person they are visiting hits them over the head with a bouquet. Admittedly, she did so without knowing that you are prone to violent fits."

"I am not!"

He knew two people who were.

And one of them was right in front of him.

"If you think about it, annoying the nurses by pressing the button that summons them over and over is not that big a deal. Same with the fire alarm at school. That button marked Don't Push is hardly the launch switch for a nuclear bomb. I'm sure she got off with a scolding. Perhaps that's what she's after: anything except happiness, including making people angry. Like ordering coffee when you want tea. Speaking of which, she almost threw her coffee at me."

She had?

So that's what Yûko had stopped her from doing.

"She had calculated that I knew her situation and was going to help with it, so I would not be all that angry."

Watanuki was silent.

"The old idea that things are going too well. Watanuki, can you understand the desire to stumble deliberately when the story looks to progress your way? 'Trouble follows fortune.' So why not trip yourself up in advance? If you're going be tripped anyway, trip yourself before anything good happens. I have no idea how conscious she is of what she's doing, but it is, to a certain extent, deliberate."

"Oh . . ."

Were there really people like that?

Someone that thorough.

"She mentioned failing to get into the schools she most wanted to attend, but she always got in somewhere else. She may have failed to get the job she wanted most, but she was hired by her second choice. She mentioned fighting the urge to throw herself in front of the train in the station . . . but she never actually did."

The most she ever did was jump out in front of a scooter that was slowing down as it approached a crosswalk.

"And when you get right down to it, the fact that she is alive now proves everything. The fact that she has survived this long is not a miracle, it is proof. The greatest taboo for a human is suicide. If you're satisfied by pretending to kill yourself, then the action cannot be taken as a violation of that taboo."

She had cut her wrists once—but only once. And the cuts had been too shallow to kill her.

"If there was a button marked Don't Push, that woman would never push it," Yûko went on. "She would just claim she would and convince herself that it was true. She's never killed anyone, she's never eaten anybody, yet she talks about violating taboos? Makes my sides hurt from laughing. Any number of children have jumped out the window of their classroom. That's not a taboo! Look at it all lined up like this, Watanuki, and you can tell just how calculating that woman is."

Avoiding happiness.

Avoiding pressure.

"A word as forthright and flamboyant as *urges* hardly describes such a slipshod methodology. What she does is simply a compromise. It seems you are among them, Watanuki, but there are any number of people who do not like being exalted, do not like being thought highly of, and the vast majority of those people invariably choose the second-best option."

The second-best option.

"A problem of balance and swift adjustment. Nobody can afford to keep the gas pedal down all the time, can they? You'd never make it around the next corner. You could boil it down to overcautiousness or underestimating oneself, but either way, refusing to accept a normal amount of happiness can hardly be described as the right thing to do."

"The right thing to do?"

"It is your duty to accept a measure of happiness equivalent to the actions you have taken. Rejecting it violates your contract with yourself. If your effort is not rewarded, your soul rebels."

"Rebels . . ."

"You could also say it overflows. If you do the work to receive the best option, then you must accept that option as your reward."

That was the fair price.

A fair price could neither be undercut nor overpaid.

Yûko pointed her pipe at the seat where Kushimura had been a few minutes before.

"Stop herself from doing what she doesn't want to do . . . a fascinating turn of phrase, and one that makes no sense. The fact that she doesn't want to do those things suggests she is already stopping herself from doing them—very calculatedly. She may well have a black belt in stopping herself. Never once leaving the realm of safety, never even going close to the fence around the realm. The only question is, to what extent is she herself aware of this?"

". . . If she puts those glasses on," Watanuki said, trying to hide how shaken he was, "will she really . . . be able to choose the path that's best for her?"

"Of course not," Yûko said, as if it were obvious. "Those are an ordinary pair of fake glasses."

"Eh . . . but . . . then . . ."

"Watanuki, you said it yourself. Have you already forgotten how pompously you lectured me for deceiving her? You must be suffering from amnesia."

Overflows The word used for rebellion or revolt is a homonym of the word for flood or overflow. Both words are read *hanran*.

"No, I mean, you're right, but . . . then what was the point of it all?"

"There is a point . . . just not a dramatic one."

Watanuki waited.

"I merely provided an opportunity."

She had not become any more involved than that.

"Watanuki, you always wear glasses. But if you were to take them off, do you think you wouldn't be able to see spirits anymore?"

"Huh?"

"Or if you close your eyes. That would prevent your seeing them. Even more extreme—you could gouge both eyes out. Would that get rid of the spirits that gather around you?"

"Now you're starting to scare me," Watanuki said, backing away from Yûko and protecting his eyes.

"I exist to scare you. Answer the question. If that would work, you would hardly need to continue your life of indentured servitude here."

"Nah, nothing like that would really solve the problem. Spirits aren't there because I can see them; I can see them because they're there. As long as they're attracted by my blood, I'm sure I'll still be able to sense them."

And that . . .

. . . meant that not only his sight but all five of his senses, and his sixth sense as well, would have to be shut down. Or nothing would change.

"Hmm, you think not?"

"Well . . . I've never tried, so I don't know for sure."

"Want to?"

"Since the procedure would be irreversible, hell no!"

And if it failed, where would he be?

Watanuki was no gambler.

"Your eyes themselves are of no importance," Yûko said, getting back to the point. "But when something unnatural enters the vision of someone without vision problems, the experience naturally demands attention. That's what makes my curse effective."

"Huh? Yûko-san, did you say curse?"

"I did not."

"You did so! You said it makes your curse effective! I heard you!"

"I said it makes my neurosis effective."

"In accomplishing what!?"

How could a neurosis be effective?

He couldn't begin to guess.

"She knew what was the best option without its being pointed out to her. She was avoiding it precisely because she knew. So . . . if you look at it a different way, all I had to do was make conscious what was unconscious. As time passes, what was unconscious may well become part of her, which would grant her wish. People who always wear glasses apparently feel them to be part of the face. It should take a few months for that to happen . . . and it won't be easy."

"Won't it? Once you get used to them, it's no big deal."

"I'm not talking about eyeballs," Yûko said, full of malevolence. "Nurie Kushimura has never before experienced normal levels of happiness; she has been busy avoiding it. It's built up inside her."

"B-built up?" What was? Happiness?

"By 'built up' I mean like sedimentary deposits are built up, and by deposits I mean mud. Despite that, she will be forced to harvest happiness—if she is physically up to the task. But there's nothing else she can do; she has to pay off the price she promised herself before the bill is settled. She won't be finished till the receipt is in her hand."

---

*Neurosis Untranslatable pun. Curse is *noroi*, neurosis is *noiroze*. I played around with using *spell* and *spelling* but ended up deciding that keeping the word as *curse* was more important than awkwardly trying to make the pun work.

Watanuki looked blank.

"The fair price she paid for the loss of her escape routes was the escape routes themselves. No matter how much pressure she is under, she will not allow herself to run away. I can only imagine how ugly that must be."

"Ugly . . . ?"

"Ultimately, it's up to her what she does next. She might choose to change nothing and keep running up her tab. If she throws away the glasses, she will continue to live a life of second-best options, as she always has. That might not be happiness . . . but neither is it misery."

When it came to happiness, Nurie Kushimura had never become any more involved than that.

She might have touched the surface of the spring, but she never dove down to the source.

Yûko's lack of involvement must be only natural, at least from her own point of view. Yûko was neither good nor deserving of being called evil; she simply was. Someone in her position had to maintain those standards, or she would eventually find herself thoroughly taken advantage of.

And presumably, she did not want that.

"Enough work! All done for the day! Ah, so draining! Watanuki, the coffee's gone cold, so make some more? Don't forget the milk and sugar."

"Okay, then . . . mm? W-wait, Yûko-san . . . ?"

"What? I'm not giving you a raise."

"I don't mean *that*. . . ."

Don't say it in italics, Watanuki thought. Makes it feel unpleasantly real.

"You mean Kushimura-san's urges were her own problem, a problem entirely related to her contract with herself . . . and nothing to do with spirits at all?"

"Exactly," Yûko said, rolling her eyes, as if this had been covered hours ago. "You couldn't see anything, could you?"

"Well, no . . . But the first time? At the crosswalk, on her shoulder . . ."

"Something sewn on her shoulder bag that reflected the streetlights into your eyes?" Yûko said, giving him a bewitching smile.

That's why she had said . . .

"I told you this would be a good experience for you, didn't I? Remember that there are people like her."

"People like her . . . ?"

Nurie Kushimura.

Calculatedly avoiding happiness.

A "good experience" for him. Yuko had said that early on.

"Even without spirits getting involved, people can cause plenty of strange events on their own. You have a healthy mind, Watanuki, and there are all kinds of people you would consider creepy. That is part of mankind, something that dwells within all humans. You always talk about spirits as if they are frightening or evil, but there is nothing as frightening or evil as humans. When you have time, Watanuki, sit somewhere alone and toy with that idea awhile. When you have finished paying off your fair price, and your eyes can no longer see spirits . . .

"Will you be able to see people?"

He could have sworn . . .

. . . he heard the sound of horrible jagged teeth snapping shut.

"Just kidding!"

Watanuki stared at her, unable to respond.

Yûko continued merrily, "Now I'm all done with work, but you, Watanuki, have just begun! When my coffee is ready, you have quite a task ahead of you! You have to make up for being late yesterday and skipping entirely the day before, or you may find yourself working at this shop for all eternity!"

"What task?"

"Flowing somen!" Yûko beamed.

As if that was the best possible choice.

Good things always brought suffering.

▼▲▼

Oh.

Oh no.

I did it again.

I wasted time.

And time is so precious.

Nobody could possibly solve my problems. Nobody could possibly grant my wish. I knew it would be pointless, so why?

Let that nice child talk me into it . . . let myself sit in that terrifying woman's gaze.

And all I got was this ordinary pair of glasses.

What was the point of that?

She had said things that sounded right, but anybody could tell these were cheaply made plastic things, the kind sold in any hundred-yen shop. The origins she had given were not remotely believable.

What was that all about?

Some sort of scam?

Taking advantage of people's troubles?

But it wasn't as though I'd lost anything. I had wasted a little time but lost nothing. Not only that, but I had been given this pair of cheap fake glasses.

Fair price.

The boy had used that phrase.

But what fair price had I paid to acquire these? I didn't feel as though I had done anything, but now that I was thinking about it . . . something felt different.

Something felt wrong.

I felt as though I had lost a tangible part of myself.

Should I throw these things away?

These glasses . . . There was nothing special about them. If I threw them away, would this strange sense of loss inside me fade away?

As though I had lost a comfortable place.

As though I had lost a comfortable escape route.

As though I had a hole opened in my heart.

Or as though I had filled a hole in my heart.

I looked at the trash can.

I should throw these glasses in there.

But then . . .

———

"Go ahead. I dare you."

———

I heard her voice.

My hand stopped.

I was hearing things, of course. I had just remembered that phrase suddenly.

But . . . why not? I thought. I didn't need to make up my mind right away.

I walked on past the garbage can, keeping the glasses.

There was a crosswalk ahead of me.

The light was red, so I stopped.

▲▽▲▽

OUTLANDOS D'AMOUR

Kouhei Kadono

Illustrations by Ueda Hajime
Translated by Andrew Cunningham

Outlandos: Remote or distant lands, other countries. An old word. Refers to nowhere specifically but denotes far-away lands in the abstract.

This short story is by one of the stars of Japan's light novel world: Kouhei Kadono. American manga connoisseurs have already gotten a taste of Kadono's cool and revolutionary style with the Boogiepop novels. The first Boogiepop novel, *Boogiepop wa Warawanai* (*Boogiepop and Others* in the United States), single-handedly changed the light novel scene upon its release in 1998, and Kadono remains a revolutionary writer whose innovative work continues to propel the light novel genre forward. In addition to the Boogiepop novels, his dream-team collaboration with illustrator Kazuma Kaneko (famous for *ATLUS* games *Megami Tensei* and *Persona*) resulted in another popular novel series: the Jiken series, a bold mash-up of mystery and fantasy storytelling. Del Rey Manga will bring this series to the United States, beginning with the first volume, *The Case of the Dragonslayer,* in spring of 2009.

The story's illustrator, Ueda Hajime, has also established a devoted following in the United States. A manga artist and illustrator, Ueda Hajime created his international reputation with the manga adaptation of Gainax's popular *FLCL* anime.

Ueda followed this triumph with original series, including *Q-Ko-Chan: The Earth Invader Girl*. The truly global appeal of Hajime's work rests on his unique sense of composition and utterly distinctive visual sensibility. The illustrations accompanying this work are wonderful examples of Hajime's instantly recognizable style.

▲▽▲

1

"What's the first thing you remember? Do you remember being born?" she asked.

Kunio Koryo didn't even hesitate.

"Red," he said. He always did.

"Red?"

"Yes."

"What was red?"

"Everything."

"The things around you?"

"Yes, and my hands were red, too."

"Your hands? You were just a baby. Did you know they were your hands?"

"At the time, I'm sure I didn't. I saw something dyed red like maple leaves, and in retrospect, I imagine they were probably my hands."

"But what you remember most clearly was the color? Which means," the woman did not hesitate either, "blood? You saw yourself covered in blood, and the area around you . . . ?"

"I imagine so. The red was a dark red, so—"

"Memories of emerging from the womb? That would explain the blood . . ."

"I don't think so. I don't remember emerging from darkness, and I have no memories of my mother at all."

Kunio shrugged.

"I don't know how I was born. And newborns can barely see. It takes some time before the brain can process visual information."

"You've looked into it, then? You're probably right. . . . It takes awhile before you can see anything clearly. And once that much time had passed . . . even if you had been left lying in the birth blood, by the time you could see, it would have dried out and been more brown than red. And that doesn't explain why everything around you was red as well. . . ."

She nodded quietly.

"This might be a bit of a reach . . . but perhaps you were simply in a red room?"

"Certainly possible. I can imagine being in a room painted the color of blood."

"So you don't have a strong conviction that it was blood?"

"Right. It's just a memory. But I feel like there was a smell as well, which is why I think it might have been blood. And I was wet . . . and left there alone."

"They left you lying in a pool of blood as a baby? I wonder why. . . ."

"No idea. Might provide some interesting results in psychoanalysis. But they would probably assume my impressions have been distorted."

"You don't deny the possibility?"

"No. I don't really care if the memory is true or not. The memory doesn't frighten me; it doesn't feel like a traumatic weight on my heart. . . ."

"It's just there?"

"Exactly."

"But where were you?"

"I don't know."

"You don't remember the place at all? Do you have any impressions of it at all?"

"Somewhere far away."

"How far?"

"Very far . . . somewhere not here."

"By here . . . you mean this building? Or this city?"

"No... nothing like that. More abstract. Just not... here."

"Another country?"

"Maybe, but every other country I've been to has felt wrong as well. The air... no, just the feeling in the air... there's something different about it."

For the first time, Kunio's expression grew ruffled, and he fell silent.

The woman, Setsuko Amamiya, noted that flicker and narrowed her eyes a little. This was the same expression she had when she had found her target. She was a professional killer.

But she did not, at the moment, have any plans to kill Kunio Koryo. She had come to see him for other reasons.

"Perhaps that 'different' feeling is connected to your unique 'talent.'"

"How so?"

"Your strange abilities have been a mystery even within our system, but it seems we've finally found a hint as to their true nature. Something I encountered on another mission suggested the existence of a world beyond our own: a world where something called 'magic' exists. This energy can be used to achieve any number of things."

"Huh?"

"You always claim your ability is not an intrinsic part of you but merely a technique, right? Do you see the similarity?"

This came out of the blue and stunned him.

Amamiya continued, "Perhaps you are a human who has come from there to here. The strange ability you can use here, what we call outlandos d'amour, is actually a technique that anyone there can use and that they call 'magic.'"

Kunio wasn't sure how to react to this. He felt like she was saying something completely unrealistic that somehow made sense to him anyway: a very strange feeling.

"... Um," he said, trying to piece his thoughts together.

"You mean my ability has no real value and is, in fact, terribly common?"

Amamiya shook her head. "No, quite the opposite."

"Er..."

"If your ability is based on an energy that can be explained theoretically, applied broadly, and used by anyone... you could fundamentally change the world. It is entirely possible that as the holder of this key, you're more valuable than anyone else alive."

Amamiya's tone was calm, and she did not appear to be bluffing or trying to get a rise out of him.

"Huh... I doubt that," Kunio said, for lack of a better answer. "But as far as using it... it's not like I do anything directly. I'm not sure how they explained it to you, but—"

"Right," Amamiya nodded. "You can sense... 'fractures,' was it? Fractures made unconsciously by others, which they themselves have not noticed. For example..."

They were seated in a lounge, and she waved her hand, indicating the entire entrance hall of the building.

"Are there any here? Anyone with one of these fractures stuck to them? Can you see anything?"

"Um... I don't really 'see' them...," Kunio said, flustered. He looked around the room as directed.

But halfway, he suddenly froze, abruptly and awkwardly, completely forgetting his surroundings.

Amamiya frowned at him. "Is something wrong?"

Kunio didn't even blink. His gaze had locked onto something across the room.

A young woman. She was wearing a suit, but she had a baby face and might even still be in her teens. She had black hair, neither long nor short, and seemed very unsophisticated. She had noticed him staring at her and looked rather alarmed.

The intensity of his gaze was enough to spook anyone.

"What? Something about that girl?" Amamiya asked, but Kunio didn't answer.

Still looking like he'd been struck by lightning, he stood up.

And strode directly over to this entirely unexceptional-looking girl.

"Hey!" Amamiya called after him, but he did not appear to hear her. He just drifted over to the girl, as if being dragged in her direction.

And croaked, "Uh, um . . . your name?"

The girl flinched. Fumbling, she stammered, "Eh, er, um, uh . . ."

His response was equally incoherent. "N-no, I'm not . . . anyone suspicious . . . I mean, I'm just . . ."

If this had happened under any other circumstances, it would have been a perfectly ordinary sight. A chance encounter, a man speaking to a girl he's just seen for the first time—happens every day.

Kunio Koryo had fallen in love with her at first sight.

He was a late bloomer, and in his twenty-six years alive, she was his first love.

▼▲▼

Kunio Koryo was first discovered buried in the earth. He was not dead. He was less than a year old and had been buried in the ground but was not dead. In fact, upon his discovery, he was the picture of health.

He was discovered at a construction site. The shovel had been roughly scooping chunks out of the ground, but the machine had suddenly stopped.

"It was like an electric crackle ran through it. Maybe the battery short-circuited," the man operating the shovel explained later, but when the machine stopped, it saved a life. The teeth of the shovel had stopped right before they touched the buried baby, which surfaced just enough to

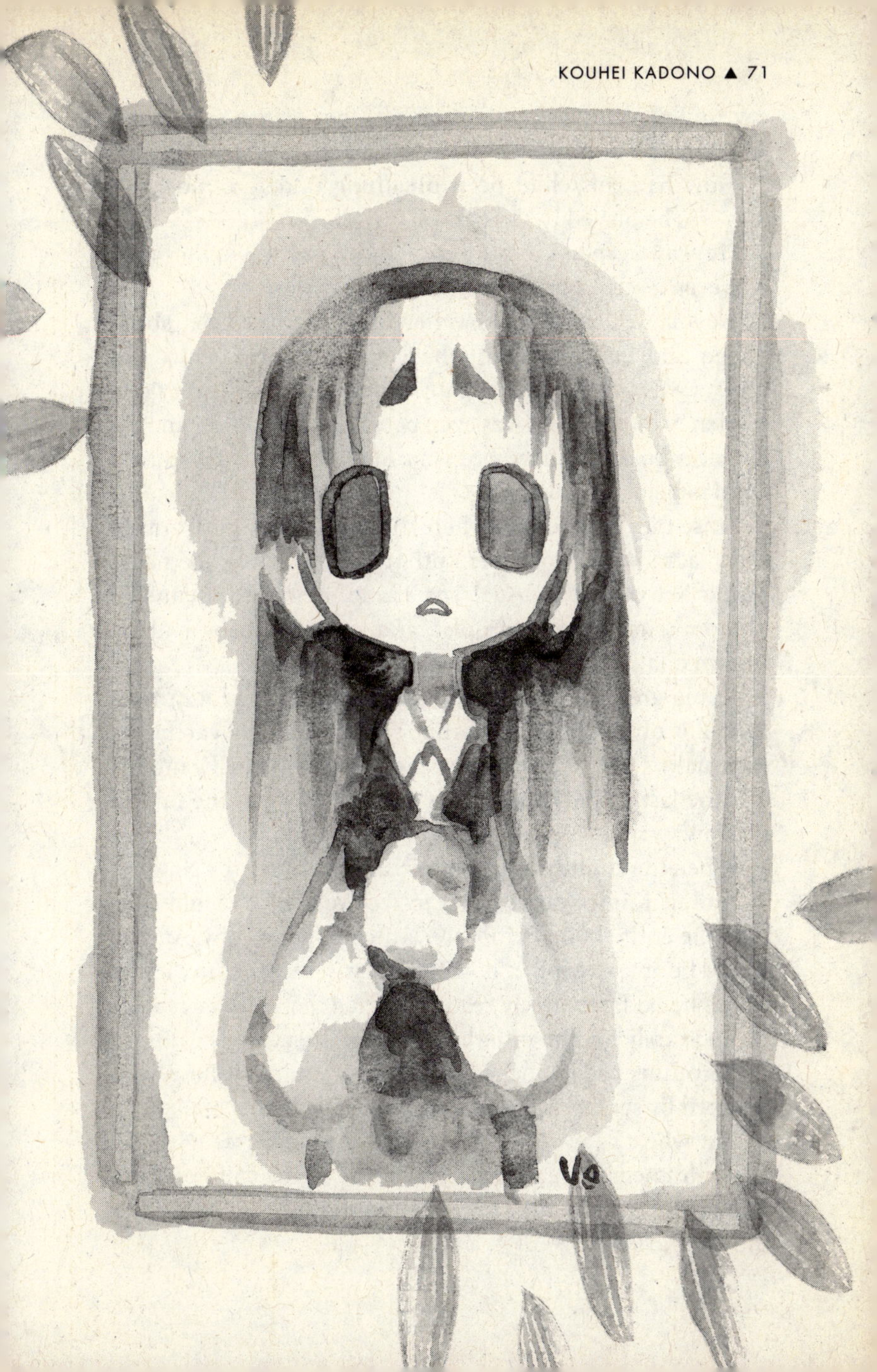

cry out—a strange cry, somewhere between a sob and a laugh.

How had this child been breathing underground? And why was he buried in the first place?

He was wrapped in a kind of sheet and was unharmed. Not even a scratch, not even a rash.

Normally, they would have assumed he had been abandoned and that his parents had clearly wanted him dead, but . . . when they saw the baby's innocent smile, every one of them wondered if it was even possible to abandon him. He did not appear to have been harmed at all by the sinister hand fate had dealt him.

Since they had no idea where the child had come from, he was placed with the proper authorities and given the name Kunio Koryo. An unusual last name, it was the name of a famous local philanthropist, and since the baby had no known relatives, there was no one to object.

Kunio grew up to be a quiet child. He spent a lot of time carefully observing those around him, and his caretakers eventually realized that he was exceptionally intelligent. He was the last of the children his age to speak but the first to read and write.

When the adults passed out picture books for the children to read, if Kunio was the first to receive his, he would have read the entire book before the last child got a copy. And he would be able to explain how the story was similar to picture books he had previously read. He had a malleable personality and rarely fought with the other children.

If nothing had happened, he would presumably have been adopted by someone eventually and led a normal life.

But when he was three years old, the facility caught fire. Arson in the middle of the night, while all the children were asleep, and by all rights, the building should have burned to the ground.

But instead . . . something strange happened.

Before the fire spread, Kunio woke up, got out of bed, and headed toward the fire.

Afterward, Kunio said, "I was so young that I don't remember much. But I don't think I was scared."

Several others woke up when they heard him padding by and followed after him, wondering what was going on. And they saw what happened.

The first recorded Kunio "miracle."

Kunio looked at the fire and began muttering something. His lips moved, but no one could hear what he said, and what they did hear seemed to have no meaning. . . .

But a moment later, a shower of electric sparks rained down in front of him. The building had been struck by lightning.

The lightning struck the fire, exploding right in the center of it.

The impact worked much like using a bomb to put out an oil fire—the fire that had threatened to burn the building down went out. But there was now a crack running all the way through the building, and the facility was no longer habitable.

Everyone asked Kunio what had happened, but he had been as surprised as anyone. He did not yet understand what he himself had done.

But what he had done attracted the attention of a certain system.

It was much too big to call it "a society" and much too abstract to really control anything. It had eyes all over the world, a kind of consciousness administration. It was just a system, moving on its own, which is why people called it the Organization.

He had always been under this system's watchful eye. His "birth" was too unique not to be. And the power that put out the fire confirmed it.

He was quickly taken in.

For a while, he was brought up in a kind of laboratory, living a life in which he was never sure if they were researching him or not, but eventually he returned to normal life.

He went to school and grew up like any other boy. He remained quiet and did not change much. It was his surroundings that changed.

▼▲▼

"You live alone, Koryo?" Kaori Nakayama asked. She was in his grade, and they had somehow ended up leaving school together that day.

"Yeah," Kunio nodded, not minding. "My parents live abroad . . . I think."

This was what he was supposed to say, the cover story the Organization had created for him. There was no proof that it was a lie. In fact, it could be proved beyond all doubt to be true in any court of law.

"You think?" Kaori asked, surprised by the lack of certainty, but then she giggled. "You're weird, Koryo."

They had been in the same class last year, but she hadn't struck up a conversation with him for a while. He rarely started conversations himself, so it was entirely possible the two of them had never talked like this before.

"Really? I think I'm normal. . . ."

"But you get good grades . . . and you're good at sports, and yet you aren't on any teams?"

"Well, yeah . . ."

They had been very clear that he was not to get involved in extracurricular activities. But he couldn't say that. "I just couldn't make up my mind."

"There wasn't anything you wanted to do?"

"Nah . . ." He was forced to be vague about this.

Only people who knew what position they would hold in

the world, who knew what path lay ahead of them, could talk about the future. He had no idea where he'd even come from and had no right to talk about things like that. He wanted to know who he was first. And that knowledge was still a long, long way off.

"Yeah..." Kaori sighed. "I see that in your eyes sometimes. You're looking at something far, far away.... When you get like that, what are you thinking about?"

"Huh?" The question took him by surprise. "What do you mean?" he asked.

Kaori didn't answer. "Koryo... have you ever been angry?" she asked suddenly. "Pissed off, irritated... Have you ever felt like that?"

"Hmm..." Not sure what she was trying to ask, he just grunted vaguely.

"I mean, you always settle other people's fights. When things start to get ugly, you show up out of nowhere and calm everyone down."

He didn't reply. It was extremely difficult for Kunio to talk about this. He had been forbidden to tell anyone normal about it, and even if he did, they would not understand.

When he said nothing, Kaori continued, "Once, when I was really, really mad, you cooled me off. Do you remember what you said?"

"Nothing important, I'm sure."

"You said, 'Who are you mad at? What is making you so angry? Do you really know?' I don't know what you meant, but... it worked. I don't even remember why I was angry now, but I can't forget what you said to me."

"Did I say that?"

"Yes. You did," Kaori said firmly. Then she suddenly said, "I don't... think I'll ever amount to anything. If I study really, really hard, I can probably go to a really good college, but I don't really want to be a doctor or a lawyer. Just because I like karaoke doesn't mean I want to take lessons and try to be a singer, and I mean, I'm always like that. Just going through the motions. And I don't really mind that. But . . ."

Kaori sighed again.

"You don't even know what I'm talking about, right?"

"Nope," Kunio shook his head. He was always honest, whenever possible.

"I knew it! You haven't decided anything, but you never seem to hesitate either! It's so unfair! I've been jealous of you for ages. . . ."

She sped up, walking ahead of him. Turning her back on him.

She started to say something else, but before she could—

"Don't move!" Kunio said, suddenly forceful.

She froze, shocked. But his expression was so grim and intent and more than a little frightening, so she did as he asked.

"On your . . . neck."

"Eh?"

Her hair was pulled back in a ponytail, exposing the nape of her neck. Kunio reached out and brushed his finger against it.

"On your neck . . . a fracture."

What a weird thing to say.

"Where'd you get this fracture? Who put it there?"

"Uh, um . . . What?" Kaori shivered, unable to understand what he was saying.

"Have you . . . felt like someone was watching you?" he asked.

Kaori gasped. She had. It was making her nervous. That was why she had called out to Kunio on her way home.

"Y-yeah . . ."

"You're in danger," Kunio said, deadly serious. "And that danger relates to your neck. Protect your neck. And don't go anywhere alone."

His words sounded like some sort of prophecy, but they sounded neither like a threat nor like he was forcibly trying to persuade her. He was just flatly stating the truth.

"Um," Kaori said, unable to hide her confusion.

At last Kunio noticed and suddenly grew much less clear. "Er . . . no, I mean . . . be careful? Lots of scary people out there, right?"

He was obviously trying to worm his way out of it. He was an honest boy and no good at lying.

Kaori felt like the boy in front of her, close enough to touch, was very, very far away.

Kunio himself had explained these "fractures" to the Organization in the following manner.

"It's not like I'm making them. They were already there."

"And you can see them? You have special senses?" The researcher listened to him gravely, accepting everything he said, no matter how crazy it sounded.

"I can't see them, nor can I sense them directly. How can I put this? . . . I know they're there because I can't see them."

"What do you mean?"

"Everywhere else is . . . saturated, except for that one place where it's split open . . . so it's like something's flowing toward the gap. . . . Augh, I don't know how to put this."

"Hmmm . . ." The flaxen-haired researcher listened with interest. "It is a little piecemeal, but you're basically trying to explain something that we do not know and cannot perceive. For example . . . a congenitally blind man perceives the world through exclusively three-dimensional senses like touch and sound and is unable to comprehend two-dimensional representations like pictures or photographs. As far as your perceptions go, we are in the position of the blind man. Our perception has yet to acquire the concept you're trying to explain, whatever this thing that 'saturates' the world is."

"Really?"

"Yes. I can't even begin to grasp what it is that saturates the world. But as far as you're concerned, it has always been there. Now . . . hypothetically speaking, what do you think is causing these fractures?"

"Um . . . I don't know."

"When you saved everyone from the fire . . . That was no accident; it did not start naturally. It was arson, an act of human evil. If I suggested that you could sense the fire because a human had started it . . . what would you think?"

"I was so little . . . I don't really remember."

"Think about it. . . . Look at it this way. Afterward it was discovered that the man who started the fire had a personal grudge against the facility. Could you have reacted to that man's feelings rather than the fire itself? Could it have been that man's intentions that triggered your reaction?"

"His intentions . . . ?"

"The 'fractures' you can detect might be made unconsciously by the power of someone's intentions—like a seal carved into them by living energy. I've heard you often step in to stop fights? When people's intentions turn ugly, you might be detecting them before they get too evil, before they get so serious. I feel like all the incidents you've explained to us fit this theory, but . . . does your understanding refute it?"

"Mm. . . . I'm not sure. But I don't feel like it's wrong either."

"It sounds like a reasonable working assumption to say that what you perceive as a fracture is a manifestation of powerful negative intentions one person holds toward another. But can we really call that an ability? There's something about what you do that feels different from the other superpowered people."

"How so?"

"You seem to be so . . . quiet. Never forced. People with

unusual power usually end up very distorted by that power, but you aren't. Why not?"

The researcher frowned, mulling it over, but Kunio could not even work out what it was that seemed to be confusing him.

... So someone was actually after Kunio's ex-classmate, Kaori Nakayama. A sexual deviant with a fixation on women's necks had set his sights on her.

He had thousands of pictures, all focused on the napes of women's necks, and there was a pile of handkerchiefs with brown stains on them in his room. Apparently, he had been boarding crowded trains, making a small cut on a woman's neck, and collecting the blood on handkerchiefs. The cut was so small that his victims barely felt a pick and were often surprised to find a scab there later on. So far, he had been satisfied with these scratches, but with Kaori Nakayama, that was apparently inadequate. The pictures he had taken of her were the only ones in his collection that showed the face and body, and there were dozens of them. And on every one of them he had drawn a sinister line across her neck, as if practicing cutting off her head. Even the most amateur psychoanalyst could tell that he had a fetish for the female neck and that he had a history of making cuts . . .

. . . and that he had been practicing.

He had been searching for the neck he should really cut and had at last found it.

When he moved to assault Kaori, the police were lying in wait and captured him—alerted through channels by the Organization, following Kunio's information.

"Th-the absolute . . . perfect instant . . . s-severed . . . cut off . . . ," the man had screamed, thrashing wildly and injuring several officers, but they had managed to restrain him in the end.

He was twenty-four, unemployed, by the name of Shoji Morita. He had no priors, and had he not been caught in the act, it would have been nigh impossible to arrest him in time. It had been a very close call.

But the location had been an unlucky one. Shoji Morita had spared no thought for saving himself once he had cut off her head and had tried to carry out his crime on a busy street. A large number of people had witnessed the commotion and seen him get arrested.

As a result of which all kinds of ridiculous stories dogged Kaori Nakayama, and she and her parents had eventually moved to escape them.

Kunio had worried about her a little, but she was far away now, so he had not dwelled on it for long.

Kunio's days as a student had continued uneventfully, and after graduation he had taken a job at a food company as a quality control supervisor.

A perfectly ordinary white-collar job, but, in fact, he had never once performed his duties. According to the official records, his job consisted of going from one warehouse to the other, inspecting the company's products, but this was all part of his cover.

His actual job was far stranger: he discovered grudges.

Acting on orders from the Organization, he never had any real understanding of what he was doing. He came into work, picked up the envelope lying on his desk, and went to the place written inside, met the person he was instructed to meet, and checked to see if there were any "fractures" on that person or his or her surroundings. That was all.

Most of the time, he found one. Naturally, since he was only dispatched to places where one was already believed to exist. He was not required to inform the people he met about what he had found, and the people he met were never told exactly who he was. His meetings were sudden and not particularly welcome—and Kunio was never told what had happened to the targeted individual or company. Kunio vaguely assumed that the Organization decided whether or not to act when they received his report. If the targeted person was of use to them, they would save him; if not, they would let him die.

Besides his "work," occasionally people would come to see him. In addition to his regular interviews with the researchers, he was questioned by these visitors. They would ask him several questions, the same questions every time, and then leave. He had no idea exactly who they were, but he knew one thing about them.

(They're all . . . killers. They have all killed an incredible number of people.)

He could tell. What he felt from them was well beyond a fracture. Instead of other people's intentions creating a fracture on them, they were carving fractures into themselves. It was like a cold wind jetting out of them.

(I imagine they had to cut part of their hearts away, so they could kill people without it bothering them. . . .)

He didn't know if they were here to kill him or not. They might just be checking to see if they needed to.

When he met these people, and when he met the powerful, haughty individuals who had no idea they were being targeted, in the corner of his mind, Kunio always wondered . . .

(Why am I alive?)

He did not enjoy life.

There was nothing much he wanted to do.

He did not know what the point of anything he did was.

No—he knew that there was no point, and that was all that mattered.

Everyone he met in his line of work was successful, as far as the world was concerned. But every single one of them had earned someone's undying hatred. The more people worked, the more they tried to accomplish something, the more fractures appeared in the world.

After he spent a few years living like this, a certain woman came to visit him. Her name was Setsuko Amamiya, and what happened that day would change his life forever.

Kunio felt nothing from Setsuko Amamiya herself.

She was different from the damaged people who had come to see him before. There was no chill from the grudges received from others and from herself. As far as his senses were concerned, she was just a quiet, calm woman.

But while he was talking to her, by the purest coincidence, he happened to meet a girl.

▼▲▼

"—Uh, um . . . ?"

The girl seemed too surprised to respond. She did not seem used to getting hit on.

"Er, I'm . . ." Kunio had no idea what to say either. He'd been driven here by a sudden heat rising out of his chest. But somehow he managed, "I'm, uh, Koryo. Koryo. Kunio Koryo. I'm Kunio Koryo."

For some reason, he was repeating his name like a campaigning politician.

"N-no, I don't . . ." The girl obviously did not want to know his name, and this served to flummox her still further.

If he had just been trying to pick her up, he would have followed it with, "Buy you a drink?" or "Join me for karaoke?" but since Kunio himself had no idea what he was trying to accomplish, he had nothing further to add. He just waited for her reaction.

"No, I'm, um . . ." She was very pale, and it did not look like he could expect any kind of positive reaction.

But Kunio was too carried away to notice.

"You . . . I, uh . . . you . . ."

"Er, um, I . . ."

Both of them were just babbling now, their conversation never managing to connect.

At which point, a voice from behind the girl snapped, "What's going on?"

Kunio looked toward the voice and saw another girl, even younger, in a school uniform.

She glared at him.

"N-no . . ." The girl was still too stunned to be able to explain anything to the younger girl.

The younger girl sighed and said firmly, "I'm sorry, sir, but my sister has little experience speaking to men. Don't try to play your little games with her."

Completely thrown for a loop, Kunio stammered, "No, I'm really not . . . anyone suspicious. . . ."

But at the same time, a voice inside him disagreed. He was suspicious, wasn't he?

Nothing in the world defined him clearly. He was a dangling man.

"I just—" he said, but the younger girl cut him off.

"Let's go," she said, and pulled her sister's arm.

The shocked expression never once left the girl's face. Even as she was dragged away.

". . . Ah, ah—"

Kunio tried to call after them, but he had no idea what to say. He wanted to run after them but had no idea what to do if he caught them, so he ended up just standing there, dazed.

"Rejected you?" Amamiya said, coming up behind him. She sounded very amused, but Kunio was too out of it to notice.

He did not reply.

"She your type? The report said you weren't that interested in girls, but I guess we'll have to revise that," she chuckled.

Kunio never heard her.

He was too busy staring after the girl.

2

Half a year had passed since Kunio Koryo married.

His work continued without change, and he had begun to realize it would never end. But since it required very little of his time, he occasionally arrived home significantly earlier than most businessmen. He had been given an apartment that, while hardly luxurious, was still more than enough space for the two of them.

He turned the key, opened the door, and realized the place was empty. His wife was out.

This was not unusual. It was only four, and he knew his wife was usually out shopping at this time of day. She always tried to get the shopping done before he was supposed to be home at six.

Kunio took off his jacket and took in the laundry hanging on the veranda. His wife had not asked him to do this, but he figured he might as well help with the housework, especially simple stuff.

When he was finished, he went to the kitchen and opened the refrigerator, looking for the mugicha.

The white door swung open, revealing its contents. Kunio was used to it by now, but if a stranger had opened this refrigerator, the contents would have been quite a shock.

There was food inside. But a very small amount, tucked away to the side. More than half the space inside was filled with giant plastic bottles filled with black liquid.

Dozens of them. Packed in rows.

At a glance, they looked like soy sauce or cola, but the liq-

---

**Mugicha* A kind of tea (*tisane*) made from roasted barley.

uid was much too thick. If asked what it looked like, most people would probably say, "Kind of like . . . blood."

Kunio did not even glance at the bottles. He just took out the mugicha and poured himself a glass.

Obviously, the bottles were not filled with blood. If it had actually been blood, it would have coagulated by now. And it smelled less like iron and more like oil.

This was his wife's "staple diet." She had been born with damaged organs, and this special nutritional fluid was the most effective way for her to receive nourishment. It contained glucose and protein and a number of different vitamins. It was perfectly safe for Kunio as well, but it did not taste very good.

Kunio opened the door again to put the mugicha back and stared at the contents for a moment.

The hospital provided this liquid. She could not go far from the place it was made. It was hard for them to go on long vacations, and she got motion sick so easily she could not even take the train.

He was never sure if he should feel bad about that.

Since the first time he had met her, and even now that they had married, she remained a wonderful being, and he did not want to feel anything negative like pity or regret for her. But from an objective, ordinary perspective, her life was certainly a difficult one.

This discrepancy had been bothering him for a while and showed no signs of resolving itself. Every time he saw the refrigerator full of black liquid, it nagged at him again.

He heard the sound of a key scrabbling at the front door.

Kunio closed the refrigerator, went to the door, and opened one of the two locks.

Then he opened the door. His wife was standing outside, a grocery bag in her hand, looking surprised.

"Ah . . . ahhh . . . W-welcome home, Kunio."

"Thanks. And the same to you, Koi." He smiled at her, but she just slid past him, head down, into the apartment.

"Ah! The laundry . . . ," she said, the moment she saw it folded in piles.

"Yeah, it was dry."

"Sorry . . . ," Koi Koryo said in a tiny voice, bowing her head. Kunio had absolutely no idea why his wife always apologized to him.

But since she did, he had no choice but to respond rather pompously, "Nah, it was nothing."

She took the grocery bag into the kitchen.

"What's for dinner? Mackerel?" he asked, peering into the bag.

Koi said, again, "Uh, um . . . sorry."

"Want me to cook?"

"N-no, I can do it. But . . . thank you."

She was less stiff than simply not used to it yet. Like she wanted to be polite but wasn't sure when to stop.

"Sure."

Kunio was long since used to this part of her.

Soon enough the rice was cooked, and the smell of frying fish filled the room. Koi had to rely on her nutritional fluid for nourishment, but she could eat normal food. Just for the taste—she digested almost none of it—but she could eat as much as she wanted without getting fat, a trait anyone on a diet would surely be envious of. But sweet things taste good because they become energy so quickly, and just as candy with artificial sweeteners is never as good as candy made with real sugar, taking pleasure in food is a physical experience. One she could never have.

After his meal was laid out in front of him, she sat down opposite him, and they began eating.

In silence. They had never had any real conversations during meals. Neither of them knew what to talk about.

He looked across the table and watched her eat her tiny portions, just enough to make sure everything tasted right. She always looked to him like she was making an effort, and this never changed about her. Not since the first time he had laid eyes on her . . .

▼▲▼

Kunio had first seen her a year before, and she had quickly been dragged away from him.

But the memory of her did not fade so easily.

Early the next day, even though he had not arranged to meet anyone there, Kunio had gone to the entrance hall of that building again and waited all day, just in case she came back.

The next day and the next day . . . On the fourth day, he drew a picture of her and started asking people if they knew her, what her name was. With no results.

He was obviously obsessed, and it was clearly alarming people.

On the sixth day, he skipped work again, but this time a girl appeared before him.

"You there."

He turned around. He'd seen her before.

"You're . . ."

It was the younger sister of the girl he was looking for. In her school uniform again.

"What are you playing at?" she scowled. "Showing people drawings of my sister . . . This is a problem. Really."

She snatched the picture from his hand and tore it up.

"Ah . . . no," Kunio said, alarmed, but then it occurred to him that he didn't need it anymore. The clue he'd been looking for was standing right in front of him.

"Y-you're her sister, aren't you?" Kunio asked, intense.

The girl's expression did not lighten. "What do you want?

To make her miserable?" she demanded. "Why won't you just leave her alone? She's easy enough to bully without you."

"N-no, I don't want to . . . Eh?" Kunio frowned, puzzled. "Easy to bully?"

"Shy and . . . What do you care? If you're looking to get laid, there's plenty of other girls around. Much cuter girls, girls who will go with anyone who looks good. That's not my sister."

"W-wait just a minute. You've got the wrong idea."

"How so?"

"I-I just want to talk to her. Really. I'm serious. I just want to meet her. It doesn't have to be in private," Kunio said desperately. If this girl rejected the idea, he knew he would never see either of them again.

She looked him over carefully.

Kunio stared back at her . . . and then shivered.

She looked like an ordinary girl, but there was something about her . . . something that made the hairs on his neck stand up.

It wasn't a fracture, nothing that obvious, but something similar, something frightening and sharp . . . that vanished a moment later.

"Tell me your name and where you work first," she said, not minding if it was rude.

It never even occurred to Kunio to take offense. He nodded quickly. "Of course! I'm . . ."

He gave her his name and his home and work addresses and phone numbers. It occurred to him later that this could get him in trouble, but at the time it never entered his head.

"Hmm . . . Well, I guess you are serious." She nodded. "Okay, I'll tell my sister about you. Come here again tomorrow," she said, and turned to leave.

"W-wait! Will you at least give me a name?"

"My name is Mai Kuran. And my sister's name is Koi Kobayashi."

Without another word of explanation, she was gone.

"Koi . . . ," Kunio said, for the first time. From that moment on, that name was incredibly precious to him.

▼▲▼

. . . And now, a year later, they were married.

Before their marriage, they had basically done all the usual things a young couple would. They'd gone on dates, he'd bought her presents, she'd knitted him a sweater, he had proposed with a ring worth three months' salary, everything. But they had hardly done any of the things lovers usually did.

They had never had a fight.

Not even a little argument.

They had not had a wedding ceremony, but this was because of Koi's complicated family situation and not by choice. Nevertheless, it was a little strange that their feelings had never once been in conflict.

And now they were in their apartment, newlyweds, eating across from each other in total silence. Not even attempting to talk.

Kunio had spent his entire life not talking to people, so silence was fine with him, but he occasionally wondered if it bothered her.

Every meal, she would eat just a few bites and be done, and sit patiently waiting for him to finish.

Kunio took a bite of fish, and as he chewed, his lips abruptly twisted slightly. A bone had poked him.

"Ah!"

Koi went pale and stood up. She always noticed instantly if he was injured in any way.

"S-sorry! Are you okay?" she asked timidly.

Kunio nodded. "Yeah, it's nothing. Just scraped my gum a little. No big deal."

"I'm sorry. . . . I should have been more careful getting the bones out. . . ."

"Nobody can get all the bones out of mackerel. I was just eating too fast," he said, completely unruffled.

For a long moment, she sat with her head down, saying nothing.

Kunio put the bone back in his mouth, chewed it up, and fell silent himself.

But this new silence lacked the transparency of even a moment before.

Kunio gazed absently at Koi, who had long since finished eating and had nothing to do, wondering what he could do for her.

She had accepted his feelings, but he had no idea if that had made her happier.

Perhaps she could have lived a more peaceful life without him . . . as long as she was provided for.

(I . . . .)

Kunio remembered what Setsuko Amamiya had said.

He might hold the key to changing the world.

(If I really am . . . a kind of bomb like that, then . . .)

He had never really thought about marriage or happiness before. But now he thought about it all the time.

(Is being with me causing her grief . . . ?)

As the thought crossed his mind, Koi looked up and said hesitantly, "Uh, um, I . . ."

"Mm?"

"There's something . . . Kunio . . . I have to tell you. . . . Um . . ."

"What?"

"I . . . um . . ." There was a long pause, and then she said

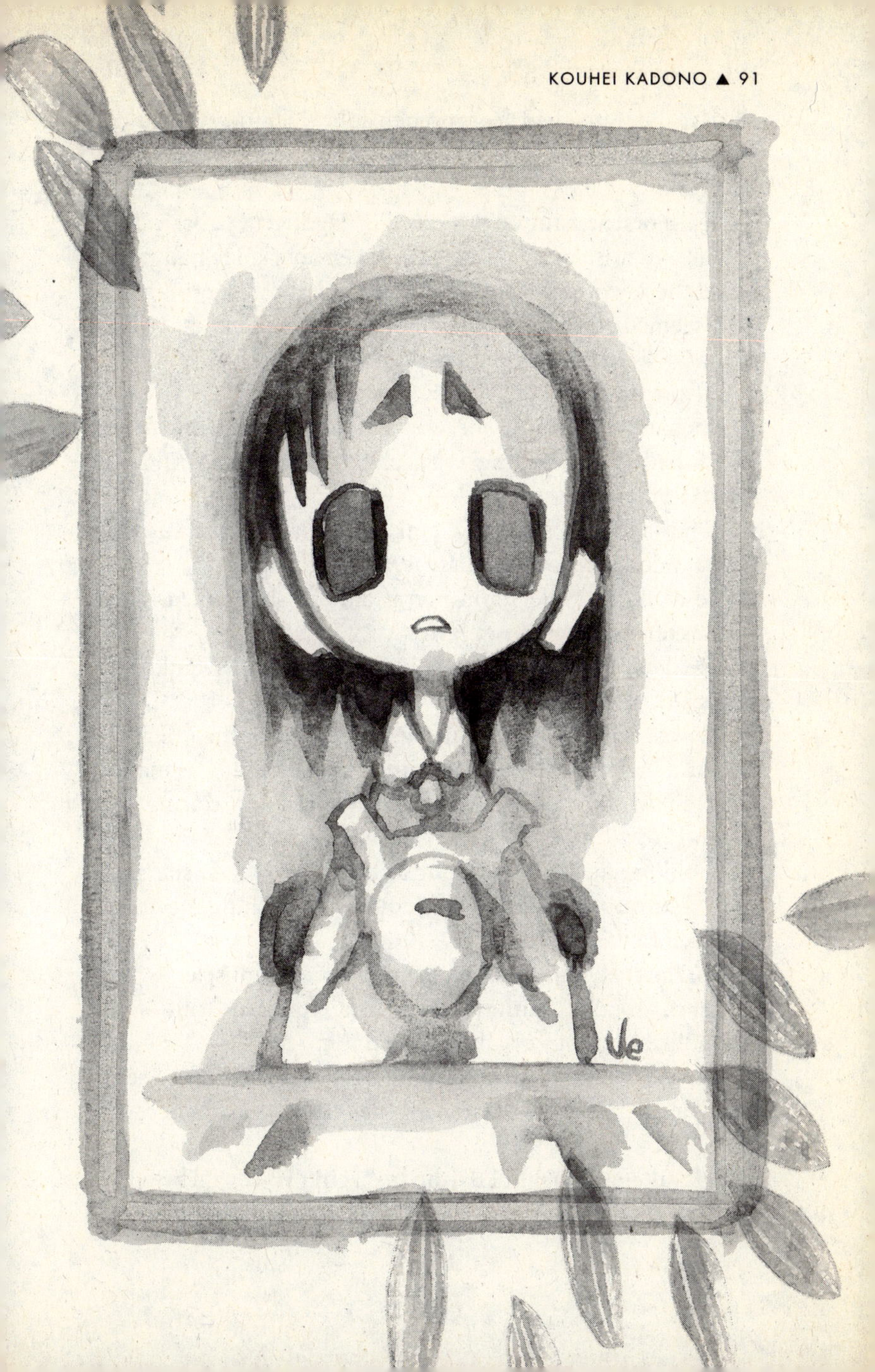

clearly, but no less comprehensibly, "I-I'm . . . um . . . a Porsche."

"Eh?"

"A P-Porsche Laufwerk . . . um . . . Jagdtiger . . . basically."

". . . What is that?" Kunio said, taken aback. He had never heard these words before. "Is that a kind of car? German?"

It seemed strange for anyone with motion sickness as bad as his wife's to talk about luxury cars.

"N-no, not that . . ."

Uncharacteristically, she was starting to get worked up. Like a child just learning to speak who can't quite find the words to communicate.

"The Jagdtiger is, um, a tank. It has a Porsche suspension . . . designed by Dr. Porsche, a very cheap . . ."

He couldn't understand her at all, but she looked like a cornered fox, which upset him.

"R-right. First, calm down. What about this tank?" he asked.

He was not a military buff by any stretch of the imagination and had never heard the name of a tank that was manufactured in very small numbers in Germany during the Second World War.

Looking like she was about to burst into tears, she said, "I . . . I, um . . ." But before she could say anything more, the doorbell rang.

Koi flinched and then froze, not moving a muscle.

"Er . . . so . . . ," Kunio said, trying to figure out if he should hear her out or answer the door.

But the bell kept ringing, so he figured he should go send them away. He headed toward the front door, where he heard . . .

"Hey there! Thought I'd drop in," a girl's voice said brightly. Mai Kuran.

Relieved, Kunio opened the door. Koi's sister came in, bowing her head.

She greeted her sister, who was still sitting at the table, and sat down next to her.

"What's wrong? You look sort of down. . . ."

"No, it's nothing. Really," Koi said, shaking her head awkwardly.

Mai glanced at Kunio. "Am I interrupting something? Wouldn't want to interfere with the newlyweds!" She winked at him.

He laughed. "No, nothing like that. Thanks for coming," Kunio said, meaning it. Being alone with Koi, as strangely as she had been behaving, had been pretty hard on him.

"So, Koi . . . ?" he asked, expecting her to continue, but she sat in silence, not even attempting to speak. Assuming she no longer wanted to talk about it, Kunio let the conversation drift away from Dr. Porsche.

"Is she looking after you properly? I had my doubts . . . ," Mai said brightly.

"Of course she is. Much better than I deserve," Kunio said seriously.

Koi hung her head.

Mai's eyes opened wide, and then she giggled. "Are you always this serious? Like a teacher . . . !"

"R-really?"

"Yeah, all straitlaced and firm."

"I don't mean to be. . . ."

"Koi, don't you think he should smile more?"

"N-no . . . However Kunio wants to be is fine with me."

"But you'd like her to smile more, right?" Mai said, turning to Kunio.

Flustered, he stammered, "No . . . I don't . . ."

Certainly, he wanted her to smile if she felt like it. But he didn't know what he could do to make her laugh more, and even if she never smiled, he loved her poker face just as much.

He didn't really know what he thought, frankly.

"Um, I'll make some coffee. . . ."

Kunio had finished eating, so Koi quickly cleared his dishes away.

"Need any help?" Mai asked.

Koi smiled faintly at her. "No, I've got it." She went into the kitchen alone.

"She still seems a little stressed," Mai whispered, leaning across the table. "Is it still a little awkward for you as well?"

"W-well . . . yeah, a little," Kunio said, smiling ruefully.

Mai never beat around the bush.

These sisters had different names and different mothers—and while Mai had her father's name, Koi was using her long since deceased mother's name. Koi was a product of what sounded less like a mistress than a one-night stand.

She was not allowed anywhere near her father's home, and Mai's visits were kept secret. If she were caught spending time with her sister, it would apparently lead to "all sorts of trouble."

Given the uniqueness of his own birth, Kunio didn't care at all about any of this, but he did occasionally wonder what Koi herself thought about it. Did it bother her? Did she suffer because of it? Or did she harbor a grudge against her father?

(Should I . . .)

How should he react to all this? He did want to know more, but was it right to ask?

Suddenly, in a quiet, cold voice, Mai asked, "Getting tired of her yet?"

He turned toward her, shocked. She glanced toward the

kitchen, where Koi was still making coffee, not meeting his eye. Her question had been less blunt than . . . relentless.

"Wh-what do you mean?" Kunio asked, but Mai said nothing more.

When Koi had poured the coffee, Mai went into the kitchen and carried her own cup back.

"Smells good," she said, so happily that Kunio wondered if he had been hearing things a moment before.

"What were you talking about?" Koi asked, seeing his expression.

Before he could answer, Mai said smoothly, "I was telling him what a great husband my sister landed."

Mai lied so well that Kunio had nothing else to add.

▼▲▼

And then one morning . . .

Kunio was leaving his apartment, carrying out the nonburnable trash, when he bumped into someone moving in.

"Hey there! You live here?" a cheery-looking middle-aged man in a suit said, holding a moving box.

"Yes . . . You're moving in?"

"Yeah. Name's Kuriyama. Nice to meet you."

As they were exchanging small talk, a woman's voice called out from behind them.

"They're waiting for you upstairs!"

"Oh, right! Sorry, gotta run," the man said, bobbing his head and boarding the elevator Kunio had just stepped out of.

Kunio watched him aimlessly, when he heard someone gasp.

"Ah . . . K-Koryo . . . ?"

He knew that voice from somewhere. He swung around and gasped himself.

It was a woman he had once gone to school with.

"N-Nakayama . . . ," he croaked . . . but not because she had become remarkably beautiful since he'd last seen her.

"I-it's Kuriyama now. Kaori Kuriyama."

The same Kaori who had been attacked by a deviant and chased out of town by rumors. She smiled at him nervously.

"Ah, yeah . . . right."

Kunio nodded, barely hearing her.

He could sense it—a huge fracture, far larger than ten years before, stretching from her neck to her chest.

3

Crimson—his earliest memories.

Presumably, he had been left alone in a place covered in fresh blood, where nothing else moved. He would never know where that place was, but if that blood was human, then this had been the site of a long and terrible slaughter. The battle had raged on and on, with everyone furiously trying to kill each other—a bloodthirsty world.

(Just like this one.)

That place that was not here, and the place he knew all too well from living in it—both of them were filled with hate, where people cursed one another just like on that bloodstained wasteland.

(Koi, do you even know . . . ?)

He thought of his wife again.

(Do you even know what would make you happy?)

He had fallen in love with her, and she had accepted it, but how inevitable had that been?

Had she needed his financial support? He sometimes wondered if that was all. He didn't mind if it was. He wanted her, and as long as he had her, he did not much care why. But—was that really good for her?

(If money is the only problem . . . you're already my wife, and if . . . something happened to me, everything I left behind would be yours. Truth is, you might no longer need me.)

What Setsuko Amamiya had said had been bothering him recently.

"You might have the power to change the world."

He had tried not to think about it. But the longer he and Koi lived happily together, the larger it grew in the back of his mind. It was starting to be a burden.

(If I'm some sort of catalyst, capable of releasing something that has been building up here, in this world . . . then I . . .)

This fact always made him shudder.

If his very existence was a calamity waiting to happen, waiting to unleash horror on the world—and more important, on one person in it, his wife, Koi . . .

In the evening, on the road between the shopping area and the apartment:

"Oh, Kuriyama!" Kunio called out, spying his married ex-classmate on her way home from shopping.

"Ah! Koryo . . . ," Kaori Kuriyama said, startled. "You're headed home?"

"Yep. Wrapped things up early today! Your husband's always home late?"

"Yes, I'm afraid so . . . these days . . . ," she replied, looking a little tense.

"He must be working hard. I tend to be quick to give up, myself," Kunio said, smiling faintly.

"I suppose . . . but I hope he doesn't work too hard." Kaori sighed. Then she asked timidly, "How's your adorable wife?"

"Oh, you met her?"

"Yes, when I was introducing myself."

"Be nice to her, will you? She's so shy . . ."

"I thought as much," Kaori said, smiling awkwardly.

From this alone, Kunio could imagine what Koi had been like. She had probably stood there unable to say a word, looking completely lost and helpless.

"Koryo, how did you . . . ?"

"She was a clerk where I work."

"Oh . . . How . . . ordinary."

"Is that bad?"

"No . . . It's just, you were always a little mysterious. I wondered what kind of person you would marry. . . ."

"We're very run-of-the-mill."

"Aren't we all? Still," Kaori raised her head and looked over at him, "you never change, Koryo. You have the same eyes you did in high school."

"Oh? You mean I never grew up?"

"No, not like that . . . You never were very childish."

"Ouch. You make it sound like I was a real bore. Was I really that stuck-up?" He laughed.

Kaori giggled. "No, not like that . . . Oh, but, yeah . . . maybe. At the time, I always thought you were very calm and quiet, but looking back . . ."

She trailed off.

Kunio had looked away from her, his attention aimed in a very different direction. She followed his gaze.

A man was standing there.

It took her a moment to realize what she was seeing.

She had done her best to repress those memories. But she had been unable to forget.

Her instincts would not let her eliminate all traces of that danger, of the man who had tried to take her life.

Eyes glazed over, the man shuffled toward them, his mouth moving constantly, muttering something.

". . . Think . . . Who do you think . . ."

They couldn't make it out. His mutter never quite became words.

That bizarrely pale face had not changed much in ten years. But the flesh on his belly and shoulders and neck had swollen, making him fatter, heavier.

"... Ah, ahhhhh—"

Kaori started backing away. Her mind had not let her remember him yet, but her body was already on the defensive.

This fat man was the same one, the same nightmare that had once tried to cut off her head.

His name was Shoji Morita. He was thirty-four. He had been sentenced to seven years in prison for assault with attempt to cause bodily harm and disturbance of the peace, and his sentence had been extended for three years for bad behavior, but he had at last been released from prison... and had instantly come after her again.

Despite his unnatural fixation on cutting off the head of a beautiful woman, he had been declared completely sane and had appeared before her without his violent obsession diminished in the slightest.

"Ah..."

Kaori remembered now, and the memory left her legs buckling under her. She collapsed to the ground. Ironically, fear had overcome her and robbed her of the self-control required to flee.

The road ran past a river and was deserted. During the day and at night, it was busy enough, but at this time of day, hardly anyone walked here.

The sun was just beginning to set on the opposite bank.

"Who do you think..."

Shoji Morita came closer to her, but his gaze was not fixed on Kaori.

He was coming straight for Kunio.

"Who do you think you are!? Y-you're nothing!"

His eyes were filled with envy.

The sight of Kunio chatting happily with Kaori had been enough to spark a jealous rage.

And Kunio . . . remained perfectly calm.

He stepped lightly in front of Kaori, putting himself between her and Shoji Morita.

"Y-you're nothing!"

As Shoji Morita advanced on them, Kunio stepped forward to meet him.

As far as Kunio was concerned, Shoji Morita's appearance was not a surprise at all. It had been exactly what he had expected . . . or more accurately . . .

(Just as I planned . . .)

Everything was happening just like he'd wanted it to.

"How dare you!" Shoji Morita shrieked, lunging at Kunio. With a butcher knife in his hand.

Kunio did not dodge. Instead, he grabbed hold of Shoji Morita.

He got a grip on the wrist of the fat man's knife hand, and they grappled together.

". . . . ."

Kaori sat there watching, dazed.

"S-son of a bitch!" Shoji Morita snarled, trying to shove Kunio bodily away from him, but Kunio held on tight, and the two of them went tumbling off the road.

Into the river, with a splash.

This area had been a mountain once, and as the area around the mountain had been leveled out, the height discrepancies had led to the river's flowing through large pipes here and there. The two men were dragged through one of them.

And emerged somewhere else entirely.

Gray concrete walls on either side of them. Until March,

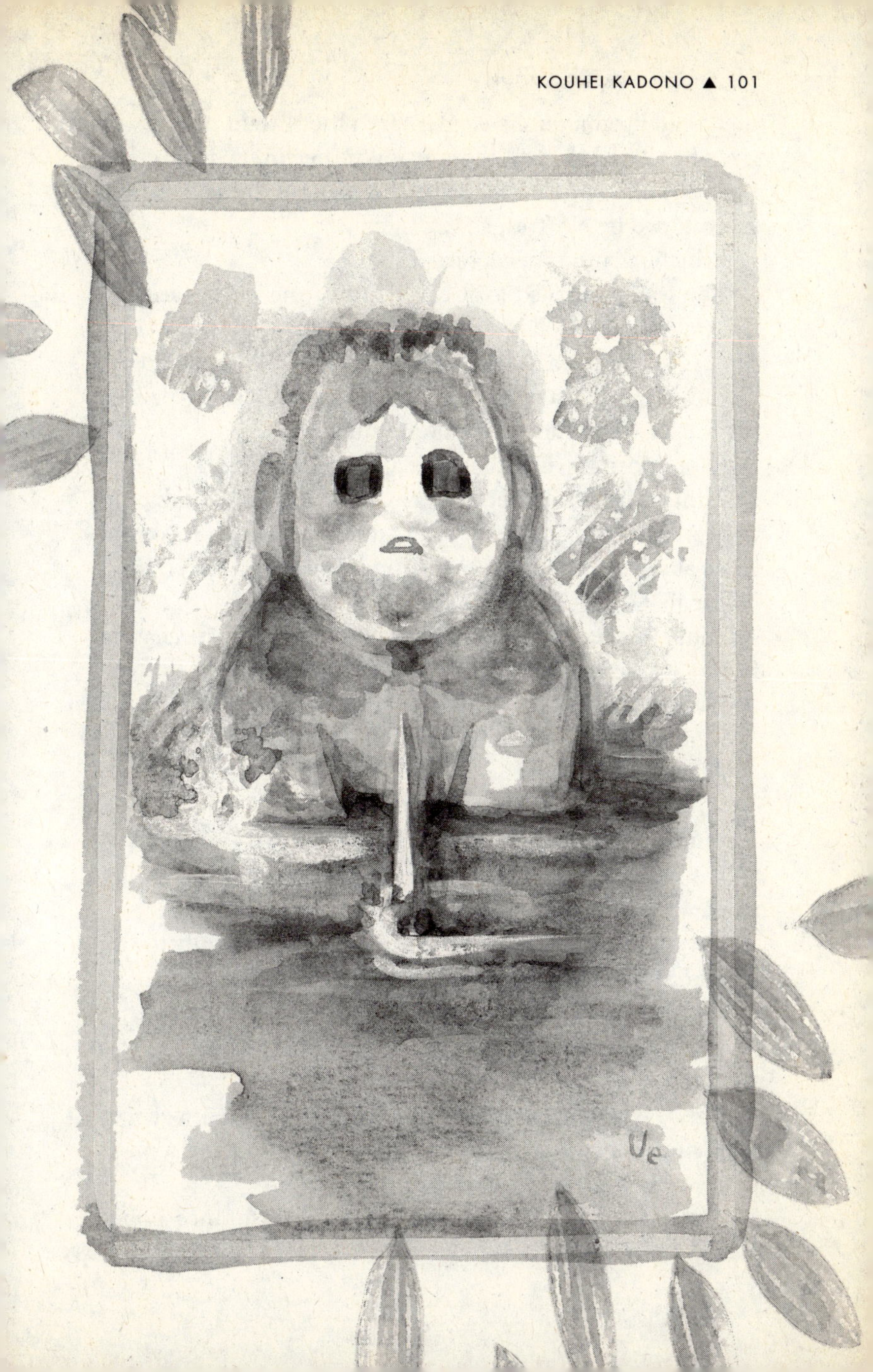
Ue

there had been a public elementary school right next to the river, but it had closed, fallout from the declining birthrate. It had yet to be targeted for redevelopment and was currently surrounded by No Trespassing signs.

Which meant it was deserted.

The water churned as it came out of the pipe, sweeping the grappling men away from each other.

"S-s-s-s-son of a . . . son of a bitch . . . !" Morita stood up.

Kunio tried to stand as well, but there was a sharp pain in his back, and his movements were sluggish.

Shoji Morita swung the knife again, attacking.

Kunio dodged desperately. He managed to scramble up the concrete embankment, out of the river. There was a tall fence along the top of the bank, to prevent the children from falling in.

Shoji Morita came out of the water really fast, chasing Kunio. Kunio dragged himself backward.

His back came up against the fence, blocking his path.

If he tried to climb it, he'd be stabbed in the back.

He was about to die.

". . . . ."

But Kunio never panicked.

His mind was not focused on the evil man in front of him at all.

He was thinking only of his wife, Koi. He was only thinking about what he could do for her.

(If I die like this, here . . . no matter how you look at it, no matter how much you try, nobody will ever believe it was suicide.)

This was beyond all doubt. It had obviously been sheer coincidence. He had been talking with a neighbor, and a madman with a knife had attacked out of nowhere.

And if he died like this, then the life insurance policy

would pay out—enough to keep even a sickly woman like Koi comfortable for the rest of her life.

And the catalyst that might be sleeping within him would vanish safely.

He had been thinking about this for a while.

He no longer had any doubts in his mind about what he had been living for.

He had met her—and that was enough. He had achieved happiness. The satisfaction of that was enough to erase all the emptiness of his life before.

Which was exactly why he could not bear the thought, however unlikely, that he might cause Koi harm.

(If I die now—if I am gone before I release danger on the world, and if that makes things better for her . . . then I don't mind.)

He had been thinking about this since he met Kaori Kuriyama again. For the last few days, he had been watching her in secret, well aware that someone else was watching her, too. Which is why he had deliberately called out to someone else's wife on a deserted street, in a very friendly manner. If he did nothing, Kaori's husband would be targeted, and in that case, his plan would not work. It was a little rushed, but Shoji Morita had come after him anyway, swinging the knife around, chasing him down.

"Wh-wh-wh-whoooooooo!" Morita wailed.

Behind his voice there was a crunch, as if there had been some sort of accident in the distance—but this place was cut off from all such outside commotion.

"Who do you . . . think you . . . areeee!"

Shoji Morita was white as a sheet. Ten years locked up, thinking of only one thing, and then to see it being so easily meddled with—all his frustration had come tearing out of him.

It occurred to Kunio that he understood how Morita felt.

He did not share the fat man's enthusiasms, nor was he as willing to do whatever it took to achieve what he desired—but even so . . . Morita had spent ten long years thinking of nothing but Kaori's neck, dreaming of cutting off her head, and that kind of emotion . . . was something Kunio could understand.

Kunio had spent his entire life not sure what it was that he longed for, and when he had met her, at last he realized—and had known that the emptiness was gone forever.

Nobody else could ever understand what it meant to him, but this man had found that same thing in Kaori. That unnameable, incomparable thing that erased all the meaninglessness of life before it.

There was no turning back and no desire to turn back—and this alone, Kunio and Shoji Morita had in common.

Both of them were aliens in this world. Forced to live, hunkered down, far from the place of peace in their hearts. The feeble little light they'd managed to find here was all that supported them.

"Y-you son of a bitch . . . !"

Shoji Morita came after Kunio with no hesitation, waving a cheap carving knife he'd presumably bought at the local supermarket, which glittered in the light of the setting sun. . . .

▼▲▼

. . . On previous occasions, it had been reported as follows.

▲▼▲▼▲

Kunio had faced the fire and had been seen to mutter something under his breath. His mouth had moved, and he looked like he was saying something, but no one could hear him, and what they could hear held no meaning.

This time he was not facing the fire in the orphanage. But there was no doubt that he was facing someone with evil, murderous intentions.

When he encountered something like this, he could always feel it—feel his tongue moving on its own.

Nobody had discovered it yet, but under his tongue, looking for all the world like capillaries, was a tattoo of a very unusual pattern. There were no chemicals or metallic particles in the ink, nothing even the most state-of-the-art medical procedures would detect.

Once, in a world far, far away, those who had looked after him as a baby had placed this charm on him, in the knowledge that he would find himself in a harsh world. A charm to protect him from all harm. In our world, charms are nothing but a small comfort for the superstitious, but in his world, charms and other spells were practical and effective in all fields of civilization. They helped crops grow, helped keep builders safe, protected travelers and merchants . . . and they had their uses in war.

And in killing.

Kunio was aware that he was chanting some words of power and that they were creating an effect, but he did not know what. He could not hear his own voice.

He did not need to.

Even if he had understood, there was no one in this world he could explain it to.

In all likelihood, Shoji Morita never understood what happened.

He swung the knife, trying to stab Kunio Koryo, ready to kill him—but the blade suddenly slipped from his fingers.

It appeared without warning. There was nothing in the sky above a moment before. But down it came. What the ancients believed to be the gods' punishment.

Lightning.

First the flash of light and a moment later the noise—but Shoji Morita never heard that thunder. Before it reached his ears, the lightning's high-voltage electricity struck the blade of his knife, coursed through his body, stopped his heart, and boiled every cell in his body. He died instantly.

Something came out of his half-open mouth, but it was not words, only an emission of fried, burned air.

His knees folded awkwardly, his body leaned backward, bending like soft candy, and the soulless thing that had been Shoji Morita a moment before collapsed on the ground.

"... I knew it," Kunio whispered, watching. He looked very tired. "Of course. This always happens." He sighed.

He had seriously thought about dying and leaving the life insurance payments to his wife, but he had known full well things would probably not turn out that way.

He had absolutely no control over the phenomenon that protected him, but he had worked out what set it off and what it could do.

If someone was trying to injure him, with intent to kill, it always activated.

Each time Kunio encountered a situation like that, this knowledge was brought home again.

He had no idea what secrets lay within him, but he needed to know that danger as accurately as possible, for one very crucial reason. . . .

He staggered upright and walked back upstream.

The sun had set, and it was getting dark.

When he climbed back out of the river on the other side of the pipe, Kaori Kuriyama was waiting for him.

"Ah . . . Koryo . . . ," she said, worried.

Kunio nodded faintly. "He'll never bother you again," he said, emotionless.

"Eh . . ." Kaori seemed a little dazed. "Then . . . that lightning . . . ?"

She had sharp instincts. It was as if she had correctly guessed what he had done.

But Kunio did not even blink. "Yeah. But leave him there till someone else finds him. You don't want him causing another commotion, do you?"

His tone was peaceful, but it allowed no argument.

"Eh . . . yes . . . yes, right," Kaori said, still shaking, nodding to herself. Less in agreement with Kunio than trying to convince herself.

Kunio seemed calm and used to this sort of thing. And that was very convincing.

He said nothing, just looked down at his neighbor's wife coolly.

He was used to this now.

He had few memories of the time he stopped the fire in the orphanage, but that was only natural. He had been very young, but even more critical . . .

(The same thing has happened so many times in so many places that it lost all significance—all the times it happened when I was a child just got muddled together, and I can't remember any of them specifically.)

Even the Organization did not know how much he knew about his own abilities. Setsuko Amamiya had called it "magic"—the ability to summon forth some kind of energy that lay sleeping in the world—and he had figured out how it worked.

If he had wanted to change the world, it would have been easy.

He plopped his hand down on Kaori Kuriyama's shoulder.

She looked up.

"Listen—no matter what anyone asks you, just say you don't know. That will make things easier for both of us."

His voice was quiet. It never changed.

"O-okay," Kaori said, nodding. She had no other choice.

▼▲▼

"I'm home!"

Kunio returned to his home, where Koi was waiting for him.

"Welcome back, Kunio . . . Mm?"

Kunio had fallen in the river and was wet and covered in mud. When she saw him, her eyes went wide.

"Ah, I slipped on the riverbank and fell in. Stupid, eh?" he said, chuckling. Trying to convince her it was no big deal. "It's about time we sent this suit out to be cleaned anyway."

"Just a minute," she said, and ran to the closet, emerging with a towel. "Please be more careful. Are you cold?"

Koi helped him take off his wet clothes, drying him off with the towel.

"Nah, I'm fine."

He pulled off his socks and wiped his bare feet with the towel and at last stepped up into the apartment.

"I'll start filling up the tub," she said, and vanished into the bathroom again.

Still wet, Kunio gazed absently around their home.

It was nothing fancy—just an ordinary, commonplace apartment.

But it was warm and more precious to him than anywhere else in the world.

There was no point in even comparing it to other places. He cared not a whit for the world, for the future. . . .

He stood there until Koi came back. "You should shower while you wait for the bath to fill . . . I think. . . ."

As always, hesitant, insecure.

"Yeah, good idea," Kunio said, nodding. He stepped into the bathroom, sat down on the stool next to the bath, and turned the tap for the showerhead.

The shower was not particularly strong, sharing water with the bath, but he didn't mind. He let the feeble stream play over his body. It wasn't very warm.

". . . Um, do you need . . . ?" he heard Koi ask.

As brightly as he could, Kunio said, "No, I'm all good."

He didn't care about the world. There was only one thing in it that mattered to him—and that was her. She was all he cared about.

And if one day she tried to kill him?

Would he, as always, call down lightning and burn her to a crisp?

That was why he had to find out more. Without the Organization knowing, no matter how much danger it put him in—just in case she ever grew to hate him, just in case she ever tried to kill him—so that he could avoid killing her. No matter what it cost him, he had to learn to control this "magic." He had to learn how not to use it, how to stop it from taking action against her. To do that, he had to know how to use it—an ironic reversal.

". . . Mm?"

Kunio noticed a thin red line in the water around his feet. Blood.

His blood. He had felt no pain and had not noticed, but the edge of Shoji Morita's blade had grazed his neck.

He knew a smile had broken out on his face.

It looked like he was making progress.

He turned off the shower.

The bath was still only half full, but he climbed on in.

He hugged his knees to his chest, as if making sure his body was his own.

"... Um ...?" Koi called out, worried. She must have heard the shower stop.

"No problems. Still all good," he said peacefully. But his body was trembling.

"Okay ... I hope you don't catch cold...."

"Yeah, so do I," he whispered, running his fingers over the cut on his neck.

He could feel the pain now.

"No problem at all, Koi."

His murmur was too soft for his wife to hear, and this time she did not answer.

▲▼▲▼▲

DRILL HOLE IN MY BRAIN

Otaro Maijo

Illustrations by the author
Translated by Andrew Cunningham

The end of a love brings a terrible choice for two boys.
The power to destroy love . . . is love itself?
Otaro Maijo has created a scene sadder than any before . . .
all linked together with a metal tower.

"Drill Hole in My Brain" is an emblematic *Faust* story, reaching beyond the boundaries of genre fiction into the avant-garde, and reinvigorating avant-garde provocation with a pop sensibility. This erotic phantasmagoria combines the surrealistic and the shocking in a way that readers of such Western authors as William S. Burroughs and Georges Bataille will recognize.

Otaro Maijo was born in 1973. His debut work, *Smoke, Soil, or Sacrifices,* won the prestigious Mephisto Award, given to new fantasy and mystery writers. He is a gigantic talent, dashing freely through the Japanese literary scene. The illustrations are by the multitalented author.

▲▼▲▼▲

My mom's a piece of shit.

Without even consulting my feelings on the matter, she married my dad, had me, and then went and had an affair with Kouji Miyadate.

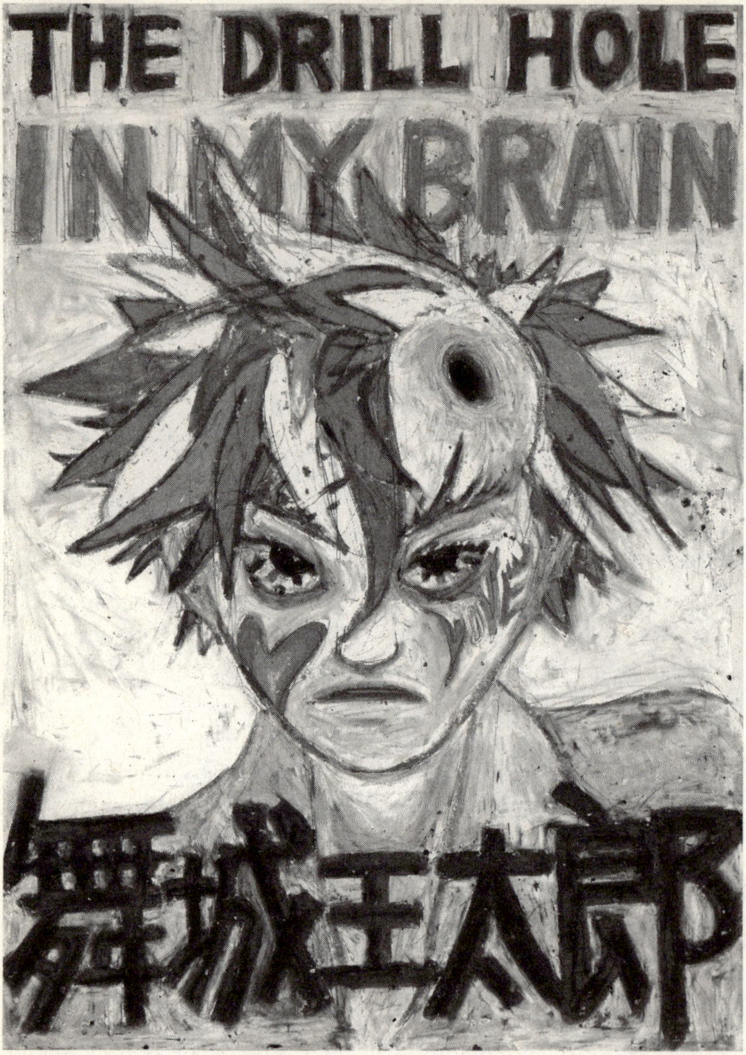
THE DRILL HOLE
IN MY BRAIN
舞城王太郎

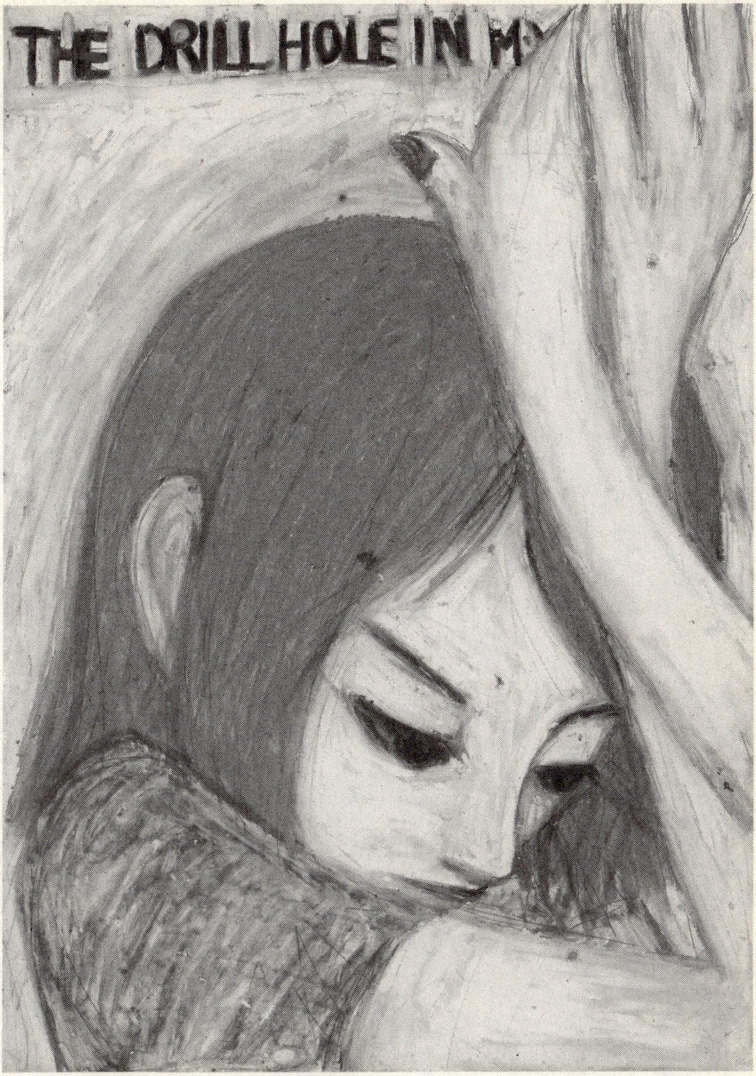
THE DRILL HOLE IN M

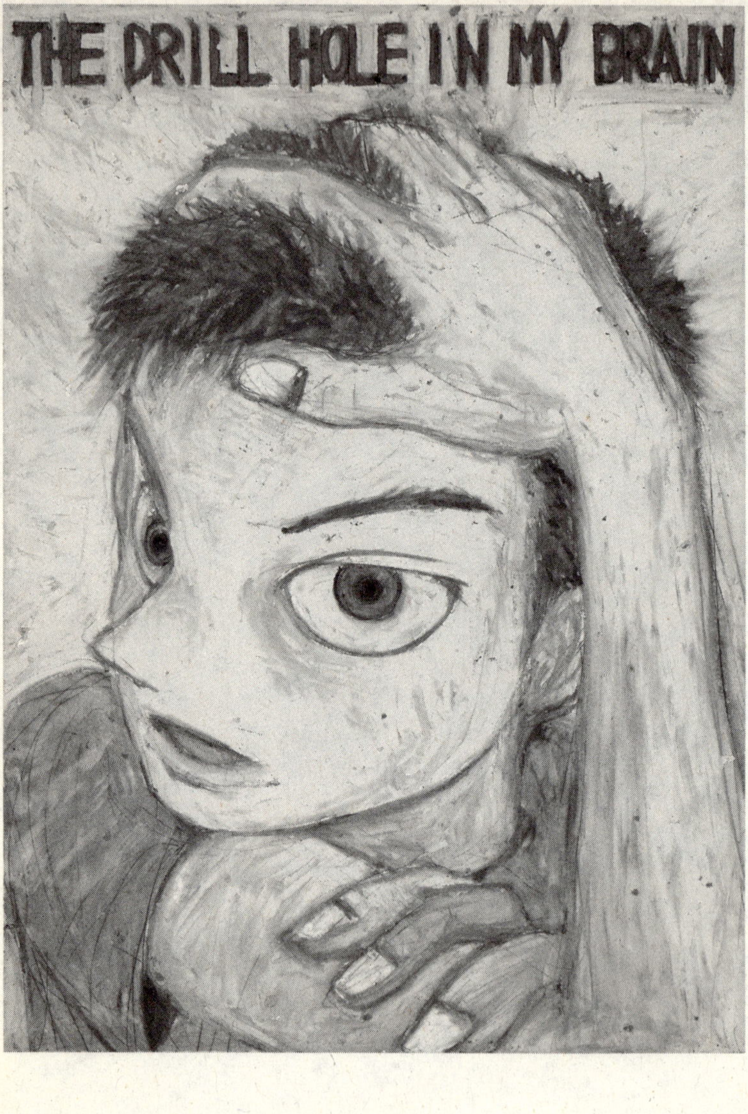
THE DRILL HOLE IN MY BRAIN

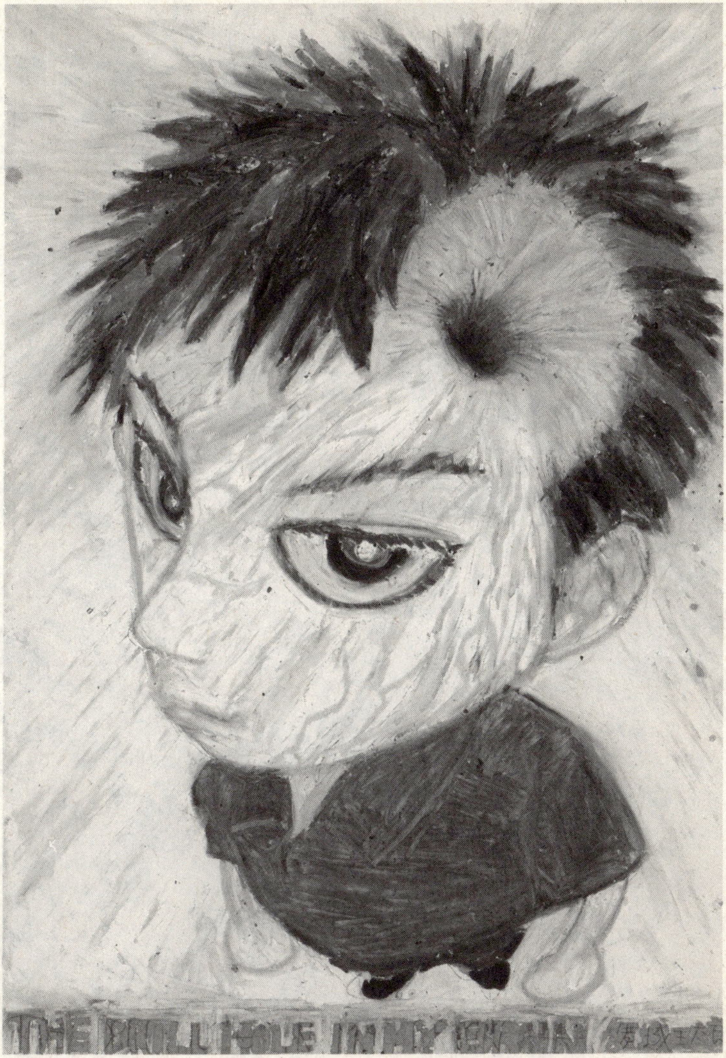
THE DRILL HOLE IN MY BRAIN

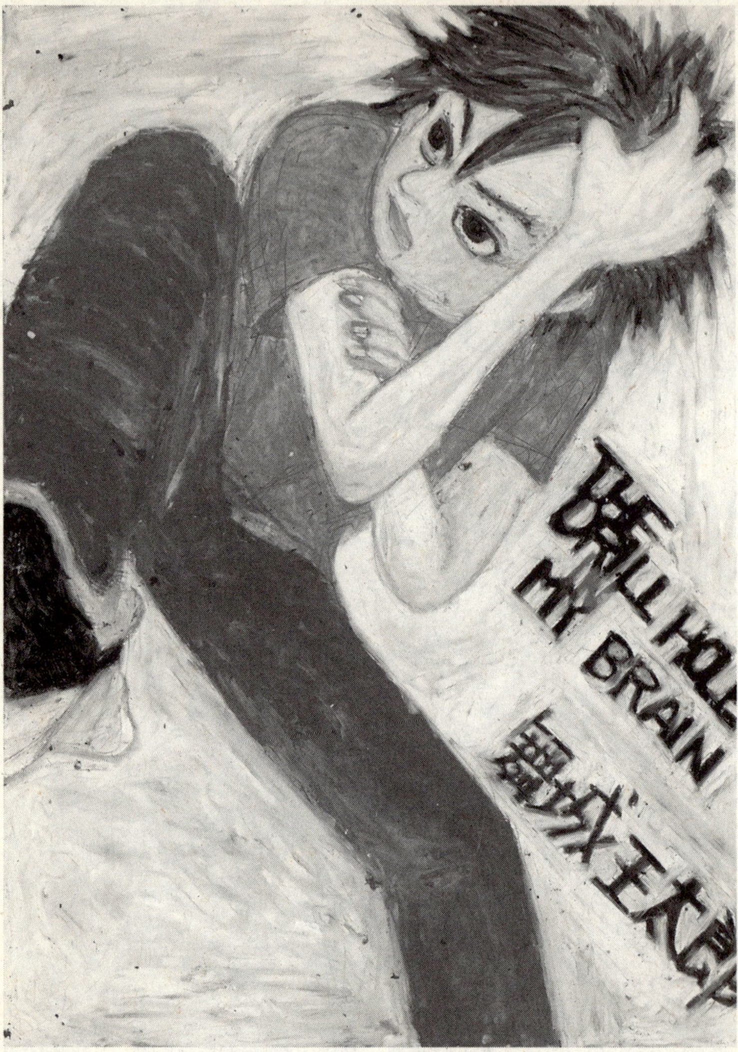
DRILL HOLE
MY BRAIN

And Kouji Miyadate is total scum. No, seriously, I mean it. What the hell did my mom ever see in him? Kouji Miyadate worked in the tatami shop near West Akatsuki Station, but he went skiing, fell, cut the palm of his hand on the edge of the ski, injured the tendon so he could no longer make tatami, and ended up working at the ice cream shop his brother-in-law in Takefu owned and drank what little money he earned off that. What an asshole. Whenever he laughed, his tiny little mouth looked just like an asshole. He was short and scrawny, his hair was always dirty, and he never shaved. And he was disgustingly servile.

My dad's a piece of shit, too. He should have just beat the shit out of Kouji Miyadate without saying a damn thing, but even though he had us, he kept on acting like it was a question of love and put himself on the block with Kouji Miyadate and demanded that my mom choose. Like an idiot. Putting himself at Kouji Miyadate's level. He should have just beat the shit out of him. Since he didn't, my mom did the obvious fucking thing and decided to try and patch things up with my dad, which gave Kouji Miyadate a chance to get really pissed off. Like he had any goddamn right to be angry.

Even pissed off, Kouji Miyadate knew he couldn't win a fair fight, so he needed a weapon. When Kouji Miyadate attacked our house on the evening of June 14, he had a basket hanging from his back. Inside the basket were a hatchet, a scythe, and two butcher knives.

Grandma and Grandpa were sleeping on the first floor, and he used the hatchet on them. Cut Grandpa's head clean off. He swung the hatchet at my dad in the living room. His brains came out. Then Kouji Miyadate went up the stairs and tried to use it on my brother in the first room, but my brother sacrificed his arm to steal it away. A moment later, one of the butcher knives slit my brother's jugular. He was then stabbed several times in the belly, pulping his organs. I came running in from the next room and kicked the bloody knife out of Kouji Miyadate's hand, then managed to steal the other knife as well, but in the commotion, Kouji Miyadate grabbed a Phillips screwdriver from my brother's desk and stabbed it into my head. On the left side, right on the border between the calvarium and the temporal area. It sank all the way in, and I heard a whistling sound inside my head. My sister hid under the kotatsu in her bedroom, and Kouji Miyadate never found her. My mom was out drinking in Sabae. Kouji Miyadate searched for her fruitlessly for a while, then tried to kill himself by slicing open his belly with the scythe just inside the front door but was too scared, mucked it up, and ended up climbing the mountain next to my house, still bleeding, heading off into the darkness without anyone the wiser.

About twenty minutes after Kouji Miyadate left my house, my sister came out from under the kotatsu and found me. I was still alive, with a screwdriver jammed in my brain. Or I was dead. I was somewhere in between, looking at flowers.

They were big, bright white flowers. No leaves, only petals, with the stamen and pistils jutting out of them. The flowers were moving, swelling, increasing in number. New flowers rose and bloomed like bubbles all around me. They welled up from the bloodstained floor, dancing all around me, all over me, swallowing me. The flowers smelled of summer rain. The flower petals were actually wet, and they touched my shoulders, my neck, my collarbone, licking me. Even if I closed my eyes, the flowers were so bright that my field of vision remained illuminated. My head. There was a dull throbbing sound echoing through both ears. There was a metal rod stuck in my head. My head was heavy, the weight of the Phillips screwdriver bearing down on it. Were screwdrivers really this heavy? If I let my guard down, I was half convinced my head would roll right off my shoulders. I was not in pain. But it did feel strange. Not because the screwdriver was stuck in my head but because, with it there, I could feel how my brain was moving. My brain was not sitting in my head gloppily like a bowl of tofu—it was pulsing. Like the mantle inside the earth. Part liquid and slowly moving. There was no right brain, left brain, cerebrum, cerebellum, just one big two-liter mass of yogurt I called a brain, and it was only slumming for an hourly wage. In one place, it worked on logic; in another, helped out with memory; and somewhere else, it was concentrating on talking. My brain cells were nothing but a bunch of temps.

Beyond the flowers, on the other side of my brother's bloodstained bed, was a huge gorilla. It had no eyes. It was flexing its muscles, resting both fists on the bed, rocking its body back and forth. It seemed to be excited that I was about to die. Or was it excited about these flowers blooming all over me? I didn't know what the flowers were called. They were something between a rose and a lily, but I was pretty sure they were my life, which is why they were growing out of me, blooming. When they withered, I would die. The gorilla reached out and grabbed one of my flowers, and tried to put it in its mouth.

"Stop!" I said.

Don't eat my life!

Across the chilly, white, rain-scented flowers of my life, I could hear someone wailing. My sister. "Are you alive? Hide!" She came pushing her way through the white flowers, but she didn't look like my sister. She was a stack of cup ramen containers, piled up in a vaguely human shape. Super Cup Miso Flavor. Bar Ramen Manaka. Pe-young Cup Noo-

---

Cup ramen Instant ramen packaged in a bowl. This convenience food can be prepared quickly, inside the packaging: pour boiling water in, close the lid, wait three minutes, then open and eat. Most of these are common ramen flavors. Kitsune Donbee is actually *udon*. *Tonkotsu* is pork bone.

dle Seafood Flavor. Kurodama Tonkotsu. Wakame Ramen. Super Cup Pork Kimchi. Super Cup Summer Curry. Super Cup Soy Sauce. Lots of Super Cup. Anyway, she was a big pile of them. I was pretty disappointed, but I called her name, and the cup ramen alien put her hand on my shoulder, so I guessed she was my sister. Apparently, the cup ramen already had boiling water in it, because her hand on my shoulder was warm, and the parts of her body that weren't touching me were warm, and everything smelled good. The gorilla that had failed to eat my flowers came over and peeled back the red grid-patterned lid on the Big Kitsune Donbee container at the top of my sister, opened its mouth wide, and poured the entire contents down its throat. I didn't stop it. With my sister in this condition, I didn't mind if the gorilla ate her. The gorilla gradually ate its way through my sister. Miso flavor, seafood flavor, tonkotsu, soy sauce, salt, soy sauce . . . More and more of my sister's body vanished inside the gorilla. While I was being impressed by how quickly the gorilla with no eyes ate, what was left of her spoke again.

"Is your head okay?"

"Of course it ain't. I think I'm dying."

"Don't die, Hide. You can't die. I'll go call a doctor."

"Sure, but how can you use the phone with the gorilla eating you?"

"What are you talking about? What gorilla?"

"This one . . . ," I started to say, but then I realized. The gorilla with no eyes did not exist. My sister's body was not made of cup ramen. I had a Phillips screwdriver jammed in my brain, and I was seeing things. The white flowers were a lie. I was just imagining them. But they looked really real. "This is amazing," I said.

"What?" she asked. But I just replied, "Nothing." The tip of the screwdriver was magnetic, in order to keep the screws attached. It was generating an electromagnetic field in my brain. Which left me seeing weird things. Ha-ha-ha. I tried to move the screwdriver. I might be able to change the channel and see something different. At least, that's what I thought, but neither of my hands would move. And not only would they not move, but I couldn't feel them. It was like my hands were cut off from me. They were no longer my hands.

"I can't move my hands," I said. My voice sounded like I was suffering. Even though I didn't mind not being able to move them at all.

"Sit still, Hide. Until the doctor gets here."

"Try moving this screwdriver for me?"

"Hell no! That's dangerous!"

"It bothers me."

"Forget about it."

"Stop that, gorilla!" I shouted, since the eyeless gorilla was still happily eating my sister. It turned its face toward me. And opened its mouth. Wondering if it was trying to eat me, I looked inside its mouth, and there was a girl behind its teeth. She was wearing the eyeless gorilla like a costume. She had pale skin; short, unruly black hair; round eyes that looked like grapes grown in some secret pleasure garden, eyes you could conquer the world with. She was so cute she could probably cut the world into pieces like a cake. She reached her long, thin arm out of the gorilla's throat and asked, "Can I twist it?"

"Sure," I said.

Apparently, she put her hand on the screwdriver sticking out of the left side of my head. The *niiiiiiiiii* sound in my head stopped. Her hand was dampening the vibrations of the screwdriver. Somewhere nearby my sister was saying, "Oh, I've been too scared to check, but I'm sure more people are injured or dead." The girl in the gorilla twisted the screwdriver in my head. There was a strange sound inside my head and a stabbing pain behind my eyes, and I was dying. Vanishing.

The white flowers enveloping me all began swirling together, and I was swallowed in a whirlpool of blinding white light. And I became Makoto Muraki, eighth grader at Tokyo Chofu Junior High, savior of the world.

The boy who existed only to save the world.

There was a hole in the left side of Makoto Muraki's head. The hole went all the way inside Makoto Muraki's brain. I don't know why he had a hole there. All I knew was that I could save the world, and that I reeeally loved a girl named Akana Sayaki in my class.

Akana Sayaki was a unicorn. She had an orange horn in the middle of her forehead, just at the hairline. She would put that horn into the hole in my head, and we would have sex. We had decided it was still too early for us to have ordinary sex. Ordinary sex was something we both wanted to try. But not yet. The sex we had with our heads was very special, and Akana and I were the only people who could have sex like that, which made us feel very close. After all, I was the only boy with a hole in his head, and Akana was the only girl with a horn on hers. When Akana's long, pointy horn thrust into my head, it gave me a strange tingling, quite different from pain or itchy sensations, that ran all the way from my head to my toes. When Akana was inside me, it felt like my entire body was being gently but forcefully twisted. It hurt a little but felt so good. It made it hard to breathe. It made me faint. I could feel Akana's horn slowly digging into my brain. While Akana's horn was in me, I could hear a sound, *niiiiiii-iiiiiiin*, inside my head. According to Akana, the inside of my head was soft and warm and wet, and when her horn was in me, it was soaking in brain liquid and felt really good, but the hard surface of her horn, with its drill-like spiral groove, made all sensations from her horn seem very far away, and she often got so impatient that her blood felt like it was flowing backward. When Akana was having sex with me, she occasionally started crying loudly. She wanted to feel me better. When we were having sex, both of us had our heads down, so her tears fell straight from her eyes to the ground without running down her cheeks. I could hear them dripping from far away. Her horn made me a little too dazed to really understand her tears. I was too busy feeling good to pay attention to Akana's immense frustration. We were absolutely the ideal partners for each other, so why was our sex so imperfect?

Since spring we have both been trying to decide if we should try ordinary sex or not. We'd discussed it. Akana said she was up for it. Even though she was the one who'd rejected it in seventh grade. I was satisfied with Akana's horn and didn't feel the need to use my penis at this point. Our sex had no climax and could go on for as long as Akana kept her horn inside my head, so I told her I didn't think genital sex would be nearly as much fun in comparison, since it had an end. But the truth, which I didn't tell Akana, was that I wasn't confident I could handle genital sex. I didn't know if my penis could give Akana anything like the pleasure her horn gave me. Akana's horn was really amazing.

But apparently, Akana had had just about enough, and she'd started to take it out on me. "It's not fair! You're the only one that gets to have fun!" "Why don't you ever think about my needs?" "Do you even love me, really?" And, "I think I'll just do it the normal way with someone else."

When she said that, I hurriedly tried to soothe her. "That will just hurt you, Akana." "It'll destroy the deep bond between us." "It's not that I don't want to do it with you. I'm just so busy fighting. . . . Please, wait until things settle down a little."

I was, in fact, pretty dang busy fighting.

Yesterday, in the Tama riverbed, I'd fought the Korean rapper Furious. He was really angry. Two days before, I'd gone flying around Chofu Tower, fighting Misaki Itabashi, telephone receptionist for the Rainbow Insurance Company near Chofu Station's East Entrance. Her left kick was so strong that the sheer speed and force of it bent space. Two days before that, I had fought some random alien. Three days before that, I had fought seven fake members of the Kanagawa Prefectural Assembly. Before that, I fought an elephant that spoke Japanese and had the ghosts of twenty-three elementary school students riding on its back. The elephant trampled seventy-six people; the fake assembly members poured gasoline on 206 people and lit them on fire; the alien I detected approaching and destroyed, ship and all, in outer space, leaving no casualties, but if it had invaded or the spaceship crashed into the earth, millions would have died. Misaki Itabashi kicked forty-two people to death, and Furious zapped 2,500 people with anger lightning, causing severe burns. I was the only person in the world who could fight enemies like this, so nobody ever dared say it to my face, but it was obvious that too many people were dying. I had to console Akana and win the next fight and the fight after that.

All of which was Makoto Muraki's ridiculous, absurd, laughable situation as it came to me, becoming my own memories. I wasn't pretending to be someone else—I had quite literally become him, which was a bizarre but powerful experience. I had two sets of memories, of completely equal importance and vividness. The hole in my head had been made by Kouji Miyadate and a Phillips screwdriver. But at the same time, the hole had been made by someone else: when Makoto Muraki was four years old, he had vanished and was found two days later in a room on the seventh floor of an apartment building near Chofu Station. Makoto Muraki did not remember who had opened it or how, so I didn't know either. But the discrepancy remained. As if I had been heading to a location that had two routes to it, each with completely different scenery, and when I reached that location and tried to think back how I had arrived there, I felt as if I had taken both routes simultaneously. I had no idea how I'd managed to be in two places at the same time on my way. I doubt I experienced both routes simultaneously. But for some reason, my memories overlapped. How could something like that happen? It was impossible, but when I was four, I was going to preschool in West Akatsuki in Fukui Prefecture and in Tokyo, in Chofu, being kidnapped and having a hole opened in my head. I was catching cicadas with my friends in West Akatsuki and having waves of pleasure as Akana stuck her horn into the hole in my head. Even though in West Akatsuki my head didn't have a hole in it yet.

This never happened to anyone else. When an actor was playing a role, everything that happened to that character onstage was experienced by the actor. But the character's background was only in the actor's mind, never actually experienced. The feelings the actor had onstage relied on his imagined version of the character's background, not on actual firsthand experience, and were very different from the real thing. Emotions build on top of one another. No matter how emotionally involved you get with a novel or manga or movie, the character's experiences never became your own. There wasn't enough information. The temperature, hunger, taste, smell, texture, pain, and so much more—it was impossible to convey all that in one moment to the reader, to the audience. These details had a big influence on the experience. So there was no way for anybody to genuinely experience someone else's life.

But apparently there was one way to do it. There was one perfect expression. First, jam a Phillips screwdriver into your head in exactly the right spot, so that you don't die. An ordinary screwdriver might work just as well. Anything pointy might do the trick. It is entirely possible the tip doesn't need to be magnetic. I have no idea. But I pulled it off with a

Phillips. Then, once the screwdriver is in your head, twist it till you find the right channel and become someone else. In my case, that person was Chofu resident Makoto Muraki, the boy who saved the world. Naturally, he did not really exist. I knew that.

The most obvious reason was that, in the Chofu city I was living in as Makoto Muraki, there was a huge, huge leaning tower made of metal. About a hundred meters across and two thousand meters tall, a giant cylinder jabbed diagonally up toward the clouds. Chofu Tower was a mystery to everyone who lived there, but not to me. There were pointed walls at the top in the shape of a plus, making it obvious that this was the Phillips screwdriver lodged in my skull. So this place was the inside of my head. My skull had been turned inside out and rolled into a ball, with everything outside it inside it swollen to the size of the earth. Since the world existed only in my head, it made perfect sense for Makoto Muraki to fly around fighting aliens. He was a hero I had invented. But I didn't remember inventing him. Which meant something in my unconscious mind had become Makoto Muraki.

Becoming Makoto Muraki was much, much more impressive than reading a novel or manga or watching TV or a movie. I was actually flying through the atmosphere and into space, and I actually killed a praying mantis the size of a skyscraper with a single punch. Much more impressive than the most flawless of performances. There was no comparison. Jam a Phillips screwdriver in your head, and while it might be kind of hard to actually choose the part, you end up remembering that character's past as if it had actually happened to you. Your emotions were real as well. I did not love Akana because that was part of the setting; I genuinely loved Akana, I thought about her all the time, she made my chest hurt, and one action on her part could cheer me up or cast me down instantly.

But Akana was starting to feel trapped in our relationship, which was extremely painful for me. My penis was so small compared to her horn, and so soft compared to her horn, but should I really try and get it as hard as possible and put it inside her?

While I was hesitating, another enemy arrived. This time the enemy was Risa Matsumoto, a third-year student at Seiraku Junior High, where I went to school. Of all people. Why would Matsumoto turn against me? Matsumoto was vice president of the art club, and both Akana and I were members, too. She taught me how to do oil paintings with a knife and taught Akana how to capture the bone structure in a portrait. I did a painting of Akana entirely with a knife. Sclurshing the oil paint onto the canvas with the three-sided blade, scraping the paint off again with the edge, swarshing more color on top of that. People were an outline and colors. Akana drew me, paying close attention to the bones beneath my flesh. It was always the bones that moved, and the flesh wrapped around the bones was moving them, but it was always the bones that moved, Akana told me. So she believed that whenever she drew flesh, she had to know how the flesh moved what bones and how it was wrapped around those bones. And Akana didn't understand my bones. She drew my bones and flesh the way Matsumoto had told her to, but my neck is not the same length as my torso, and my arms do not grow out from behind my ears. My right leg is not twisted around my left leg, and there isn't a gaping hole in the middle of my belly. My hole is in my head. But in Akana's picture, my head was smooth and flat with no opening anywhere.

"Maybe that's what you look like to unicorn eyes," Matsumoto said, standing next to me. I thought that Akana had chosen to fill in my hole. My erotic hole, gone with a brushstroke. It was quite a shock. Where did Akana plan to put her horn? My hole had been designed for her, but she'd covered it up. I started crying, certain I was going to lose her, and I felt Matsumoto's warmth against my elbow. Her tiny breasts were pressed against my arm. There was something hard under the uniform's sweater and shirt, and I could tell Matsumoto wasn't wearing a bra, and her nipples were pressing against me, against my elbow, and that maybe they had been hard before they touched me and Matsumoto was deliberately pressing her hard nipples against my skin. Staring at the picture of me Akana drew, like a warped image of an anchor upside down, I called out to her silently. Akana, Matsumoto is pressing her hard nipples against my elbow! Come and save me! I knew that Akana's left kidney could hear my screams. But no matter how long I waited, she never came. Matsumoto's sharp nipples seemed to be slowly stabbing themselves into my arm, paralyzing it. Akana, I called again, don't ignore me!

"Muraki," Matsumoto said. I couldn't take my eyes off the anchor me that Akana had drawn. I couldn't imagine that bizarre version of myself saving the world. I couldn't imagine that boy overcoming all his physical problems and defeating his enemies, protecting the earth. I was powerless. And not just the version of me in the picture, but Matsumoto's nipples had me pinned down, equally powerless. "Muraki," she called again, but the only thing I could do was pretend I was still looking at the picture and refuse to turn and look at Matsumoto's face. Matsumoto was a beautiful girl. She had long eyelashes and a pointy chin. Small shoulders and thin arms and legs. The breasts on which rested the hard nipples that were pressing against my elbow were small but very soft. The hole on my head was getting hot. My brain was melting, changing shape. Well aware of that, Matsumoto reached her hand out to the hole on my head and brushed her cold fingertips against it. "I thought your skull would make it hard, but the bit around the hole is actually soft. And warm. It feels good," Matsumoto said. "It's so wet. Is it always wet like this?"

It was only when Akana had her horn inside. "Please don't touch it," I said.

"Does it hurt?" Matsumoto asked. But her fingers showed no signs of moving away from the edge of my hole. They just brushed against it, teasing the edge.

". . . It doesn't, but . . ."

"It feels good?"

I didn't say anything.

"Heh heh. This is the world's exit. Amazing. The entire world spills out of here? I'll leave through here eventually myself, right?"

Oh, I thought, and Matsumoto's thin middle finger, like cold plastic, slid into my head. That *niiiiiiiiiiiiiin* sound came again, to my surprise—the same sound I heard when Akana's horn was in me. We thought that made us so unique. . . .

Matsumoto's middle finger stroked my skull and brain. It was shorter and thinner and smoother than Akana's horn, and the tingle that ran through me was different than I got from Akana's horn, but it was just as powerful. The back of my neck went numb, and my shoulders slumped. My right leg pulled backward on its own. "Oooh," I moaned.

"Feels good, doesn't it, Muraki?" It felt like a big, warm hand was yanking roughly on my tailbone, and I almost fell to the floor. There were seven members of the art club there besides us, and they were all watching us. Akana was out with our teacher, doing her duties as class representative. But she would be here soon. Akana, Akana, I called. Matsumoto's put her finger in my hole. It feels good! Akana, Matsumoto's finger feels so good! Ahh! Why aren't you here?

But if she did come, I'd be in trouble. I didn't want her to see me like this. I didn't want her to see me with someone else's finger in my hole. Not with anything besides Akana's horn inside me . . .

Akana, Akana, come here. I can't push Matsumoto's finger

away. My body's paralyzed, and I can't stop her from poking around inside my hole. Akana, save me. Come to the art room.

Matsumoto's middle finger dug gently into my brain. Mixing a bit of the yogurt in my head. Matsumoto scooped a bit of my brain off with her crooked finger, and a shrill sound echoed through my skull. She pulled her finger out, leaving the hole empty again, and I wanted her to put it back in. When I turned my tearstained face toward Matsumoto to make that request, Matsumoto had a bit of my brain on the middle finger of her right hand, which she put in her mouth, finger and all. "Eww!" one of the girls in the club yelled. "What the hell are you doing, Matsumoto!?" Matsumoto slowly licked her finger clean. When she pulled her moistened finger out from between her round lips, there was no trace of my brain on it. She had eaten it.

"Mm . . . the world is pretty tasty," Matsumoto said. "Kind of tastes like mangoes."

A thought struck me, and I looked out the windows of the art room. Chofu Tower was still there. The scenery around it had not changed. No, of course not. It was not my brain she'd just scooped out but Makoto Muraki's. But somewhere a world had had a piece dug out of it and vanished down Matsumoto's throat, into her stomach.

"Bend over, Muraki," Matsumoto said. "I want to put my mouth on that hole and suck out the world inside, eat the whole thing."

I was about to ask if she was crazy, but she reached out her hand again and stuck her wet finger into my hole.

Niiiiiiiiiiiiiiiiin.

Once again, that powerful tingle and numbness washed over me. It was like a single thread running right up my spine had been yanked upward directly from my neck, and my legs had been pulled right off the floor. Like my body, from the hole in my head to the tips of my fingers and toes, was made out of hundreds of tiny sleeping spiders, and they had all woken up at once and started swarming all over as my body crumbled away. Aaaaah. Aah. Matsumoto's middle finger was digging around in my brain again, but at the same time, her index finger was sliding into my wet hole. With a slurping sound, it entered the hole in my head. Her ring finger followed. Schlp. My hole was full of fingers. Matsumoto's three fingers were thicker than Akana's horn. They were shorter but softer—they might not reach all the way in, but they could tease the brain around the entrance. I could barely stand. My mind grew hazy, waves of bliss racing over me, unable to resist.

Akana! Akana! Come here! Please come! Look! This is so amazing! Come and see! Aaaaaaah! Akana! Akana! Akana!

Ahahahah I couldn't close my mouth I was drooling.

Akana! Akana! Oh god, I love sex with this hole in my head! I'm sure it is so much more sensitive than your vagina oooh Matsumoto's fingers feel so good! Aaaaugh! I was sure your horn was the only thing that would work! But anyone could do it, anyone's fingers could do it! Aaah, Akana! Come and see! This is so amazing! Aaaugh! Akana!

"Muraki, this feels good, right? So very good? Heh heh. You're drooooling. Ah-ha-ha! You should see your face, Muraki. Aren't you embarrassed? Getting all ecstatic with everyone watching," Matsumoto said, putting her other hand on my crotch and squeezing my penis. "Ew . . . wow, you're hard down here, too. You're such a slut. How'd you ever get to be such a whore? Standing in front of everyone, feeling so good with your dick all hard. Touched by a girl who isn't even your girlfriend. How did this happen? You want to cum? You want to cum down here, too?"

What did she mean by cum? I wondered, trying to make my yogurt brain work. Was she going to take my penis out of my pants? My penis was so small compared to Akana's horn, but was she going to take it out in front of everyone? It was hard now, and bigger, but my dick was still nothing next to Akana's horn. . . . Please don't do that. . . .

Still clutching my penis from outside my pants, Matsumoto's left hand rubbed up and down the length of it.

"Ah ah aaahh!"

"Such an embarrassing moan. Stop it! Everyone's watching. And you're so ecstatic you're drooling. What's going to happen next, Muraki? Should I stop? You want me to stop?"

I shook my head. Akana! Akana! Help me!

"How far down does this go? This feels like the edge of your skull, so if I try something impossible, I might just do it," Matsumoto said, and then, even though there was no space left for her thumb and pinkie, she jammed them in anyway, twisting them in, forcing my hole open wider. My skull creaked, everything went dark in front of my eyes, and with a glop Matsumoto's entire fist went into my head, all the way to the wrist.

Akana!

I was sure both my eyeballs had popped right out of my head. I was sure both my knees had exploded and everything below them had fallen into some deep ravine. I was sure my crotch had split open, and the split was gradually working its way up my chest. I was sure my ketchup was spurting out of my eye sockets and liquid fire was raining out of my knees and salmon roe the size of softballs were falling out of the split in my crotch and piling up underneath me.

"Ew, dirty!" Matsumoto said, and took her hand away from my crotch, so it must still be in one piece. "You came? Muraki! Ah-ha-ha! Gross. Really? Wow, you really are the worst! I'm not even your girlfriend! Why did you cum? Spilling your filthy sperm in your pants, the shame! Don't you just wanna die?" As she said this, Matsumoto took the fist she had jammed inside my head and opened it wide. All five of Matsumoto's fingers slushed out into my brain. Everything from my rectum through my large and small intestines to my stomach and esophagus stretched out like a shape memory alloy cooled with water, tearing right out my ass and into the ground, and the tip came popping out of the ground on the other side of the world. Aaaaaaaaaaaahhhhhh!

"Now I get to eat the world," Matsumoto said, and grabbed a handful of my brain. She yanked it right out. Nnnnnnnnnnnnnnnnnnnnnnnnnnnnnna!

Matsumoto's fist popped out of my head clutching my brain, and for that brief moment while she conveyed it to her mouth, I was free of the tingle and the numbness and was able to shake off the reverb long enough to karate chop Matsumoto's neck. I couldn't let her eat any more of my brain. Ffwip! Splat!

Makoto Muraki lived in the world inside my brain, and I had no idea what kind of world there was still deeper in his brain. But if there was a world inside Makoto Muraki's head, like Risa Matsumoto hoped there was ("I want to put my mouth on that hole and suck out the world inside, eat the whole thing"), then it was just like the one inside my brain. An imaginary world filled with imaginary people. Since I was Makoto Muraki, it was possible there was another imaginary Chofu and Chofu Tower and boy named Makoto Muraki, savior of the world, inside Makoto Muraki's head. It was not at all strange for Makoto Muraki to have the same thing inside his head that I had in mine. Which meant that when the Makoto Muraki in this world had his brain pulled out, at the exact same moment inside him, another Makoto Muraki was having his brain pulled out as inside him yet another Makoto Muraki had his brain yanked out at the same time and in the same fashion. . . . The same events might well be happening in each world in tandem. I didn't know. And at my level, that wasn't a problem. Even if there was another Makoto Muraki inside the Makoto Muraki inside me and a certain event happened at the same time in a different dimension of us, I was unable to sense the Makoto Muraki inside the Makoto Muraki inside me and had no way of telling if that event actually was happening, which meant it was entirely without meaning. No matter how badly the world inside the Makoto Muraki inside me was damaged, it did not put me out in any way. Hmph. Eat all you like, Risa Matsumoto.

Keeping an eye on Matsumoto's severed head, I bent over her body, wiped my drool, pulled her hand open, transferred my brains from her hand to mine, and slowly shoved them back inside my head. The brain containing the world was warm and soft and probably did taste a bit like mango.

The other club members were either stunned or crying, or crouching with their eyes closed and their hands over their ears, but I just took out my cell phone and dialed. I was calling Kouji Miyadate, at the Saving the World with Makoto Muraki Unit (the Muraki Unit for short), who was in charge of cleanup after an incident. Tworurururu. Tworururururu. For some reason, my crotch was cold and wet. Something must have actually happened with my penis back there when Matsumoto rubbed it and it felt like my crotch had split open and giant salmon roe were dropping out. I'd have to change pants later.

Kouji Miyadate? I thought. Why was Kouji Miyadate in this world? Why was Kouji Miyadate in my head!? Tworururururu. Was Kouji Miyadate going to answer? That piece of shit?

He was here. I knew he was. The Miyadate who worked at the Muraki Unit was also short, scrawny, unshaven, and looked like a grinning asshole. This Miyadate was Kouji Miyadate. Tworurururu . . . but he was fighting on my side, to save the world. Furious and Misaki Itabashi corpses, the remains of the spaceship, the elephant's body—all of these had been dissected and hauled off to the incinerators by Miyadate. He was a really good guy. There was no ski scar on his hand. He did not spend all his time drinking.

This was Chofu. The west side of Chofu, in Tokyo . . . so was he also in Fukui Prefecture, in West Akatsuki? Was my house there and my family and my dead body?

Tworurururuchii. "Disposal team." Kouji Miyadate's voice. It was really him. The hole in my head tingled, but not like it did when Akana's horn was in it or Matsumoto's fingers or fist were in it, and there was no numbness. "Kouji Miyadate?" I asked. "Yes, speaking . . . Makoto?" "Hideaki Kato, fucktard. You know who I am, right?" "Hideaki . . . Kato? Sorry, I don't recognize the name. . . . How'd you get this number? Is Makoto Muraki with you? Put him on." I hung up.

This was bad. Miyadate was going to report this weird phone call to the head of the Muraki Unit, to the information and public safety bureaus. In about ten minutes, the Muraki Unit would assume I'd been defeated and spring into action. Chofu would be placed under martial law, and the allied forces would adjust the orbits of the surveillance satellites to cover the Chofu area. Those pictures would show I was safe, but they would also be aware there was a chance the enemy had the ability to change shape and become me, like that Snake Person a while back. Chofu would be filled with armed men. Once there, they would not leave. And if the enemy after Matsumoto appeared, Chofu would be total chaos. Even more people would die. Chofu had managed to be relatively peaceful so far because I was fighting all the enemies single-handedly, but if everyone saw not only the people who always got killed but the people trying to fight back getting killed, then panic would spread explosively. Nobody would be able to live in Chofu ever again. But with me fighting and always winning, even if I got hurt or lost an arm or leg, then one or two hundred people dying was no problem at all.

I left the art room and went to the teachers' room and asked our teacher, Komai, where Akana was, but he didn't know, so I pressed down on my left eyeball through the lid. Behind it was a sonar system that let me track down people's souls, and the *niiiiin* reverb still echoing from Matsumoto's fingers changed to an *uuuuuuuuuuuunn,* and I started looking for Akana. *Niiiiiiuuuuuuuuuuuuuunnnn* . . . There she was. In the nurse's office. I took my hand away from my eye, and the eyeball returned to its normal position. I left the teachers' room and went down the hall, down the stairs, turned left, and went into the nurse's office, where I found Akana's bloody kidney lying on the bed. The kidney that received my telepathy. The left one. I could smell it lying there the moment I walked into the nurse's office. There was an equally bloody scalpel lying next to it. Under the bed was Takamura, the school nurse, apparently drugged. The enemy had attacked. Someone who knew that I couldn't find Akana without her kidney had become an enemy and taken Akana away, I thought. Then it hit me.

I was wrong.

Akana had held the scalpel herself, had cut out her own kidney. So she would never hear my voice again. So I would never find her again. So she could run away from me. Her feelings had driven her to it.

This was not the best timing, I thought. I was sure she wanted me to chase after her. She was hoping I would wander around aimlessly, searching for her without so much as a clue. When she saw me doing that, she would be sure I loved her. But by this point in our relationship, we shouldn't need to constantly check on each other's feelings. I had other things I wanted to do. I had to go to West Akatsuki. I had to see if I existed in this world. I had no time to waste on a lover who cut out her own kidney and vanished in a storm of sex-related angst. She had two kidneys and could afford to lose one.

I took Akana's tiny kidney off the bed. Blood dripped off it. It was still warm and heavy. The kidney that had linked me to her. This was Akana's heart. Akana had left her own heart here and taken her vagina and horn away from me. I put Akana's forlorn kidney in the pocket of my uniform. The blood would dry soon, and it would start to rot.... No, unicorn kidneys didn't rot. It would dry out, swell up a little, and then shrink down again, all without going bad. Would it shrink out of existence? I didn't know. Akana was the only unicorn I knew. I loved Akana's horn. But now that I'd tasted Matsumoto's finger, Akana's horn was not as special to me. Until now my hole had only known her horn, had only thought about her horn, but now it knew other things. Anyone's fingers could fit in my hole. Anyone's hand could slide into my brain, all the way to the wrist. That could really happen to my hole. And I could make it happen. Akana's horn was wonderful. But Matsumoto's fingers were amazing, and other people's fingers and hands would probably be wonderful in their own way.

With the weight of Akana's kidney pulling my jacket a little to the left, I left school and walked home. My home was on the twelveth floor of a massive apartment building at the far end of a massive apartment complex near the Tama River. My father and mother and sister and brother had all been killed by enemies, one after the other, so I lived alone. I looked out the window at the Tama River and saw high school students playing soccer. It was fall, and some people had already broken out the long sleeves. I took off my jacket and laid it on the sofa. On a whim, I touched Akana's kidney in the pocket, but it was like a potato, dry and hard. I was a little excited to have part of her body lying on my sofa. It was out of the question for a boy to invite a girl over without a family around to chaperone, so Akana had never been in here. Akana had always peered into the room from the entrance like she wanted to come in, but I was afraid that if I let her come in, we'd end up having genital sex on the sofa or my bed. But we could have head sex outside. I couldn't figure out what possible reason I could have to refuse if we were alone inside together and the mood started to go in that direction, and sex wasn't the sort of thing you could avoid by just saying no. It sometimes happened even after saying "no" but usually happened before you even had a chance to stop. I had already learned that much from head sex. I had kind of forced her into head sex when she was saying no, and I had also noticed she wasn't in the mood and pretended I had no idea. Akana was nice, so she would always end up putting her horn into my head.

But Akana didn't matter now, so I flew out of the window.

As I headed into the air above the apartment complex, the smell of autumn in the air grew faint, and that weird moist scent of outer space replaced it. Space smelled like an unclean damp rag boiled with an orange peel. The smell bothered me at first, but after defeating two or three aliens, it no longer bothered me. Hovering between space and the upper edges of the atmosphere, I briefly thought about Akana again but quickly shook my head, forgot about her, and dived back downward, landing in the rotary outside Chofu Station. Using some of the monthly allowance provided by the government, I bought a ticket. My full abilities only really worked in the Chofu area. So if I was going as far as Fukui, I had to take the train.

I went to Tokyo Station and boarded the Shinkansen for the first time. I'd been so busy saving the world that I'd never been on it before. I'd almost never left Chofu. Ever since I passed through Tsutsujigaoka Station, and while I was changing trains at Shinjuku and riding the Central Line to Tokyo Station, I'd been quite excited. But the Shinkansen looked different from the other trains, and the atmosphere was sort of uptight, so I got a little nervous. Most of the other passengers were middle-aged men in suits, so it felt like everyone around me was part of the same group and knew exactly what they were doing, and I had somehow got mixed into their party without a clue what was happening. I felt like the businessmen and women around me had all noticed that I was in the wrong place and were wondering if they should point this out to me, which made me a little antsy. I was afraid of nothing back in Chofu, but without my full powers, I was apparently quite a wuss. Everyone else appeared to be perfectly calm and not worried about powers or lack thereof. When I had my full powers, I had to fight all these crazy enemies to save the world, a life of pain, suffering, and great inconvenience, and never got to leave Chofu, and when I did leave, I always ended up all nervous and wondering exactly what the point of being all-powerful and saving the world was. Wondering this again, I boarded the Hikaru express to New Osaka Station. But I knew full well there was no point. I fell asleep as the train neared Nagoya. Matsumoto's fingers had made me feel so good that I was exhausted. Even if I was awake, I would just stress out, certain all the businessmen around me were staring.

And in Makoto Muraki's dreams, I met that girl in the gorilla again. She was so cute jar lids would release their seals for her, with her beautiful black hair, short and permed, and her small, pale face with those shockingly large eyes. She had taken off the gorilla costume and was wearing a blue T-shirt. But she wasn't wearing a bra, so the nipples on her thin chest were tenting the fabric. She wasn't wearing pants or a skirt or even underwear, and her pubic hair was clearly visible beneath the edge of the shirt. "Hey, that's pretty hot," I said, as Makoto Muraki in the dream. The girl did not appear to be embarrassed. She just stood there, staring at my face. "Mm? Where's the gorilla?" I asked. The girl said nothing but shifted one leg sideways, opening her legs. I could see down underneath the tufts of pubic hair. The girl looked up through her lashes at me, and I wondered if she was about to pee, but what emerged from behind the hair was not piss but a thick, long, black . . . no, not poop, a finger. It looked like a finger-shaped cock coming out of the girl's crotch, but it was probably the gorilla's finger. The gorilla. The gorilla with no eyes, I guess. This time it was inside the girl and poking its finger out of her crotch. I didn't have a great deal of experience with gorilla hands, so I wasn't completely sure, but it was probably the gorilla's index finger, so it was like the gorilla was pointing at the ground under her feet from inside her snatch. I looked down, but there was nothing on the ground. We were both standing in the middle of the grounds of some school. There was a track laid out around us. There was no one here but the two of us. I'd seen this place before. It was Seiraku Junior High. Not the school I was attending but the school Makoto Muraki went to. But I was glad. I had no idea who this girl the gorilla was wearing was, but I kept my eye on the gorilla's finger, even as I glanced around at the school. I wondered if other fingers would emerge until all five were out, followed by the palm, and then the wrist, the arm, and then the entire eyeless gorilla body, and if the gorilla would have anything to say for itself once it had taken the girl off, but nothing of the sort happened. The gorilla's finger remained pointing downward from the girl's snatch without moving at all, and the girl just stood there staring at me and not moving at all. I got tired of waiting and spoke to her.

"So, what's your name?" The girl said something, but I couldn't hear her. Mm? What was that? This time the girl shook her head. She said something else, but it had no meaning in my ears. I gave up. So I said, "Come on out, gorilla. What the fuck are you hiding inside a girl for?"

Then something terrifying happened and I woke up. Makoto Muraki's eyes opened. I was on the Shinkansen, and the loudspeaker was just announcing that we were approaching Maibara Station. This is the JR Tokaido Shinkansen bound for New Osaka Station. Approaching Maibara Station. If I got off the Shinkansen here, changed to the Hokuriku Line, took the express to Tsuruga, and then changed to a local train, I would get to West Akatsuki Station. Hideaki Kato's house was there. While I was heading there, I was in the eighth grade at West Akatsuki Junior High, and it was about 5:00 P.M., so I would be swinging a shinnai around at kendo practice. I think. I might have skipped. This was four years ago for me. But I didn't remember much that happened four years ago. Makoto Muraki had a hole in his head, and that might have damaged some of my memories. I couldn't remember what happened at the end of the dream, either. When I woke up, I was covered in sweat. My heart was beating quickly, like it was trying to vibrate its way up my ribs and escape. Something had happened to me in Makoto Muraki's dream. That girl, with the gorilla finger sticking out of her crotch. The gorilla inside the girl. I was sure that girl/gorilla had done something to me. The Shinkansen pulled into Maibara Station, and I put my hands on my crotch, near the back of my ball sack. About where the girl's snatch had been. But there was no terrifying gorilla finger sticking out of me. Good. But then I gasped—there was no one sitting next to me, but across the aisle there were a couple of businessmen getting ready to get off the train, busy getting bags down from the luggage rack, so I quickly undid the clasp on my pants, and took a look at my penis through the fly on my boxers. It was not a gorilla finger. But it was also not my penis. Makoto Muraki had castrated me while I was dreaming.

Peeking out of the fly of my boxers was not Makoto Muraki's tiny, hairy cock but that glowing white flower. Makoto

THE DRILL HOLE IN MY BRAIN

蛭児王太郎

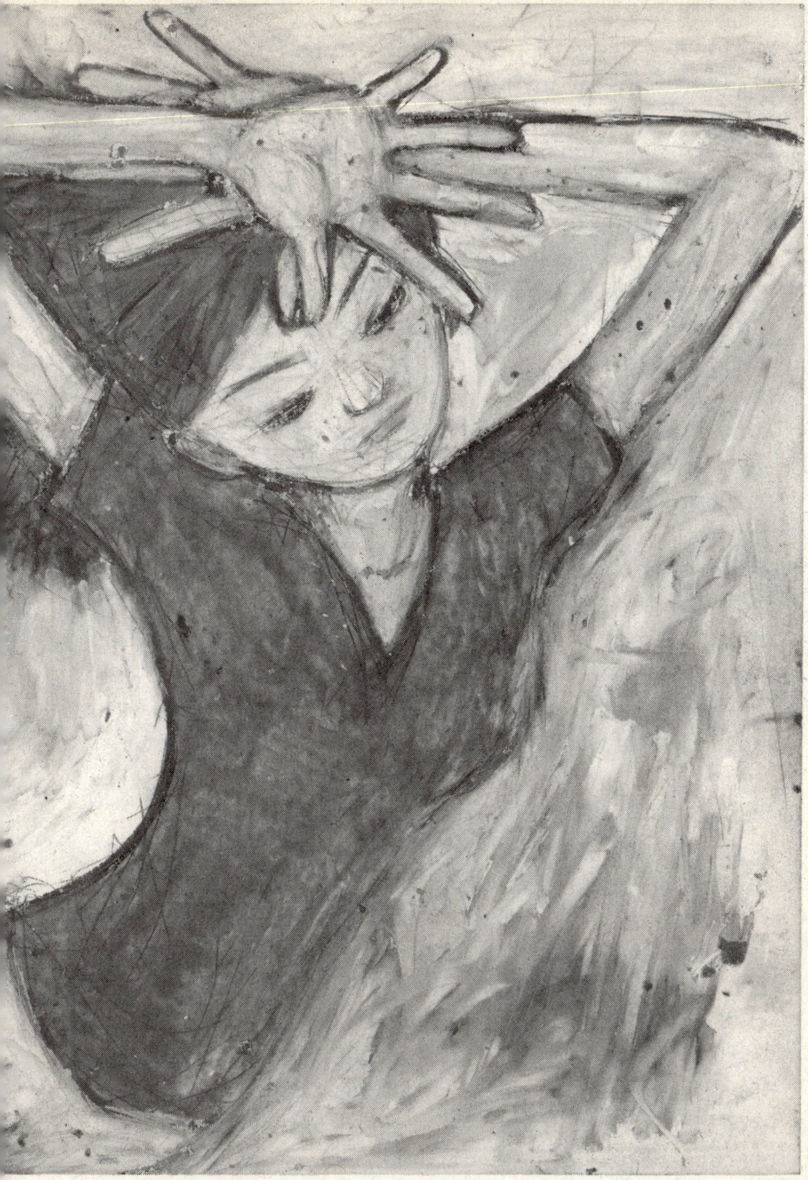

Muraki had never seen that flower before. I gasped in surprise and didn't say anything for a minute, but then I thought about Akana. This way, even if I wanted to have genital sex with Akana, I couldn't. I couldn't make Akana happy. Akana had wanted to have genital sex so much. I could still have head sex, but I could never have genital sex now. But if I could never have genital sex, then I could hardly ask for head sex. I could never do anything for her. I would take and take and never give back, which was out of the question... except that that was what I had been doing all along. I had never done anything for Akana at all, just done what I wanted to do. Take take take take and never once given. And now I could never give. I mourned the loss of my penis. I felt sorry for Akana. The thing she had wanted was no longer in this world. The thought that Akana would no longer want me now that I no longer had a penis, only a hole, crushed me. She would leave me. The very thought broke my heart, and I almost burst into tears. But I didn't have time to cry. I was surrounded by adults on the Shinkansen, and the clasp on my pants was undone, and a glowing white crotch flower was sticking out of the fly of my boxers. I couldn't just sit there crying.

So I reached down to close up my fly, but the tip of my finger brushed against one of the moist flower petals, and *vvvvvvvv* it felt like waves of electricity ran out across my entire body. In a second, the shock wave reached every bit of my body, numbness spreading all the way to my core. At first, I mistook it for pain. Presumably out of sheer surprise. But it wasn't. I had grown another set of genitals. The clitoris girls were supposed to have must feel like this. No male organ was this sensitive. Hot damn! I grew a clitoris! I was thrilled. But once I thought about it a minute, I realized that a clitoris this big could be hard to handle. I couldn't close my pants. And if the hole in my head was my vagina, a clitoris at my crotch meant I was like a giant upside-down set of female genitals with arms and legs attached. But maybe my arms and legs were extra; maybe they were the large and small labia. Which made me a walking . . . snatch. By this point, my mental image of Makoto Muraki, boy savior of the world, was a junior high eighth-grade upside-down cunt. I rose from my seat with my glowing white flower clitoris exposed and got off the Shinkansen, bathing everyone in the light of my beautiful clitoris.

Maibara was in Shiga Prefecture. It was October, still early afternoon, but nice and cool. The sky was a pale blue, with only a few scattered clouds moving quickly in the wind. The breeze hit the moist flower at my crotch. It felt chilly. I walked empty-handed along the platform after the Shinkansen pulled away, heading for the walkway to the other train. The attendants and other passengers all saw the glowing white clitoris flower sticking out of the fly of my trousers. But everyone was too polite to stare, so I got carried away. It's not like anyone knew this was a clitoris. So I thought I might as well play with it a bit. I crossed the walkway, went through the gates, and across another bridge toward the platform for the express, but on the way, I touched the glowing white flower at my crotch again.

Zap! "Aah! Hahh . . . !" It felt like someone had shot a bullet right down into my genitals. My legs twisted, and I fell backward, landing on the ground on my ass. Wow. No girl had a clitoris like this. It felt much too superamazingly great. This flower, like a cross between a rose and a lily, was connected to every single nerve in my body, to my sensory, motor, and relay neurons. The people walking behind me in the passage looked surprised as they passed me. That's when I realized my mouth was hanging open and drool was coming out.

I wiped it with my hand and realized it wasn't drool at all.

It was white bubbles. I was blowing bubbles. I put my face down and tried to spit the bubbles out, but what I thought was a mouthful turned into a torrent of bubbles spewing onto the ground. Some sort of liquid was churning up out of my throat, turning into bubbles as it reached the top, swelling and filling my mouth, and then spilling out into the world.

"Yikes! Are you okay?" someone asked. I nodded. I was all-powerful in Chofu, could beat down any enemy. Nobody would ever worry about me. Everyone admired me, praised me, thanked me, or occasionally heckled me, but not one of them was ever worried about me. Not even Akana. I was so much stronger than all my enemies that I'd never even had a close call. I always won. Saving the world carried no sense of danger at all. Humans would only leave the future of the world in the hands of someone who could defeat any enemy without even breaking a sweat. I never did. The sweatless victor. The savior never lost. Everyone cheered me on, without ever worrying about me. But I had a hole in my head and had just discovered that if someone stuck their fingers or hand in it, like Matsumoto had, then my body would be paralyzed. I had managed to cut Matsumoto's head off somehow, but if another enemy went after my hole, I had no idea if I would be able to turn the tables on them again. Well . . . it was my job to save the world, after all, so I would probably figure something out.

But I wasn't in Chofu now; I was in Shiga Prefecture, not all-powerful, and I had a flower clitoris blooming out of my crotch. And now I was touching it and experiencing waves of such intense pleasure I had bubbles coming out of my mouth. They were still spewing out of me. Were these bubbles a side effect of the ecstasy that touching the flower clitoris produced? What the hell were they? They wouldn't stop flowing out of me. It was getting hard to breathe. Even if I tried breathing through my nose, the bubbles were still in my throat and would get stuck in my windpipe. But just before I had to take a breath, the geyser stopped. I collapsed against the wall, took a deep breath, and then coughed violently. When that subsided, I looked up again. The man who had spoken to me a minute before was gone, and the other passengers were avoiding me. They were stepping carefully over the bubbles on the floor, heading down the stairs to the express train platform. A few of them glanced at me in passing, but I didn't mind. I didn't care about the bubbles either. I didn't care about not being able to breathe. I reached toward the crotch flower again. My finger trembled, moving closer to one of the flower petals. I was trying to brush it gently, but I stabbed my clitoris instead. Lightning ran down me, my skin crackled, my flesh convulsed, my bones melted. But once the initial shock wore off, the sea of blood that the lightning brought with it seemed to ebb away, and fitful pleasure beamed out of the flower that I was able to receive, barely, using my entire body. I couldn't bear to look at that blinding white flower anymore, so I closed my eyes, but I couldn't pull my hand away. I left my finger on the flower, sprawled on the concrete walkway in Maibara Station, with crowds of people passing me, stabbed through by the beam shooting out of my flower, enjoying myself.

Bubbles were pouring out of me again. If I put my face on the floor, I would drown in them. But even with my face up, it was hard to breathe. Each blast of the beam shook my breath, knocked the timing out of whack, so that even if my lungs gasped for air, there might not be air for them to breathe. The bubbles made me cough and gasp, but even as my consciousness started to fade out, I stroked the edge of the petal again, rubbing my finger against it, tweaking the edge. I was a giant pussy. I wanted someone to do this for me. Oh, right! Akana! The hole in my head was numb right now, but it longed for Akana, far more than it ever had, far more powerfully than ever before. Akana's horn. The unicorn cock. Aahhh! But the unicorn's horn was not a sexual organ. It was just a horn, and I had only been using it like a penis, taking pleasure from it. Akana had said it felt good to her as well, but I'm sure that was a lie, something she only said to make me feel better, and all she had really wanted was to make me happy, and, in fact, she had felt absolutely nothing when she stuck it into my wet head hole. If something was a sex organ, it was used to have sex with, and when you had sex with it, you would know that's what it was supposed to be used for, because it just felt so good, it just fit perfectly, and you wanted to use it like that forever, and afterward you wanted to use it again as soon as possible. But Akana never thought any of that about her horn. It was just a horn, not a sex organ, and nothing she should ever have put inside my head. As I toyed with my crotch flower, floating in that incredible sweetness, I thought of Akana and pitied her. Inside my pity there was pleasure. Even as I felt sorry for her, I still desired her horn. I wanted her horn inside me. Even though Akana's horn was not a sex organ, even though she did not particularly want to stick it in me, even though my constantly asking for it was hurting her, making her sad, making her miserable, I still wanted Akana's horn. Or Matsumoto's hand. Other people, other things might work, too. The handle of a mop or a broom might do just fine. But out of infinite possible choices, I had chosen Akana's horn. Wasn't that love?

If you loved someone, was it okay to hurt them?

What choice did I have? I wanted what I wanted.

It was up to Akana to decide what to do about it. I admitted it was selfish of me, and Akana knew that, and if she didn't know that, I would be glad to tell her. It was up to her to decide if she wanted to leave me or if she was willing to be with me. She could make her own choice. But whatever her choice was, I would still want her. As long as I wanted her, I would try to have her. As I thought this through, my fingers constantly brushed against my flower. I couldn't stop. I wanted it. I wouldn't stop. I had no intention of stopping. I didn't care about anyone else. They could think whatever they wanted. The clitoris blooming on my crotch was making all of me explode. It was as if the upper layer of my skin all over my body had been peeled away, leaving only the most delicate layer exposed, and everything that touched me came as a shock. Obviously, it didn't hurt, and I did not feel any pain, but I thought I did. It felt like all the blood vessels in my body had twisted into spirals, into intricate patterns, but the blood flowing through them was being forced to go faster and faster, and at any moment it would tear free and spray all over the place. My temples throbbed horribly. I was sure my brain had hardened, had turned smooth like ivory. Like a phone. Had I died? Was I dying? Could people die from orgasms? I'd heard people say sex felt so good they'd almost died, but was that referring to an actual possibility? I wanted to die. I wanted to drop dead at the peak of this ecstasy. I touched my flower again, genuinely prepared to die. The white flower dug into my body with a million tiny fingers. Chiseling away at me. I could smell death around me. It smelled a lot like outer space. That mix of wet rag and orange peel. Did people go to space when they died? Did the souls of dead humans collect in space? Was that empty vacuum actually full of souls? Which meant souls consisted of nothingness, nothing but a smell of wet rags and orange peels? If the liquid in the bubbles coming out of my mouth was not coming from my lungs but my soul, then each one of these bubbles contained a vacuum, had nothing inside it but a moist citrus smell, empty space, a void. Outer space was growing out of my throat, which meant space and the world were all inside me. The universe around me existed simultaneously within me, and in that universe there was another me, and perhaps in the miniature universe bubbles I was spewing out was a miniature earth and a miniature me that just happened to be invisible but were really there even though I couldn't see them.

Inside Makoto Muraki, I wondered why we were thinking about this. But if the big universe existed simultaneously inside the small universe, then the Makoto Muraki that existed inside me, and the world in which Makoto Muraki existed, might also be more than just my delusion and might actually really exist somewhere. But that didn't answer the question of whether I existed in Makoto Muraki's world inside me. Me being me and me being Makoto Muraki at the same time in the same world was different from the idea that the small universe was the same as the large one. Discovering Makoto Muraki inside myself, as a part of myself, and finding myself inside myself were two very different things.

This was no time for me to be jerking off in the Maibara Station hallway. No time to be drowning in pleasure, blowing bubbles, and pondering unnecessary, meaningless, mistaken things.

I dragged my hand away from the white flower Makoto Muraki'd been frantically stroking, quickly shifted it to the glistening root of the thing, and plucked it right off my crotch. A crackle of lightning shot from the balls of my feet all the way up my spine and into my brain. I felt like a single tree in the middle of a field, lightning slamming down on me and turning me into a ball of fire. I split open, fractured, burned, and became ash. Reduced to ashes. The glowing white flower clutched tightly in my right hand, it occurred to me that this sensation was really the ultimate orgasm.

Without realizing what I was doing, I brought the white flower to my mouth and shoved it right inside, not even stopping to smell it, chomped down on it a few times and swallowed. It squished against my teeth like a tangerine, tasted a lot like cucumber and a little like paper. Not particularly pleasant. That gorilla with no eyes had eaten a bunch of them, but . . . had all those white flowers been some other people's clitorises? No, I had just called it a clitoris, but it wasn't, really, just something easy to mistake for a clitoris. Was it something entirely different that only functioned as a clitoris when it happened to be growing out of someone's crotch?

What did I care? I was dumb enough to eat the thing. I am not like that eyeless gorilla! Damn it. I tried opening and closing my eyelids a few times. They were still there. I touched my eyes with my trembling left hand. I still had eyeballs. Tears were running down my cheeks. While I checked that my eyes were still there, I wiped them. My vision cleared a little, so I held up my other hand. My right hand was still covered in the clear goo that had been stuck to the flower petals. I held it up to my nose and sniffed. It smelled like gauze. I licked it. It tasted like nothing. But when it entered my mouth, the stickiness slid aside and vanished. Like snow. I licked my hand a few more times, enjoying the sensation, but I knew this was not the time for that. I had a train to catch. I forced myself upright.

I looked down. My crotch flower was gone, but that didn't mean my cock had come back, just a little white hole where I'd yanked the flower out, but not a tunnel like the hole in my head, more closed off, like I'd been stung. I zipped up my fly and fastened my pants again, then convinced my quivering legs to stand. They shook like jelly. My head was spinning. I almost lost my balance, but I felt like I'd never make it upright again if I let myself fall, so I held on. With my left hand, I pulled a handkerchief out of my pocket and wiped the goo off my right hand, then leaned against the wall for a minute catching my breath. At last I started walking, down the stairs, onto the express platform, stood there till the Shirasagi express bound for Kanazawa pulled in, and I got on. There was a restroom near the link between cars, and I washed my face in the sink. My face was a mess, covered in tears and drool and bubbles. But washing my face helped put some distance between me and the white flower. The Shirasagi pulled out, and Maibara Station vanished in the distance. The farther it became, the closer we were to West Akatsuki Station. To my house. To me. This was a Tuesday, when I was in eighth grade—I should be in school. If I as Makoto Muraki met me as me, would I cause a paradox and make the world explode? No matter how hard I ransacked my memory, I had no memory of meeting myself as Makoto Muraki. Would I even be able to meet myself? Or was this really a different world from my own and I did not actually exist here as myself? But Chofu and Maibara Station and West Akatsuki all existed. But there was a giant Phillips screwdriver sticking out of the ground in Chofu, and I was the boy savior of the world, and there were flowers growing out of my crotch. But Tokyo Station and Maibara Station and the Shinkansen, everything except Chofu—or, more accurately, everything except Chofu Tower—was perfectly normal, the way it should be. As Makoto Muraki, I lost my special powers when I left Chofu. Makoto Muraki's world really didn't look any different than mine. This world was the world inside my head. Was it possible that it was the same as the world outside my head? Did I exist inside myself as a different personality called Makoto Muraki but also exist simultaneously as myself? Could two of the same thing exist at the same time? That was much too complex.

If the inside and the outside were the same, then what possible meaning did the boundary between them have? If everything except for me was exactly the same, then I was the only thing dividing inside from out, and I would have to live as a kind of antibeing, neither inside nor outside. I had no reason to exist; I might as well not exist; but was this true for everyone? Did we all have a world inside ourselves that was exactly like the world outside, and did we all exist only as the border between the inside and outside world, as if we didn't actually exist at all? As far as I was concerned, Chofu was an alien world. I lived there as Makoto Muraki, savior of the world. All kinds of crazy enemies charged in, one after the other. There was a girl with a horn named Akana. None of that was possible in my world. But now that I had left Chofu, the world looked like it always had, the same as it did in my world. Only Chofu, and me, as Makoto Muraki, were alien. What was Chofu to me?

There was a giant Phillips screwdriver jammed into Chofu. Which meant this world's Chofu was in the left front of my head? If Kouji Miyadate had stabbed the screwdriver into the right side of my head, Makoto Muraki would live in Osaka or New Zealand, would have fought somewhere other than Chofu? Would I have been someone other than Makoto Muraki? Would I never have met Akana?

If I stabbed someone else in the head, would they also become someone else somewhere and fight enemies and fall in love with girls?

Akana.

I took Akana's kidney out of my pocket. Akana's kidney was dry, shrunken, and hard, only about the size of a Ping-Pong ball. How small would it get? I had to solve this mystery before it shrank away to nothing. Was Hideaki Kato in West Akatsuki?

I left the washroom and sat down in the first empty seat. It was a reserved seat, so it was possible someone had a ticket for it, but I'd deal with that if they showed up. For the moment, I wanted to close my eyes and rest. Between Matsumoto's fingers and my flower-induced endless orgasm, I was completely exhausted. But I had to stop myself from falling asleep. I didn't want to dream about that cute girl and the eyeless gorilla again. I didn't need another glowing white flower that felt really good. I would have to eat it again, and I was afraid I would turn into that gorilla. I didn't want to sleep again. I was too scared of dreaming to sleep. . . .

I got off the Shirasagi at Tsuruga Station. My head was still fogged over, but my legs had stopped shaking, and I could walk normally. I went down the stairs to the connecting tunnel, over to the platform for the local train, and sat down on a bench. I had an idea: I took Akana's kidney out of my pocket and put it in my mouth. If it was shrinking because it was drying out, then if I kept it wet, it wouldn't shrink as fast, I thought. Akana's kidney was about the size of a large hard candy but tasted like Fanta Lemon. Sweet, sour, tingly on the tongue. The surface of it was rough like a potato skin, but in my mouth, it soon became slick and seemed to suck my tongue and the sides of my cheeks into it. This was the kidney my Akana had used to hear my voice when I was far away. She'd had her horn since she was born. There were no other humans with horns; she was the only unicorn in the entire world, and everyone around her had marveled and laughed, and when she realized that it was my voice she had been hearing her entire life and found the hole in my head— in that very first moment, she fell in love with me. Of course, it was the hole in my head that clinched it. Her long horn, an extra bit other people didn't have, and the hole in my head, a missing bit everyone else had. Surplus and absence. She was convex, I was concave. Which was why, less than two days after we met, we had head sex. The notion that her horn belonged inside my hole was a very strong one. We both wanted to see if it would fit. And when she first put it in, we both knew how right we had been. The size and depth of my hole was exactly the same as the length and thickness of her horn.

Akana was overjoyed to have discovered why her horn existed. The intense pleasure her horn gave me made me dizzy. I almost pissed my pants. I couldn't feel my legs. Ah, Akana. We were both so happy then, certain that we existed only for each other, but now I'm so far away from you, sucking on your kidney. My voice will never reach you again, and I'm not even looking for you.

How did things turn out like this? I asked myself, but I knew the answer now. Now that I had lost my penis, I could answer. My penis was in my way. I didn't need it. Since I had it, I couldn't focus on head sex, and I got caught up in a weird sense of duty, wondering if I should use it to have normal sex with Akana, and developed a complex about Akana's horn. But now that I had no penis, I felt totally free. I could never have genital sex. No matter how much Akana wanted it, no matter how much her genitals longed for mine. It was simply a fact that genital sex was no longer a possibility for me, which meant Akana might never come back to me. She might go to some other boy and get him to insert his penis in her vagina. But there was nothing I could do about it; I had no right to stop her, and honestly, I felt like her horn was not the only thing that could fit in my hole. Matsumoto was an enemy, but her fingers and hand worked fine. All girls had vaginas and might want to have genital sex with a boy, so maybe I should go out with another boy. If a boy put his penis in the hole in my head, and the hole in my head was warm and wet and felt good like Matsumoto said it did, then I could probably satisfy a boy. And the boy's penis might satisfy me. It made sense. But thinking about it a little more, there was no need for it to be genitals. Fingers and hands were good enough. I could simply go out with people who had no particular interest or no interest at all in genital sex, people incapable of having sex, and get them to play with the hole in my head. Right. Then the whole problem of genital sex was done with. I could also ask all kinds of different people to play with the hole in my head, avoiding the issue of genital sex entirely. Dicks, finger, hands, sticks, even carrots or cucumbers, anything. As long as I felt good, I didn't really care what went in there.

Why didn't I just play with my own hole?

Because if I did that, then I would be complete in and of myself, and I would curl up, turn over, get sucked into the hole in my head, swallowed up completely, and vanish, leaving no trace of me to be found anywhere in the world.

And if I was sucked into the hole in my head, would Makoto Muraki and I find ourselves in yet another world inside Makoto Muraki's head? That terrified me. Worlds inside heads . . . The farther back you went, the deeper you went, the more layers you passed through . . . the less sense things would make. I could barely handle the Chofu in Makoto Muraki's world, the world inside my head, and if I went further back, into imaginary worlds and even more imaginary worlds . . . It was beyond my imagination.

So I never touched the hole in my head myself. There were so many secrets there that I had yet to uncover, and I did not particularly want to find them out.

The local train pulled into the station. Only three cars long, white, with a blue line. The box seats at the back of the last car were each occupied by a single high school boy, and the other boxes and the long benches were completely empty. The last car had stopped in front of me, and sitting on the nearest empty seat left me on the long bench next to the four high school boys. I sat at the end of the bench, leaned my head against the wall, closed my eyes, and rolled Akana's kidney around on my tongue, being careful not to fall asleep. The speakers crackled to life, announcing that the train would be waiting in Tsuruga Station for five minutes. Then I heard people speaking Fukui dialect. The four boys were all friends and were chatting across the aisles, each taking up an entire box seat. Which meant they had to talk rather loudly, and I could hear everything they said.

"Dang phone still won't connect."

"Give it up already."

"Seriously, relax. We all gonna die anyway."

"Yeah, but I really wanna hear Yuka's voice one last time."

"Shimazaki's probably still in school. Takefu South won't tell the students shit, so Shimazaki don't know what's going on, still has her phone off. She ain't gonna answer, won't even notice till after school."

"Just message her, Ogaya."

"Not enough! This is the last time, I need to hear . . ."

"We got thirty minutes more? Only thirty minutes till the end of the world. Don't much matter what you do. It'll take us like thirty minutes to even get to Takefu."

"Makoto Muraki's a fucking retard. Keeps saying he'll save the world, but he ain't saved shit. Just put it off like ten years."

"Yeah, right. Only lasted ten years. Makoto Muraki's a pussy!"

"Lay off him. He saved the fucking world every day for ten years. The fucking world should have ended ten years ago; only lasted this long because of him."

"Fuck that. You got the power to save the world, everyone trusts you to save the world, then you've gotta go and save it, right? Nothing else is important. Letting the world last a measly ten more years don't even count."

"You try beating down enemies every fucking day for ten goddamn years. You'd get fed up with it, too. Saving the world is hard fucking work."

"But saving the world's not the kind of job you can just up and quit 'cause you're 'fed up.' You can't ever quit. Never. You've gotta save the world. It's your fucking responsibility."

"Yeah . . ."

"No point in defending him, Shuichi. Defend him all you like, world's still gonna end in thirty minutes."

A new enemy had appeared, I thought. I had known it was possible, and it obviously had happened. Another enemy attacking right after Matsumoto. Before, there were never two enemies attacking Chofu in the same day. They were really out to kill the world. That's why they'd come the first time I ever left home. They'd never come more than once a day before, but that might just have been so they could catch us off guard today. I was in Fukui now, and it had taken me, like, four hours to get here from Tokyo. If I went back now, the enemy would still wipe out Chofu. And the death of Chofu meant the death of the world. I couldn't get there in time. I didn't have my powers. I could do anything when I was in Chofu but nothing anywhere else. I couldn't just fly home, nor could I warp. If what these four high school boys bitching about me said was true, Chofu would be gone in thirty minutes, and the world would end as well. That's why there was no one on the train. They were all spending their last half hour in a way that meant something to them. They only had thirty minutes.

But in thirty minutes, I could get to West Akatsuki. I might as well go. If I ran all the way from the station, I'd reach the junior high in time. If the school knew the world was about to end and had canceled classes and sent the students home, then I'd just have to find a cab that didn't know the world was ending and see if I could get home in time. There might be some taxi drivers who knew the world was ending but were still operating anyway. People were like that. I would find myself. If I didn't exist here, that would be fine with me. I just wanted to know if I existed in this world. The world was in danger? Fuck it. It had put these four boys within earshot, blatantly hinting that I should hurry back to Chofu and save the world like I always had, but I had no intention of doing what the world wanted this time. I didn't give two shits about the world. I was done protecting it. The world would die in thirty minutes. I had thirty minutes left to live.

Humans were such selfish creatures, I thought. When you got down to it, the question of whether I existed simultaneously as Makoto Muraki and myself in the world inside me might not really matter. With the world about to end because of me, maybe trying to check up on this was not the last thing I should be doing. Maybe I didn't really need to specifically ascertain the state of my existence. I highly doubted knowing was going to change anything at all.

Oh, well. No matter what I wanted to do, Fukui was too far from Chofu, and there was no way for me to save the world. The local train started moving, and I closed my eyes. If the world was going to end, let it. If I was going to die, then so be it. But first I had to check, I had to know. . . . And the train pulled into West Akatsuki; I went down the hallway that looked exactly like I remembered it and down the stairs and out the gates. There was a TV next to the gates, tuned to the news. Broadcasting that the world was going to end. The station waiting room was filled with old men and women, sitting on benches and watching it, obviously not planning on getting on a train anytime soon. Akana was on the screen, in her uniform. Her left side was stained with blood. It was still bleeding from where she'd cut her kidney out. Akana was running around the school grounds, chasing the other Seiraku Academy students with her horn. She was stabbing them in the chest, stomach, through the neck, and tossing them in the air. I stopped rolling her kidney around in my mouth.

Akana was attacking students in our school at random, killing them. The last enemy to attack Chofu was Akana.

Who came up with that plot? This was getting stupid. The world was reeeeeally trying its damnedest to get me to save it. Trying to get me to fulfill my function as Makoto Muraki, boy savior of the world. That's why it had turned Matsumoto into an enemy, driven Akana into a corner, torn out her kidney, and made her an enemy, too. Forcing me to make a choice: my identity or the world?

I took Akana's kidney out of my mouth and put it in my jacket pocket.

Poor Akana. Manipulated by the world in a desperate attempt to summon me. Even putting the world's scheming aside, it hurt to see Akana crazily slaughtering everyone around her. It saddened me. It was painful to watch. I wanted to put her out of her misery. In doing so, I would save the world, which was exactly what the world wanted, but okay. Akana had been nice to me, she had said she loved me, she had meant a lot to me, and to see her covered in human blood and slaughtering boys and girls was too much. I could not bear to see the horn that had felt so good when she put it in the hole in my head being used to kill people at such astounding speed. I began trying to think of a way to get back to Chofu in thirty minutes. Seriously trying. It was impossible by Shinkansen. But if the government knew where I was, they could send a Harrier from the base at Kanazawa in a couple of minutes, pick me up, and have me in Tokyo in fifteen minutes. If I had five or ten minutes, I could easily kill Akana. Two minutes, one minute, hell, ten seconds would be plenty. She was killing people so blindly she might not even be able to hear me, but I'd say my last words to her and kill her as painlessly as possible. Argh. I'd been sure there was no way to save the world, but there had turned out to be one. I'd been planning on letting the world end, but I couldn't do that now. Of course not. The world was bound and determined to make me save it. There was no escape. The world controlled the timing perfectly. There was always a chance to save the world. All I had to do was call. I could save the world with a phone call. I would lose Akana, but in a sense, I had already been making myself ready to lose her, and losing her like this today was better than losing her yesterday, and thanks to Matsumoto, I felt a lot better about it.

Akana's horn was hardly the only thing that could fit in the hole in my head. That idea alone meant my love for Akana was not as thoughtful and tender as it used to be, meant it had turned into something that was sort of hard to really call love.

I could kill Akana. I could save the world one last time. I could come back to Fukui after I'd finished Akana off. I could meet this other me I imagined was somewhere in Fukui's West Akatsuki after I was done with her.

"Excuse me? I'm Makoto Muraki. It's an emergency, so can I borrow your phone?" I asked the station attendant. I'd left my phone in Chofu. I have to admit that part of me had wanted to make it hard for the government to contact me in the event of an enemy attack while I was away. I really didn't give a damn about the world. But it had never occurred to me that the next enemy would be Akana Sayaki.

The woman behind the ticket window just gaped when she heard my name, so I jumped in through the window, picked up the phone, and dialed the prime minister's office. Tworurururu. The red phone on the prime minister's desk was ringing. But not for very long. The prime minister had nothing better to do than sit around next to the phone waiting for me to call. It rang one time, and the prime minister, Miyashita, answered.

"Hello!?"

"Hey, it's Muraki."

"Muraki! Oh, were we ever waiting for this! Where are you?"

"Fukui."

"Eh? What are you doing there? No, never mind. Where in Fukui? Give me your exact location!"

"West Akatsuki Station."

". . . Right. We just confirmed it on this end. You're using the station manager's phone? Don't move! Military transport is on its way. Looks like they can land in the parking lot next to the station. Stay on the line. Are you safe, Muraki?"

"Sure. Safe and sound."

". . . So you weren't kidnapped or held hostage?"

"Nope."

"You know what's happening in Chofu right now?"

"Yeah, basically."

"Just to be sure, here are the facts: Enemy 1,937, as I'm sure you've noticed, is Akana Sayaki. We're still working to confirm that, but at the moment we're 78 percent sure it's her. Which means we're sure. She's in Chofu's Fuda, slaughtering the entire student population of Seiraku Academy, using her unicorn horn as a weapon. The slaughter began at 2:15. In the last hour and twenty-five minutes, 234 people have died—that we've been able to confirm. There are still 300 students and faculty in the school. Akana Sayaki destroyed the school security systems and has used glue or charms to seal off the doors, windows, seven entrances to the underground tunnels, emergency exits, emergency escape chute, roof doors, hidden SWAT team entrances, fourth-dimensional hall, spirit world tunnel, and the psychic corridors residing in twins, clones, and organ/cornea transplant recipients. Our psychic team is attempting to establish control over the humans inside, but Akana Sayaki has everyone in a state of panic, and they have had little success. . . ."

While Prime Minister Miyashita was explaining all this, I could hear the shrill whine of an engine approaching. A Harrier. I glanced at my watch. Three minutes. One hell of a scramble. The army and government had been working really hard to improve their emergency response time over the last five years. If they could respond this quickly not only around Chofu but in Ishikawa and Fukui as well, then that was the real deal. The scream of the Harrier turned to a roar, hovering over West Akatsuki, and in my ear Prime Minister Miyashita shouted to be heard through the racket.

"Military transport has arrived! They'll land in the station parking lot in ten seconds! It's dangerous, Muraki! Wait by the phone!"

I crouched down, and the Harrier started to land, dropping to thirty centimeters in one burst, the wind from the engines shattering every window in the station. The old men and women in the waiting room shrieked and cowered on the floor. The lunches and souvenirs and newspapers on the stand were blown off the shelves.

"Okay, Muraki. Leave the station office and climb on board that Harrier! The rest is in your hands! I know today's battle will be unusually painful for you, and I am sorry, but all I can do is ask you to try. We'll be sure to supply counseling afterward. Muraki, save the world. Please," Prime Minister Miyashita said.

I stood up. "Don't worry, your excellency," I said. "I will save the world." I was the boy savior of the world, and I existed because the world had created me to save itself, and as long as the world had created me, that meant it was obvious the world had no intention of ending just yet. I hung up the phone, thanked the woman curled up on the floor and covering her head with her hands, and went out into the gale, past the waiting room and out of the station, where the Harrier was hovering. I jumped on board, and the soldiers inside grabbed me, belting me into a seat. One of them turned around and shouted, "Muraki secured! Go Go Go!" The Harrier rose straight up, then shot forward suddenly, breaking the sound barrier, and headed for Tokyo. The seat was hard and the g-force insane, but I was only thinking of Akana. Of my lover Akana, whom I was about to kill.

Yeah. I had always loved her.

Until I transferred into Akana's class in the third grade, everyone had picked on her, and when I stood next to the podium to introduce myself, her horn was inside a plastic bottle. A 1.5-liter Aquarius bottle, and on the see-through surface someone had written in magic marker, "Danger! Do not touch." The mouth of the bottle was Scotch-taped to her head, and someone had written "Take this off = 100 yen" on her forehead.

With my powers, I could instantly tell who had done that to her. Before I even said my name, I took care of those five idiots. I grabbed a pencil from each of them, buried it perpendicularly in their foreheads, and sealed over the wound. The pointy end up. The skin on their foreheads was pulled up like a tent, and they all started crying.

"Don't cry, dumbass. I just pulled your skin up a little and made a tent over the pencil," I said. "Like a pencil rocket, hissss bang!"

They cried harder. That felt good. No matter how hard they cried, no matter how much the teacher yelled at me or pleaded with me, even when everyone in class got mad at me, I wouldn't take the pencils out. I didn't put the pencils in there to teach them what it felt like to get hurt or anything. I was just really pissed off at the dumb shit these five idiots had done to the girl with the horn.

I ignored the crying and screaming and went over to Akana, carefully peeled away the tape, and took the bottle off her horn. Then I touched her horn gently. I'd never seen a girl with a horn before. I knew then just how important she was to me. I knew how close Akana and I were going to be. Akana was staring shyly at the ground, but after a minute, she managed to look up and say, "Thanks. This is so strange. I never thought something like this would happen." Did she mean me taking the bottle off her horn? Or beating off the bullies? Or how I'd managed to put the pencils inside the skin of their foreheads without breaking the skin? Or did she mean meeting me? I didn't know then, and I don't know now.

A plastic bottle! An empty plastic bottle! When I saw Akana's horn stabbing the bottle, I realized her horn could go inside the hole on my head. But even though I'd freed her from the Aquarius bottle . . . making her put her horn in my head may not have been much different, as far as Akana was concerned. I was also empty, dangerous, and would exact a lot more then a hundred yen from her if she pulled out. When Akana asked Emi Inoue for help when she wanted to have genital sex but I would only agree to head sex, Emi told me to think about Akana more, to take better care of her, so I changed her memories and moved Emi Inoue to New Zealand and then corrected all of Akana's classmates' memories as well. When Daiki Sawada said he liked her despite her horn and tried getting closer to her, I changed Akana's and her classmates' memories and turned Daiki Sawada into a rabbit and put him in the rabbit pen at the nearest elementary school. Kazuo Ito, Toshimasa Yoda, and what's-his-name Kitakura are all doing just fine as a carp, a goldfish, and a chow chow.

Makoto Muraki was a dick. Far as I was concerned, he was a piece of shit, too. Such a complete shithead I could use every insult I knew and not be done abusing him. All he ever did was embarrass and abuse Akana, just like that Aquarius bottle. And now the piece of shit was on his way to kill her.

Sure, just like Makoto Muraki, Akana was an imaginary person living in the world inside my head, and I shouldn't really care if she lived or died or got herself killed, but I couldn't think like that because for some reason I loved Akana, and there was no hole in my head—this whole stupid complex about head sex versus genital sex all belonged to

Makoto Muraki, boy savior of the world, and not to me, Hideaki Kato. I have my own love, and sure, it may have been Makoto Muraki who actually met Akana and fell in love with her, but I had those memories, too, and I felt those same feelings for her, and I still loved her just like always. I didn't give two tugs of a dead dog's dick about head sex. I could take pleasure in it when Makoto Muraki did, and I knew just how intense that pleasure was, but ultimately that pleasure belonged to Makoto Muraki, not to Hideaki Kato. We were the same person at the moment, but our names and personalities were different, and our feelings did not always match up either. Makoto Muraki and I had briefly merged, but we were beginning to pull apart again. I had my own love, and I was fucked if I was going to let Makoto Muraki kill Akana!

"Sorry, but go back to Fukui! To West Akatsuki!" I shouted. I was able to shout this. This world was only in my head, and Makoto Muraki was just a character in it, so I could control him. I could let this world end. It was fine with me if my beloved Akana destroyed the world. The end of this world might mean my death. I might suffer brain death the second it ended. But I didn't care. I already had a Phillips screwdriver jammed in my head and I was as good as dead anyway, and I loved, loved, loved Akana, and my love for her had not changed the way Makoto Muraki's had, and judging from my memories, head sex was a blast, but as Hideaki Kato, I'd had normal sex, and I'd be happy to do that with Akana, even now. But according to Makoto Muraki's memories, once someone had become an enemy, the process could not be reversed, and anyone who had become an enemy lost all their memories, had a very different personality, and the person on a rampage in Chofu had been Akana but was not her anymore. I had lost the one I loved. But I still loved Akana, and I damn well wanted her to smash this stupid world apart. And if the end of the world meant the real me would die, I wanted to know more about the me in this world first. Maybe the end of this world just meant that one of the programs the Phillips screwdriver in my head allowed me to see would end forever, and if I twisted the screwdriver in a different direction, I could see a different channel, a different program. But if that happened, I would still have Makoto Muraki's memories and know all kinds of things about this world. I didn't give a damn about Makoto Muraki, but I wanted to find out for sure about Hideaki Kato before the channel changed and I could never know for sure.

I was probably a little lonely, waking up here as Makoto Muraki, living in Chofu instead of West Akatsuki, in a world I didn't know filled with insane shit. Maybe that was why I was so fixated on closing that distance from myself. That was all I really wanted.

But the Harrier showed no signs of changing direction. The soldiers aboard were all staring at me, not moving.

"Go back to West Akatsuki!" I roared. "Go back!"

An impossibly placid man emerged from behind the soldiers. "My name is Shogo Shimada, squad leader for Third Airborne Unit, Eighteenth Division. What's the problem, Muraki?"

"I want to go back to West Akatsuki before we go to Chofu."

"Look . . . Chofu is fifteen minutes from West Akatsuki. We left West Akatsuki almost ten minutes ago. If we went back to Fukui, it would take us twenty minutes to get here again. I have no idea what you want to go there for, but by the time we reach Chofu, the world would have ended. Is there no way this can wait until after you've gone to Chofu and defeated the enemy? I promise we'll make sure you get back to West Akatsuki."

"Nope." I did not want all those people begging me to kill Akana. I did not want to see how much Akana had changed, now that she was an enemy. I did not want to see the scene of slaughter where Akana had been trying to end the world. It was all my . . . Makoto Muraki's fault. "Go to West Akatsuki. It's important."

"What's so important? More important than the end of the world?"

It was. The world didn't matter to me at all. Not anymore. But I couldn't tell him that. "The fate of the world depends on it," I said.

"I see. But what is it? Will you tell me?"

What was it? "My partner." The other me. If he existed.

"Partner? I had no idea you had one, Muraki. You're absolutely sure you need this partner to win today?"

"Absolutely."

"But we don't have time to go get that partner. For the moment, we're going to take you to Chofu and have you fight enemy 1,937. If you can hold out for ten or fifteen minutes, the army will get that partner to you."

"No, without him—"

"Muraki. You are the only person in the world who even stands a chance against the enemy. This is the only way. First, you start to fight the enemy in Chofu. Buy time until your partner arrives. When your partner gets there, you can join forces and defeat the enemy. You have to try, Muraki. You're our only hope. I know that leaving everything up to you reflects badly on humanity. I know we make things very hard for you. But, Muraki, that's all we can do. Please. Do what we cannot. You're the only one who can do this, so you have to try. Well, Muraki . . . what do you say?"

I fell silent.

Shimada got some sort of communication on his headset and said, "Wait. 651-7 round." We were almost over Chofu, and they had decided to delay the Harrier's arrival. I had failed to answer clearly. In a moment, I'd be over Chofu, Makoto Muraki's full powers would be restored, and they must be worried that I would take control of the Harrier. They were right.

"I'll be honest. I'm considering taking over this Harrier. Second we enter Chofu and I get the almighty back, I take y'all out, snatch how to fly this thing out of the pilot's brain, and get the fuck back to West Akatsuki."

"You can't. Not enough fuel," Shogo Shimada said. "You won't make it to Fukui."

"Dumbass. I'm Makoto Muraki! There's an airport in Chofu. Fuel'll jet out of that, into here, and we're good."

"We can blow Chofu airport up now."

"I can siphon off enough from the airplanes in the sky over Chofu."

"We can divert all flights away from Chofu."

"In time? The world's about to end."

"No time to think about it. Your world's done for. I protected it ten years. You lived ten years more. You're just gonna have to be satisfied with that."

I might die, too. But I wasn't scared. I'd much rather be killed by Akana Sayaki than Kouji Miyadate.

"Go on, take me to Chofu. You do that, I promise you won't suffer when I kill you. Maybe I'll even just turn you into an idiot and make you forget everything that happened."

"Is that a threat?"

"Yeah."

"That attitude makes this easier."

Shimada raised his elbow and made a fist, then yanked it back, pumping his fist in the air. The soldiers behind me grabbed my arms and shoulders. Silver duct tape bound my legs to the seat. Outside of Chofu, I was an ordinary eighth grader and could hardly fight off trained soldiers.

"Muraki, your powers as a hero have gone to your head. You look down on us humans," Shimada said, glaring down at me. I couldn't move. "Humans are frail creatures, but we've put a lot of time into discovering how to defeat stronger creatures. No matter how many times we lose, we never give up hope."

I could only glare back at him. The world was about to end, and he was making speeches?

"How can we win? Every time we lose, we run away again. But we do not just run. We observe our enemy. We study them. We discover their weakness. We search for a weak point. And we have been studying and observing more than just the enemy, Muraki. We have also been observing and studying the powerful hero who saves us all."

As Shimada said this, the soldiers behind him brought out a grotesque machine. It was long and pointed, a mechanical device modeled on Akana's horn. They also handed Shimada a black box. It was very simple, just one button and a handle that went up and down. Presumably a wireless controller. Shimada took it and pushed the button. The fake Akana horn began whirring, wriggling like a giant metal caterpillar. Shimada pushed the button again, and the caterpillar stopped moving. I got it. This was a Makoto Muraki–only vibrator.

"I put this in you, you won't be able to move," Shimada said, sticking that horrible machine into the hole in my head. It was always wet inside the hole, so it slid smoothly into my brain. The size of it matched Akana's horn with hateful perfection. That shrill *niiiiiiiiiiiiiiiiin* sound echoed through my head again. Again. Even Matsumoto's fingers had been enough to make me feel good. But I didn't like this. A mechanical cock jammed into my brain by some crazy man . . . I didn't want to react to that!

Fuck, it felt good!

It was exactly like Akana's horn. My beloved Akana. Her horn had given me so much pleasure . . . for five years, since we were nine. The hole in my head knew it very well. Even the waves of pleasure felt familiar. Until Matsumoto jammed her fingers in there today, I had only had that horn, only let that horn inside my hole, only wanted that horn in me, and thought I never wanted anyone other than Akana inside me. I felt more than a little grateful for this sweet artificial penis that was giving me that exact same pleasure. I really did love Akana's horn. I loved Akana. I felt like I had been given a powerful reminder of why I had. A specific, practical, clear explanation of exactly why I had loved her. I really wanted to thank them for it. I had looked at no one but her for five years. I had thought of no one but her. I loved no one but Akana!

"Enjoying yourself, Muraki?"

Shimada pushed the button again, and the mechanical version of Akana's horn, which had just been resting quietly in my brain, began to vibrate. It shook my very spine, destroying it.

"Aaaahh! Ah ah ahh . . . ah . . . aaaaaaahh!"

I almost peed my pants. Wow. This was wow. The real Akana's horn never moved like this. It felt good. So good. Too fucking good. The fake horn wriggled away inside my head. The mechanical horn's surface was covered in little studs that dug into my brain, making different bits of my body shudder, contract, flail around wildly. My body no longer belonged to me. I really didn't know what was going on. I was well on my way to breaking forever. My body seemed ready to tear itself apart. Any second now, kabooooom! Explode into a shower of gore.

Oh, I wanted this. I wanted this fake Akana horn so much. Would they give it to me if I saved the world? How much did it cost? How many times did I have to save the world before they gave it to me?

"We know exactly how much pleasure it takes to stop you

from moving, and how much leaves you still capable of movement. We have no time to test this. We have to get to Chofu. For us, for you, for all mankind—everything depends on this fight. If we do nothing, the world will end in a few minutes. Cast your dice, Muraki. You'll find out what you rolled when the dice stop."

The Harrier stopped circling and entered Chofu. I knew this, because my full powers returned. But my incredible power was dispersed by the sound of the motor in the fake Akana horn. If Shimada eased the control bar down a little, some of it came back, but when he pushed it up again, my body simply would not respond. I was completely under the control of the fake horn writhing around in my brain. And as long as Shimada held the controller, he controlled me, standing in for all mankind. Trying to force me to kill Akana.

Was that okay? Killing Akana? I could kill her like nothing.

Once again, I had completely stopped caring about Akana. About her or the world. I just wanted the vibrator they had jammed in my head.

Would they give it to me if I killed Akana?

The Harrier reached the airspace over Seiraku Academy and began hovering. The soldiers opened the doors; Shimada said, "Good luck, Muraki"; and another soldier pushed me out. As I fell, the vibrator stopped wriggling and I managed to stop myself just before I slammed into the roof of the school, avoiding a messy death.

Good luck?

I was entirely ready to kill Akana. I was gonna save the world. Ooooh. The beautiful machine in my head cast aside all hesitation. I was me. Makoto Muraki. The boy savior of the world. That was the role I'd been given. I had to fulfill that role. I was happy to save the world. From now on, I might always live under the control of this mechanical horn, but I wanted that, I wanted a life of constant pleasure with this horn jammed in my head. I would fight. I would kill every enemy that appeared, one after the other, and get them to make the horn move as a reward. Make it move till I pissed myself. I might finally climax. I might finally pass over that ultimate peak. What fun. Too fun. My body might fall apart completely, but that didn't scare me. I wanted it to break me. I wanted it to drive me mad with pleasure and kill me. When I died, the world would probably end, but if they wanted me to save the world, they had to make the horn move inside my head. The world, the humans, and I were about to start a game of chicken. My heart thrilled. All that lay in store for me was a huge and vast ecstasy. It would continue till I died or the world ended, whichever came first. Fantastic. Aaaaaaaahh!

Shit, I couldn't move. The pleasure the cunt in Makoto Muraki's head was radiating was much too powerful. Just having the vibrator in there numbed me, made it hard to think, and if it started to wriggle, it was a tidal wave, a massive earthquake, a towering inferno. I couldn't breathe, I couldn't stand, my body grew hot and seemed about to catch fire.

I had definitely underestimated humans. Not only because they'd jammed a vibrator in my head—I had never realized how much humans were controlled, manipulated, paralyzed by their sex drives. Anything was fine. Didn't matter if your sex partner was going out with you. Could be a total stranger. Didn't have to be a person. Could be a broom handle. Didn't matter what as long as it made you feel good. So very greedy. I was scared. The cunt on my head was going to swallow the world.

An army helicopter had landed on the roof of the school, and a special ops squad was in position. But Akana's barrier was probably too strong for any ordinary methods to break through. The door on the roof and the windows on the classrooms and hallways were impenetrable, obviously, but I highly doubted they would even be able to dig a hole through the roof. I was sure they could not break down the walls, and they could not dig up from below the building.

Okay, I thought. The stronger and tougher the barrier was, the better. It should be next to impossible to get in. I was Makoto Muraki, the boy who saved the world. It was a given that I would save the world, and now that she was an enemy, there was no way Akana could escape me. There was always a way in. I would find a way into the school, a way to stop her. When almost all those methods were sealed off, my omnipotence came in. I stood in the center of the roof, surrounded by soldiers. No . . . I didn't stop to stand. I slid right on down. The soldiers gasped, but I just sank right on into the floor.

Through concrete.

If you threw a ball against a wall, the odds of the ball's passing through it were extremely remote, but when the ball was destined to reach the other side of the wall, and the only way to do that was to pass through the wall, then the ball would go right through it. All the miracles I performed worked on this principle. I used the fact that the outcome was predetermined and the fact that there was no other way for that result to be achieved to fly, time-travel, warp space. . . .

I emerged from the ceiling onto the fourth floor. It was a bloodbath.

Akana's horn was no longer a sex organ that went into the hole in my head. It was now a unicorn's weapon. Students from our school were folded over, stacked up, torn apart, flung aside, exploded, beaten to a pulp, washed away, rubbed away to stains or splots. Akana was demolishing them thoroughly. The glass windows were covered in blood, and the room was dark, but none of them were alive. Even if they played dead and hid in the pile of bodies, there was so much blood flowing around that they would have drowned in it.

But despite the piles of corpses, the fourth floor was hardly silent. Their screams were still echoing. Reverbs from death screams tend to linger. They seemed particularly loud today. I already had the constant *niiiiiiiiiiiin* in my head the fake horn was creating. Over that whine there was the *rrraaah* of dead children's lingering screams, and those two sounds refused to harmonize, bouncing off each other instead. My ears hurt, so I waved a hand, and the screaming stopped. I just waved my right hand diagonally down from the left, and all sound on the fourth floor ceased. The world in Chofu obeyed me.

With the fourth floor quiet, I could hear the screams below. Where there was screaming, there was Akana. What should my last words to her be?

As I picked my way between blood-covered walls and past piles of dead bodies, trying not to get any of the blood on me, I decided to get Akana to help me. I took her kidney out of my pocket—it was now the size of a bead—and popped it in my mouth. It was bitter now. I coated it in spit. Just a few minutes longer.

I found Akana near the library on the second floor, running two girls through at once, with their bodies hanging down and blocking her face. Akana's horn had missed their hearts, and they were hanging from her head puking blood and sobbing. "Akana," I said, and Akana shook her head, dropping the girls onto the floor. I heard the screams of the survivors in the distance as the new *rrrrraaah* around me bounced off the *niiiiiiiiiin* in my head, but I spoke through the ruckus, saying, "It's me." But Akana did not appear to know me and just stared at me, eyes glazed over, then swung her horn around and lunged at me. This made me sad. She had been so important to me. She had wanted so much from me. But I had a different horn stabbing my head, and there was really nothing left that I wanted from her, so I would have to kill her and then call Miyadate at the Muraki Unit like I always did after I defeated an enemy and have him dispose of the corpse. There was no more hesitation or doubt or any other strong emotion left concerning this. I realized there was nothing left for me to say to her. Any bond between us had long since been lost.

Fuck it, I thought. Just kill her and get it over with. There might be another enemy soon. I dodged her lunge and spun around, aiming to chop her head off. I swung my hand to do just that.

Instead, I stabbed my hand into her left side. Akana shrieked. I pulled my hand out again and jammed her tiny, tiny kidney into the wound. Then I used Makoto Muraki's ridiculous powers to put it back where it used to be, connect all the blood vessels again, make it function again—in miniature, but Akana had her kidney back. The same kidney she'd cut out herself, the one that could hear my voice.

Akana, Akana.

This was the only way to make her hear my voice now that she was an enemy. This was the only way I could reach her.

Akana.

"Makoto."

Akana's voice. Her own voice, emerging from her own throat. Aaaah. I wanted to cry with joy. I still loved her.

I'm sorry, Akana. I'm really sorry.

"Makoto. It hurts. I don't want this. It hurts too much."

Sorry.

"I don't want this. Why did you put the kidney back? Don't do that. I don't want to hear your voice anymore. It hurts."

Sorry. I've been so selfish. . . .

"No more. Just kill me. I've had enough. I'm tired. I

wanted to be with you, I wanted to help save the world, but you don't need me anymore, do you? You'll be fine without me, won't you? You don't need me anymore."

I want to be with you. Really.

"That's not true."

Really.

"Enough. I don't want to be with you anymore. I just want it all to end."

Don't die, Akana. I don't want to lose you.

"Kill me, Makoto. You have to save the world. If you don't kill me, I'll destroy the world. I will!"

Don't do that.

"No. You already know, don't you? Once you become an enemy, you can never turn back. You have only two choices. Kill me or let the world end."

I don't care about the world.

"Don't be stupid! Makoto, if the world ends, then I'll die, and you'll die. You have to kill me. Come on! I want you to kill me!"

No. I won't kill you, Akana. I'd rather both of us died along with the whole world.

"How can you say that? You were made to save the world, so you have to kill me and do just that. You have to. It's your destiny!"

I won't kill you. No matter what.

But I'll kill you. I can kill Akana. Hideaki Kato and I were only overlapping temporarily, and we've separated now. Hideaki Kato and I have different personalities. But these powers belong to Makoto Muraki, to me, not to Hideaki Kato. When I realized that, I used those powers to shove Hideaki Kato aside. To keep him from getting in my way.

Stop!

"Go ahead, Makoto. Kill me."

Goodbye, Akana. I really did love you.

Stop!

"Thank you, Makoto. I really do care about you. I really do love you. But it just hurts too much. Bye."

Aaaaaaughhh!

My hand cut Akana's head clean off. Her neck was soft, and all I had to do was swing my hand across on a level and it cut right through like a sponge cake and landed on the floor a couple of meters away.

The world would continue. I would wait for the next enemy. I would manage to defeat it, too. I was Makoto Muraki, savior of the world. Saving the world was my destiny; it was preordained.

Shitbird! Fucktard!

I screamed and cursed, but my curses had no power. I was sealed off inside Makoto Muraki's head, and even though Makoto Muraki was only in my head, I was also inside his head.

How did that work?

I released the barrier around Seiraku Academy, freed the surviving students, and waved the army in in their place, then I called Miyadate. The army had entered the scene first, which meant he had his job cut out for him, but Miyadate was the one who should take care of the enemy corpse. Akana Sayaki's corpse was on the second floor, outside the library. I cut off her head. She had a horn, so it should be easy to find her head, but the body was wearing a uniform and was covered in blood like everyone else's, so it might be a bit trickier, but she had a name tag on, so I was sure he could work it out.

Then I found the Harrier jet, still hovering in the air above, and jumped on board. As Shogo Shimada had promised, they took me back to Fukui, to West Akatsuki. In classroom 2-B of West Akatsuki Junior High, I found Hideaki Kato, obliviously taking math. I went to the gym, found a bat, went back to 2-B, into the classroom, and beat Hideaki Kato to death with the bat. His voice inside my head was gone. I dropped the blood-covered bat in the school yard, ran back to West Akatsuki station, rode to Tsuruga Station, Maibara Station, Tokyo Station, Shinjuku Station, and back to Chofu, my uniform still covered in blood. My full powers returned again. Enemy 1,938 had still not shown up.

I remained alive inside Makoto Muraki, saying nothing. I was outside Makoto Muraki and inside him as well. Makoto Muraki was inside me and outside me. I understood that now. The only way to make this contradiction noncontradictory, in other words, for me and Makoto Muraki to disappear simultaneously or become one thing, was for me to stab that giant Chofu Tower into the hole in Makoto Muraki's head. That giant metal tower was the Phillips screwdriver that was jammed inside my head, so if I jammed the same thing inside Makoto Muraki's head, Makoto Muraki and I would fuse. I didn't know what would happen if we did. The hole in Makoto Muraki's head could take more than the fake Akana horn, more than fingers and hands—it could take much, much more than that, even Chofu Tower, but the intense pleasure he would get from jamming Chofu Tower in there might finally kill him. Then I might die, too. I might wake up as Hideaki Kato again, in my brother's room, with a Phillips screwdriver jammed in my head. I had no idea what would happen.

Inside Makoto Muraki, I looked up at Chofu Tower. Waiting for Makoto Muraki to notice the overwhelming pleasure it held in store for him. At the moment, his escalation was not proceeding very quickly, and the vibrator was good enough for him. I hoped he reached Chofu Tower level soon.

Stab more things into your head.

    Stab it.

                                  Stab it.

        Stab it.

STAB IT.

F-SENSEI'S POCKET

Otsuichi

Illustrations by Takeshi Obata
Translated by Andrew Cunningham

What if you could . . . ?
Everything you ever dreamed of . . .
All of it, everything come true?

In some ways, American readers will need no help appreciating "F-sensei's Pocket." This compelling story has an inventive plot and two memorable heroines to recommend it. And yet Japanese readers would have a significantly different experience with this story, for one important reason: It refers constantly to a uniquely Japanese pop-culture icon. That icon is Doraemon, a time-traveling robot cat from an enduringly popular manga that has spawned its own multimedia and merchandising empire. The ubiquity and popularity of Doraemon in Japan is hard to overestimate; Mickey Mouse might be our closest analogue. So Japanese fans would recognize instantly that all of the devices the two girls discover are references to Doraemon; footnotes are provided for the benefit of American readers. The "sensei" in the title refers to Fujiko F. Fujio, the creator of *Doraemon*. "Sensei's" literal translation is "one who came before," and it can be used to refer to not only a teacher but to any person who has achieved true mastery of his field, including manga-ka.

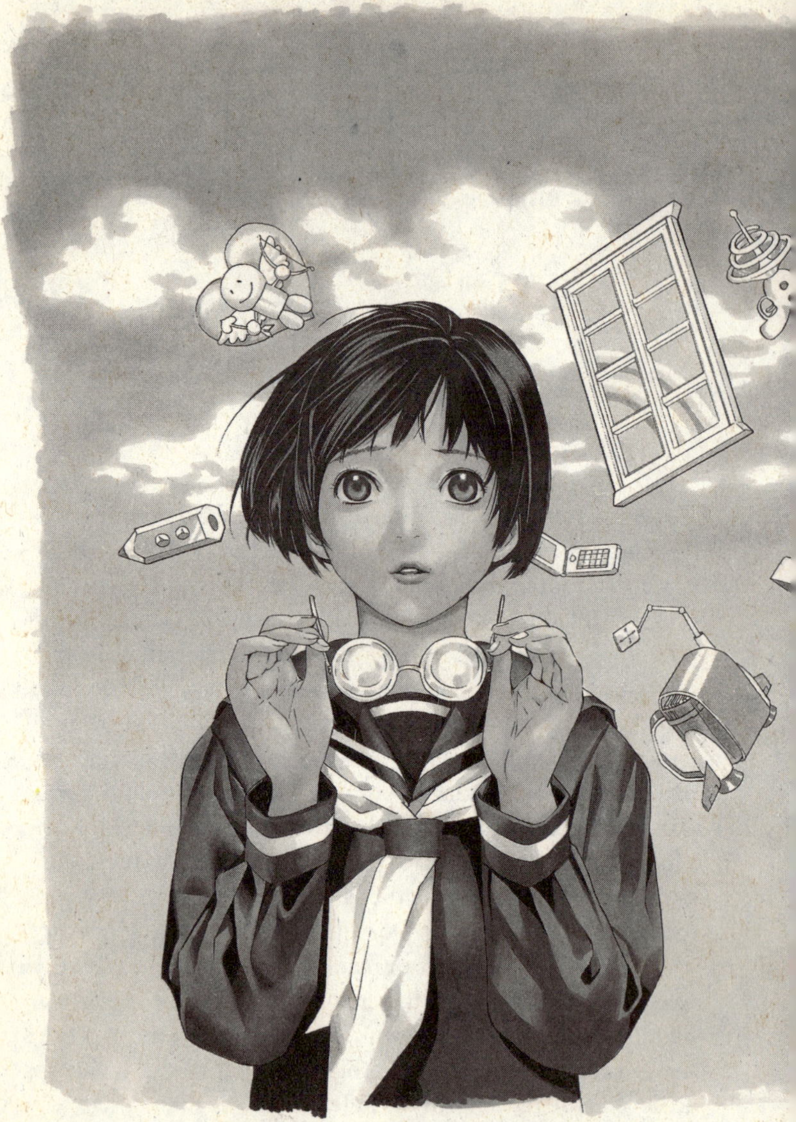

Continuing in the *Faust* tradition of bringing together Japan's top talents, "F-sensei's Pocket" matches hot novelist Otsuichi with superstar artist Takeshi Obata. Born in 1978, Otsuichi was an award-winning novelist from the start, with his debut *Summer, Fireworks, and My Corpse* winning the 6th Jump Novel and Nonfiction Award's grand prize. This was

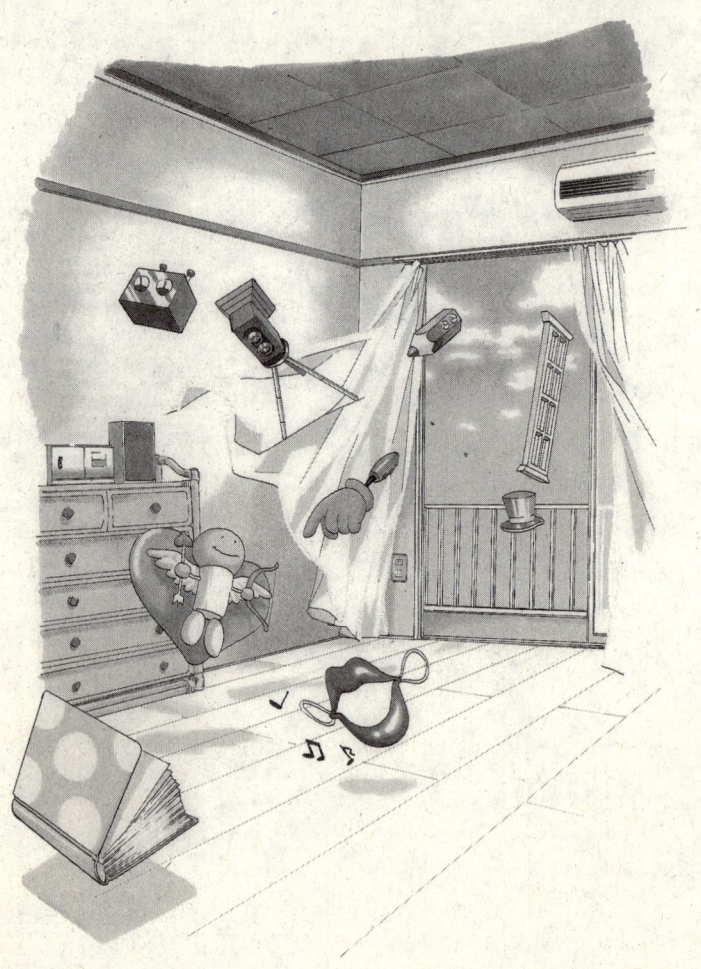

followed with another triumph in 2003: His novel *Goth Wristcut Case* won the 3rd Honkaku Mystery Prize. Typical of his work are the novels *Gun and Chocolate, Ushinawareru Monogatari,* and *ZOO*. Recent years have seen a spate of his books being adapted into movies, with *Goth Wristcut Case* being optioned by Hollywood. He has recently published a novelization of Hirohiko Araki's world-famous manga *JoJo's Bizarre Adventure*.

Illustrator and manga artist Takeshi Obata's masterpiece *Death Note* (co-created with writer Tsugumi Ohba and published by Shueisha) has become a major cultural phenomenon. It is considered one of twenty-first-century-Japan's most iconic works, and has been adapted to multiple media platforms, including blockbuster feature films, TV anime, video games, prose novels, etc. This popular artist's work presents a true picture of modern Japan. His most recent project is the manga series *Blue Dragon: Ral Grado*.

▲▼▲▼▲

Prologue

Probably because it was built on a hill, my room was always very windy, and if I opened the window, I never needed a fan in summer. If the floor got dusty, I just had to open the bay window opposite the veranda and the wind would gust right through the window and carry all the dust away. When I got out of the bath, I could stand in front of the window and the wind would dry my hair in seconds. But it wasn't all good—the wind brought its share of problems.

If I put a wind chime near the window, it would ring continuously and annoy the neighbors. When the wind was particularly strong, it would slam up against the glass so hard I was often afraid it would shatter. And when such gales passed, the veranda would be full of leaves.

Leaves were not the only thing that collected outside my window. Mixed in with the leaves I would find strangers' mud-covered underwear, socks, and skirts, lying on my veranda or plastered against the window. My veranda window was like the nets fishermen use. Just as their nets collect massive quantities of smaller fish, the grille of my veranda collected anything the wind brought it. When I opened my curtains in the morning, I might well find some strange man's boxers hanging right in front of me, which is a problem no high school girl should ever have to deal with.

It seemed a shame to throw away the clothes that blew here, so I washed them. After I ironed them, I gave all the men's clothes to my father. Unaware of their origins, my father was happy to wear strangers' boxers. Some of them were expensive brand names, which my mother was overjoyed to get as presents. Occasionally, I even went out wearing only clothes collected by my veranda. Nobody ever noticed that everything I was wearing had been carried to me by the wind.

On the night of November 6, with winter approaching, my little brother—very little brother; he wasn't even in preschool yet—said he wanted to sleep with me.

I lay in bed next to him, brushing his head and listening to the wind shaking my window. The wind had picked up as night fell, and the constant wailing outside grew even louder.

When I woke up that morning, I slipped quietly out of bed, trying not to wake my brother up. I went out on the veranda and looked down at the town below the hill. Last night's wind had vanished like a lie, and the veranda was piled high with leaves again.

My yawns were interrupted by a strange object half buried in the leaves. It was yellow, shaped like a T, about twenty centimeters across. I pulled it out of the leaves and looked at it closely: the cross section of the T was a propeller. The bottom of the vertical line widened into a half sphere so you could stand it up like a lamp.

At a glance, it looked like a bamboo copter, but on closer inspection, the first thing my mind connected it to was the Take-copter from a really famous manga. This manga was about a cat robot (which looked nothing like a cat) from the future that used many devices to help out the hapless main character. The Take-copter was one of the most famous devices, and the cat robot used it whenever they needed to fly.

From the weight and feel of it, I couldn't tell if it was metal or plastic. I went back into my room, vaguely impressed that they were making toys like this now. This was definitely one of the stranger things to sweep up on my veranda.

At the time, I had not yet noticed the white fabric that had caught on the edge of the roof. If it had blown away before I noticed it, Kyoko Inoue would never have brought such horrors upon the town.

1

Friday, November 7.

I was a class representative, so after school, our teacher, Tsukamoto, summoned me and ordered me to take care of a few things. The male representative, Kuraki, helped me finish them off, and only then could I leave school. It was a fifteen-minute walk home. When I got there, I said hello to my

---

Bamboo copter *Take tonbo* (literally "bamboo dragonfly") is a Chinese toy that flies when it spins.

Really famous manga The narrator is referring to the massively popular Doraemon series. See the chapter introduction. *Take-copter* literally means "bamboo copter." One of the more popular devices used in *Doraemon*, the copter was worn on the head, allowing the user to fly briefly. (The batteries have a short life span.)

mother and brother, fetched the Take-copter from my room, put it in my shoulder bag, and went out again.

"This morning I found a Take-copter toy on my veranda," I'd said at lunch.

Kyoko Inoue was a big manga fan, and she instantly cried, "Let me see!" Rather forcefully. "Matsuda, you don't have it with you?"

"I'll go home and get it after school. You wait in the usual abandoned building."

"You're so nice!"

"Well, you loaned me *Glass Mask*."

It was four o'clock by the time I reached the abandoned building at the end of the arcade. It was an old three-story building between the fruit shop and the toy store. When the big department store went in near the station, lots of customers had stopped coming to the arcade, and all the shops in this building had been forced to close. Now there was nothing but concrete walls, turned red in the setting sun.

I slipped inside the building, careful not to be seen. The first floor was filled with naked mannequins, the second with empty bookshelves, and the third with abandoned office furniture. Kyoko Inoue was waiting, like always, in a chair near the windows, gazing at the sunset. It was hard to tell through her awful glasses, but judging from the drool on the collar of her uniform, she had fallen asleep again.

The area was filled with an almost overpowering citrus scent. Kyoko Inoue had brought an air freshener in, attempting to bring some life to the place.

It was Kyoko Inoue who had told me about the empty building in the first place. She had been napping here after school long before I got to know her. This building was her equivalent of the hill behind Nobita's house.

---

*Nobita The main character in *Doraemon,* also a fan of midday naps.

"Wake up, Inoue. I brought the thing I was talking about at lunch."

I shook her shoulders, disturbing her citrus-scented dreams. She wiped away her drool and then stretched like a cat.

I took what I'd found on my veranda that morning out of my bag. Inoue adjusted her glasses, staring at the thing in my hand.

"See? Obviously a Take-copter," I said, handing it to her.

"You really found this on your veranda?"

"I find all kinds of stuff there when the wind's strong enough. Once I even found some Chinese money mixed in with the leaves. I bet it was blown right across the ocean. And even weirder stuff: a few weeks ago, I found next year's newspaper, just lying there on my veranda."

"Next year's? Not last year's?"

"Next year's. According to the date on it," I insisted.

Inoue did not seem that surprised. "Hmm... I guess that's possible," she murmured. She looked down at the Take-copter in her hands. "There's a manufacturer's logo, but I've never heard of the company...."

"Did they make it without a license? Ignoring copyright. You make something like this without permission from Shogakakan, they'll sue you."

"Yeah. They'd better look out."

"You can say that again. Can't let their guard down for a second. I want to stand on the roof screaming, 'Protect copyright!' Wait, we've cleared this story, right?"

"Yes. Mm...?" Inoue touched the bottom of the Take-copter, and her expression got really weird. In the manga, the characters would place that part of the device on their heads when they were ready to use it. The manga never showed it in

---

Shogakakan Major Japanese publishing company and the publisher of *Doraemon*.

any detail. Inoue was touching it and pulling her hand away, over and over.

"If you touch it here, it sort of sucks your skin in like a magnet. How'd they do that? Oh, a button . . . ," she said, pointing at the bottom of the Take-copter.

Like she said, there was a little button near the base. She pushed it, and the propeller suddenly began to spin. A little faster than any toy I'd ever seen.

Wow. This thing was really well made, I thought. But my surprise quickly gave way to concern.

"Uh . . . ," I gasped.

Inoue's arm, the one holding the Take-copter, was rising into the air—as if it were being pulled upward by invisible string. She was trying to pull her arm back down, staring at it in disbelief. But her arm kept rising. She was short anyway, so a moment later, she was on tiptoes.

"Wh-what is this thing!?" Kyoko Inoue almost never spoke in class, but this was enough to get her screaming.

Her finger hit the Take-copter's switch again. The propeller stopped suddenly, and the mysterious power that had lifted her up vanished.

Inoue landed on her backside, the Take-copter slipping from her grasp and rolling away across the floor.

I went after it and picked it up gingerly, as if it were a poisonous snake. It had hit the concrete pretty hard, but there wasn't a scratch on the yellow . . . whatever it was. It gleamed softly in the light of the evening sun.

"Inoue, I saw it happen . . . ," I said, looking down at her. She was adjusting her glasses, not making any effort to stand. "I'm pretty sure I wasn't seeing things. . . ."

Just before she'd managed to turn the Take-copter off, Inoue had been standing on tiptoes . . . and the Take-copter had pulled her upward even farther. She had been at least five centimeters off the ground.

Until a month before, I had never so much as spoken to Kyoko Inoue. We went to the same school and were in the same class, but that was all—just classmates. Nothing more, nothing less—the kind of cast member forgotten as completely as a random passerby the moment you graduated.

I was representative for class 2-A. Not because I liked working for everyone else. Purely because being class representative made a good impression on the teachers and meant they would write good things in your letters of recommendation. I had made the calculated decision to serve as class representative at least once while I was in high school.

In manga, you see lots of young people putting themselves forward as candidates and actively campaigning for the job. But nobody I knew was that weird.

"Anyone want to be class representative?" Tsukamoto, our homeroom teacher, had asked at the beginning of first semester in our second year. Nobody raised a hand. In the middle of that silence, I raised my hand high, and a little stir ran around the room.

"Who is she?"

"Matsuda. Kozue Matsuda."

As far as I was concerned, classmates were simply a part of the background that occasionally happened to move across my field of vision. The noise a certain segment of that background was making was not unlike the sound a tree makes in a strong wind.

So I was class representative. From that day forth, I was the teacher's dog. Seriously, the way they worked me? Anyone alive would say the same. If I found cigarette butts in the classroom, I would take them to the teachers' room and give them to Tsukamoto.

"Nice job, Matsuda. Allow me to reward you. Tell me . . . what do you want?" Tsukamoto said with a satisfied nod.

"I need no reward. Instead, make sure to write a good letter of recommendation."

"Of course. You need not worry about that."

"Thank you very much."

"You may go."

"Aye, aye!"

Several female students saw us playing evil overlord and loyal servant and squawked in protest. Tsukamoto taught math, but he was kinda cool. Which meant he was popular with the girls. I was working as his minion for the pure, noble cause of making my letter of recommendation a good one, but the girls who had a crush on him appeared to view our interaction as flirtatious.

But I paid no heed to voices of protest from one segment of the background. Anytime there was a problem in the classroom, I headed right for the teachers' room, found my evil overlord banging away at his laptop, and filed a report. First, the girls who had a thing for Tsukamoto started calling me "dog." Then the boys who had been suspended for smoking in school started calling me "the rat."

Cold-blooded informant, police dog, teacher's hotline. The nicknames they came up with for me spread throughout the school, and soon enough nobody ever spoke to me.

One day I found obscene language carved into my desk. Phrases so dirty even Kodansha refuses to publish them. This happened several days in a row, so I hid in the broom cupboard after school and caught a girl in the act. I grabbed her wrist and dragged her off to Tsukamoto, and she burst into tears and wailed, "I just hate Matsuda so much!" Her portable CD player had been confiscated after I reported it. It was returned to her eventually, but she'd been nursing a grudge anyway.

Even with no friends, I was perfectly fine. Did anyone really enjoy talking to mailboxes and shrubs by the side of the road? If they spoke to you, wouldn't you just be annoyed? It was the same thing. Not having anyone to talk to in class was nothing to get upset about.

Then one day after school, a few days after the rainy season ended . . .

As always, Tsukamoto had piled on the chores, and I was taking care of them with the male representative, Kuraki, and reminding myself that this was all for my letter of recommendation. When we were done, I went to report back to Tsukamoto and then back to the classroom to pick up my shoulder bag and head home.

But there were several girls in class. They were standing in a circle around a short girl with awful glasses. They did not appear to be playing ring-around-the-rosy. They were engaged in what the masses call "bullying."

The bullies turned around, flustered by my sudden appearance. Watching them out of the corner of my eye, I hoisted my shoulder bag over my head and left the room. I want directly back to the teachers' room and filed a report.

And then I went right home, so I did not really know if the girl in the awful glasses had been saved from her bullies or not. I really wasn't interested. I had simply reported it and had never once been concerned by any of the problems that occurred in the classroom. So until Tsukamoto mentioned it a week later, I had honestly forgotten anything like that had ever happened.

"Matsuda, that bullying incident you reported last Thursday . . . Kyoko Inoue insists she was not being bullied."

Tsukamoto had conducted a secret investigation and interviewed those involved. He cupped his cheek in one hand, rested his elbow on the desk, and sighed.

"Matsuda."

"Yes!" I replied, like a dog addressed by its master.

"I really hate kids."

Careful not to let my posture droop, I decided that Kyoko Inoue must be the girl with the awful glasses. I had not bothered to learn most of my classmates' names, assuming that it was simply a waste of my valuable memory.

This girl, Kyoko Inoue, did not stand out. If I had not seen her being bullied, and Tsukamoto had not mentioned her name to me, I would probably have graduated without ever learning her name.

But because this had happened, for some reason Inoue began entering my field of vision. Like me, she was always alone at lunch. Not that she was reading or anything; she would go straight to sleep, not even taking off her glasses. Her desk was often covered in drool, which she would quickly wipe away the moment she woke up. But everyone had noticed, and they all giggled when someone drew a picture of her drooling on the blackboard.

All her classmates found her thick glasses hilarious. These glasses were like someone had cut the bottoms off a couple of milk bottles, like something that only existed in old-school manga. You know what I mean? Just like the meat on a bone primitive people always eat in manga, they were fantasy glasses, comically deformed. And Takeshi Obata's got to draw them for the illustrations, poor thing.

Anyway, I knew no life-form more pathetic than Kyoko Inoue when the class was packed. She would hug her textbook to her chest, hunch down, and sneak over to the corner of the room. Like a tiny mammal terrified of a storm. Her plain bowl cut and awful glasses were presumably a result of her deep desire to survive this unpleasantness unnoticed.

There was only one other astonishingly distinctive feature to Kyoko Inoue's pathetic life. Namely, that when she removed her awful glasses, she was—you guessed it—beautiful. I first noticed this astounding bit of cliché when she woke up from a nap and let out a yawn so huge it was embarrassing to even look at. After her yawn, she briefly removed her awful glasses, rubbed her eyes, and then put them back on. When I saw her face, I almost stood up, pointed at her, and screamed, "You've gotta be kidding!" but I was grown-up enough to stop myself. And this part of her profile has absolutely no bearing on this short story, so there was no real reason for me to get angry.

But I was the only one who knew this about her, and I only knew because I happened to see her yawn. The other students almost never even glanced in Kyoko Inoue's direction. She was shunned by the class, treated like a smelly creature that was always lurking at the corner of the eye. Her innate timidity was obvious and aggravating to everyone. Adolescents had a lot of energy to burn, and she was a good way to vent.

"Didn't expect your room to be so plain, Matsuda. No posters at all?"

"Can't. They'd rip right off the wall if I opened the window."

"Why is there an outdoor broom standing in the corner?"

"To clean the veranda with. Ignore it."

"So, um, who exactly is the child clinging to my leg?"

"Yuuya, of course. My brother."

Yuuya always clung to the legs of any visitors. I assume he was a koala in his previous life. Kyoko Inoue was looking around my room with interest, dragging him along after her. I opened the window onto the veranda. Instantly, the crisp November wind slapped against my cheeks.

Her bowl cut flapping, Inoue cried out, surprised, "Wow, that's some wind!"

"I found the Take-copter here."

Kyoko Inoue dragged Yuuya over to the window and peered out onto the veranda. "Out here?" she said. It was still covered with leaves—I hadn't cleaned that morning.

Given the sheer length of that flashback, you readers might be a trifle confused now. To clarify: We are now some thirty minutes after the Take-copter lifted Kyoko Inoue's toes off the ground. The clock read 5:00, and it was already starting to get dark out. I had brought her here because she insisted she wanted to see my veranda before she went home.

The last time I brought a friend home, I was in elementary school. So my mother was very happy to see Inoue, but she was about to run some errands.

"Take this," she said, handing Yuuya to me like a deliveryman passes over a parcel, and away she went. My father wasn't home from work yet, so it was just the three of us.

"Matsuda, what do you think about . . . what happened?" Inoue asked, peering at the leaves on the veranda.

I knew what she was driving at.

"Well . . ."

I thought about the yellow T-shaped thing in my bag again. I was beginning to wonder if it had just been my imagination and it had not lifted her at all. It was easy enough to check—we just had to hit the switch again—but both of us were a little too scared to try.

That was when a sudden blast of wind shot through the veranda window. I barely managed to keep my uniform skirt from blowing up, and Inoue completely failed. Her skirt ended up on top of Yuuya's head. His grip on her leg never loosened. About a third of the leaves piled up out there came sailing into my room, carried right up near the ceiling, filling the air, spinning and dancing across the room. Gusts like this were not unusual, but it clearly caught Inoue off guard.

"Like the catbus going by," she muttered.

No sooner had the words left her mouth than we heard

something hard fall outside. It landed on top of the remaining leaves. Inoue and I turned toward the window.

There was what appeared to be a flashlight lying there. But a very colorful one—it looked like a toy.

"That wasn't there a second ago . . . ," I pointed out. It felt like the flashlight had been born of darkness. Inoue and I approached it. Fear of the unknown welled up inside me. Only Yuuya remained happily clinging to Kyoko Inoue's leg.

"Does that look like the Small Light to you?" Inoue asked nervously, trying to detach Yuuya. But Yuuya just shook his head no, and she gave up. The Small Light was one of the secret devices that appeared in that famous manga—a particularly dangerous device with the ability to shrink anything it shone upon.

I moved toward the veranda to pick the light up. I bent down and reached out my hand, and a shiver went down my spine.

"Matsuda!" I heard Inoue shriek.

It was suddenly dark, so I looked up, and a massive board of some kind was about to fall on my head. I did a backward somersault, and a red door slammed to the ground where my head had been. If I had reached a second later, I would have died. I never imagined the basic gymnastics they had mercilessly forced us to perform in elementary school would save my life.

I looked up at the edge of the roof where it jutted out over the veranda. There was a bit of white cloth stuck there, flapping in the wind. It was a semicircle, only about thirty centimeters across, but on closer inspection, it appeared to be a kind of pocket. The gust a moment before had opened the mouth of it, and as I watched, something else began sliding out of it.

---

*Small Light Another fabulous device from *Doraemon*.

A moment later, a phone booth landed on the veranda. It was not toy-sized. It was a perfectly normal size for a phone booth, the same size you saw all over town . . . yet I had seen it come out of a tiny pocket. Nothing that large could ever have fit inside something that small. But both of us, and my leg-clinging brother, had seen the pocket bring a phone booth into the world.

2

Kyoko Inoue and I spoke for the first time on the class trip in October. The entire second year went to Kyoto by Shinkansen,* but the class was divided into six groups. Each group had six or seven students in it, and we were supposed to stay together during our free time. The students were free to form their own groups, so most of them were composed of people who liked each other.

But—big surprise—since neither Kyoko Inoue nor I had any friends, we remained unaffiliated. Naturally, we were forcibly added to a group that had only managed to assemble four. They greeted us with welcoming smiles. And on our second day in Kyoto, the moment we were allowed to go where we chose, they smiled at us again as they bade us farewell. At Kinkakuji. I will never forget.

"I'm gonna hit the can."

"Me, too."

"I want some souvenirs!"

"Wait, I'll come with you. Oh, we'll be right back. Matsuda, Inoue, you wait here."

And with that, they scattered. Kyoko Inoue and I gazed across the pond at the golden pavilion, waiting for them to come back. Half an hour later, there was still no sign of them.

---

*Shinkansen The bullet train.

"So that was their plan!" I growled.

Next to me, Kyoko Inoue's shoulders twitched. Surprised to hear me suddenly speak.

"P-plan?" she stammered. I'd never heard her voice before, but it wasn't a bad one. But even away from school, she maintained an aura of cloddishness, like a high school girl from the Showa era brought here via time machine.

"They meant to ditch us all along! No point in standing here any longer. I'm leaving. You do what you like, Inoue."

"Ditch us...?" Kyoko Inoue murmured, and then fell silent, staring into the pond, heedless of the crowds of tourists around us.

Seeing the sights of Kyoto on my own suited me just fine, so I left her there. But when I glanced backward, she was trailing along after me, maintaining a fixed distance.

So that was their plan!

Oh, well. I dragged her along, following the schedule we'd chosen in class. While we walked through the temples and rode buses around, neither of us spoke. Occasionally, we encountered groups with the same uniform as ours. They passed by us, beaming, singing songs of youth. When they were gone, Inoue and I remained silent. Readers, close your eyes and imagine two high school girls, not particularly friendly, standing absently in a temple with nothing to do.

I glanced down at the girl next to me, in her awful glasses, resigned to the fact that our class hated both of us enough to ditch us. Everywhere we went, captions appeared in my mind: "The two most hated arrive in Honganji" or "The two most hated leave Arashiyama, purchasing nothing," or "The two most hated eat McDonald's hamburgers in silence."

I continued this even after our meal.

"The two most hated enrage some delinquents from some other school when one of them trips in a souvenir stand at Kiyomizu-dera."

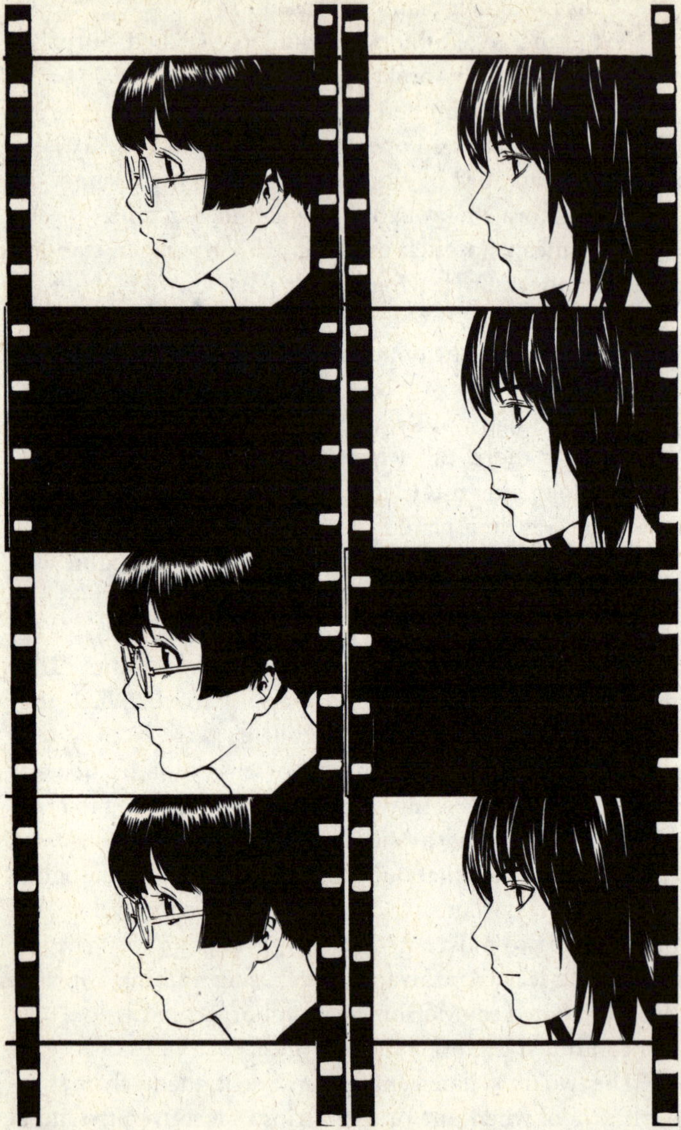

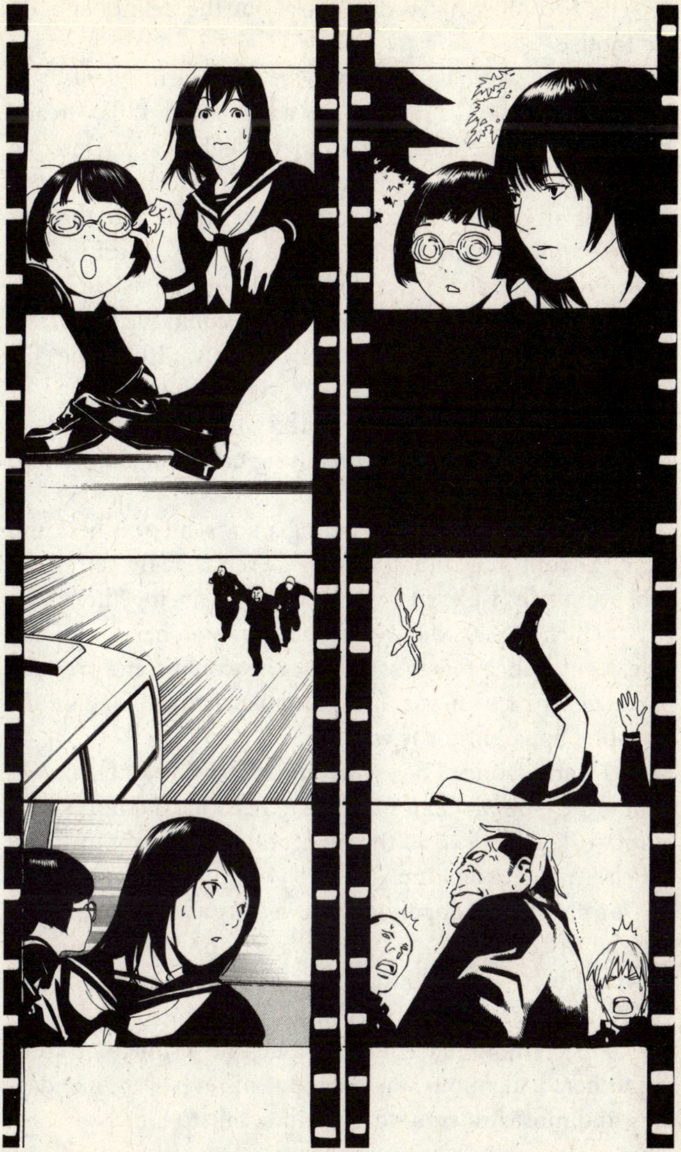

"The two most hated apologize, but the delinquents do not forgive."

"The two most hated run away from the delinquents."

... As Inoue and I ran, we saw a bus ahead of us, already in the bus stop. Behind us a group of slightly scary-looking high school boys with hair dyed blond or brown were in hot pursuit. Half crying, Kyoko Inoue threw herself onto the bus. I jumped on after her and yelled to the bus driver, "Drive away! Quickly!" The driver closed the door and stepped on the gas, and in the rearview mirror, we could see the delinquents giving up in despair. Seeing them vanish in the distance was a great relief.

"The two most hated escape successfully," I said aloud.

Inoue was doubled over, breathing hard, but she glanced up at me and smiled.

After that, we began exchanging a few sentences here and there. We continued doing so after we returned from the trip, and, eventually, we even began walking home together.

By which I mean she would follow me on her own. Likewise, we ate lunch together because she would come over and sit down across from me. I was completely fine being on my own, but, apparently, she was not.

As I learned once I began talking to her, Kyoko Inoue was even more pathetic than I had imagined. She did not do any homework, fell asleep all the time, and never spoke to any of her classmates except me.

Our classmates apparently viewed us as a pathetic little community of hated ones, but I was not one to be bothered by what the background thought.

"You're amazing, Matsuda. None of the other students can talk to Tsukamoto like equals," Inoue said at lunch. According to her, Tsukamoto was cool, but his eyes were like daggers, and most students were afraid to talk to him.

"We aren't equals, and I barely ever speak to him. I simply report what happens in the room. I'm going to see him now. . . . Want to come?"

"Oh no!"

"Why not?"

"If my eyes meet his, I will turn to stone," Inoue explained, deadly serious.

Kyoko Inoue's hands slipped, and the phone booth we were carrying tipped over. The top of it struck the fluorescent light hanging from the ceiling, and the light in the room swayed. Once we had successfully carried both the red door and the phone booth into the room, we both sighed. They were made of the same lightweight material as the Take-copter, but if they had fallen on my head, I probably would still have been seriously injured. The phone booth and the red door were enough to make my room feel very cramped.

"Matsuda, we should get the Fourth-Dimensional Pocket before anything else falls out . . . ," Inoue said, reaching up and trying to grab the white scrap of fabric. But she was much too short, and her hands got nowhere near it. I brushed her aside and carefully took hold of it.

"Inoue, you called this a Fourth-Dimensional Pocket, right?" I said. The fabric felt different from anything I'd ever touched before. It was very comfortable, a feeling equivalent to the first time I squeezed a Tempur pillow in the bedroom section at Tokyu Hands. I looked closer but could see no threads at all—it was like a metal or plastic, but neither.

"I'm sure of it! It is the famous Fourth-Dimensional Pocket! We have all the proof we need!" Kyoko Inoue said,

---

*Fourth-Dimensional Pocket In *Doraemon,* it's the magic pocket attached to the cat robot Doraemon himself, where all the devices are stored.

waving at the phone booth and the red door. According to her, these were the spitting image of the What-If Booth and the Anywhere Door, secret devices from that famous manga.

I had noticed this as well, but I found her theory hard to believe. I said as much. "Hard to believe."

"Just to be sure, why not put your hand inside that pocket?" Inoue said, pointing at the white cloth in my hands. She called it a pocket, but it was just two white semicircles attached to each other. The curve was attached, and the straight line was not. It could easily have been called a bag. A mystic bag that could summon doors and phone booths.

I hesitated for a long moment but at last slipped my fingers into the pouch. I timidly pushed them farther down, waiting for them to hit bottom. But my wrist went in, my elbow went in, and my fingers still felt nothing.

Inoue watched me, her hands clasped over her mouth, stricken. I glanced toward the window and saw a reflection of myself with a white scrap of cloth eating my arm. There was nothing left beyond the shoulder—one of my arms had been completely erased.

The skin on my missing arm was inside the pouch, touching air that was warm and somehow comfortingly familiar. No, not air . . . It was almost like lukewarm water. My arm and fingers, even under the tips of my nails, were wrapped in darkness, which clung to me softly. I was getting spooked. I knew there was a lot more space inside that pouch than could be seen from the outside.

"No mistaking it," Kyoko Inoue said, confident. "That is the Fourth-Dimensional Pocket from Fujiko F. Fujio-sensei's internationally famous manga Doraemon . . . !"

I yanked my arm out of it and sat down on my bed. I held

What-if Booth and Anywhere Door In *Doraemon,* the What-If Booth is a magic phone booth that can alter the world according to a hypothetical idea—and change it back again, while the Anywhere Door is a pathway to anywhere in the universe.

the pocket out toward her, and Inoue took it, glittering with curiosity.

My mind was starting to overheat, so I thought about the South Pole. Blue sky, white Antarctic ice. Beautiful. Enchanting. My heart grew calm again as I filled my mind with the kind of landscape images NHK always runs in the middle of the night, after they've gone off the air.

The Fourth-Dimensional Pocket. A warehouse filled with countless secret devices belonging to a round blue robot from the future. It looked like an ordinary pocket, but the inside was infinitely large, a fourth-dimensional space. It was usually attached to the robot's belly, but it was apparently easy to remove, and I had seem him take it off and wash it any number of times in the anime. But why had it been hanging outside my window? Obviously, I knew how it got here. The wind had picked it up somewhere and carried it to us.

Kyoko Inoue pulled the flaps of the Fourth-Dimensional Pocket apart and peered inside.

"Like a well," she said, impressed. Then she yelled into it. I could hear her voice bouncing around inside, echoing. "I want to dive right in . . . mm? Matsuda, what is it?"

"The South Pole. The South Pole. I'm busy broadcasting that image in my mind, so please do not speak to me."

"The South Pole?"

"It calms me. Ah, but this time that may be impossible. Yuuya, come here."

When even the South Pole failed me, the only option was to hug Yuuya. In class, they called me the cold-blooded informant, but at home, I was alarmingly clingy, constantly doting on my brother. The sight of Yuuya staring confusedly at his own reflection, proudly using the TV remote control, jumping in surprise at the sound of the front doorbell . . . how could I not smile?

"Mm? Yuuya?"

There was no sign of him. I looked carefully at Kyoko Inoue's legs, but he was not attached to either of them. He was also not attached to mine or to my Kokuyo desk. Had he left the room since we weren't playing with him? I went out into the hall, looking for him, when the phone rang.

"I'll get that. Inoue, try to find him."

"Okay."

I went downstairs and answered the phone.

"Ah . . . Kozue . . . ?"

It was my grandmother's voice. She lived in Kyushu. I'd last spoke to her three months ago, when we visited for Obon. But I was more alarmed than happy to hear from her now. She sounded really rattled.

"What is it?" I asked.

"Is your mother home?" she asked hesitantly.

"No."

"Well . . . Kozue, listen carefully. . . . Yuuya just showed up here."

"Yuuya?"

"Yes. We were just eating dinner when he came padding down the hall. Quite a shock. 'How did you get here? Is your mother with you?' we asked, but Yuuya just looked blank. I can't imagine he took the train all the way here by himself, but . . . how on earth . . . ?"

At this point, she suddenly broke off. Something had clearly happened on the other end of the line, and there was a little ripple of panic. I could hear her talking to someone else . . . my grandfather? The two of them lived alone, so . . . But what I could hear sounded like a much younger voice. It must be someone else.

"Hello?" a girl's voice said. To my surprise, not my grandmother's. "Matsuda? Can you hear me?"

I knew that voice.

"Yeah, I can hear you. But why are you in my grandfather's house? Kyoko Inoue! You should be upstairs!"

"The Anywhere Door was open a crack. I figured Yuuya had gone through there accidentally and didn't bother closing it behind him. So I followed him here. . . ."

The Anywhere Door. One of the many items from F-sensei's manga. If you visualized the spot where you wanted to go and turned the knob, the door would open onto that place. This device was extremely popular. In *Shosetsu Subaru*'s November issue, for the feature "We Asked 106 Writers," a great number of them gave it as their answer to the question "What would you bring to a deserted island?" But of course, the Anywhere Door only existed in manga, just like meat with bones sticking out of it and milk bottle glasses. It should not exist. And yet . . .

"So Yuuya's clinging to my leg again," Inoue said.

I went through the red door in my room and found myself on the porch of my grandparents' house. I greeted them both, and they said we must eat dinner before we went home. Kyoko Inoue, Yuuya, and I all went back to Tokyo after dinner. We opened the door on their porch, and they came to see us off.

"They're inventing such amazing things these days!" my grandfather said, gazing at the door in admiration. My grandmother forced some homemade pickles on us, and we were back in Tokyo.

"Getting late," Inoue said.

"I'll walk you to the station," I said. "The streets around here are a maze."

Inoue adjusted her awful glasses, grinning. "No need," she said, and opened the red door. On the other side was a room I'd never seen before. "My room," she said.

"Pretty big," I remarked, poking my head through the door. Not particularly feminine. No stuffed animals at all. Everything was the same drab color.

"Smells . . . good?"

A lot better than the citrus air freshener in the abandoned building.

"Probably the incense I was burning last night."

"What's that big tank?"

"I used to have tropical fish. They all died. Don't look."

Embarrassed, Kyoko Inoue awkwardly stepped into my line of sight, passing through the door. She waved goodbye. When she closed the door, it vanished, melting into the air. The Anywhere Door appeared to follow whoever had passed through it. But a few minutes later, it appeared again.

"Forgot my shoes," she said. She'd left them inside the front door.

After that, we played with the devices in the Fourth-Dimensional Pocket every day. Went to foreign lands through the Anywhere Door, saw the pyramids, some penguins, the *Mona Lisa*. We even sneaked into the White House and were almost caught but managed to get safely home. Kyoko Inoue brought a piece of paper back from the White House. It appeared to contain top secret information, but her English was crap and she ended up throwing it away unread. Oh, and the actual South Pole was much too cold and failed to calm me at all.

We used the Indoor Fishing Hole and caught some fish in my room. The Adaptation Beam gave us bodies that could survive anywhere, and we went deep-sea diving near Okinawa. We even used the Watermelon Straw to drink the fruit of a watermelon without worrying about seeds.

---

*Shock Gun, Air Cannon All of these devices can be found in *Doraemon*.

We lined up empty cans on the roof of the abandoned building and fired the Shock Gun at them. It was really hard to hit, so next we put the Air Cannon on our arms and fired that. All five cans were blown away in a single blast.

There were a number of Take-copters in the pocket. We each put one on our head and practiced flying. But they were kind of embarrassing. Sticking a bamboo copter on your head just made you feel like an idiot. Just like Hatabou from Osomatsu-kun! I thought.

I always tensed up when I hit the switch. The propeller would start spinning really fast, and I could feel my entire body rising into the air. Inoue and I were free from gravity, floating above the ground. It did not feel like we were using wind pressure to achieve levitation. The wind from the spinning propeller was no stronger than that of a box fan, but this gentle breeze was enough to defy gravity.

But we never flew more than two meters high. Human beings like the ground. Having nothing beneath our feet was more frightening than either of us had imagined, and there was always that lingering anxiety that the Take-copter would come off. If it let go of us ten meters up, our flesh would hit the ground, our bones would crack, and we'd end up covered in blood like this writer's other stories. Because of this I rarely used the Take-copter. Instead, I just stuck it in the corner of my shoulder bag and forgot about it.

At school, I continued exposing other students as Tsukamoto's minion. Kyoko Inoue maintained her awful glasses and drab exterior, hiding from the delinquents.

Kyoko Inoue kept the Fourth-Dimensional Pocket in her home, not telling anyone about it. I had found it, but her love for that mystic pouch was far greater than my own.

Inoue seemed to be fundamentally far more enthusiastic about the secret devices than I was. She used them like a child whose dream has come true. As I watched her happily chase penguins around at the South Pole, I realized that if anyone who knew Inoue only from school saw her now, they would be stunned.

Somebody hid Kyoko Inoue's indoor shoes on the morning of November 25, about twenty days after we found the Fourth-Dimensional Pocket.

I couldn't read her expression behind those awful glasses, but she appeared to be used to this. She quickly went to the teachers' room and borrowed some visitor slippers. I didn't know who did it, but there were five girls grinning at her in the classroom. A group who had often caused problems in class before. I stood bolt upright in front of Tsukamoto and informed him that they were probably behind this.

"You have no proof," Tsukamoto said calmly, staring at me through long, narrow eyes. "How unusual . . . You aren't one to speak based on a guess. For your friend?"

I wasn't sure how to respond. He smiled faintly.

"Never mind. I simply rejoice in this change."

Change. His word echoed inside my mind.

"Excuse me," I said, bowing my head, and left the room.

"Let's use the secret devices and get some evidence," I suggested when I got back to the classroom. But Kyoko Inoue just smiled vaguely, unsettled.

The next day, November 26, two of the girls who had laughed at Inoue did not come to school. The next day, all five of them were absent. We thought they were skipping or had come down with the flu. There was a nasty bug going around, and the news had said a number of schools had been forced to close.

Indoor shoes Japanese students wear these inside the school and their own shoes outside. Visitors wear slippers, which have no heels and are much less comfortable.

I learned otherwise at lunch. After Inoue and I finished eating, I went to the teachers' room, summoned by Tsukamoto.

"This isn't public knowledge yet, but all five of them are missing," he said, resting his cheek on one hand.

I left the teachers' room, weaving my way through chatting students. I wanted to speak to Kyoko Inoue as soon as possible. The sky through the hallway windows was gray and dark, and the chill in the air served as a reminder that December was almost here.

All five of the girls had vanished from their bedrooms in the middle of the night. Their shoes were still there. The only things missing were their pajamas and them. Kidnapping? Runaways? Nobody knew. If it had been kidnapping, how had the culprit entered the house?

I remembered the devices in the Fourth-Dimensional Pocket. We had even made it into the White House, so it would be incredibly easy to get inside someone's bedroom.

On the landing, I ran into Kuraki, the male class representative.

"Is it true they're missing?" he asked.

"How do you . . . ?"

"Everyone's talking about it."

According to him, one of the missing girls' parents had been calling other students.

"Probably true," I said, and hurried onward.

When I reached the classroom, lunch break was almost over. The students were starting to file back inside. Kyoko Inoue was sitting alone at her desk, avoiding the other students. In slippers—her indoor shoes were still missing.

Normally, when we talked, she would come to me. This was the first time we'd ever spoken near her desk.

"What did Tsukamoto say?" she asked when she saw my expression.

"All five girls have gone missing."

"Oh," she said, looking up at me through her glasses. The incredibly thick lenses distorted her big eyes.

Did you do it?

I did not say anything. I had reported any number of student crimes to the teachers and never once hesitated. But with Kyoko Inoue, I just stood there in silence.

The bell rang, and the Japanese teacher came into the room. The students began taking their seats, and I was forced away from Inoue. Even when class started, I could hardly pay attention. I needed to know for sure. Had she done it? I kept glancing at Kyoko Inoue, and her eyes met mine several times. She was equally worried about how I would react.

About halfway through class, the teacher happened to pull open a drawer and found something stuffed inside.

"What's this?" he asked, pulling something out and holding it up. It was a pair of very small indoor shoes. "Who put shoes in here?"

He looked around the room. Several students looked at Kyoko Inoue.

Inoue stood up in front of everyone and went to take the shoes from him. She was bright red. Even her ears. When she sat down again, class resumed. I stared at her the whole time, not listening at all. Inoue put the shoes on the floor and stared out of the window, head in her hand. She had a window seat. It was almost winter, and the darkened view was nothing much to look at.

After class, I went over to her, about to speak.

"Sorry, I've got to use the toilet," Inoue said, and ran out of the room, still in the slippers she'd borrowed from the teachers' room. I crouched down and looked at her indoor shoes. They'd been stomped flat.

The hand on the classroom clock moved forward. Kyoko Inoue did not return.

I went to the restroom to look for her, but she was gone. She'd used the same trick our group had used on the class trip. I went back to the classroom and called her on my cell phone. Her ringtone sounded from her bag, which she'd left sitting next to her desk.

At last the break ended, and the bell rang, signaling the start of the next class. Inoue never came back. Her bag remained where it was.

The next day was November 28. When I got to school, the number of students had been reduced by half.

3

During morning homeroom, with the classroom feeling uncomfortably roomy, Tsukamoto informed us that classes were canceled, but this failed to cheer anyone up. Those students who had come to school were gazing around them at empty seats, trying to come to terms with what had happened. Kyoko Inoue was not here either—her bag and indoor shoes were right where they'd been the day before.

"If any of you know where the missing students are, come to me after class. The police might want to speak to you at some point, so tell them what you know honestly," Tsukamoto said, gazing around the room.

Other students were peering through the windows from the hall, having heard the rumors. Half the class going missing was unthinkable.

"A TV crew!" somebody yelled, staring out the window. We all stood up and peered out with them. Several people were standing near the school gates, and one of them was shouldering what was clearly a TV camera.

"That was fast," I heard Tsukamoto mutter over the noise my classmates were making. From this distance, the camera looked tiny, but the moment it appeared, this became a huge story.

Tsukamoto left the room as soon as homeroom ended. But none of the students got ready to leave. They all sat with their remaining friends, exchanging information. But none of them knew where the missing students were, and the more they talked, the more scared they got.

"Did you hear? Sato and Fujiwara from C class are absent today . . . ," said one of the students in the huddle that had formed in the middle of the room. I was not taking part in this, but there weren't many people in the room, so I could hear them well enough.

"You're sure they're not just sick?"

"No . . ."

Their conversation ended there, but it reminded me of something Inoue had said.

"In junior high, they used to throw erasers at me."

We had been walking together down the hall, and Inoue had suddenly hidden herself in the shadow of a vending machine, apparently because she'd seen a pair of girls walking toward us. When they were out of sight, I had asked if she knew them, and she had answered as above.

"Sato and Fujiwara. They're in C class now." She came out from behind the vending machine and brushed the dust off her skirt.

"Now the police!" somebody yelled. He'd been staring out the window and seen a patrol car pull through the gate. I left the classroom and headed for the teachers' room. I had decided to tell Tsukamoto about Inoue and the Fourth-Dimensional Pocket. Like a faithful police dog, I would tell my master who was behind this. That was my job at school.

If I had played my role as informant yesterday, things might never have gone this far.

Biting my lip, I opened the teachers' room door. The teachers were all working flat out, answering phones. The room was usually so quiet, but now it was like there was a tornado loose inside. The principal, who usually wandered the hallways guffawing loudly, was now gripping a phone, grimly talking to someone.

I looked for Tsukamoto, but he wasn't in the teachers' room. I stood staring down at his empty desk, cursing my poor timing. He must be busy teaching some other class.

"Matsuda," called Tamura, hanging up her phone. She was a young teacher, in charge of the first-year students, and there were lots of rumors that she had a thing for Tsukamoto. She glared at me and snorted. Apparently, she also had the wrong idea about me and Tsukamoto.

"What is it?" I asked.

She handed me a scrap of paper. "Tsukamoto left this. Said to give it to you if you came."

Tsukamoto's note said, "Gone to Kyoko Inoue's house." He had clearly realized she was involved as well. Now that I thought about it, it was pretty obvious.

On the twenty-fifth, I had told him those five girls had probably hidden Inoue's indoor shoes. Anyone would suspect her when they turned up missing.

I would have to go to her house, too. I didn't know her address, but it would be written in a book somewhere in Tsukamoto's desk. I started flipping through the files, and Tamura spoke up again. "And Tsukamoto said to give you this if you started messing up his desk."

She held out another note. It had Kyoko Inoue's address written on it.

I went back to class, grabbed my shoulder bag, and left

school. There were three TV cameras outside the school gates, and a reporter headed toward me with a microphone. I shook him off and hurried toward the station.

Kyoko Inoue lived fifteen minutes from school by train. Her house was at least twice as big as mine. Even the door was twice as big. She had never said a word about where she lived, but, apparently, she was rich. A four-eyed secret beauty and a pampered rich girl? Too many tags!

I pushed the button next to the sign reading Inoue. I could hear the bell, but there was no answer. I opened the giant black door anyway. Fortunately, it was unlocked.

The entrance hall alone was the size of my bedroom. There were rows of shoes. I recognized one pair. The sneakers Tsukamoto always wore. Nervously, I gulped.

"Matsuda. You told him about me, didn't you?"

The voice came from down the hall. A short girl came walking quietly from the back room. For a moment, I didn't realize that I knew her.

". . . Are you . . . Kyoko Inoue?" I asked, not really sure.

She nodded.

"You wear contacts at home?"

Her awful glasses were gone. The clothes she was wearing were adorable, and her back was straight. Without her high school uniform, she could easily pass for junior high . . . or even elementary school.

"I'm always like this at home."

She stood bolt upright, and there was no trace of the drab, pathetic Kyoko Inoue I knew. The girl in front of me looked like God had done his best to create the most beautiful girl possible. There was even a trace of elegance to her adorableness. If she came to school with contacts, everyone would have gasped and, cowed, would have let her have the right of way.

"Why no glasses only at home? Some sort of secret identity?"

"No. I prefer looking the way I do at school. I don't stand out, and people don't come near me, and I feel much more comfortable."

Inoue scratched her head, a little embarrassed. Her hair was still the same bowl cut. But weirdly, it no longer looked so dated you wanted to compare her to Wakame-chan. Now it looked like something out of a glamorous French film.

"I was kidnapped when I was in elementary school. Ever since, I've done my best not to get noticed. I don't want anything that scary to happen again. These days, my motto is 'Avoid eye contact at all costs.'"

"So you weren't born so timid...."

If anyone else had said they'd been kidnapped, I would have found it hard to believe, but the way Inoue looked now, it seemed pretty likely.

"But my father makes me dress like this at home. Sheer vanity. When he brings his subordinates home with him, he always makes me sit in."

"Inoue, where is Tsukamoto? Where is everyone?"

She stared back at me, eyes like jewels. Without the glasses in the way, her eyes had a genuine power, and my underarms started to sweat.

"... In here. They're all in here."

Kyoko Inoue beckoned. Pretty much admitting she was behind this. I took off my shoes, stepped up into the house, and followed her into the living room. A ridiculously nice living room that really slammed home how middle-class I was. But there was no sign of Tsukamoto or the missing students.

"Where?"

"In here."

She pointed to a low table. There was a massive tank on it.

The same one I'd seen through the Anywhere Door in her room.

From a distance, it looked empty, but when I looked closer, there were a number of black specks at the bottom. They were moving around, so at first, I thought they were ants.

"Use this," Kyoko Inoue said, handing me a magnifying glass. What I had taken for ants proved to be people . . . five-millimeter-tall human beings. Through the glass, I could see one in his pajamas, waving at me to save him. I recognized his face—he was one of the classmates I had always considered part of the background. My classmate was standing on a vast field of clear plastic. I barely managed to avoid collapsing.

"Matsuda, see . . . over there . . . ," Inoue said, peering into the tank with a different magnifying glass and pointing inside with the tip of a pen. There were a lot of little black dots clustered together. But when Inoue pointed the pen at them, they scattered like baby spiders—assuming she was about to attack. I aimed my glass at them and found Tsukamoto enlarged by the lens. He waved one hand at me in greeting.

"Tsukamoto!" I yelped, and everyone in the tank clapped their hands over their ears, wincing.

"I shrank them all down with this," Kyoko Inoue said, pulling out what looked like a flashlight. One of the devices created in the future world—the Small Light. "My father's in there, too. He caught me in the act. . . ."

I looked around with the magnifying glass. There were a lot of people I didn't recognize. Kyoko Inoue plucked a bit of bread off the loaf next to the tank and dropped it in. The shrunken people could probably eat off that for three days. Then she dropped a little water in with a sponge. Thirsty people gathered around the drops.

Some people were trying to call for help on their cell phones, presumably shrunken down with them, in their pockets. But phones smaller than a sesame seed could not get a signal, and they were unable to talk.

There were a number of what looked like tents scattered around. That manga had longer story lines, and the characters would have adventures in all kinds of places. These were the temporary living quarters that often showed up then. They had bathrooms and showers in the tents, so it was clear they had been given the bare minimum needed to survive.

"What are you going to do with them?"

Kyoko Inoue sat down on the sofa and let out a thoughtful sigh. She pondered it for a long moment, toying with her hair, and then said, ". . . What do you think?" She clearly had no idea.

"You didn't kidnap them for any grand purpose?"

"Sheer impulse."

Pathetic! I almost yelled that at her, but I bit it off. I had been watching; I knew just what had made her do this. I had no right to scream at her.

"Give me back the pocket."

Inoue shook her head, took out the Small Light and pointed it at me. I stared it down for a few seconds, but ultimately, she did not shrink me. When she put the light away, I gave a great sigh of relief.

"I knew you would come here eventually, Matsuda. But I hope you won't tell anyone they're here. Keep it secret."

"Why would I do that? I'm an informant. I'm telling the news crews all about you."

". . . Thought as much. That's why I took a hostage." Leaning back on the sofa, the beautiful girl stretched out a slender arm and pointed at the tank.

"Hostage?"

"See for yourself."

I began hunting for a hostage. But there were so many specks, and they would not stop moving. I couldn't find anyone who looked likely. I felt like I was playing Where's Waldo?

"Er . . . you still can't find them?" Inoue said, five minutes later, unable to stand it any longer.

"Wait! Don't say anything. I'll find the answer myself," I insisted.

Through the glass, I found Tsukamoto again. He was looking up at me and shouting, but his voice was too small for me to make out. I shook my head, and he gave up. Instead, he pointed at his leg. There was something really small clinging to his leg. My parents and Yuuya were in the tank.

I began spending my days at Kyoko Inoue's house. We took turns cooking, washing dishes, and doing laundry. I planned to snatch the Fourth-Dimensional Pocket when she let her guard down—I was sure she had it hidden down her shirt. But she kept the Shock Gun on her hip and was ready to shoot if I made any funny moves.

The Shock Gun was one of the future devices from the Fourth-Dimensional Pocket. It was shaped like the ray guns from old sci-fi films, and when you pulled the trigger, it fired a beam of light. It was not strong enough to kill someone, but it could easily knock you out.

This beautiful girl would sleep on the sofa, her legs and arms sprawling out . . . but the weapon always at her side. If I tried to take the pocket by force, I'd get shot and wake up in the tank. And then there would be no one left who knew her sin. So I did not throw myself at her.

Inoue and I spent all day staring down at everyone in the tank. There were so many of them, and they all looked so anxious. Everyone loved Yuuya, and he was clinging to a different leg every time we saw him.

"I'm sorry, Daddy," Kyoko Inoue said. But she kept her father trapped in the tank. She did, however, explain her motives for shrinking her classmates and the story of how we'd found the Fourth-Dimensional Pocket.

Her father was a dignified man. He went around bowing his head to everyone in the tank, apologizing for the trouble his daughter had caused them. But all the students who had bullied Inoue looked guilty and refused to blame him. Oh, her mother had apparently died when Inoue was only one. Her father had been so busy at work that she had spent the bulk of her time alone in this huge house reading manga.

They could hear our voices, but the tank people's voices were too small for us to make out. Instead, they had to explain what they wanted by waving their arms and bodies around. They were all getting really good at this.

When my parents pointed at the TV and waved their hands as if they wanted the channel changed, I picked up the remote control and did just that on the massive TV on the wall opposite. The walls of the tank were clear plastic, so when the TV was on, they could all watch. Tiny people gathered along the wall to watch, like iron fragments gathering around a magnet.

I turned to the news, and there was a report on the mysterious mass disappearance. All of us, including those in the tank, watched with bated breath. All the information we had was what the anchors were able to tell us.

They broadcast the names of the missing, like the names of the dead in an airplane crash, rolling on and on across the screen. When the tank people saw their own names, they looked uncomfortable.

The bulk of the reports showed images of the police in charge of the investigation and interviews with the families of the missing people.

Then, on one afternoon gossip show, they had a crew out doing interviews with the locals about the night most of the children had vanished. Outside the bookstore by the station, they pointed their mic at the owner, a middle-aged man with glasses.

"Oh yeah . . . In the middle of the night, I saw a girl looking up at the window of that house. Wonder if she had anything to do with it . . . ," he said, pointing at a house where, presumably, someone had gone missing.

The reporter asked what the girl had looked like.

"She had really thick glasses."

Inoue jumped up and walked out of the living room. She came back a few minutes later and lowered her hand carefully into the tank. I looked inside with the magnifying glass, and it was the bookshop owner we'd seen a few minutes before.

When the number of missing people passed forty, the town began to panic. The number had reached that high because Kyoko Inoue had snatched up anyone who gave an eyewitness report to the TV crews, shrunk them down, and brought them back with her.

"The people interviewed have all vanished!"

"The mysterious disappearances may never end!"

Articles like that started showing up in the weekly magazines. Soon, nobody would let the media interview them.

"A girl with glasses behind it all . . . !?"

One newspaper sifted through the interviews and settled on that idea. The day that paper came out, Kyoko Inoue went through the Anywhere Door and came back with the newspaper reporter and editor, tiny.

The culprits were foreigners! They were kidnapping citizens and turning them into spies! People actually believed this. Other people were convinced that it was supernatural or that they were all being kidnapped by aliens. The papers and TV were filled with wild rumors and speculation. But the truth was that a high school girl was shrinking everyone down and keeping them in a tank.

Inoue and I tried improving the tank. We did not want Yuuya inconvenienced, so we tried to make things easier for him. First we put grass on the bottom of the tank. We took a chunk of turf from Inoue's garden and shrunk it down with the small light. We also brought in some swings and a bench from the park, and a few trees. The boys played with a tiny soccer ball, and the adults with go and shogi boards. Soon the interior of the tank was a grassy field where the forty-plus tiny people could live as they pleased.

The newspaper reporters alone carried right on working inside the tank, interviewing everyone around them. Inoue and I watched them through the glass, pointing at us and asking Tsukamoto what kind of students those giants had been in class.

When it grew dark out, I always went home.

"I can't let you spend the night here, Matsuda. You might try to steal the Fourth-Dimensional Pocket while I'm asleep," Kyoko Inoue insisted, looking very sleepy. She was the kind of girl who usually napped through class. But not anymore. With me in the house, she couldn't let herself nod off.

I did what she asked and went back to the empty house on top of the hill.

When I lay in bed with the lights off, I could hear the wind swirling around outside my window. Every night, I stayed awake until very late listening to it moan. Staring up at the ceiling, thinking about Yuuya, my parents, Tsukamoto, my classmates, and everyone else trapped in the tank.

The Fourth-Dimensional Pocket was something that should never have fallen into our hands. With the future devices from that pocket, we could conquer not just Japan but the world. I read through the manga, checking, and there was even a bomb in that pocket large enough to destroy the world.

I remembered that warm, familiar darkness I had felt

when I put my arm into the pocket. She had fallen into the pouch but not noticed until too late. I stared up at the ceiling, remembering what I had seen in town earlier that day.

The cops in the patrol cars were all carrying guns and glaring at the faces of everyone who passed by, watching their every move. The extreme caution everyone displayed as they walked through town showed how terrified everyone was that they would be the next to vanish. There was an awful tension in the air, and everyone in the country was focused on one little town.

Anyone who lived here, anyone who talked about the disappearances at all, would vanish, one after the other. Swings and trees were vanishing as well, impossibly. All these phenomena were being carried out by one tiny little girl named Kyoko Inoue, but the only one who knew that . . . was me. I had to get that pouch back from her. With that thought, I closed my eyes.

The afternoon of December 3, two police officers visited Kyoko Inoue's house, and events began moving again. This was a full week after the first people had disappeared.

4

I woke up and looked out my window. The skies on December 3 were clear, with long, thin clouds looking like they'd been spread out with a spatula across the upper reaches of the atmosphere. I closed the curtains, changed, and got ready to leave the house. I glanced at my watch—it was almost noon. I had been at Kyoko Inoue's until very late the day before and had gone to bed even later, so I had overslept more than usual.

Hoisting my shoulder bag over my head, I left the house. It was even colder than last week, and my heavy coat could not keep me warm. The leafless trees between the houses spread their wiry, bare branches, trembling in the wind.

I hurried toward Inoue's house. I was worried that something might have happened to Yuuya in that tank. That beautiful idiot might have flushed him down the drain on a whim. The only way to stop her was for me to be with her, watching her every move.

I reached the house and rang the front doorbell, but Kyoko Inoue did not emerge. Was she out somewhere with the Anywhere Door? I went right on inside. I had long since figured out where the front door key was hidden. But Kyoko Inoue was inside.

She was lying on the sofa in the living room, sound asleep and drooling. I had arrived so late that she had let her guard down and fallen asleep. The winter sunlight was streaming through the window onto her cheek.

The tank was on the low table near the sofa, just like it had been the night before. I took a look through the magnifying glass, and everyone seemed fine. Several of the boys were gazing in rapture at the sight of Kyoko Inoue asleep on the sofa. I found Tsukamoto. He was pointing at her and trying to tell me something.

I turned my attention back to the sleeping girl. I could see a bit of white cloth sticking out of her jacket pocket. I knew what Tsukamoto was trying to say. Kyoko Inoue was asleep, and I could not miss this chance. Taking care to make no sound, I reached out toward her jacket. All the five-millimeter-tall people in the tank stood up, watching me closely.

My fingers grasped the white cloth. That strange, indescribable texture. Nothing else but the Fourth-Dimensional Pocket felt like that. Kyoko Inoue's tiny face was right in front of me, sound asleep. I pulled the white cloth slowly out of her pocket.

The front doorbell rang. A beautiful electronic chime echoed through the house. The noise did not wake her up. But it surprised me enough that I spun toward the door, and my shoulder bag swung around and smacked her on the hand. Kyoko Inoue's eyes opened.

"Augh!" she shrieked, and snatched the Fourth-Dimensional Pocket out of my hand. Then she grabbed the Shock Gun and pointed it at me. Her aim was all over the place. We had played with the Shock Gun and the Air Cannon once before, in the abandoned building. She had nearly shot her own feet then as well.

"How could you attack me in my sleep!?" she yelped, genuinely hurt, the top of the Shock Gun wobbling.

"More important, we have company. What now?"

The phone had rung a few times during the week, and Kyoko Inoue had answered politely, insisting that she was not missing.

We knew the media were gathering around the homes of the missing people. That was why she had been so careful to keep herself off the lists of the missing. Which meant Kyoko Inoue had to go answer the door as well.

The chime rang again.

"You stay here, Matsuda. Do not follow me," Inoue said, and walked backward into the hall, keeping the Shock Gun aimed at me.

Careful not to tip her off, I stood at the living room entrance, peering into the front hall. I could see her back ahead of me.

"Who is it?" Inoue called out, without opening the door.

"Hello. We wanted to ask a few questions . . . ," said a woman's voice, muffled by the door.

"A few questions?" Inoue asked, opening the door. A man and a woman were standing outside. They were both wearing suits and appeared to be in their twenties.

"Are you Kyoko Inoue? Your school gave us your address. Whew . . . When you took so long to answer, we thought you were already gone," the man said. The word *already* echoed around in my mind.

He pulled out what looked like a badge and showed it to Inoue. Both of us suddenly realized that they were police.

"By the way . . . what is that?" the woman asked, pointing at Kyoko Inoue's hand.

She was still holding the Shock Gun. "This? Just a toy. I was playing with a friend of mine . . . ," she said, putting the gun down on top of a shoe box. She seemed a little nervous about talking to the police and never glanced at the Shock Gun once she let go of it.

I could feel my heart beating faster.

"Are you aware of the recent string of disappearances?" the woman asked.

Inoue nodded. I took a deep breath and silently bent my legs a few times before stretching my Achilles tendons.

"According to our investigations, half the missing people are in your class. So we are making the rounds and speaking to those members of the class who remain."

Kyoko Inoue listened in silence.

My Achilles tendons were stretched thoroughly, so I left the living room and began walking down the hall. Being careful not to make a sound, moving closer and closer to Inoue's back.

The male policeman noticed me and said, "Who is that?" Kyoko Inoue turned around just as I bolted forward and tackled her. She fell forward onto the cops in the doorway. My socks slipped on the floorboards, and I nearly toppled over as well but managed to catch myself and grabbed the Shock Gun from the shoe box.

As Kyoko Inoue tried to get up, I pointed the tip of the Shock Gun at her and pulled the trigger. Light gathered around my hand and then flashed. Inoue's terrified expression briefly gleamed white.

But the light the Shock Gun emitted missed her body. Kyoko Inoue's shoes were lying near the cops' heads, and the light hit those. There was a flash, and the shoes leaped like they had firecrackers in them. They bounced off the walls and tumbled to the floor again—with burn marks on them, smoking slightly.

I pulled the trigger again. But Kyoko Inoue got to her feet faster and bolted out of the door without any shoes. The second blast brushed by her, scorching the edge of her skirt.

I vaulted over the fallen cops and raced after her—without putting shoes on either. I could not let Kyoko Inoue get away. I had to knock her out with the Shock Gun and steal the mystic bag hidden in her pocket. The cops had clearly realized that what I held was no toy, and I heard them shouting, "Wait!"

Chasing Kyoko Inoue, I ran down the street. I fired the Shock Gun after her, but there was no way I could aim while running. I glanced back, and the cops were right behind me. They had clearly taken me for the bad guy, but I had no time to explain myself.

A few blocks down, Kyoko Inoue turned the corner. I followed after. When I rounded the corner, I raised the Shock Gun. I'd intended to fire a warning shot, but what I saw surprised me so much I forgot to pull the trigger.

Around the corner was a narrow alley with walls on either side. It was a dead end. Kyoko Inoue was nowhere to be seen. She had vanished into thin air.

I sniffed: there was a vivid smell in the air—the citrus scent from the air freshener she'd left in the abandoned building. She'd used the Anywhere Door. She was in the abandoned building now. The door had linked the two places. And the smell had come here, lingering in the air.

The two cops caught up with me. When they noticed the alley was a dead end, they relaxed. They glanced at each other and nodded—they had me cornered.

I, on the other hand, still had my shoulder bag with me. Which explained why it had been so hard to run. What a stroke of luck.

I took the Take-copter out of the corner of my bag, stuck it on my head, and pressed the switch. This was no time for fear. The cops watched me, puzzled.

The propeller began spinning, kicking up a breeze. My entire body felt like it was floating. The feeling of the ground beneath my feet disappeared. The telephone wires overhead came toward me. I barely managed to dodge them, but now I was off balance. I kicked off the roof next to me, stabilizing myself. The cops' shocked faces grew small underneath me, and the houses around them began to look like miniatures.

Before I knew it, I was way up in the air. There was nothing around me in any direction but down. There was wind blowing around me, but no walls, no fences. The roads and alleys of the town were far below me, and the only sound I could hear was my own breath. A swallow flew past far below me, then swooped up and brushed past my nose, wheeling high above. I followed, heading higher.

The future device needed little control—it followed my thoughts. Holding the Shock Gun tightly, making sure I didn't drop it, I flew forward, my body streaming out behind me. The wind the propeller generated wrapped around my body. I felt like my body was melting into the wind, becoming part of the sky.

Landing on the roof of the abandoned building gave my legs a numbing shock. I hadn't practiced enough and had failed to properly control the speed of my landing. I flipped the switch on the Take-copter, took it off, and shoved it in my coat pocket. It was at least fifteen minutes from Kyoko Inoue's house to here by train, but the Take-copter had brought me here in no time at all.

The staircase to the third floor was decaying from disuse, but I went on down. The air inside was cold, like a refrigerator. And I had no shoes, so the chill of the concrete went right through my socks. Clutching the Shock Gun, I stepped onto the floor, that citrus scent all around me.

I was in some company office, filled with desks and chairs. There was a girl sitting in a chair near the window. Luck was with me, and she was staring outside. That neatly trimmed bowl cut definitely belonged to Kyoko Inoue—I'd seen the back of her head in class a hundred times. She was only wearing a light jacket and looked very cold. She did not appear to notice me, just stared down into the town she had plunged into chaos.

I pointed the tip of the Shock Gun at her. Just as I pulled the trigger, she wiped her eyes. From behind, I couldn't see very well, but I guessed she was wiping her tears away. The light left the Shock Gun and burned the back of the office chair next to her. I had hesitated, and the aim had gone wild.

Kyoko Inoue jumped up and spun toward me.

"Why are you here!?" she yelped, reeling. She hid behind the desk.

"Following you, of course!"

"What for!?"

"To kick your ass!"

Holding the Shock Gun ready, I stepped forward across the floor, headed toward her hiding spot. But she had moved away from the desk and was no longer there.

"To kick my ass!?" Kyoko Inoue's voice came from behind a different desk.

"Can't let you screw things up anymore!"

"No fair!" Kyoko Inoue stood up.

Thinking this was my chance, I took aim. But then I saw the tube on her right arm and aborted the attack. It was a cylinder, like the tip of a tank cannon.

"Boom!" she said, and the mouth of the tube shook. I jumped aside, sprawling on my belly. A second later, a massive blast of air gushed past where I had been standing, and a dull thud shook the room. I could hear glass breaking and chairs falling over. A shower of tiny stone fragments fell on my back and head. The blast of air from her right hand had struck the wall and broken a chunk of it away.

It was a future device called the Air Cannon. It looked like an ordinary tube, but if you put it on your arm and said, "Boom!" it would fire a destructive blast of air. You had to speak aloud because the thing had no trigger. According to the manga, it wasn't strong enough to kill anyone. But it was definitely strong enough to crack a few ribs. I was furious.

"What if I got hurt!?"

I crawled along behind the desks. It was dangerous to stay in one spot.

Boom!

You've got a lot of nerve!

▼▲▼

"Then I can use the Time-Wrapping Cloth to send you back to before you were hurt! Boom!"

A second after her shout, there was a rumble, and a powerful shock wave came tearing through the air toward me. I rolled across the floor and started moving behind the desks again.

"You just don't get it! We should never have used the future devices!"

---

*Time-Wrapping Cloth In *Doraemon*, a cloth with two sides, each with clocks printed on it. Wrap something in one side and it becomes newer, wrap it in the other and it becomes older.

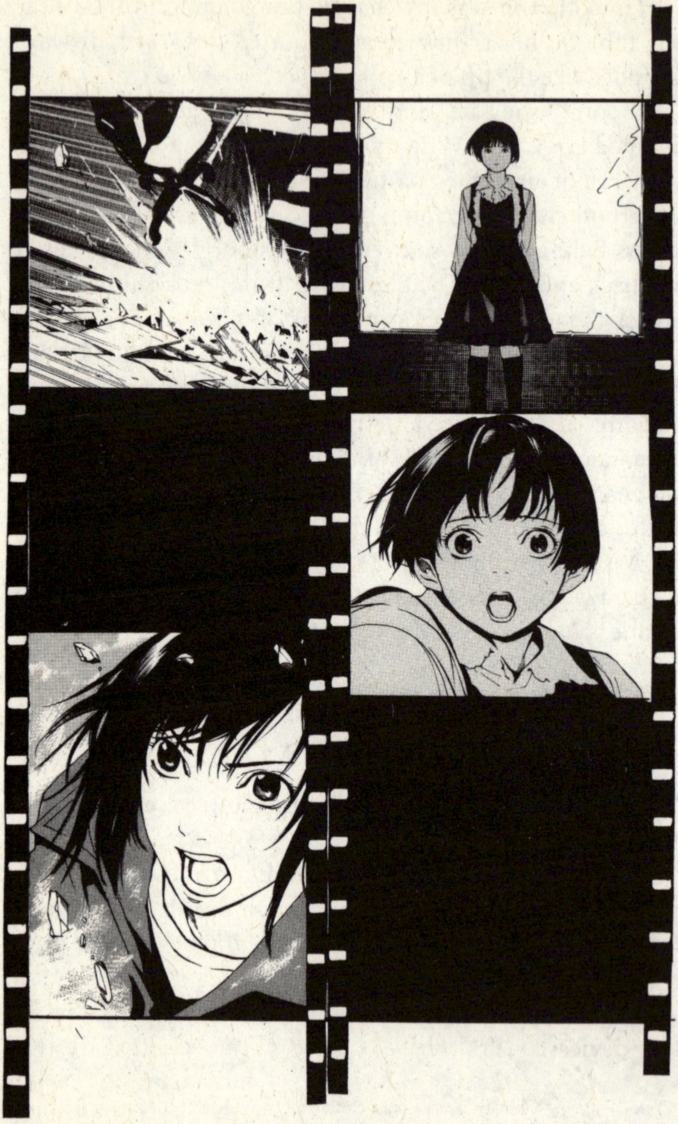

I crawled along the concrete floor, dragging my shoulder bag after me, getting dust all over my coat. Sweat mixed with the dirt, rolling down my cheek and getting in my mouth. I spit on the ground and shouted, "Drop the pocket or we aren't friends!"

Then I caught a glimpse of Kyoko Inoue through the gap between two desks. She was crawling along the floor, tears and dust muddying her pale cheeks.

I aimed the Shock Gun carefully and pulled the trigger. The filthy floor turned momentarily white. A ball of light passed over her shoulder, almost touching it, and slammed into the wall. A few strands of Inoue's hair fluttered into the air, but that was all.

Before I could fire again, she pointed the Air Cannon at me. I tried to run, but my shoulder bag caught on the corner of the desk and slowed me down. Inoue's lips moved, whispering the word.

The desk in front of me exploded, sending the chair and my body flying. I was blown across the room like a rag doll. The world seemed to spin around me, and the Shock Gun slipped out of my hand.

I was sure I was about to slam into the wall, but instead, I crashed through the window, flung right out of the building. The gray floor revolved away, replaced by blue sky. The desk came after me and lodged in the window frame with more than half the desk jutting out of the building. My body, the desk chair, and a shower of broken glass spun in the air. Three stories up.

The fall would kill me. No sooner had the thought crossed my mind than something caught me, and I stopped falling. I could see the desk and shards of glass vanishing into the depths below me at terrifying speed and smashing into the ground. The ruckus had clearly been heard outside the building, and there were people gathered around like ants round a piece of mochi. They scattered, avoiding the falling objects.

My fall had been stopped by my shoulder bag, which was still caught on the desk. The desk was caught in the window frame, half out and half in, and I was dangling off the outside end of it, supported by nothing but the strap of my bag.

"Matsuda!" Kyoko Inoue's head popped out of the next window over, staring down at the ground. Her face had gone white as a sheet. "Damn you, Matsuda! How dare you go and die!" she shrieked at the street below, leaning out the window.

Still clinging to the strap of my shoulder bag, I reached in my pocket and pulled out the Take-copter.

"I'm the main character. How can I die?"

Kyoko Inoue finally noticed me. "Matsuda? That is you hanging there, right? It is! Matsuda! The famous informant!" she cried, beaming happily.

"Kyoko Inoue! You made me mad. You've got a lot of nerve," I snarled back. The desk above me shifted. There was an ear-piercing scream of metal scraping across the window frame.

"Don't move! The desk is gonna fall!"

"And whose fault is that!?"

I put the Take-copter on my head. My chest was burning with sheer fury.

"Kyoko Inoue, we are no longer friends! You're an unpleasant, pathetic weakling! Go away!"

She stopped smiling and clapped her hands over her face. But my fury was not going anywhere yet.

"Don't you see!? Everything you've done is pathetic, childish revenge! It's stupid! Idiotic! Completely wrong! I never want to see your face again!"

Mochi A Japanese sweet made by pounding sticky rice.

I sniffed. My nose was running. . . . Apparently, I was crying.

"Are you listening? I'm done liking you! I have no more sympathy! I hate your goddamn guts! The readers hate you, too! We don't need a character like you!" I yelled, wiping my tears.

I thought she would argue back, but Kyoko Inoue just took it in silence, saying nothing. She was leaning out the window, looking at me, her bowl cut flapping in the chilly breeze.

"It makes me sick just looking at you! I'm sure the readers would be far happier reading about my adorable brother or the prickly protagonist! Our pairing has ended! Such a shame! I thought we might get a series out of this concept, but oh, well! That can never happen now, not even if the editors ask for it! Even if the readers love it! Obata doesn't even want to draw you anymore! People like you die alone and unloved! I really, really hate you!"

I hit the Take-copter switch, and the propeller began to spin. The gravity that had been pulling me down vanished, and I was floating. Now the desk could fall whenever it wanted, and I'd be fine.

Then something tightened around my neck, and I lost my balance. My shoulder bag was still attached to the desk.

I swore, stopped trying to fly, and started trying to free my bag. I yanked it a few times and heard an ominous scraping sound.

"Look out!" Kyoko Inoue shrieked. Pulling on it had shaken the desk loose. It was no longer a desk, really—just a mass of metal as wide as my arms could stretch. As I hovered in the air, it started tipping forward.

The force of the Air Cannon's blast had twisted the steel, and it was slipping out of the window frame with a horrible screech. The strap of my shoulder bag was still wrapped around my neck and arm. The Take-copter was hardly strong enough to lift the desk as well. If the desk began tumbling down the side of the wall, it would pull me after it and we would both slam into the pavement below.

The sun was burning the desk's shadow onto the building wall. It was sliding downward. The strap around my neck was pulled taut. This time I really was going to die. There was nothing I could do but close my eyes.

But no matter how long I waited, the moment never came. I was still hovering, and the Take-copter was whirring away on my head. I had no idea what was going on. I opened my eyes to see, and the shoulder bag strap was still wrapped around me. The bag was still caught on the desk. But the desk was now the size of a key case. I looked back at the window, and Kyoko Inoue was standing there, holding the Small Light.

"Come down from there, both of you!" someone yelled from below, through a megaphone. We looked down, and police had surrounded the building. They were looking up at us, and several had already entered the building. They would be up the stairs and onto the third floor in a few minutes.

I moved over to Kyoko Inoue and the window and climbed through. Once I was inside, I took the Take-copter off my head and put it back in my coat pocket.

"Kyoko Inoue!" My voice echoed through the abandoned office. Her shoulders shook.

"Y-yes?"

"Grit your teeth!"

And I slapped her.

She rubbed her cheek, tears in her eyes, and held out the Fourth-Dimensional Pocket. She did not look inclined to resist. I took the white semicircle . . . and it was all over.

Epilogue

"My, Kozue! I was getting worried. Every time I call these days, nobody answers," my grandmother said when she opened the door. "But what is with those clothes? And that girl . . . You came here with Yuuya before, right?" she added, looking at Kyoko Inoue. We were both covered in dust.

Inoue bowed low. "I'm surprised you recognized me."

"Don't be silly, I recognized your scent."

Inoue blinked and then sniffed her underarms.

"What happened to your glasses? They were so cute. And why is your cheek red?"

Kyoko Inoue winced and rubbed her cheek sheepishly.

My grandmother led us inside. We took off our grime- and mud-blackened socks inside the entrance, and threw them away. When I shut the door, I could see the wild grass growing beyond their garden. My grandparents lived in the south end of Kyushu. Way out in the country—the nearest house was a good twenty minutes' walk. At the end of their land was a huge overgrown thicket—nobody knew who owned it—in the middle of which was a red door. The Anywhere Door Kyoko Inoue and I had left there.

As we walked down the hallway, Kyoko Inoue rubbed her cheek. Our fisticuffs had reached their climax only a few moments before. I could have handed her over to the police, but I couldn't quite bring myself to do that, so we had fled through the Anywhere Door. And when I opened the door, what popped into my head was my grandparents' house.

In the living room, we turned on the TV, and it was showing the abandoned building we had been in a few minutes before. The crowd had clearly been watching my midair exploits closely, and they were describing them in excited detail.

"Looks awful," my grandmother said, making tea.

"So many terrible things these days . . . ," Inoue replied. I glared at her, and she quietly sipped her tea.

We took turns in the bath and put on some of the clothes my mother had left here. They were just my size but much too big for someone as tiny as Kyoko Inoue. The sleeves were hanging down comically. Feeling much better, we watched the fuss back in our distant hometown on TV.

"They must be checking your house now."

"Wonder what they made of the tank. . . ."

I was worried they might dissect Yuuya in the name of science.

"We should go save them," I said, standing up.

But my grandmother said, "Don't be in such a hurry." Obviously, she only said that because she thought I meant we were going home.

"If we go to my house now, we'll run right into the police. We should probably wait and see," Inoue said, wrapping her baggy sleeves around my neck.

In the end, Kyoko Inoue and I stayed the night at my grandmother's house. We ate dinner, built a fire, and sat under the kotatsu eating sweets and watching boring TV. We even played Old Maid.

In the evening, my grandmother laid out futons for us both in a small room. The room had a porch, and if we opened the shoji screens, we could see the red door outside. Kyoko Inoue borrowed a cup of water and dropped her contacts inside. We undressed and piled the clothes at the side of the room. I placed the Fourth-Dimensional Pocket on top of our clothes. Kyoko Inoue no longer looked tempted to touch it.

We lay down on the futons and talked about what to do next. We both felt that after we put the tank people back, we would have to flee for foreign lands. There was no way we could just go back to school. We had turned the entire town upside down. I was sure Tsukamoto would write terrible things in my letter of recommendation.

We talked until two in the morning.

"It's getting late.... We should sleep. We'll go save Yuuya in the morning."

I turned out the lights. The moon was out, and the shoji screens were bathed in white light. We snuggled down inside our respective futons. Even in southern Kyushu, December nights were still cold.

Just as I was about to sleep, I heard a voice from the other futon.

"Matsuda, are you awake?"

Slightly annoyed, I answered, "I almost wasn't."

"I'm sorry I almost killed you."

"Oh, that? Don't worry, I won't forgive you."

"You are mad at me."

"I almost died."

"Matsuda, why didn't you turn me over to the police? Normally, you always reports students when they do something wrong...."

I stared up at the ceiling, thinking.

"Tsukamoto called it a change. From now on, it might be hard for me to keep informing."

"Too bad."

Your fault.

Since this house was in the country, there was no traffic outside. The tiny room was very, very quiet. Her cheeks were white in the moonlight coming through the shoji screens. I remembered seeing her in class, in her slippers, staring out the window at the winter landscape.

"We should sleep."

"Yes."

At last, I heard Kyoko Inoue's breathing slow. A little while later, I dropped off to sleep as well.

I don't know what I dreamed. When I woke up again, it was not yet dawn and still dark out.

The sound of the shoji screen sliding open pulled me out of my slumber. My eyes flickered open, and the screen onto the porch was open.

I held my breath, watching, and a big, round shadow at least four feet tall stepped into the room. A fat, round body I had seen countless times before. I hid my shock and pretended I was still asleep.

The shadow moved past our pillows and reached out to where our clothes were piled. Its hands were just round balls, with no signs of fingers. It picked up the Fourth-Dimensional Pocket, attached it to its belly, and gave a satisfied nod. Like it had been looking for it ever since the wind snatched it away.

It left the way it had come in, turned to look at the two of us for a moment, and then closed the screen behind it.

The next day, Kyoko Inoue and I got on the Shinkansen Nozomi, headed back to Tokyo. We passed through the gates at Hakata Station and sat next to each other on the train.

"I wonder where the pocket went . . . ," Kyoko Inoue murmured, sipping tea from a plastic bottle, as the train pulled out. She'd said this over and over all morning long. She found it hard to drink tea with her ridiculously long sleeves. Before we'd left, my grandmother had given us paper bags to carry our dirty clothes.

"The Fourth-Dimensional Pocket, the Anywhere Door—all of that stuff should never have existed outside of manga. The moment they took form and appeared in our world, they were impossible. Just like ice always melts at room temperature, the pocket itself vanished naturally."

"Such a shame," Kyoko Inoue murmured, gazing out the window at the land slipping by.

"Not really. Everything's back the way it was. I'm tired, so I'm gonna nap awhile."

We'd had quite a time getting from my grandparents' house to Hakata Station. Not because it was all that far but because every bus or train we got on, I could sense all the men staring at Kyoko Inoue. She'd been hunched over and hiding behind me, but without her glasses, she still attracted attention. Clichés were more of a problem than I had previously thought.

"Matsuda, was it all a dream? A strange dream that only we had?" she asked seriously.

"Dunno. I'm sleepy, so don't talk to me for a while," I said, leaning back and closing my eyes.

We had noticed something wrong that morning. When we turned on the TV, none of the news programs were reporting on the commotion and disappearances in our hometown.

This had flustered us, but then my grandmother said, "Kozue, phone call from your mother."

I took the phone, and my mother, who should have been in the tank, was on the line. "Kozue, you and Inoue will be back today, right? School starts tomorrow, so don't forget. Yuuya misses you!"

According to my mother, classes had been canceled on account of the flu. Inoue and I had used the vacation to visit my grandparents.

While I was on the phone with my mother, Kyoko Inoue got my grandfather to find the last few days' worth of newspapers for her. She had been unable to find any mention of the panic in our town—all the articles had been replaced.

Everything connected to Kyoko Inoue's crimes had vanished, and except for the two of us, everyone's memories of the last ten days had been changed. All traces of the future devices had vanished so cleanly it was easy to believe what we had gone through had been just a dream.

But it had really happened. I knew it had. Just before we had left my grandmother's house, I had put my clothes in a paper bag, and a yellow thing with a propeller on it had fallen out of my coat pocket and rolled across the tatami. The Take-copter, absently shoved in my pocket after Kyoko Inoue saved me.

The cat robot who had visited the night before had erased all memories of the incident from everyone in the world before the sun rose. And had taken the future devices with him. But it had never occurred to him that the Take-copter was still in my coat pocket. Even in the manga, he always missed the most important things.

I had stared at the Take-copter a minute and then shoved it in my shoulder bag, which still had a miniature desk hanging from it. Kyoko Inoue had been busy with her own packing and did not notice. I had decided to keep it a secret from her.

"Almost in Kyoto," Inoue said, packing away her station lunch. The Shinkansen had passed through Shin Osaka and was almost at Kyoto Station. It was slowing down, and we could actually look at the scenery near the train comfortably. The train pulled into the platform, and several passengers stood up.

"Come to think of it, when we came here for the class trip, you were sitting next to me," I said when the train had come to a full stop.

She nodded, pressing her face against the window pane. Everyone in class had hated us, and we had ended up sitting next to each other, all the garbage gathered in one place. I didn't care who sat next to me, and I imagine she felt the same. So neither of us had objected.

"We didn't talk at all."

"If I'd known you were this pathetic, I would never have let you sit next to me."

Kyoko Inoue glanced at me and smiled and then looked out the window again. She had the window seat; I had the aisle. "We had so much fun in Kyoto," she murmured.

The crowd was moving past outside, their breath white in front of them. It looked very cold.

"Matsuda, you know Doraemon had an ending?" she asked suddenly.

"Eh, really?"

"Yeah. Showa 46. All three magazines it was running in each had a different ending. One of them was 'Goodbye, Doraemon,' from volume six of the Tento Mushi Comics edition."

"Didn't they make that into a movie?"

"Yeah. They connected it to a few other stories and made a movie. In *Goodbye, Doraemon,* Doraemon ends up going back to the future."

Kyoko Inoue bent over, leaning her cheek against the window.

"That was a great story. You really should read it, Matsuda. My personal recommendation."

She covered her face with her overlong sleeves.

"Promise me you'll read it. Nobita . . . was so cool. It's a beautiful story. . . . You won't be able to . . . stop crying. . . ."

Sobs began breaking up her speech. Gasping and sobbing, she pressed on, keeping her face covered.

"A really good story. Not like ours. Those children were so much better. . . . Nobita . . . he did the right thing, faced down his feelings, never . . . never asked Doraemon for help. But I . . . why did I . . . I'm sorry. I'm sorry, Matsuda. I'm sorry, Mommy. Can't I get out here? Can't I just stay in Kyoto?"

She wrapped her arms around herself, barely keeping it together.

"Inoue . . ." I put my hand on her shoulder, worried. I could feel her trembling. This trembling had probably been with her every day in class. I gulped.

Still sobbing quietly, she wiped her tears. She never once wailed aloud. The way she cried was just like a child with a cold who can't stop sniffing. It was so quiet that none of the other passengers even noticed. She had cried all the time, and nobody in class, nobody in the entire town, had ever noticed. Muffling her sobs, keeping it all inside, bearing all that torment alone.

The buzzer rang. The train was about to pull out.

I made up my mind and put my arms around the girl next to me. Her body shuddered. She briefly tried to pull away.

But I didn't care. I just tightened my grip. Squeezing her tiny shoulders in my arms. This time, her fear would melt away in my arms.

The train gathered speed, and the platform slid past us.

In my arms, she felt hot, feverish. I held her so tightly I almost broke her bones.

"Think about the South Pole," I said.

In my arms, she nodded. Kyoko Inoue's ragged breathing began to subside. The strength left her arms, and she sighed.

The train left the station, and we could see the town we'd been forced to explore together passing by outside the window. The sun was shining brightly down on it, and I had to squint. But that view slid by as well. The Shinkansen moved forward, carrying us with it.

▲▼▲▼▲

THE GARDEN OF SINNERS
A View from Above

an excerpt

Kinoku Nasu

Illustrations by Takashi Takeuchi (TYPE-MOON)
Translated by Paul Johnson

The *Garden of Sinners* is a novel with a unique history—and a dazzling future. The novel was first serialized on artist Takeuchi's website, beginning in 1998. But the novel did not begin to find its true audience until the creators featured an excerpt on the disk for their visual novel blockbuster, *Tsukuhime*. A visual novel is a special kind of video game, an interactive, electronic novel that combines text and visuals; the best-known example in the United States is perhaps *Phoenix Wright: Ace Attorney*. It is entirely appropriate that *The Garden of Sinners* should have gotten its start in the world of the Web and visual novels: This hyperactively inventive novel has a true twenty-first-century sensibility that shows a tremendous anime and video game influence. Its dazzling imagery, in fact, cries out for visual interpretation, which has arrived in the form of a magnificent anime. *The Garden of Sinners* is currently having all seven chapters adapted into an unprecedented full series of complete animated movies, with the first chapter being released in December 2007. It looks set to be a record-breaking hit for the creators Kinoku Nasu, a scenario writer and novelist; and Takashi Takeuchi, an illustrator with the game company, TYPE-MOON. Takeuchi and Nasu have been friends since middle school. Takeuchi has illustrated not only *The Garden of Sinners*, but other works by Nasu, such as *Tsukihime* and *Fate/stay night*. The creators talk about *The Garden of Sinners* in an interview, including exclusive remarks on its publication in the United States, in the bonus features at the end of this volume.

The first chapter of *The Garden of Sinners* is presented here. The novel will be published in the United States, in its entirety in two volumes by Del Rey Manga, beginning in 2009.

▲▼▲▼▲

One day, I took the main street route home. This was unusual for me, just a whim of the moment. I had been walking, not thinking about anything in particular, down the street—that street whose buildings I was so tired of looking at—when someone fell from above.

I hardly even had a chance to hear it. The muffled splattering sound.

But it was obvious: someone had fallen from one of the buildings above . . . and was now dead.

Deepest crimson gushed down the asphalt. Only the long black hair still retained its former appearance. Thin, fragile, white-looking limbs. And a lifeless, smashed face.

This series of images was like pressed flowers, trapped flat between the old pages of a book. I guess. Probably.

Only because the corpse, its neck twisted into a fetal position, looked to me like a folded lily.

A View from Above

1

On the night it turned August, Mikiya suddenly dropped in out of the blue.

"Evening. You're looking as fatigued as always, Shiki."

The unexpected visitor stood in the entranceway. He smiled as he shot me this lame greeting.

"Actually, yeah, there was an accident just before I got here. A girl committed suicide. Jumped off a building. There's been a lot of that going on lately. But you never think you're actually going to see one, huh? . . . Here you go. For the fridge."

As he unlaced his boots, he tossed me a bag from a convenience store. There were a couple of cartons of strawberry

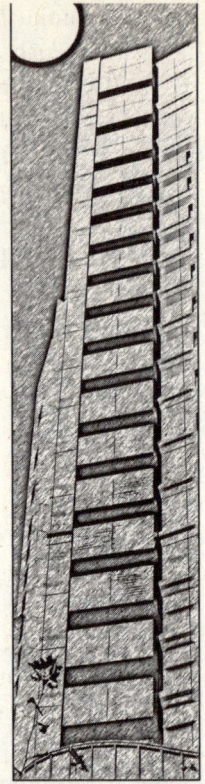

Häagen-Dazs inside. I guessed I was supposed to put them in the fridge before they melted.

Mikiya had finished undoing his shoes and was over the threshold before I'd finished groggily inspecting the bag.

▼▲▼

I lived in a studio apartment. Not counting the three-foot-long hallway leading from the entranceway, the door led straight into my room, which served as both bedroom and living room.

Glaring at Mikiya's back as he strode hastily into the room, I followed suit.

"Shiki, you cut class today, right? I don't care about grades, but if you don't at least watch your attendance, you won't be able to go on to a decent school. You haven't forgotten, have you? We promised to go to college together."

"Yeah, like *you* have the right to lecture me about school," I replied. "For starters, I don't actually remember making that promise. And besides, didn't you drop out?"

". . . Uh, well, I guess I *don't* really have the right, now that you mention it," said Mikiya awkwardly, sitting down. Yeah, he always did betray himself when backed into a corner. That's something that came back to me recently.

Mikiya sat down in the dead center of the room. I lowered myself onto the bed behind him and lay sideways on it. Mikiya stayed like that, facing away from me. He was pretty short, and I absentmindedly gazed at his tiny back.

His full name was Mikiya Kokutō, and it had somehow happened that he'd been a friend of mine ever since high school. He was kind of boring: it was like he'd been permanently frozen in the shape of a student or something. But he was a real treasure compared to most guys today—the ones who show off all the latest fashions, one by one, like it's some kind of race, before ultimately burning themselves out. He didn't dye his hair or let it grow long. He wasn't tanned and didn't accessorize. He didn't carry a cell phone and didn't fool around with girls. He was only five five. His features were on the "cute" side, and his black-framed glasses strengthened that impression even more.

He'd graduated now and was wearing everyday clothes, but if he were to get dressed up and walk down the street . . . he might be so good-looking that people would stop on the street to stare at him.

"Are you listening, Shiki? I saw your mother. You should at least drop by your house, shouldn't you? You've been out of the hospital for *two months* now, and you haven't even called?"

"Yeah. I don't have any reason to, that's why."

"Uh . . . You don't *need* a reason for a happy family get-together, you know. You haven't spoken to them in two years. All you need to do is sit down and have a proper talk with them."

". . . Nah. I can't see it happening, so forget about it. If I saw them, it would just make us all feel even more distant from each other. I even feel weird around *you*. So how do you expect me to carry on a conversation with total strangers like them?"

"Look, nothing's gonna get fixed like that, is it? Things'll stay this way your whole life if you don't make the first move and open up to them. It's a tragedy to not be able to even meet up with your own parents when they're living so close by."

I frowned at his judgmental tone.

No good, he said? What was no good about it? There was no funny business going on between me and my parents or anything like that. The case was simple. Their daughter had been in a car accident. She lost all of her memories from before the crash. That's all. Biologically speaking, and according to the census register, I *was* still family. I didn't see any problem with just leaving it at that.

But Mikiya always worried about people's emotional well-being. Even though stuff like that held zero interest for me.

▼▲▼

Shiki Ryōgi has been my friend since high school. It was a private school, famous for sending students on to good colleges.

You don't see a name like *Shiki Ryōgi* every day, so it stuck in my mind when the application results were being posted, and then I ended up in the same class as she was. After that, I became one of Shiki's very few friends.

Since our school was a prep school without a dress code, I think everyone expressed themselves by wearing different things. In that kind of crowd, Shiki really stood out like a sore thumb in school.

The reason was because she always wore a kimono.

The modest, informal look really complemented her slender shoulders, and she only had to walk in to make the classroom feel like a classic samurai castle. That's how powerful the effect was. It wasn't just the look either. Her movements and the way she acted were all perfect. Only in class did she utter anything resembling words. I think that was the only thing that gave us any idea of what Shiki was like as a person.

As for her actual looks, well, they were too good to be true.

Her hair was as pretty as dark black silk, cut in a half-hearted fashion, then left to its own devices. The result was a short cut just long enough to hide her ears. Strangely enough, it suited her so well that a lot of pupils mistook her for a boy.

Shiki was so good-looing that if a boy looked at her, he thought she was a girl, and if a girl looked at her, she thought it was a boy. Her features were more awe-inspiring than beautiful.

But if you asked me, I would say that she had something even more fascinating than these characteristics: her eyes.

Her expression was slightly sharp yet tranquil. Her brows were delicate. She had a way of always seeming to be gazing at something invisible to us. In my opinion, this summed up her entire personality.

That's right. Until she ended up the way she did.

▼▲▼

"Jumping..."

"Huh...? Ah, sorry. I wasn't listening."

"Suicide by jumping. Does that count as an accident, Mikiya?"

My mumbled, bored-sounding words jolted Mikiya out of his silence and back to his senses. With that, he thought seriously about the question. His answer was naïvely straightforward.

"Yeah, I'd definitely say that's an accident...but... it's...I don't really know how to put it.... If a person commits suicide, they're dead and gone, right? They do it of their own free will. The responsibility is theirs alone. But if you *jump* from a high place, the responsibility doesn't completely belong to that person. Hard to distinguish it from falling. That's more like an accident."

"So not murder and not accidental death," I said. "The line seems pretty hazy, if you ask me. But if people are gonna kill themselves, I just wish they'd do it without bothering others."

"Shiki, it's not nice to speak ill of the dead."

Mikiya's tone didn't sound scolding, nor was it cold or blunt. It was so boringly predictable that I could tell he was going to say it even before he opened his mouth.

"*Cocteau,* I really hate how you generalize stuff."

A sudden and brutal objection. Mikiya didn't take offense, though.

"Aah. You haven't called me that in a while," he said.

"Really?"

Mikiya nodded like a particularly well-mannered squirrel.

I had two names for him—*Mikiya* and *Cocteau*—but I didn't really like the sound of *Cocteau*. . . . I don't really know why. My musings had brought about a lull in the conversation, and Mikiya clapped his hands like he'd remembered something.

"Speaking of which! It's a bit weird, but my sister saw it."

"Hm? Saw what?"

"You know, *her* again. The girl at the Fujō Building, flying. You said you saw it, too, didn't you?"

I didn't say anything. But, yeah, I remembered it. It had all started three weeks before and was something of a ghost story.

In the business district was a high-class apartment complex called the Fujō Building, and I saw what looked like a person in the sky above it. If Mikiya's sister Azaka had seen it, too, then it wasn't just me. The thing had to be real, it seemed.

After my accident, I'd been in a coma for two years. Ever since, I'd been able to see "things that shouldn't be there." Well, according to Tōko, it was more like I'd become able to *perceive* them rather than *see* them; basically, my brain and eyes had been raised to a new level, become more acute somehow. That was all. Not that I thought it was interesting in any way.

"If we're talking the Fujō Building," I said, "then I saw it plenty of times—not just once. Obviously, I don't know if I'd be able to see it now, though, since I haven't walked that way in a while."

"Hmm. I go that way a lot, but I've never seen anything."

"It's because you wear glasses."

Mikiya pouted, saying it had nothing to do with his glasses. His response was warm, with no hint of maliciousness. And that was why it was hard for him to see such things.

Even so, it just kept on happening: the mind-numbingly dull phenomenon of people jumping—or falling or whatever. I didn't know if there was any meaning behind it, so I'd asked Mikiya's opinion.

"Mikiya, why do you think someone would jump?"

Mikiya shrugged dismissively.

"Jumping, falling . . . I don't understand either," he said naturally. "They're not something I've tried yet, are they?"

2

On the night August ended, I decided to take a stroll.

Even though it was the end of summer, the open air was quite chilly. It was long after the last train had departed, and the town had fallen silent.

Quiet, cold, desolate: it was like an unfamiliar ghost town, even. Devoid of pedestrians and all human warmth, the scene looked as artificial as a photo and made me think of an incurable illness.

Sick, diseased, abnormal.

It felt like everything, from the dark-windowed houses to the brightly illuminated convenience stores, could crumble at the sound of a cough.

Amid it all, the verdant moonlight accentuated the night. The moon was the only thing that looked alive in this totally anesthetized world. It made my eyes hurt horribly.

That was what I meant by *abnormal.*

When I left my house, I'd put on a black leather jacket over my light blue kimono. The sleeves of the kimono were tucked up in my jacket, and I was sweating. Despite that, I wasn't hot. . . . In fact . . .

The weather hadn't felt cold to me the whole time.

▼▲▼

Even walking out so late at night, I would meet people.

Someone just looking at the ground, walking briskly onward. Someone else standing morosely before a vending machine. A small group, congregating in the lights of the convenience stores.

I cast around for a meaning to these actions, but, after all, I was an outsider looking in. There was no chance of my understanding. For one thing, I myself had no reason to be walking out at night like this.

I was, after all, just repeating my old self's habits. Nothing more.

It had happened two years ago.

I, Shiki Ryōgi, was just about to move up to the second year of senior high school when I had a traffic accident and was hauled off to the hospital, just like that.

It happened on a rainy night. Apparently, I was thrown from the car. Fortunately, it was a nice, clean crash: no major injuries, bleeding, or broken bones. On the flip side, all the damage ended up unluckily concentrated in my head.

I was in a coma from that point on. Maybe it was because my body was pretty much in perfect condition, but the hospital decided to keep me alive, and my body desperately carried on breathing as I lay there unconscious.

Then, two months ago, Shiki Ryōgi came back to life.

The doctors were apparently as shocked as if Lazarus himself had woken up in their hospital. Just from that, I knew, after all, just how hopeless my condition must have been. I was in for something of a shock myself, though not as big as theirs.

I'd go so far as to say I didn't know who I was. My memories up until that point were strange, somehow. To put it simply, I couldn't trust my own memory.

It's different from a simple memory defect that prevents you from recalling your past . . . the kind of defect that's called amnesia.

Tōko told me the word *memory* refers to four processes the brain carries out: encoding, storage, recall, and authentication.

"Encoding" is how an image you've seen is written onto the brain. "Storage" is how you retain it. "Recall" is retrieving stored information. In other words, recalling memories. And "authentication" is how the brain checks that the recalled information is consistent with previous memories.

If you are physically unable to perform just one of these four mental processes, the result is a defective memory. Naturally, because there are lots of ways it can go wrong, you get a lot of totally different kinds of memory defects.

But in my case, all of the four processes were working fine. My memories of the past didn't feel real, but they were still in total agreement with the images I'd built up back then. Which means my "authentication" process was working, too.

Even so, I was completely unsure about my past self. I didn't feel that I was *me* at all. Even if I recalled the Shiki Ryōgi from the past, I could only think of her as a different person. Even though I was definitely, without a doubt, Shiki Ryōgi.

Shiki Ryōgi disappeared during that two-year blank.

Perhaps not as far as the rest of the world is concerned, but my contents were hollowed out all the same. My memories *and* the personality I used to have. Those links had been hopelessly severed beyond repair.

My memories have become nothing more than vacant images. But since I still have access to those images, I could still pretend to be my former self. I could pass myself off to friends and family alike as the Shiki Ryōgi they knew.

As you'd expect, this wasn't especially nice for me, though. It tormented me with an unbearable suffocating feeling.

It's just like I was copying. I wasn't living at all.

I was like a newborn baby. I didn't know anything. I

hadn't acquired anything of my own. Yet my seventeen-year-old memory proved that I was a fully grown human being.

Fundamentally, emotions that I should have felt from various experiences *were* there in the form of memories. But I didn't experience them. Try as I might to make them real to me, they were still things that I already knew. If they evoke no reaction, it doesn't feel like you're alive.... It's the same as when a magician's sleight-of-hand tricks fail to surprise you anymore.

And so I repeated the same routines my former self used to do, all the while feeling like a zombie.

But I went on doing it for a simple reason: if I did it, then maybe, just maybe, I'd be able to go back to being who I was. If I kept at this, maybe these nighttime walks would start to mean something to me, too.

Yeah, that's right. I might even be able to say that I loved my old self.

▼▲▼

Feeling like I'd walked a fair distance, I looked up. This was the business district, the source of all those rumors. A row of buildings, all neatly lined up the same height. The glassy surface of the buildings now reflected only moonlight. The buildings, standing in formation along the main street, felt like nothing more than a meandering phantom world of shadow images.

Among them was a conspicuously tall shape. This twenty-story-tall, ladderlike structure looked like a long, narrow tower and seemed so tall it almost touched the moon. It was called the Fujō Building.

It was an apartment building, but no light shone from it. The residents must all have been asleep. The time was close to two in the morning, after all.

And at that very moment . . . a tedious shadow came into my field of vision. A humanlike silhouette, floating into view. No, it wasn't a simile: the girl was actually floating.

There was no wind.

The night air was strangely chilly for summer. My neck shuddered from the cold.

Of course, this was all just my imagination.

"Well, look at that. Here she is again," I said.

I wasn't happy about it but couldn't help seeing it. With that, the girl in question flew, as if leaning against the moon.

A View from Above

An image of a dragonfly. Flying away, restless.

A butterfly followed it, but the dragonfly didn't slow down. All of a sudden, the butterfly couldn't keep up and fell, powerlessly, just as it disappeared from my field of vision.

It formed a bow in the air as it fell. It fell like a flattened lily, in a snakelike arc. That image was heartbreakingly sad.

Even if we couldn't go on together, I at least wanted to stay beside it for a while. But that was impossible. Because my feet weren't on the ground, and I couldn't even stop.

Someone was talking, and I resigned myself to waking up.

My eyelids were heavy. Proof that I hadn't slept even two hours. It was touching that my body still wanted to get up and be active despite that fact, though. And this touch of vanity was enough to secure my victory over sleep. . . . Seriously, I'm always getting into trouble like this.

I remembered for sure that all last night, I'd stayed up to put the finishing touches on some plans. I must have fallen asleep here in Miss Tōko's room.

I rose up from the sofa energetically. Sure enough, the sight of the office met my eyes.

Shafts of summer sunlight. It seemed that it wasn't even

noon yet. And amid those shining rays, Shiki and Miss Tōko were deep in conversation. Shiki was leaning against the wall, while Miss Tōko sat cross-legged on a fold-out chair. As always, Shiki was wearing a kimono as though it were the most natural thing in the world. As for Miss Tōko, she was wearing plain, tight black pants and what looked like a snazzy new white shirt. With her short hair and plunging neckline, she really did look like some kind of presidential secretary. Though, that said, her expression whenever she took off her glasses was so indescribably ghastly that she'd probably never get a job like that even if a disaster wiped out every other woman on earth.

"Morning, Kokutō."

The glance that Miss Tōko gave me was ... well, the same as always. From looking at her glasses-less face, I could guess that she and Shiki had been having one of *those* conversations.

"I'm sorry. I guess I overslept."

"Stop with the pointless explanations. I've got eyes, you know," she replied bluntly, cigarette in mouth.

"Make some coffee since you're up. It'll be good rehabilitation for you."

Rehabilitation? What, like, back into society?

I didn't know why she felt I needed something like that, but Miss Tōko was always like this. I wasn't about to ask her to elaborate.

"Do you want anything, Shiki?"

"I'm fine. I'm off to bed any minute now."

It looked like Shiki was definitely suffering from sleep deprivation. She had probably gone off for one of her nighttime walks after I dozed off last night.

▼▲▼

Next to Miss Tōko's private room, which served as the office, was what looked like a kind of kitchen. Maybe it had been some kind of lab originally, as it had three faucets in a row. In short, it was more like a drinking area at a school than like a kitchen sink. Two of the faucets were tied up with wire and out of use. I didn't know why. Miss Tōko simply said it made things easier, but it struck me as pointless and just annoyed me.

Okay, I thought, firing up the coffeemaker. The first thing I did when getting to work was to make the coffee. I'd now progressed to the point where I could do it in my sleep. Almost half a year had passed since I, Mikiya Kokutō, had become an employee here.

Actually, no. It felt strange to put it that way. This wasn't a company, in any case. The reason I'd barged my way in anyway, despite knowing all that, was solely because I was hopelessly fascinated by Miss Tōko's work, I guess.

After Shiki had sealed herself away in a perpetual seventeen-year-old time bubble, I had graduated from school, clueless, and drifted into a college. I'd promised Shiki I'd get into that college. Even though it looked like she would never recover, I wanted to keep that vow, at least.

But after that, nothing. Once I became a university student, I was just counting off days on the calendar. And while I was blankly idling away the hours, I dragged myself to some event or other a friend had invited me to, and I found a doll.

This doll had been so elaborately crafted that it was pushing the limits of ethical decency. It was like a human being had been frozen still. Yet, at the same time, it obviously felt like a mere fabrication of the human shape—something that would never move on its own.

A human shape, clearly not a person. Yet simultaneously impossible to see as anything but.

Someone who would come back to life at any moment. That's how it looked. But it was a doll; it had never been a living thing. And yet I couldn't help but feel it was alive, but in a place human beings could never reach.

This contradiction captivated me. Most probably, it reminded me so much of Shiki's condition.

The identity of the person exhibiting the doll was a blank. The accompanying pamphlet didn't even offer a hint. I frantically dug around for information, and it turned out to be an unofficial display, the maker an unknown name in the industry.

Her name was Tōko Aozaki. She was a recluse. Though she was an expert doll-maker, it seemed she also did plans for buildings. In any case, despite the fact that she would do anything to just *create,* she didn't accept commissions. The work always came from her side. She'd go to the people in question, say "I'm going to make this," get payment in advance, and then go off and set about making it.

Either she was a bona fide libertine or else a real eccentric. My interest was piqued. Even though I really shouldn't have, I looked up her address.

▼▲▼

It was far from the heart of town: neither a residential area nor an industrial district. No. In fact, Tōko Aozaki's house was hardly what you'd call a house at all.

Frankly, it was a ruin. And I don't mean it was just a little bit run-down either. Construction had started on it many years ago during the boom years, but the economy had gotten worse, and they'd given up on it partway through, leaving a genuine abandoned building, in every sense of the word. The exterior "building" shape was pretty much done, but the insides were a different story, with all the walls and floors totally bare, consisting of nothing but their raw materials.

They were probably aiming for six floors if they'd actually finished, but now there was nothing from the fourth floor up.... It may be more efficient to construct a tall building from the top floor down, but this one must have been built using old-school methods. Because it had been abandoned halfway, the partly completed fifth floor now made for a makeshift rooftop.

The building site was surrounded by a high concrete wall, but I doubt it would have kept anyone out. It was a deeply mysterious building, so much so that it was a miracle the neighborhood kids hadn't turned it into a secret base or something.

Well, in any case, it seemed that Tōko Aozaki had bought this abandoned place that nobody else wanted. The kitchenesque room in which I was currently pouring coffee was on the fourth floor. The second and third floors were where Miss Tōko did her work, so we all usually communicated up here on the fourth.

... Anyway, back to the story.

Eventually, I got to know her and dropped out of college to come and work here. Amazingly enough, I was being paid wages and everything.

According to Miss Tōko, you can break humans down into two diphyletic categories: *makers and searchers* as well as *users and destroyers.*

"You've got no talent as far as creating goes, Mikiya," she'd said to me bluntly. But she'd employed me anyway. I must have had some skills as a "searcher," I guess.

"What's taking you so long, Kokutō?"

A demand rang out from the next room.

When I looked, I found the coffeemaker had been filled with dark, black liquid for some time.

▼▲▼

"Seems that yesterday was the eighth one now," said Miss Tōko suddenly, stubbing out her spent cigarette. "It's about time the rest of the world started noticing the connection."

She probably meant the recent epidemic of female high school students jumping to their deaths. I doubted she was talking about the harsh water shortages we'd been having this summer. As topics of woe went, that wasn't one she'd normally go for.

"The eighth one . . . ?" I ventured. "Uh, don't you mean the sixth?"

"The number went up while you were spacing out. Starting from June, there've been three a month on average. I wonder if there'll be another one before three days are up."

Discretion clearly wasn't her strong point. Miss Tōko cast a glance at the calendar. There were just three days left in August. . . . That left three . . . There was something not quite right there, though, and doubts immediately surfaced in my consciousness.

"But they're all unrelated, though," I said. "The girls who killed themselves were all from different schools, and they didn't even know each other. Well, I guess the police could be keeping information from the public, though."

"How cynical of you. That's not like you, Kokutō. Mistrusting others like that."

The corners of her mouth raised as Miss Tōko teased me. The glasses-less person I was looking at now became the most malicious-looking individual imaginable.

". . . But they haven't released any suicide notes," I continued. "Six people . . . no, eight, you say? If that's all, then they could at least make an official announcement or something like that, but they're keeping a lid on it. That's concealment of information, surely?"

"That's what I mean by *connection*," Miss Tōko replied. "Actually, *common features* would be a more accurate description. Of the eight, most of them were seen jumping of their own accord from various places by multiple eyewitnesses. None of the girls had any evident personal problems.

None were taking drugs or under the influence of shady religions. There's no doubt that these were spontaneous suicides, inspired by individual anxiety. Therefore, they didn't *want* to leave any last words, and the police probably don't consider the factors they have in common to be important."

". . . So, it's not that they aren't releasing the suicide notes. There never *were* any from the start?"

Miss Tōko nodded at my incredulous question, not looking a hundred percent certain. But was that really all there was to it?

Something wasn't right there. I took hold of the coffee cup and let thoughts run through my head as I sampled the bitter beverage.

Why weren't there any suicide notes? A person doesn't kill herself without leaving a note.

Speaking from pure logic, a suicide note is a sign of lingering regret. When people who don't want to die but see no other choice decide to finish themselves off, they leave their reasons behind in the form of a note.

Suicide without a note.

Having *no reason* to leave a note. To no longer have any kind of view on the world and just bow out . . . vanish without protest. That's total suicide. Such a complete suicide would leave no suicide note from the start, and wouldn't, I felt, even draw attention to fact of the death itself.

Which meant that jumping to one's death *wasn't* actually total suicide.

Dying in front of onlookers like that felt in itself like a form of suicide note. Surely it was because they wanted to leave something for the world to remember them by . . . because they wanted to *announce* their deaths in some fashion? So it only made sense that they must have left suicide notes.

So what was going on? Had a third party taken the girls' last notes away, since none had been found? No, then we'd have been leaving the realm of suicide altogether. What, then? There was only one reason I could think of.

In short, that they had literally been accidents.

That the girls had never intended to die. In that case, there would have been no need to write notes. It would be like just heading out for some shopping and getting hit by a car through pure bad luck. Just like Shiki had gone out last night.

... But, still, I couldn't for the life of me think how someone could just go out shopping and end up falling off a building.

"Mikiya, it'll stop with the eighth jumper. There won't be any more for a long time after that."

Shiki's words cut off my runaway train of thought.

"What, you *know* they're going to stop?"

The question was out of my mouth before I knew it.

"I saw it, that's why," Shiki said. "There were eight of them, flying."

"Aha. There were only that many at the building, huh? So you knew how many there'd be right from the start, Shiki?"

"Yeah," Shiki said. "I took care of *her,* but the girls will still be lingering around there for a while. Pretty miserable state of affairs, though. Hey, Tōko ... do you think that's the fate people get stuck with if they go throwing themselves off buildings like that?"

"I wonder. It's hard to say. There are so many factors involved. But, historically speaking, though there have been a lot of experiments, no human being has ever managed to succeed in flying under their own power. The words *flying* and *falling* are actually closely interlinked. But for people who are truly obsessed with the sky, however, that fact doesn't register. The result is that they end up aiming for the clouds after they die, too. Rather than falling to the ground, it's like falling up into the sky."

Shiki frowned, not happy with the answer.

... She was angry. But at what?

"Um, excuse me," I interjected, "but I'm not following this at all."

"Huh? Oh, just the Fujō Building ghost story," replied Miss Tōko. "I was thinking that I'd have to see it for myself to see if there's any substance to it or if it's just a bunch of reflections. I was going to go take a look when I had some free time, but Shiki killed it. So I won't have a chance now."

... Aha. *That* story, like I thought.

When Miss Tōko took off her glasses and got together with Shiki, it was usually this kind of occult stuff they talked about.

"You heard that Shiki saw a floating girl above the Fujō Building, right? There's more to the story. It seems there were human-looking shapes bustling and flying around the girl. Since they don't leave the building, we were talking about whether the place acts like a net, trapping them."

They'd lost me. My face clouded over. What I was hearing was just too strange and difficult to understand.

Miss Tōko must have seen my expression, because she broke it down for me.

"So, there was someone floating at the Fujō Building, with the figures of all the suicide girls around her. And those girls looked like ghosts, right? That's all there was to it. Pretty simple, eh?"

I nodded in tentative agreement.

I grasped the essential point of the story, but it seemed I'd joined in after the tale had ended yet again. From what Shiki had said earlier, it looked like she had done away with the ghost or whatever it was herself. Miss Tōko and Shiki had known each other two months now. In my position, I usually only ever heard the endings of these kinds of stories.

I wasn't like these two women. Incredibly average old me

didn't want to get mixed up in stuff like that. But I didn't like being completely out of the loop either, and so this state of affairs was pretty much just right for me. It's what they call "making the best of a bad situation."

▼▲▼

"It's like something out of a pulp novel," I said, and Miss Tōko agreed.

Only Shiki didn't seem convinced. Her eyes filled more and more with annoyance, casting sidelong glances and glaring at me.

Had I done something to make her mad?

"Hey . . . speaking of Shiki seeing ghosts . . . It started in July, didn't it? And weren't there four of them at the Fujō Building back then?"

I was asking the obvious, just for the sake of clarification, and Shiki shook her head moodily.

"Eight," she said. "There were eight of them flying there from the start. I told you, didn't I? That there wouldn't be more than eight jumpers. Because the order goes in reverse for them."

"What, so you could see eight right from the start? Hey, you're like the amazing future-seeing girl."

"Yeah, *right*. I'm normal. It's the other side that's messed up," Shiki argued. "Yeah, weird. Like fire and ice living as roommates. So . . ."

Miss Tōko wasted no time in picking up where Shiki's vague statements had left off.

"So, time works strangely on the other side. Time doesn't pass in one solitary way. The mileage things have before decaying away is uneven. So it's a fact that there's a time lag between the breakdown of the human body and the memories that fill that body. Do a person's memories disappear after their body dies? I don't think so. Nothing just disappears abruptly, as long as there are observers left, watching. Things fade away gradually.

"Memories of a person . . . no, a record, in fact. Say the observer isn't a person but the environment surrounding that record. In that case, it walks the streets as a unique, phantom vision after death, like those girls. This is one aspect of the whole 'ghost' phenomenon. The ones who end up seeing these visions are those who have something in common with them: friends or family of the deceased. Shiki's the exception. Well, that's 'trace time expiration' for you. But in the case of that building rooftop, it happened slowly. The trace of the girls from when they were alive hasn't yet caught up to their original time.

"The result is that their memories alone are still living.

"What we have is probably the extremely delayed-action reality of those girls, projecting itself onto that place as phantoms."

At that point, Miss Tōko lit the latest in who knows how many cigarettes.

In short, even if something disappears, as long as someone remembers it, it isn't gone. And if something is remembered, it's alive. And if it's alive, you can see it. That was my best guess.

Which meant that they *were* illusions at the end of the day. No, actually, the way Miss Tōko herself labeled them "phantoms" meant they were definitely something more otherworldly and impossible than that.

"It's a good theory. No harm in running with it," said Shiki. "The problem is *her*. I got a good hit in, but if she's corporeal, it'll just happen all over again. And I'm sick of protecting Mikiya already."

"Agreed. I'll take care of Kirie Fujō," Miss Tōko said. "You just walk Kokutō home. He's still got five hours until quitting time, so use that bed over there if you want to sleep."

The bed Miss Tōko was pointing at hadn't been cleaned once in a whole half year and looked like the inside of an incinerator packed with wastepaper.

Shiki, naturally, ignored this.

"Well, what was she, then, in the end?"

A cigarette in her mouth, Tōko the sorceress gave a considered "hmph" and stepped soundlessly over to the window.

▼▲▼

She surveyed the outside world from there.

There were no lights in the room, which was illuminated solely by the daylight from outside, making it difficult to tell if was daytime or evening inside.

Beyond the window, by contrast, it was clearly day. Miss Tōko gazed out at the summer afternoon streets, standing in silence for a while.

"She probably used to be one of the 'flying' types, too."

The cigarette smoke was absorbed into the white sunlight. Her back was to us as she looked down over the landscape. Like a mirage amid a white, misty haze.

"Kokutō, when you look down at the ground from somewhere high up, what image does it make you think of?"

My absentminded senses snapped back into focus at this sudden question.

Somewhere high up, huh? There was always the time I'd visited Tokyo Tower as a kid. I couldn't remember what I'd been thinking at the time, though. The most I could remember was frantically trying to find my house from up there but not being able to.

"Er . . . smallness?" I ventured.

"That's a stretch, Kokutō," came the blunt rebuttal.

I pulled my thoughts together and offered a different suggestion.

"... Well, I guess it doesn't really suggest anything to me, but it's beautiful, isn't it? Scenery is incredible when you see it from high up."

I guess this seemed a more heartfelt answer than my last one, because Miss Tōko nodded slightly in approval.

Then, her eyes absolutely unmoving from the view outside, she began to speak.

"Looking down at a landscape far below is a magnificent spectacle. Even bog-standard scenery becomes something wonderful. But that's not the impulse you feel when you see a panoramic view of the whole world you're living in. No, there's only one impulse you get from that view from above...."

Miss Tōko paused slightly when she said the word *impulse*.

An impulse isn't based on reason or intelligence. I don't think an impulse is something that comes from inside you, like your thoughts do, but rather something that swoops down from outside. Something that sweeps over you. Like a violent mugging. No matter how much you try to resist. That's what we call an impulse. But what kind of violence could there be in a view from above...?

"It's *distance*," Miss Tōko said. "That panoramic view is far too spacious, too expansive. It creates a definite sense of estrangement from the world. And humans can only draw peace of mind from the things around them, even at the best of times. No matter what elaborate maps you may have, no matter the fact that you know you're in such and such a place, it's still nothing more than basic information. To us, the world is nothing more than what we can touch and feel. We cannot feel the connecting points in what our brains register as this planet, this country, or this city. We'd have to go and physically visit those linking points for that. And, in fact, that's fine. Our awareness is supposed to work that way.

"But if you get a view that's too spacious, it throws a spanner in the works. You've got thirty feet that you can touch and feel around you, but you're looking down over thirty thousand feet. They're both the same, both the world that you live in, but the former seems much more real.

"See? There's a contradiction right there, isn't there?

"It's proper and natural to recognize the vast scenery you're looking out over as being 'the world you live in'—more than the confined space you can actually feel with your body's senses. Yet you just cannot for the life of you feel that you are part of what you're looking down at.

"Why is that? This is just my hunch, but I think people always give priority to the information they get from their surroundings. So, at this point, 'sense,' or knowledge, and 'feelings,' or experiences, chafe against each other. Before long, there's friction, and your senses start acting erratically.

"*The city looks so small from up here. I can't believe my house is down there. So that's what that park really looks like? I never knew there was a place like* that *over there. It's like I never knew this town at all. It's like I've ended up somewhere far, far away....* —A view from too high up makes feelings like those surface. The person feels like they're somewhere miles and miles away, even though they're still standing in their own town."

A high-up place is a distant place. I understood that distance aspect completely. But what Miss Tōko was talking about was probably more of a psychological thing.

"So, basically, it's not good to look at things from high up for too long?" I asked.

"It's not good to take things to extremes. The sky has been thought of as a separate world since time immemorial. Flying is the same as going to another world. If you don't arm yourself with civilized thinking, you get influenced by deviant perceptions. Common sense literally goes out the window. Protect your awareness, and, naturally, you avoid such bad influences. If you have a firm footing, there's no problem. Once you're back on the ground, everything's normal again."

Now that she said this, I thought about when I used to look down over the sports ground from the roof of my school. I'd suddenly be struck by the inexplicable thought of what it would be like to just leap off.

Of course, I'm joking. I never had the slightest intention of actually doing it, but why, I wonder, would such a clearly deadly thought jump into my head like that?

Miss Tōko said that everybody's different, but I don't think it's especially rare for anybody to picture climbing up somewhere high and jumping off.

"... So it's a case of your thoughts temporarily going crazy?"

As soon as I voiced the notion that had surfaced in my head, Miss Tōko gave a dry laugh.

"Everyone dreams about doing taboo things, Kokutō. People like imagining things they don't do; we have a staggering capacity for self-satisfaction, after all. Only ... Yeah, we were getting closer just then. The important thing is that the temptation of the taboo only rears its head in the appropriate place and not elsewhere. That's just common sense. Your example just now ... It's not that a person's senses go crazy; it's that their reason becomes paralyzed."

"This is dragging on now, Tōko," said Shiki, clearly unable to put up with anymore.

As I thought about it, the conversation had certainly moved far off the original mark.

"It's not dragging," Miss Tōko said. "If we take it as the

classic four-step narrative structure of *introduction, development, twist,* and *conclusion,* we're still only in phase two."

"I'm only interested in the end. I'm not wasting my time joining you two and your inane banter."

"Shiki . . ."

Harsh but honest. Shiki carried on, though, despite my one-word interjection.

"So, if there's a problem with looking at landscapes from high places," she said, "then how do you explain our everyday sight? When we're walking around normally, we're still *higher* than ground level, aren't we?"

Shiki's attitude was all wrong, but her words, in contrast, had hit the mark. People's eyeballs are definitely placed higher up on their bodies than the actual ground. Which means that we basically get a view from above even by simply standing at ground level.

Miss Tōko nodded, taking Shiki up on this challenge.

"But the earth's surface, which you think of as ground level, is still an unreliable viewpoint to go on. And anyway, that aside, you still wouldn't exactly call our normal field of vision 'a view from on high,' would you?"

"*Field of vision* doesn't mean the images that our eyes can see but rather the images our brains take in. Our field of vision is protected by our common sense, so our standing viewpoint doesn't feel to us like we're high up. Even that's governed by common sense. There's no notion of height there. But on the other hand, we all of us live with a view from above. Not physically speaking but spiritually. There are a lot of individual differences at work. Those with the most expanded minds aim for great heights. But, even then, they don't leave the box they're in.

"Human beings live in boxes and *can only* live in boxes. We're not meant to see from God's viewpoint. If we cross that line, we become the monsters we're warned about.

"*Hypnos,* the personification of sleep, and his twin, *Thanatos,* the personification of death, switch places. No one knows one from the other, and in the end, it becomes impossible to distinguish between them."

As she continued, Miss Tōko herself was looking down at a world below. As she looked down, her feet were fixed to the ground. That felt to me like an extremely important point.

All of a sudden, I remembered a dream I'd had.

▼▲▼

At the end of it, a butterfly had fallen.

If she hadn't tried to follow me, she could probably have flown even longer and more gracefully.

Yes, if she'd just fluttered her wings and floated along, she would have been in the air for so much longer. But she'd realized what it was to really fly. She couldn't bear just floating there, weightless. That's why she fell. She just stopped floating.

I tilted my head as I thought all this. So, there'd been a poet hiding inside me all along, had there?

Miss Tōko cast her cigarette away out the window.

"The disturbances at the Fujō Building might well have been the world the girl was seeing. I'd hazard a guess that the difference in atmosphere that Shiki sensed is the wall separating the inside of the box from the outside. It's like a weather discontinuity line, detectable by human senses."

Finally, with Miss Tōko's speech at an end, Shiki's irritated look lifted.

She looked away with a sigh.

"Discontinuity line, huh? I wonder which one she thinks is the warm front and which is the cold one?"

In sharp contrast to the serious-sounding speech she'd just heard, Shiki really didn't sound like she was remotely interested.

"Obviously, it'll be the opposite of whatever you think," retorted Miss Tōko, adopting the same kind of nonchalant air.

▼▲▼

Her neck shivered. Was the shaking due to the chill she felt outside or the chill within?

Shiki Ryōgi couldn't tell. So she didn't dwell on it and calmly advanced.

There were no signs of life at the Fujō Building. It was two in the morning, and the apartments were lit only by white electric lights. Their glow illuminated the cream-colored walls, appearing to continue down into the depths of the passageway. There was no human warmth in the artificial light that swept away the darkness so completely. It felt more ominous than the dark it was supposed to keep at bay.

Shiki passed through the card-check entranceway and boarded the elevator.

There was no one inside. The interior was mirrored, evidently set up to allow those riding in the elevator to see themselves.

Reflected in it was a languid-eyed figure in a black leather jacket over a light blue kimono. The eyes were laid-back, showing no interest in anything around. Facing her reflected self in the mirror, Shiki pressed the button for the rooftop.

The world around her began to move upward, accompanied by a faint mechanical whir. The mechanical box was on its way up to the roof. A secret room for all of a few seconds. Right now, Shiki was cut off from anything that was happening outside these four walls and had no way of engaging with any of it. This feeling managed to slightly penetrate the void that was her heart.

Right now, this tiny box was the only world that was real to her.

The doors parted soundlessly. Ahead was an utterly black space, completely at odds with what had come before.

Shiki emerged into a small room. There was only one door—the one to the roof—and the vacant elevator returned to the ground floor as she stepped out.

There was no light, and her surroundings were chokingly dark. Her footsteps echoed as Shiki moved through the tiny room, opening the door that led to the roof.

▼▲▼

The deep black was replaced by a dim darkness. A panoramic outlook of the nighttime city leaped into view, filling her eyes in every direction. The roof of the Fujō Building had been built blank and featureless. The bare concrete floor stretched out, dead level, surrounded by a wire-mesh fence.

Apart from a water tank on top of the small room from which Shiki had just emerged, there was nothing else to draw the eye.

The place itself was a completely ordinary rooftop. Yet the landscape struck her. The roof was about ten floors higher than the surrounding buildings, and the view was more lonely than pretty. Climbing the thin ladder, Shiki found it to be like looking down over the world.

The city was like a dark, deep ocean where no light could penetrate, and it was certainly beautiful to behold. Burning lights here and there looked like the twinkling of deep-sea fish.

—*If my field of vision is the whole world, then the world is sleeping right now.*

Forever, for all I know. Though I bet it's only temporary. More's the pity.

This stillness grips my heart more than any cold does.

So much it hurts—

The stillness of the night sky was conspicuous against the streets and houses far below.

If the city was the deep sea, then the sky was purest darkness. Stars twinkled among the black, as if they were scattered jewels.

The moon was a hole. Shiki could only see it as a huge, remarkably alluring opening that pierced through the black drawing paper that was the sky. This was because she had heard, back at the Ryōgi family home, that the moon wasn't actually reflecting light from the sun at all. Instead, they said, it was merely scenery from the other side beyond, showing through the opening.

The moon, it was said, was an open door to another world.

The moon represented sorcery, the female gender, and death. Against that backdrop, a single human figure was suspended, floating.

Around the figure flew eight girls.

▼▲▼

Rising there in the air was the pale figure of a girl.

White clothes, so florid and brilliant they could have been mistaken for a showy dress, and black hair down to her hips. Slender limbs protruded from her garments, making her look all the more graceful.

Her indifferent eyes and thin eyebrows would probably have secured her a place in the most prestigious of beauty pageants.

Shiki guessed her age to be in the early twenties. Of course, she doubted whether placing someone's age was applicable when it came to ghosts. But, in any case, she doubted that the translucent girl was a ghost.

She was definitely there. The girls twisting through the night sky around her . . . *they* would be the ghosts. The girls, drifting randomly through the air, felt more like they were swimming than flying. Their forms were vague, though, and faded into translucency occasionally.

A shining white woman with a mass of girls swimming around her in a seemingly protective formation, there above Shiki's head.

This series of images was not repellent.

Rather, it was . . .

"Hmph . . . This sure is magical," Shiki scoffed mockingly.

The woman's beauty was unearthly, inhuman. Her black hair was as magnificent as strands of silk thread, smoothed out one by one with a comb. Had it been stirred by a strong wind, her billowing hair would perhaps have been a vision of mystic beauty.

"In which case, I'd better kill you," said Shiki, and the woman must have heard this because she cast her eyes downward.

The rooftop of the Fujō Building was over three hundred feet above ground, the woman another ten feet above that. Their eyes met as Shiki looked up.

No words were exchanged. No mutually understood language even.

Shiki reached into her jacket. She pulled out a lethal weapon: a seven-inch blade—more a knife than a sword.

A murderous intent filled the eyes looking down from above. Instantly, the white garments flickered. The woman's hand swept smoothly down, her fingertips pointed at Shiki. What her frail, willowy limbs suggested, however, was not a living white color.

"Bones or lilies."

A voice echoed long into the windless night air. The outstretched fingers were full of the intent to kill.

Suddenly, the white fingers were pointing at Shiki's body.

Shiki's head swam with a pulsing clamor. She staggered, as though her slender frame were about to tumble down.

But only once.

The woman above faltered slightly at this.

Her subliminal suggestion, urging her victim to fly, wasn't working on this girl.

Her ability to force the image of flying into a person's very consciousness was beyond the realm of hinting and was more like full-fledged brainwashing. There was no resisting it. As a result of the inevitable suggestion, whether they believed it would actually happen or not, people simply ran over the edge of the roof, secure in the firm belief that they could fly.

Shiki had brushed this urge aside after only slight dizziness.

Maybe, the woman pondered, it had just been a glancing blow. She resolved to try once more.

It would be much stronger this time.

Not "You can fly" this time. A strong compulsion: "You *will* fly."

And yet . . .

Shiki looked up at her before she could do it. Two arms, two legs, one torso. One small spot slightly to the left of the center of the chest. Shiki could clearly see the cross section before her eyes: a blueprint for death.

The chest, above all, would be the best place to aim for. That would mean instant death. Illusion or no, Shiki was determined to prove she could be killed . . . even if this girl was a god.

She raised the knife in her right hand. Holding the hilt in a backhanded grip, Shiki narrowed her eyes at the opponent in the sky above.

As she did, an impulse welled up in her once again.

. . . *Fly. You can fly. You've always liked the sky. You were flying only yesterday. Maybe you can fly even higher up today.*

To freedom. To peace. To laughter. You have to go. Where to? To the sky? To freedom?
—It means...
...*An escape from reality. A yearning for the heavens. Reversing gravity.*

Your feet aren't on the ground. Flying unconsciously. Let's go, let's go, let's go, go, go, go, go, go, go, go, go, go, go, go ... go, now!

"You must be joking," muttered Shiki, and raised her empty left hand.

The lure of the sky had no effect on her. She no longer even felt dizzy.

"I don't have yearnings like that. I don't feel alive, so I don't know what actual suffering is. That's right. To be honest, I've got no interest in the likes of you either."

Her words were melodic, dismissive.

Shiki didn't feel the bittersweet joys and sorrows or various binding restrictions associated with life. So she didn't feel any kind of fascination with the prospect of liberation from suffering.

"Still," she went on, "I can't have you taking a certain someone with you. If you want a reason, it's because *I* saw him first, so I'll be taking him back now."

Shiki's empty hand grasped the open air. The woman and accompanying girls were drawn toward her, just like that, while she pulled her hand back as though reeling in a line.

They were like fish being hauled up onto land in a net.

The woman's features changed, and she hit Shiki with redoubled force of will. If she could have vocalized her intention, it would probably have come out as a scream of "Fall!"

Disregarding the woman's rage entirely, Shiki gave an angry retort.

"*You* fall."

Her knife stabbed through the chest of the rapidly descending woman. It was as simple as stabbing fruit; the pierced woman was entranced by the sheer sharpness of the blade.

There was no blood.

Paralyzed by the shock of the knife, which had thrust all the way through her back, the woman twitched only once. Shiki merely tossed the dispatched body away. The woman's form sailed past the fence and plunged soundlessly.

Even on the verge of falling, her hair made no fluttering motion, and her clothes billowed in the wind as she melted into the darkness. She looked like a white flower sinking down into the ocean depths.

▼▲▼

With that, Shiki left the rooftop.

Even now, the figures of the floating girls remained overhead.

3

After being stabbed through the chest, I came to.

It had been a huge shock. That girl must have been incredibly strong to just pierce someone's heart like that.

And yet, it hadn't been an angry, frenzied strength.

She had simply sliced through bone and muscle, calm and collected, as though it were nothing.

A terrible sense of unity.

The sense of death was sweeping my body. Again and again, the sound of my heart being run through. To me, that sensation hurt more than the pain.

Because it was both fear and indescribable pleasure. My body was shaking, a chill running down my spine to the point of insanity.

I felt anxiety and isolation of tear-inducing magnitude

and a clinging attachment to life. Then, soundlessly, I started to weep.

Not from fear or pain.

It was because I, who would pray each night to see tomorrow morning, was experiencing firsthand something I had never felt—death. Most probably, this chill would be with me for eternity. I would never be able to escape it.

Or, on the other hand, I wouldn't escape as long as I myself was in love with this sensation.

▼▲▼

The sound of a door opening.

It was afternoon. There was a trace of sunlight shining in through the closed windows.

Medical consulting hours were over, so this must be someone on a social call, I thought.

My room was a private one, and I shared it with nobody.

The only things here were the rays of sunlight that had just poured in, the static cream-colored curtains that had never known a breeze, and the bed I was in.

"Excuse me. You must be Kirie Fujō."

The visitor seemed to be a woman.

After speaking out in an incredibly husky voice, she came over to my bedside, not bothering to sit down. She must have been standing over me, looking down. Her gaze felt cold.

. . . This woman is terrifying. She'll destroy me for sure.

Even so, inside I was rejoicing. It had been so many years since someone had come to visit me. So what if it was death, come to finish me off? I couldn't send her away.

"You're an enemy, aren't you?"

The woman nodded in agreement.

I focused my senses and tried with all my might to make out the figure of this visitor.

It must have been the sun's fault, but all I could see was a vast silhouette.

She was minus a jacket, but her pristine, wrinkle-free clothes made her look like a teacher. I relaxed a little at this. Only, I had to take points off for the strong orange tie around her white shirt. It was too gaudy.

"Are you one of that girl's acquaintances?" I asked. "Or are you her?"

"No, I'm a friend of the one who attacked you and the one you attacked. Honestly, of all the weird people to get mixed up with. You've really . . . well, we've *both* got bad luck."

Having said this, the woman took something out of her breast pocket and immediately put it away again.

"No smoking in hospital rooms, huh?" she said regretfully. "It looks like your lungs are gone already. Smoking wouldn't do you much good."

It must have been a box of cigarettes then.

I had never touched cigarettes, but I wanted to see what this woman looked like smoking. Maybe . . . in fact, definitely, it would have suited her, like lizard pumps and a snakeskin bag on a shop mannequin.

"It's not just your lungs that are bad, though, is it? That's the cause, but I can see tumors all over your body. Extremities show sarcoma . . . and your insides are in especially bad shape. Your hair looks to be the only part that's unaffected. Even so, you've got remarkable physical strength.

"A normal person would have died long before the disease ate them away to this extent. . . . How many years has it been, Kirie Fujō?"

She was probably asking how long I'd lived hospitalized. But I didn't have an answer for her.

"I don't know. I stopped counting long ago."

There was no reason to, after all.

Because I could never leave here. Not until the day I died.

The woman gave a short sigh of resignation.

There was no sympathy there but no revulsion either. I hated it. The only thing anyone could give me was pity. This person wouldn't spare me even that.

"Are you okay where Shiki stabbed you? From what she said, it was from the left ventricle to the midaorta. You must have been sliced through the bicuspid valve."

Her voice was perfectly calm as she spoke these incredible words. I couldn't help but crack a smile at the strangeness of it.

"You're weird. We'd hardly be talking like this if I'd been stabbed through the heart."

"Perhaps," she replied. "We'll see soon enough."

Yes, that's right. I'd been wondering if this not quite Japanese, not quite Western-style woman would finish me off, and her words had just confirmed it.

"But you'll feel its influence. Shiki's got good eyes. If what she saw was a secondary entity, then its collapse will probably reach your real body. I have two or three things I'd like to know before that happens. That's why I came out here."

A secondary entity. She must have been talking about the "other me."

"I haven't seen the flying you. Can you explain what you are?" asked the woman.

"I don't understand, myself," I replied. "All I can see is the scenery outside this window. But maybe I shouldn't have looked. I was always looking down at the outside from here. The trees showing the changing seasons, and people coming and going from the hospital . . . always changing. Even if I raise my voice, nobody hears, and I can't reach anything if I stretch out my hand. I've been gasping and wheezing for so long. Hating the scenery outside for so long. That's what a curse is, isn't it?"

"... Hmph. The Fujō blood, eh?" said the visitor. "You're from a pure bloodline going back into antiquity. They specialized in prayers, but it seems that curses were their real bread and butter. It's possible that your surname was originally *fujō*, as in 'unclean,' but they changed the way it's written."

Lineage. My family. That ends with me, too.

When I had just been hospitalized, I lost my parents and brother in a car crash. Since then, my medical bills were being paid for by someone who used to be a friend of my father. This person had a complicated name that sounded like a priest or something, so I didn't remember what kind of person he was.

"But this isn't a subconscious curse you're not aware of," the woman pointed out. "What on earth did you pray for?"

... I didn't understand that, myself. I doubted even this woman could comprehend it.

▼▲▼

"Have you ever stared out at the landscape for a long time? For year after year, kept on looking out until your consciousness stopped? ... I hate the outside. I hated it, and it terrified me. I was always looking down from above, the whole time. And after that, one day my eyes went all strange. It was like I was in the sky over that courtyard over there, looking down at the ground below. It felt like my body and my mind were still here, and just my eyes were flying. But, because I couldn't move from here, all I ended up able to do was look down at this spot from above, though."

"... So, your brain took in the surrounding landscape. Which meant you could then see it from any angle at all, I imagine.

"Did you lose your eyesight around then?"

This was a shock. The woman had noticed that I could hardly see anymore.

I nodded.

"That's right. Everything got gradually whiter, until I couldn't see anything. At first, I thought everything would be pitch-black, but it wasn't. There's just nothing. That's what it's like to be blind.

"But I didn't have any problem with it. My eyes were up in the sky already. I could only see the area around this hospital, so I could never escape from here in the first place. Nothing changes. Nothing—"

At that point, I coughed violently. I hadn't talked this much in a long time. And my eyelids felt hot.

"I see. That's how your consciousness got up into the sky. But . . . then why are you alive? If that apparition over the Fujō Building was your consciousness, you should have been killed by Shiki."

Yes, I'd wondered the same thing.

That girl . . . Her name was Shiki, by the sound of it. How was she able to cut me?

In exchange for not feeling anything, that other me had never been injured. That girl, Shiki, had killed the other me easily, as though my other body were truly solid and tangible.

"Answer me. Was the you at the Fujō Building really Kirie Fujō?"

"The one at the Fujō Building isn't me. There's a me who is always looking out at the sky and a me who was up there in it. The other one gave up on me in favor of flying, in the end. Even my own self abandoned me."

The woman by my bed gasped. It was the first time she had displayed anything like emotion.

"Split personality . . . No, it's not that. You were one originally but were then granted a second vessel.

". . . One personality controlling two bodies. Certainly, I can't think of anything else to explain it."

Now that she said that, it sounded probable. I had abandoned the myself here in this room and gone looking out over the city. And yet neither of my two selves was affixed to the ground, and both were merely floating. I, who was so isolated from the world I saw outside the window, couldn't break through my sense of detachment, no matter how hard I wished for it.

Though we were split, in the end the two myselves were connected.

"... It all makes sense. But why weren't you content with just projecting into the outside world? I don't think it was necessary to kill those girls."

Girls ... Yes, those girls I envied so. They had done a terrible thing. But I was innocent. After all, they only jumped because they wanted to.

"The you at the Fujō Building is like a body of consciousness," the woman stated. "You used it, didn't you? Those girls could always fly, right from the start, couldn't they? Whether it was just in their dreams or they could actually fly for real.

"There are a great many people who don't sleepwalk but sleepfly. It isn't a problem, though. Why? Because they show those symptoms only when they are unconscious. Because they fly without any malicious intent while asleep, and the thought of flying never enters their minds when they're awake. Those girls were special, even in such a group. Though we aren't talking Peter Pan here, they were especially light during adolescence. One or two of them were probably flying for real, but most would only have been doing it in a dream sense. You made them conscious of this. You drew out that subconscious impression and made it real.

"The result was that they became aware of the fact that they could fly. And, yes, of course they could fly. But only unconsciously. Unpowered flight is difficult. Even I can't fly without a broom. The success rate for conscious flight is about 30 percent. Those girls just tried to fly as though it were as simple as anything and, naturally, plummeted."

That's right. Those girls were flying around me. I thought they could be my friends. But they weren't even aware of me and just floated there like mindless fish.

It wasn't long before I realized they weren't conscious. Even though I thought they'd notice me if I made them aware.

That's all I wanted. So why . . .

"Are you cold? You're shaking."

The woman's voice still felt like plastic. I hugged myself, unable to stop trembling.

"I'll ask one more thing. Why did you long for the sky even though you hate the outside world?"

The reason was probably because . . .

"Because the sky is endless. I thought that if I could keep going, fly far away, then I'd find a world I didn't hate."

Then came the question, asking if I had found it.

I couldn't stop trembling. It felt like someone was physically shaking me, and my eyelids were becoming hotter and hotter.

I nodded.

"Every night before I fell asleep, I feared that I wouldn't be able to wake the next morning. Wondering if I would be alive tomorrow terrified me. I knew that if I slept, I wouldn't have the strength to wake up.

"Every day was like walking a tightrope, and all I could do was dread death. But, on the other hand, that's what made me actually able to feel that I was alive. The smell of death was the only thing that filled my empty days. But I relied on that alone to live. . . . Because I'd shed my old self like a cast-off skin. I can only feel alive by staring death in the face."

That's right. That's why I yearned for death more than life. To fly, as far as I could. To leave this place. That was why.

"Did you take the boy from my place to keep you company?"

"No. I didn't even notice at the time. I was clinging onto life, wanting to fly while I was still alive. I thought that I could manage that with him."

". . . Shiki's just like you, then. In choosing Kokutō, there's still hope for her. Well, I guess there's nothing wrong with feeling alive through someone else."

Kokutō. Of course. That Shiki girl had come to take him back from me. His savior had been absolute death to me.

Still, I didn't regret it.

"That boy is a child. He's always looking into the sky. Always perfectly upright. That's why, if he felt like it, he could fly anywhere he wanted. Yes . . . I wanted him to take me with him."

My eyelids were hot. I didn't really understand, but I must have been crying.

Not from sorrow or anything like that . . . If I really could have gone off somewhere with that boy, it would have made me so happy. Because it would never happen—because it was a dream that could never come true—it was all the more beautiful, and it filled my eyes with tears.

That was the sole dream I had had in all these years.

"But Kokutō's not interested in the sky or anything like that," the woman said. ". . . Hmm. Someone who yearns for the sky, yet can't approach it. Ironic, isn't it?"

"It is. I've heard that human beings hold on to lots of things that they don't need. I just floated. I can't fly. . . . All I can manage to do is float there."

The burning vanished from my eyes. It would probably never happen again.

Because the only thing that governed me now was the shivering coursing down my back.

"Sorry to have disturbed you. This really is the final question: what are you going to do now? I don't mind treating the wound that Shiki gave you."

I didn't answer. I merely shook my head.

The woman, I think, frowned slightly.

". . . I see. There are two kinds of escape: fleeing aimlessly and fleeing with a goal in sight. As a rule, I'd call the former floating and the latter flying.

"Only you can decide which one of the two your view from above is. But if, by some chance, you choose based on feelings of guilt and self-reproach, then that's a mistake. We don't choose our path *because* of our sins; we carry our sins down the path we choose."

And then the woman left.

She hadn't told me her name the whole time she had been here, but I understood why. There would have been no point.

. . . That woman had doubtlessly known how I would end things. Because I could never fly. I could only float.

Because I was weak, I couldn't have done as she suggested.

That's why I couldn't beat this temptation.

Back then . . . the flash I felt in the instant my heart was pierced.

The overwhelming torrential pounding of death and the throbbing of life. I hadn't thought anything of it, but I still had that simple, important thing left to me.

What I had was death.

This fear gripping my spine. I had to crash into death headlong and, in doing so, feel the joy of being alive. All for the sake of every ounce of life I had—the life I'd shown nothing but disdain for up until now. Yet it would probably be impossible for me to go out to meet that nightlike death. Most probably, that intense, vivid last moment was beyond my reach. That death which went through like a needle, like a sword, like thunder.

And so, I tried to get as close to it as I could. No plans

came to mind, but I still had a few days left to think, so it would be okay. Besides, I had already decided on the method.

I hardly feel it necessary to say, but for my final moment... naturally, jumping to my death with a view from above would be wonderful.

▼▲▼

After the sun set, I left Miss Tōko's run-down building. Shiki's apartment was nearby, but my place was about twenty minutes away by train.

Perhaps because of her lack of sleep, Shiki plodded along with a wobbly gait, nestled up close to me.

"Is suicide okay, Mikiya?"

The question came out of the blue.

"... Hmm. I'm not sure," I replied. "If I'd been infected with a retrovirus that meant that just by my living, everyone in Tokyo would die, then I think I might kill myself to save everyone."

"What's that about? That's way too far-fetched to use as an example," Shiki said.

"No, it'll do," I insisted. "But I'd do it because I'm weak, though, I think. I wouldn't have the guts to survive and have everyone in Tokyo out for my blood, so that's why I'd kill myself. That way would be easier. It's the difference between a second's worth of bravery, and courage you have to keep up forever. Anyone can see which one's harder. It's a bit extreme, but death is easy, I reckon. It's just a matter of why you do it. But there will be times when the person in question feels a terrible urge to run away. I can't deny that or object to it. Because I'm a weak person, too."

... Yet, still, self-sacrifice of the sort I had just mentioned *is* justified and would probably be seen as heroic, even.

But no. It doesn't matter how just or how noble it is; choosing death is foolish. Maybe we have to live on, no matter how ugly or how wrong we are, to correct our mistakes. Live on and accept the consequences of our actions.

That's what takes real courage. I didn't think I could do that, so I shut my mouth and stopped talking so brashly.

". . . Er, anyway," I said, finishing up, "everyone's different in the end, aren't they?"

It was pretty halfhearted, as conclusions go. Shiki glanced at me doubtfully.

"But you're different," she said, like she'd seen straight through to my real feelings. Even though it sounded cold, there was a sort of warmth in her words, too. I felt kind of awkward and walked on silently through the town for a while.

The sounds of the main street came closer. The bright lights, the hustle and bustle, the lights of the busy cars, and the sound of engines. A surging crowd of people, a babble of noises.

The station was straight ahead, past the main street's mass of department stores.

Shiki stopped abruptly.

"Mikiya, stay over tonight."

"Huh? What's with this, all of a sudden?"

Shiki pulled me along by the hand as if to say "Just come on, dammit." . . . It *would* be much less of a hassle, since Shiki's apartment was so nearby, but I felt morally awkward about spending the night at her place.

"No, really, I don't have to," I protested. "There's nothing in your room anyway. It'll just be boring. Besides, don't you have stuff to do?"

I knew full well that she didn't.

I knew what I was talking about, and Shiki wouldn't have a chance to counterattack . . . or so I thought. But she looked at me sternly, like I was the bad guy, and voiced her objection.

"Strawberry."

"Huh?"

"Strawberry Häagen-Dazs. Two cartons. You brought them with you and just left them. Clean up your damn mess."

". . . Yeah, now that you mention it . . ."

They were still there. The presents I'd brought because I was feeling a bit hot on the way to Shiki's place last time. Still, I wonder why I'd brought something like that in the first place. It was almost September, after all.

Well, that was beside the point now, though. It seemed I would have to resign myself to it and just go along with her. Still, I was a little irritated and decided to offer some counteroffensive, at least.

Even though being sniped at like that annoyed me, I had a weakness around Shiki that meant I would just shut up and take it. And even though this showed my real feelings—a cry from the real Mikiya Kokutō—Shiki still wouldn't acknowledge them.

"Oh, all right then. I'll stay the night. But still, Shiki . . ."

Shiki looked at me questioningly, and I turned to her, a serious look on my face.

"Don't say 'Clean up your damn mess.' You should clean up your talk. You're a girl, you know."

Shiki was reacting to the word *girl*.

She turned her back on me angrily and muttered something like "I can talk however the hell I want, dammit."

▼▲▼

One day, I took the main street route home. This was unusual for me, just a whim of the moment. I had been walking, not thinking about anything in particular, down the street—that street whose buildings I was so tired of looking at—when someone fell from above.

I hardly even had a chance to hear it. The muffled splattering sound.

But it was obvious: someone had fallen from one of the buildings above ... and was now dead.

Deepest crimson gushed down the asphalt. Only the long black hair still retained its former appearance. Thin, fragile, white-looking limbs. And a lifeless, smashed face. This series of images was like pressed flowers, trapped flat between the old pages of a book. I guess. Probably.

Only because the corpse, its neck twisted into a fetal position, looked to me like a folded lily.

I knew who the person was.

In the end, *Hypnos,* or sleep, had, after all, become *Thanatos* ... death.

Ignoring the gathering crowd of onlookers, I was walking away when I heard a pattering sound, and Azaka caught up with me.

"That was a jumping suicide, wasn't it, Miss Tōko?"

"Yeah, looks like it," I replied vaguely. To be honest, I didn't really have any interest.

Whatever the victim's decision had been, a suicide was only treated as a suicide in the end.

That girl's final act of will hadn't been summed up by the word *fly,* or even *float,* but rather *fall.* The only thing in that act had been vain futility. There was no need for me to pay it any attention.

"I heard there were a lot last year," said Azaka. "Maybe suicide's coming back into fashion? But I don't understand people who kill themselves. Do you, Miss Tōko?"

I nodded another vague "yes."

I looked up at the sky and answered, as though gazing at an impossible vision.

"There's no meaning in suicide. She probably just couldn't fly today. That's all."

▲▽▲▽

H PEOPLE
An Evolving World

Kozy Watanabe

Illustration by TAGRO
Translated by Paul Johnson

Faust has found an appreciative audience among Japan's manga, anime, and video game otaku (*otaku* = extremely devoted fans). It has done so by creating new, exciting fiction that's deeply influenced by otaku pop-culture tastes. But in "H People," it addresses a social issue important to otaku: the *hikikomori* phenomenon.

Hikikomori is a type of acute social withdrawal, and the Japanese term refers both to the condition and the person suffering from the condition. A *hikikomori*, for a variety of personal and emotional reasons, isolates himself completely from the world, often refusing not only to leave his home, but even his own bedroom, for periods ranging from months to years. The condition has been reported in ever-increasing numbers in Japan, though actual estimates have varied, from hundreds of thousands to one million—or one percent of Japan's population. *Hikikomori* are often heavy consumers of media such as anime and video games, with which they fill the time they spend wholly isolated from society. "H People" vividly describes the emotional state of a *hikikomori*.

The author, Kozy Watanabe, was born in 1962. A highly active novelist and writer, as well as one of video game company GTV's major talents, Watanabe is a senior figure among gaming generations and has many TV appearances under his belt. His most popular works include *Kaijin 21 Seiki Nakano Broadway Tantei Yuu & Ai* and *IKILL*.

Manga artist TAGRO provided the illustrations. His books include *Uchuu Chintai Sarga Sou* (*Square Enix*). TAGRO's works often feature depictions of twisted youth —which has enabled him to seize hold of a devoted fanbase.

▲▼▲▼▲

During the time that I've been living with the night as my daytime, stepping outside has become a real trauma. Recently, it's worsened to the point where just thinking about going outside makes me feel sick.

The doctor whom my parents took me to see didn't say the word *illness*. He did say that if I was to continue this way, then I was going to become a genuine *hikikomori*. Hearing this just made me want to go out even less.

I decided to try not to think about what other people say and to pull myself together. I have a lot of time anyway.

First, I wondered why I was all right in my own room but the outside world was so scary.

I knew the reason. The only things in my room are my things. I know everything, and there is nothing unnecessary to my day-to-day life. The desk, the chair, the bookcase, the futon. My books, my magazines, my videos. Even the comics spread across my floor. Every single object has meaning to me. No one else comes in, and I won't allow it to be cleaned.

Next, I wondered why I couldn't go outside yet I still loved to walk around game worlds.

The answer to that was clear to me, too. The thing with a video game is that the graphics may be amazing and the sound effects great, but nevertheless, it isn't real. It's virtual. Even in a superb video game, there are no unnecessary things in that world. Everything has meaning and use. Buildings, roads, robots. If it doesn't need to change, then a wall is a wall, a bed is a bed, and they all look the same. With each individual object, you can distinguish at a glance, whether you can touch it or not, whether it is friend or foe. Only the essential points stand out. So the game world had become an extension of my mind.

In contrast to that is the outside world, the real world. Even if it has no use, the features of a town are confusing and people's appearances and actions haphazard. Thus, I can't help but be surprised and worried by all the things that have nothing to do with me.

Following this train of thought, I wanted to find a solution.

I have a monitor in the shape of a pair of glasses, where the lens part is in fact a display. It makes the real world in front of my eyes look more like a CG. Fish swim in the sky and fairies dance. And the faces of the people I see are superimposed with those of idols.

Because it has a built-in GPS that can calculate my current position, when I turn my head and the world moves, the CG also moves with it.

I can walk around now, wearing my glasses. The real world is painted over by the CG.

I say CG, but it will be painted completely white. If I look at anything undesirable, anything that has no value to me, then it's blanked out.

For example, when I'm walking down the street and I accidentally look at a group of trees or a bulletin board, or perhaps I enter a building that has no potential for me to do anything there—anything like that is painted over so nothing but a silhouette remains. It works with people, too. People I don't know have no features. However, people with whom there is a possibility for me to get acquainted, such as rich people with salaries of over thirty million yen a year and unmarried women under the age of twenty-two, are not blanked out.

On a daily basis, the world is painted over, becoming whiter and whiter. Only things of value and people of value are in color. It's comfortable.

What about when you are taking lots of time off from school and you bump into a teacher on the street? In that case, he would be exactly the same. In other words, everyone would be the same. There's no need to distinguish, so "Prof." will be written on the teacher's white face.

Also, in a game, enemy characters with the same skills use the same CG. That way, you don't get confused and the game is easier to play.

Even with people you know, those over sixty years old are all bundled in as "old people," which is all you need to pick them out. Same with women under twenty-two—they only need to be divided into two types: the beautiful and the ugly.

In this way, using these glasses improves the world, and I can enjoy walking outside again. I don't see things that frustrate me. Irritating people don't try to talk to me. They might actually talk to me, but I will just ignore them, so everything is fine.

My world is becoming so much whiter and simpler.

This world began with chaos and confusion. From that point, to progress is to move toward the simple. The end of civilization will probably prove that we are but one mathematical phrase in the whole of the universe.

By using these glasses as an external compressor, I have modified my mind. I am evolving. The parts that are white are what I have already completed.

I wonder if the world wasn't perfectly white right when I was born and was just a baby. Perhaps it was as information dirtied this blank page that I became confused.

I now spend my days happily. Everything around me is white. It's such a beautiful world. I'm so happy.

Oh? Some white, featureless thing is next to me. It looks like it wants to say something.

"Can you see me? Hey, can you hear what I'm saying?"

I ignore it. Because I know that it has nothing meaningful to say to me.

There is another featureless thing now. It looks like they're talking.

But, anyway, none of that matters to me. Paying attention to that sort of occurrence only gets in the way of higher thoughts.

"You know, he really can't see us. He looks well, he's not blind, and his ears seem to hear. I mean, he can pick out the cute girls when he's walking about and actually follows after them."

"There must be something wrong with him. . . . The old man must just be senile."

YABAI DE SHOW

Ryusui Seiryôin
Translated by Paul Johnson

This story, though brief, presented one of the toughest translation challenges in the *Faust* anthology. Its humor depends on the use of the common Japanese slang word *yabai*, which is both the main character's name and a word used heavily in dialogue. Though *yabai* has been in use for a long time as an adjective meaning "bad" or "dangerous," just as with the American words "bad" or "wicked," it has also come to mean just its opposite—"great" or "awesome." The story puns constantly on the term *yabai*, which we've rendered as "bad" here.

Ryusui Seiryôin was born in 1974. He surprised the Japanese literary world in 1996 when his debut work *Cosmic Sekimatsu Tantei Shinwa* won the *2nd Mephisto Award*. His twelve-month novel serialization *Perfect World* reached its grand conclusion in 2007.

▲▼▲▼

Masashi Yabai, who was running a little late for his meeting with Seiryôin, entered the café and with a smile on his face declared, "Today is gonna be bad again!" Because this sort of thing happened all the time, the waitress laughed. It was a small shop with five seats at the counter and two booths, so any conversation could be clearly overheard.

Master: "Yabai, what's so bad about today?"

清流院流水の
BATTLE 01
挑戦者 北海道 甲田和弘

Yabai: "C'mon, Ryu P, stop looking at me with those bloodshot eyes. You look so serious. I can't relax like this. . . . Waitress, tea please."

Of course, Masashi Yabai was probably not his real name. Likewise, Seiryôin Ryûsui would go by the name of "Ryu P" in front of Yabai. Neither of them knew the other's real name.

▼▲▼

Yabai sat down opposite Ryu P and looked at the first photo that was on the table. "This is pretty bad, huh . . .", he said, looking delighted. This was a photo that Ryu P himself thought was pretty bad. They didn't mind if they quarreled. Even their greetings were that way. They would always jump into battle straightaway.

Ryu P: "You think this one is pretty bad, too, eh?"

Yabai: "The one where Mr. Bear is going to gobble up Mr. Crab? Think of it from Mr. Crab's perspective! It doesn't get much worse than this!"

Ryu P: "Mr. Crab . . . You know he's not real, right?"

Yabai: "Ryu P, are you blind? The dynamics of this picture could not be faked! The only real things are Mr. Crab and Mr. Bear. The rest are just miniatures."

> This is bad. . . .

Just then, with strange timing, Ryu P's phone rang. His ringtone ... was the song from a commercial for the crab cuisine restaurant Crab Crazy. The "Crab Palace" in the picture was also a crab cuisine restaurant.

When Yabai heard the ringtone, his eyes sparkled.

Yabai: "The age-old battle between the monkey and the crab. You would have thought we, who evolved from monkeys, could understand crabs by now. . . . Ryu P, do you eat crab?"

It seemed that the conversation had taken a bad turn. To stop Yabai's delusions would be tantamount to admitting defeat. As he feared, today he would lose yet again. . . . Ryu P rolled his eyes.

But the next photo was powerful. With that photo, just maybe . . .

YÛYA SATÔ'S COUNSELING SESSION

Yûya Satô

Illustrations by Icco Sasai
Translated by Paul Johnson

The Japanese edition of the *Faust* anthology is what's called in Japan a "mook"—a combination magazine and book. In the fashion of a magazine, it has regular features, including a series of "counseling sessions," which are something like the advice columns that are so commonly found in magazines. Except that *Faust* is no ordinary magazine, and so it plays with the ordinary magazine conventions. This "counseling session," written by the popular novelist Yûya Satô, is more of a conversation between the author and himself than between a counselor and his readers. This hugely self-referential piece also includes numerous references to the world of *Faust* and its publisher, Kodansha. For example, the author wishes for the popularity of NISIOISIN, a superstar novelist heavily associated with *Faust* and Kodansha.

Yuya Sato's debut work *Flicker Shiki—Kagami Kimihiko ni Uttetsuke no Satsujin* won the 21st Mephisto Award. After that, Kodansha Novels published his Kagami-ke Saga series, which continued on from his debut story. With that, he gained enthusiastic support from other young readers born in the 1980s. His story *1000 no Shousetsu to Bugbeared* then won the 20th Yukio Mishima Award. He is the representative author of Japan's "lost generation"—youth who have become so immersed in virtual reality that true reality becomes too terrifying.

This is not illustrator Icco Sasai's first collaboration with Yuya Sato; he also produced the artwork for Yuya Sato's Kagami-ke Saga series.

▲▽▲▽▲

I want a job.
I want to eat rice.

I want to eat a lot of rice.

Nice to meet you. I am Yûya Satô, age twenty-two, and I live alongside the Chuo line, where all the dodgy types hang out. My favorite word is *upstart,* and my least favorite word is *entertainment.* My main hobby is playing the cell phone version of Tetris. At the moment, my goal is to receive a fan letter with a photo attached. I aspire to be a Docomo subscriber. In the future, I want to be a rock musician. I've entered the National Health Insurance program, but the monthly charges are not cheap, so if I don't work, then I'll use up all my savings.

The other day, I was headed toward Shibuya, and with the awkward gait of a newborn pony, I climbed Dogenzaka. I was going to a certain studio. There I inspected the dubbing of a certain PC game that was being made by N-san, to whom I owe a lot. Thinking to myself that being a voice actor must be difficult and that it wasn't just me who was working hard, I made a resolution that tomorrow I would try harder. As I was thinking this, I glanced at the remaining money in my wallet and heard a voice in my mind saying, "There is no tomorrow." Lost in gloom, I sulked in bed.

---

*Docomo Known in Japan for being an expensive cell phone service.
*Dogenzaka An area in Shibuya.

Well, then, in this volume of *Faust*, the exciting hikikomori author has written an article in which he answers a reader's question. Yes, it's counseling! Straightforward, cheerful, with cruel and effective words, he turns those readers who were lost and stumbling toward life's dead ends onto the correct path. Wow . . . Sounds so cool, doesn't it?

When I was leading an ordinary life, I wouldn't have been able do that kind of work. However, now I'm an author. (Why are you laughing?) Now I'm qualified to help my readers. I can take letters from young boys who've made a mistake and young girls whose makeup is running from their tears. "Timid youth! Take the north-northwest road!" is the kind of helpful and appropriate advice I will give. And my readers who will be reading far too much into it will go "I knew that Yûya Satô would release us from all our pain with a single utterance!" "A problem that has plagued me for years, clear in a moment!" "Yûya Satô is a genius!" they will shout.

Thank you for the food!

While imagining the masses hanging on my every word, I brought up my plan for a "Yûya Satô Counseling Session" to that dark man Ota-san (even the editor in chief, even *Faust*'s editor, and even that Abe Futoshi do not want anything to do with him), during a phone call that came in the middle of the night when I should have been sound asleep.

And so: "What? No one is going to write to you about their problems. That's not going to work." His reply was underlined with a cruel snigger, and my wonderful plans were crushed in an instant.

When I tried to protest: "How about the readers solve your problems instead? Ha-ha! Yes, that's a good idea. Now that would be interesting! Instead of "Yûya Satô's Counseling Session," "Counseling for Yûya Satô" would be better! That is brilliant. Well, then!"

After burbling my new orders, he hung up. Somehow the very opposite of my plan had been adopted. I gripped the phone, which was emitting that hateful dial tone. Still thinking of the sadness and the bitterness and that imbecilic laugh, I remembered a lesson I had once learned: yesterday's enemy is today's enemy.

Not reader asking author, but author asking reader. That is the untold story behind the birth of "Yûya Satô's Counseling Session." A twist on the norm, a world's first (I have no proof to back up this statement), started mysteriously and rather pathetically.

However, Ota-san's decision might not have been wrong. In a counseling session, I need some good phrases to say. A good example would be that line from Kenzô Kitakata.

Yes.

Go to a Soapland.

---

*Ota-san Katsushi Ota, the editor of *Faust*.
*Soapland Similar to a Turkish bath but basically a brothel.

Q. Because of "restructuring," I lost my job, and now I can't pay back the loan on my house.
A. Go to a Soapland.
Q. I haven't had a conversation with my family for over half a year now.
A. Go to a Soapland.

Wow! Those are the simple, magic words that would fix any situation. That was a real catchphrase. However, I don't have one. No matter how hard I try, all I have is "Go to Tokyo!"

Q. Because of "restructuring," I lost my job, and now I can't pay back the loan on my house.
A. Go to Tokyo!
Q. I haven't had a conversation with my family for over half a year now.
A. Go to Tokyo!

I don't understand.

Well, I suppose that the meaning behind "Go to a Soapland" isn't clear either, but in those words there is a strange power and a forward-looking nature. In the faces of the men who have come from a Soapland, I bet, without exception, that there is a smile on every one of their faces because there they found a definite hope. It's so easy to have that image in your mind. But my "Go to Tokyo" just sounds like an escape route. Anyway, the place that I escaped to was even darker than where I started.

Oh, that's right, he had another phrase.
That was it.
Read my book.

Q. Because of "restructuring," I lost my job, and now I can't pay back the loan on my house.

A. Read my book.
Q. I haven't had a conversation with my family for over half a year now.
A. Read my book.

This is the same kind of reply as "Go to a Soapland," in that it doesn't really count as advice exactly. It's a little surreal. It's like asking what the sound of one hand clapping is. If it were a celebrity, it would be Itao. But then again, the truth is that I'm oddly happy with that. I wonder how he does it?

. . . Even so.

Read my book.

There is something fiery about those words. The beauty of the overflowing passion of a man. Still, "Read my book" hasn't got quite the bite that Basara Nekki did, does it? Read my book. . . . Ho ho ho, read my book. Read my book, read my book, read my book, read my book, read my book, read my book, read my booooook!!! You Quail idiot! You 8 byte! You who are so satisfied with munching potato chips while you read XX. You who are happy with chugging down a can of alcohol while you read XX. You XXX who made out that I didn't even exist! READ MY BOOK!

Okay. I'm calm again.

Anyway, I guess it's possible you don't even own my book in the first place.

Sigh . . . I think being a counselor would have suited me. A dry voice, a hunched back, umm . . . I have the perfect appearance. Yes, I would have been really good. And also, I'd make the readers laugh, they would make fun of me, they would snigger, and they would love me, their Yuyatan. (That's my pet name, apparently. Thank you, channel 2.) A

Basara Nekki A character from the anime *Macross 7*.

born victim. I would be able to empathize with them. Destined to be a joke until I die. At least, be ready.

However, counseling . . . is not something to be proud of. (A preamble is something to be proud of.) I've never come completely clean to anyone. The problems that normally come up during counseling like love, friendship, sex, the future, money . . . I've never talked to anyone about that stuff.

I'm just not the kind of person who would think about going to counseling.

So, I'm a little embarrassed about it.

For example (well, of course it's an example, but a real real example), even though I really, really like Y-chan, she hasn't even remotely glanced in my direction, so if I had asked someone about it, then people would find out that I like Y-chan.

Here's another example. . . . When I was in my early twenties, my hair started to get very thin. I tried various kinds of hair-growth products, but none worked. If I told people that I counted the number of hairs left on my pillow, then people would know that I was worried about losing my hair.

That would be so embarrassing! There's no way I could do it!

I don't attract attention from anyone, but I make a special effort for people to look at me and have a good opinion of me. When I pass cute girls on the street, I don't slouch. When I'm talking to friends, then I strain to use difficult words. When I'm wearing a three thousand–yen shirt, I say that it cost five thousand yen. I dress correctly even when I'm only going to the convenience store. That's the kind of person I am, so how could I ask for help from anyone else?

Come on!

Why me?

I'm getting mad!

To tell friends and lovers your worries . . . Is it really that easy for you lot to tell people your problems? Is there any value in it? Do you use talking over your worries as part of a communication tool? No . . . To say it straight out, I'm jealous of you.

But, if you never speak of your fears, your friendship will never evolve; thus, I want to do my best and come clean. Of course, I'm going to avoid the sort of problems that an author faces. The great majority of readers won't have heard of me, and I'm sure that this is the first time that most of you have come into contact with one of my articles.

I have confidence.

I don't sell very well. It was no mistake that I outright won the "Negative earnings battle of those published in *Faust*." I won first prize by a large margin.

Thinking about it . . . when I was in kindergarten, I remember singing "Even though I'm the worst, I'm in first place." I still remember it.

I want work.

I want to eat rice.

I . . . I want to write in *Mephisto*. Let me do a JDC tribute. At the very least, a few reprints would mean that joy would conquer sadness. Kodansha novels? It has such a sweet ring to it. Listen to me, please. You know, it might be the result of no sleep, but recently, I've been hearing things. "They're out to get you. They're out to get you." The sound of my dead grandmother in my ear twenty-four hours a day . . . Oh, shut up! You're so annoying! Haven't I told you before?! Yes, the newspaper man is coming to kill me. Because I found a gap in the drawers, then Kaori's curse is on me. It's 4:00 A.M. now. When I give myself a paper cut with the vegetable grater, then I've done it. Ah, I forgot to watch *Tomorrow's Nadja*! I don't have a television at home, but I'm always there in spirit.

---

*Mephisto A Japanese literary journal published by Kodansha.

So now I feel like a lost soul. I want a little of NISIOISIN's popularity. I like Nishio, who although asking for a plate of cheese for some reason, only eats crackers with no cheese for some reason.

Here we go.

▼▲▼

My problem is: What should I do to make the quality of my camera picture better?

▲▼▲▼

TATSUHIKO TAKIMOTO'S GURU GURU COUNSELING SESSION

Tatsuhiko Takimoto

Illustrations by Chizu Hashii
Translated by Paul Johnson

In another counseling session piece—a feature similar to the preceding selection—Tatsuhiko Takimoto once again addresses the *hikikomori* phenomenon. This is certainly an appropriate topic for novelist Takimoto to address: His most popular book is *Welcome to the N.H.K.*, a series which started publication online in 2001 and addressed the voiceless suffering of the *hikikomori*.

The phrase *guru guru* in the title means to "spin, twirl, or go round and round," and describes the dazzling dizziness a reader might feel while navigating this giddily humorous story. But for all its humor, the story ends with a piece of advice useful not only to *hikikomori*, but to anyone with unfulfilled dreams.

Takimoto was born in 1978. His debut *Negative Happy Chainsaw Edge*, was a breakthrough success, but he achieved a new level of popularity with *Welcome to the N.H.K.*, which has been adapted into popular anime and manga versions.

Illustrator Chizu Hashii's manga serialization of *Soshite Gonin ga Inakunaru* (by writer Kaoru Hayamine), is running in the Japanese version of *Faust*. He also worked on illustrations for the novel version from Kodansha's novel arm. He was the character designer for the anime *BLOOD+*, and *Tantei Gishiki*—the story on which he collaborated with Ryusui Seiryôin and Eiji Otsuka—is currently ongoing in monthly *Shonen Ace*. His characters are full of personality, and have really taken off with readers. Hashii's website address is http://www.interq.or.jp/ol/chizu.

▲▼▲▼

Tatsuhiko Takimoto's Guru Guru Counseling Session

"I've become a hikikomori. What should I do?"

"Get yourself together! You're just worrying about nothing. If you have that much free time, then just go out and get some fresh air!"

It'd be nice if the article could be over with that outburst, but of course, the problem isn't that simple. The fact is that "hikikomori" have become a symbol of our troubled modern society.

To understand why someone would be afraid of going outside is not easy. Of course, the answer is not to go start using the sex industry. I know many examples of people who have become spiritually and financially ruined by consumer goods.

Therefore, because I understand all the subtleties of life, I must offer some useful advice regarding this problem.

I called Asuka, the helper inside my head, with the mysterious transceiver in my brain.

In a few moments, she appeared in a sailor uniform. It looked like she had just come home from school.

Looking at the countless books on hikikomori that were on the desk, she said, "Huh, what is this? What's wrong with being a hikikomori? It seems pretty popular these days. As long as you have enough money to live. You should just tell them something like they're lowlifes and should go and get a job! Tee-hee."

. . . I clenched my fists. It isn't that simple. It just isn't. For her not to understand how other people feel and just dub them all "lowlifes" even though she knew nothing about them. I grabbed her thin white neck. . . .

"Ngh . . . What are you doing?!"

Ignoring her, I started reading the beginning of the show to the camera.

"Do you have worries in your life? But you are so beautiful. Why don't you tell me your worries? If we put our heads together, then we're bound to come up with a good answer. Now the long-awaited start of *How Do You Live?* brought to you by Tatsuhiko Takimoto and his assistant, Asuka. . . . Woah!"

A spray of blood hit the TV camera. At some point, Asuka had grabbed a small knife in her right hand. My assistant, Asuka, was a fierce girl.

"Summoning me all of a sudden and then trying to strangle me, what the hell do you think you're doing?!"

"Shh, they've started rolling. Why don't you put down the knife and read us the problem that came in from a reader? Call me Dr. Takimoto, and after that fetch a bandage for my forehead."

". . ."

Asuka noticed the presence of the camera. She feigned a cool expression and then read the letter out loud that I had handed to her.

The rest is a summary.

> Through Tatsuhiko Takimoto's appearance, not to mention the no-good people who have appeared on NHK, some unfair rumors about the possibility of living on royalties have become topics of conversation between my parents.
>
> Because of those annoying rumors, their expectations of me rose daily and I quit technical college. I'm now an unemployed idiot who locks himself away in a small room in my parents' house. My parents retired this year, which has caused more problems. There is nothing scarier than silent pressure. . . .
>
> I used to have a dream about making films. However, the script that I wrote, in which thousands of hikikomori return to society in only three weeks, was nothing more than amateurish scribblings ripped off from the plot of *Yomigaeru.*
>
> I'm most happy when I'm dreaming of appearing on NHK. . . .
>
> And so, what should people who are locking themselves up in their rooms for their whole lives to escape reality do? Please tell me how idiots can face the real world.
>
> —K.T., Fukushima Prefecture

"I see. . . ."

I tried to think of something that would ring true with him.

Something like "What's the matter with being a hikikomori?" or "Loneliness has value" was too superficial. On the

---

*NHK Japanese television station.
*Yomigaeru A 2002 Japanese film in which the dead come back to life.

other hand, "Get a job" or "Join a support group" was not going to be supportive in the slightest. The advice I was aiming for was basic advice that would shoot straight to the essence of the matter. Enlightenment that would with very little effort change the world as we know it, much as Copernicus did. Anyway, my knowledge and experience only pertained to giving realistic advice. To be honest, I could really relate to his problem.

"I can see the core of this problem right away. Do you understand it, Asuka?"

"... In other words, he wants us to tell him how he can stop locking himself away in his room and go outside again?"

While the camera wasn't on her, Asuka checked that her hair was in place.

I snorted.

"You really are a bimbo. To you, his story looks so simple, doesn't it? The root of the problem is his uncertainty regarding his own problem. See, look at this. In two whole pages, he doesn't ask one real question. Of course, he has 'My dream of making films was ripped apart' and 'I'm a hikikomori.' On top of that, his parents have retired, so things are financially difficult. But the writer doesn't take any kind of stance whatsoever. He doesn't ask, 'Tell me a way to escape being a hikikomori.' Or 'Help me find the will to follow my dreams.' He stops short of asking practical questions. It is this indefiniteness of 'What should I be doing now?' that is keeping him going. I'm very sure of this."

"... So, what difference does it make?"

"You don't get it. This needs specific advice. This beautifully written letter may be taken in jest and speaks of the writer's high intelligence, but it doesn't actually ask for advice. At the very end, it does ask how he can face the real world again, but even this question sounds just too wishy-washy, it feels too hollow. Perhaps he doesn't really want to know the answer. To make a long story short, he doesn't have a problem that other people can help him with."

"Wh-what? . . . But this is already over, then. . . ."

"Please don't get the wrong idea. Of course, it is upsetting him. But it's something that just can't be expressed. Without being able to grasp an idea himself of what is causing him this angst, then neither I nor anyone else will be able to help him."

". . . It's not just him locking himself away?"

How do I live?

"You are an idiot. That's the opinion of a bimbo. First, he is stressed, and the result of this stress is that he developed an illness in which he locks himself away. Without first dealing with the stress that is at the root of this, then even if he manages to stop being a hikikomori, he will still not be properly happy."

"So, what is the stress at the root of it?"

"As I've been saying, we don't know! If we knew, then there wouldn't be a problem! He doesn't know. I don't know. No one knows!"

". . ."

Asuka rubbed her temples and thought for a while.

"Umm, let me get this straight, what you're saying."

"Call me Dr. Takimoto!"

"What you're saying is that the reason for him locking himself in his room is that he has stress at the root of it all. And that this stress cannot be understood by him or by anyone else?"

"That's right." I crossed my arms and gave a firm nod.

"In that case, the conclusion is that he's doomed forever?"

"That's right." I crossed my arms and gave a firm nod.

Asuka started kicking down the three video cameras in order.

"I'm going home."

"Wait a minute, if you go, then . . ."

"Let go of me! I don't need any more of your nonsense! There is absolutely no reason why I should be working this ridiculous, low-grade counseling service! Who the hell thought of this stupid idea anyway?! You've all got something wrong upstairs!"

As Asuka headed for the door yelling those ridiculous things, I tackled her.

"No, I can't let you go home!"

Asuka, who had been knocked to the floor, didn't hesitate to try thrusting her index and middle fingers into my eye sockets. I had predicted this. I pushed her hands away and started to cry on her chest.

"If you go, then who will help me? Without you, I'll be doomed forever! Please, Asuka, help me!"

I begged her like that. She alone was the spider's thread. There was no way she would run off. . . .

But when I looked, I saw the fallen Asuka's open eyes looking up at me.

". . . Let me go. I hit my head."

She pushed me away and stood up. Behind her back, she took hold of the doorknob.

"You want my help that bad?"

She really was a kind girl. I nodded.

The spider's thread A reference to Ryūnosuke Akutagawa's story "The Spider's Thread." In the story the soul of a criminal is led to paradise by a spider's thread.

"Then, what do you want me to do?"

"... I don't know. I don't understand what the problem is."

"It doesn't matter if you understand or not. Just say what you're thinking."

"It's just . . . It's just, I'm scared. I don't have any kind of enthusiasm. The worry and the lethargy mean I'm idle and ambiguous, and it's rubbing away all my emotion. Recently, I don't even know what I've been thinking. So I can't give advice to other people. I rack my brains and think of an answer, but all of it sounds like crap and I just can't write. 'Get out,' 'Get a job,' all of these opinions. Are all of them correct, or are all of them wrong? However hard I try to think of some concrete advice, my mind wanders after five minutes and I'm thinking of another idea, and they all seem right. I just can't settle on one opinion. I can think of so many interpretations and explanations. An intellectual explanation, a cultural explanation, a scientific explanation, a religious explanation, I just go from one to the other...."

Hikikomori and the associated deterioration of the psyche is the reason for family lifestyles' becoming strange. Before anything else, the parent-child relationship is primary, so we should correct that first. Let's remember the traumatic memories and then deal with them. But, above all else, you need to look after your body. It's your primary asset. If you're carrying extra fat, then you're going to tire easily, your hormones will be unbalanced, and you'll become depressed. So, in other words, the reason for hikikomori is fat. Of course, even if you have your health, if you don't have life goals, then you won't enjoy each day of your life. At the most, you start doing temp work and spend your days like that. So let us work on building up concrete dreams. But if you aim for the far future, then your hard-working lifestyle will become a source of nihilism. Look to the present. If you don't give your hundred percent to the present, then peace will not come to you. This doesn't mean you should only be living in the pleasure of the moment. It is the transpersonal transcendence of the flow of consciousness living in the lie that is time. Maybe you should go and train at a temple or attend some kind of workshop. Recently, I've heard that there has been systematic research into "enlightenment" and "faith experiences." According to William James's *The Varieties of Religious Experience,* even people who have spent every day until they die depressed can gain the saving grace of God. In that instance, they can achieve happiness and spend the rest of their days on this earth happy.

I screamed, "G-GOD HELP ME! . . . But it's still so childish. After thinking about it so hard, I've come up with so many ideas. And I don't think any of them are quite right. They're all so worthless. No, it isn't that they're worthless. . . . In the end, fatigue . . . fruitless effort . . . meaningless . . . Damn, I'm so tired. If I look after myself, then I'll get better. I'll take a hot bath, and I'll get better. . . . I'm sorry to worry you. You can go home now."

". . . Right. I'm going."

"NO! I can't let you go!"

"What is this?!"

"Pl-please. Help me. . . . I can't . . . not like this . . . A-argh . . ."

I clung to Asuka and cried. I pushed my face into her ample chest and cried.

Surprisingly, Asuka didn't jump away. She gently patted my back. I looked up, and Asuka was looking at me with a face full of rage and hatred of me.

". . . Satisfied? Stop this pretend crying now."

I did as she said.

"I'm going to tell you this one thing. It's very simple. With just this, you'll be able to overcome this miserable feeling. I think you should just cheer up."

Having said such a ridiculous line, Asuka took my hand. Her hand was so warm.

". . . Do you understand why? It doesn't matter if it's your work or a person—as long as you love something from the bottom of your heart, then you'll soon start to feel better. . . . But whether you love something or whether you at some point fall in love with someone, that's fate. It's not something you can choose even if you want to. Even so, fate is a funny thing. So I guess it doesn't make for good advice. But you'll be happy."

" . . . ?"

Asuka grinned mischievously.

"If you like me."

" . . . ??"

She was right.

And I was saved.

At some point, with the voice of Kenji Ozawa playing in my room, my eyes overflowed with warm tears.

"Someday I'll live with someone loving me and someone I love back."

It was such a simple thing after all. . . .

▲▽▲▽▲

So, I beg you.

Even if it is just this one thing. Find someone whom you can really like from the bottom of your heart. Find someone with whom you know it's the real thing and then jump straight for it. And then you will understand that the bad feeling and powerlessness that have bound you were all just a

---

*Kenji Ozawa Japanese musician born in 1968.

delusion you created yourself. And you will be able to say that in this world, love is the only thing that exists.

Because of that, you will be able to face the real world head-on. There is no need now for you to spend your time meaninglessly. Pick yourself up and go out to find your destiny.

APPROACHING TWENTY YEARS OF OTAKU

Kaichiroō Morikawa

Illustration by the author
Translated by Paul Johnson

The word *otaku* has become common currency among American manga and anime fans, who have developed their own version of otaku culture. Here, the term specifically refers to fans of Japanese anime and manga, and is often brandished with pride, but in Japan, the term carries a lot more cultural baggage.

Though it's also an honorific second-person pronoun, used as a slang term, the word *otaku* in Japanese broadly refers to a person with any obsessively pursued interest. That interest can be a hobby or a topic, ranging from music to manga to martial arts to computer games and so on. But in referring to otaku culture, the term is more strictly limited to obsessive fans of a certain kind of pop culture (manga, anime, video games, etc.). This essay explores the evolution of this term, and the subculture it represents, since the word first acquired this particular usage in Japan roughly twenty years ago.

Kaichiro Morikawa was born in 1971. His book *Shuto no Tanjou-Moeru Toshi Akihabara* is an architectural account of how Akihabara—the Tokyo neighborhood that's become the unofficial headquarters of otaku culture—came into existence. He made the news in 2004 when he served as producer for the *Venezia Biennale* Japan Homes exhibition. He was the youngest person ever to serve as commissioner.

▲▽▲▽

Spirited Away has won an Academy Award.

Ten years ago, if you were an adult who played video games or watched anime, you had all the qualifications you needed to be an otaku. However, watching *Spirited Away* or owning a PlayStation 2 is just not enough anymore to get you scorned as an otaku. Now the image of the otaku has shifted: today, it implies the kind of person who's interested in *moe* and *bishōjo*. What does this shift mean?

If otaku were just a word for fans of anime and video games, then even as the worldwide recognition for the things that otaku loved increased, their love shouldn't diminish. Moreover, as the popularity of these things increased, then wouldn't the status of the otaku who were raised on them increase? This has not been the case.

As soon as anime, manga, and video games gained mainstream popularity, otaku started to create subcultures within manga, anime, and video game fandom that are even more "incorrect" to enjoy, such as *yaoi, moe* manga and anime, *bishōjo* games (dating sims featuring beautiful girls, some-

---

*Bishōjo games Computer games in which the focus is on interaction with beautiful girls, often with romantic seduction and sometimes pornographic content.

times focused on romance, and sometimes pornographic), and *eroge* (erotic video games). In the last ten years, bookstores have started to stock more and more of this "incorrect" material, such as bishōjo manga, *eroge* magazines, *moe* magazines, and *shonen-ai* (boys' love) novels.

The Trend of Otaku toward the "Incorrect"

When we call this material "incorrect," we do not mean to say it is of low quality. It is the extreme obsession with this material that is socially incorrect.

Adult men who spend large sums on *moe* anime artwork and *eroge*. Men who may even get upset and cry over the romantic stories in them. From a woman's perspective, this behavior is only a step away from an unhealthy interest in adult videos. But the trend has been leaning toward this incorrect material; otaku continue to shy away from science fiction and anime and lean instead toward *moe* and *eroge*. The development of these various genres has allowed us to understand the true personality of an otaku.

If it really is true that otaku enjoy anime, fully knowing that their interest is incorrect and yet still persisting in their enjoyment, then we can conclude that otaku enjoy anime precisely because it is incorrect to do so. In other words, otaku are not interested in anime and video games for their own sake but because it's something they should not be interested in. Putting the issue this way makes the otaku sound like a counterculture, in opposition to the mainstream culture. However, there's a subtle distinction between otaku culture and the "Yankee" subculture: the otaku culture lacks a rebellious quality.

To be a rebel is cool. And the world's obsession with cool and fashionable beauty has caused otaku to fear that, after this invasion of their space, they will be lost. Hence, otaku have headed toward "incorrect" materials. Or these materials satisfy their desires as they try to become one with eternity. From *Yamato yo towa* and *Eien ni Amuro* to *Kimi ga Nozomu Eien,* it would appear that otaku have a desire for the eternal that the "incorrect" movement supports.

Otaku and Japan

If we accept the popular notion that it was Akio Nakamori in *Manga Burikko*'s June 1983 issue who first coined the term, then the slang term *otaku* is approaching its twentieth anniversary. If we count from August 1989, when the word truly came into common usage with the capture of Tsutomu Miyazaki, then it has been fourteen years. Since then, a lot of new words have been created to label particular movements—Goths, Happy, New Man, Strawberry Club, Amuro fashion, Gal fashion—but the majority have disappeared from usage. However, even as the decades march on, the word *otaku* is still with us. The thing is, the idea of the otaku has had more staying power than its contrasting figure, the "New Man." There is clearly something more permanent in otaku culture. That the anime and video games, which make up the otaku's interests, unmistakably embody something inherently Japanese has been demonstrated over and over again. The trend of otaku toward the "incorrect" started in Japan. It may be that otaku's interests in the parts of "Japan" that are "incorrect" is a deeply rooted undercurrent of Japanese society.

---

* *"Towa" and "eien"* Mean "eternity" in Japanese.
* *Tsutomu Miyazaki* A notorious Japanese serial killer who was known as "The Otaku Murderer." Much was made of his interest in anime and manga by the Japanese media when he was apprehended for the murder of four young girls.

BONUS FEATURES

▲▽▲▽

THE GARDEN OF SINNERS
An Interview with
Kinoku Nasu and Takashi Takeuchi

Interview by Katsushi Ota
Translated by Paul Johnson

This interview was conducted with the creators of *The Garden of Sinners* novel, Kinoku Nasu and Takashi Takeuchi, on the occasion of the theatrical release of the first anime adaptation of *The Garden of Sinners*. This revolutionary novel required an equally revolutionary anime treatment, which was what studio ufotable gave it: Each of the novel's seven chapters will be adapted as fifty-minute anime features and released to theaters. The interview also includes the creator's thoughts on the American debut of their work in this edition of *Faust*.

The interviewer is Katsushi Ota, the editor in chief of *Faust* and one of Japan's most prominent fiction editors. Born in 1972 in the town of Kurashiki-shi, Okayama prefecture, Ota joined Kodansha, Japan's largest publisher, in 1995. His first assignments included editing shojo manga, but he then moved to Kodansha's literary department as an editor of mystery novels. In 2003, as part of Kodansha's 100th anniversary celebration, Ota was awarded Kodansha's top honor when he won the Kodansha New Magazine Prize. When Ota launched *Faust* magazine in the same year, he became Kodansha's youngest-ever editor in chief. *Faust*'s eclectic mix of genres—

including literary and popular fiction and comics—and innovative editorial style has made it one of the most notable and influential magazines in Japan. In 2006, Ota launched his newest publishing program, the Kodansha Box line, which he hopes to bring to readers worldwide.

▲▼▲▼▲

OTA: *The Garden of Sinners* movie has just been released [in Japan], so I'd like to ask you, if I may, about the details leading up to its creation.

NASU: Back in 1998, Takeuchi told me he was opening up a website and asked me if I'd write a monthly serial for it. What I wrote was the first chapter of *The Garden of Sinners*. Takeuchi wanted something that would go on for a year, so I thought of starting out with a grand plot and then breaking it down into monthly episodes that would come out on staggered release over the course of the year. *The Garden of Sinners* was an experiment in fusing romance and the modern detective novel—something I'd been dreaming of trying for a long time.

OTA: Text-based sites really took off on the Internet in 1997 and '98, didn't they?

TAKEUCHI: They did. I think that's just when individuals were first getting their own websites and starting to put all kinds of stuff up on them.

OTA: Tatsuhiko Takimoto and Takekuni Kitayama were publishing essays and works on websites about then, too. So what was the result?

TAKEUCHI: Hmm... Well, *The Garden of Sinners* wasn't exactly easy on the eye to read online. It had alternate readings for some words written above the kanji, so we had to write them in brackets after the word instead when we put it online. Back then, just putting something out on the Internet was fun in itself. I'd found myself a job but then came back home to Tokyo after the company I was working at went under, and Nasu was still just an amateur writer back then, so I contacted him and asked if he wanted to put the story up on a website.

OTA: But the response wasn't very good. And when you collected the serialized parts and tried to sell them at comic markets, I hear that only five copies sold and Mr. Takeuchi became incredibly depressed about the whole thing.

TAKEUCHI: That's right. Thanks to the Internet, people could now display their works all over the place. Nasu and I were all fired up and tried to take the Web by storm, but there were far too many places now where people could show off and sell their work, and ours just didn't get a second look. Having no one read our work was frustrating like you wouldn't believe.

OTA: So you turned your attention to making dating games and made your big break with *Tsukihime*.

NASU: Visual novels for the PC were really taking off at the time. Takeuchi had played them and was like "There's this whole culture here!" He said that if people wouldn't read our original novels on the Web or at comic markets, they'd definitely read them if they were in visual novel form, so we should make one. Reactions to *Tsukihime* were slow but solid, and after a while, we made our breakthrough with it. There was a novel afterward based on the foundations of *Tsukihime* . . . but the fans know all about that. The webpage on which we'd put *The Garden of Sinners* was long gone by then, so to get it out as a book, we published it ourselves as a fan job.

OTA: I could really feel the love for Kodansha Novels when I saw the self-published version of your book. It had a really suggestive cover and contents . . . but there was a mushroom logo on the cover where Kodansha's dog would have been, and the typesetting was identical to Kodansha's, too—two sets of eighteen lines with twenty-three characters per line. And it was a hybrid of romance and modern mystery. . . . Anyway, that did it. I had to meet you. "This is where I come in," I thought. [*laughs*] I remember sending you a really psyched-up e-mail.

NASU: We were both excited, but at the same time, we were dreading it, too. It was like the executioner we'd been waiting for had finally shown up with his ax.

OTA: I got a reply from the two of you right away. "Let's meet in Akihabara." I was thinking, "Aah, so it's Akihabara after all, huh? It's kind of far out there."

NASU: Cafe Corona in front of Akihabara station, wasn't it?

OTA: Just an average, everyday coffee shop. I got a good understanding after talking to you in detail and asking about your personal history. We were similar in age, had read the same books, and I'd become an editor while you'd become a writer. That's why, despite the fact that I felt strongly about wanting you to write something new, I also really wanted you to let Kodansha Novels publish *The Garden of Sinners*. Oh, that's right... because I knew you were making girlie games at the time, I was really worried that a couple of super–otaku geeks were going to walk in.

NASU: What, you expected me to be all like "How fare you this fine morn, my liege?" [*laughs*]

OTA: If thou were, I wouldst have been in trouble! [*laughs*] But you both turned out to be fine, upstanding guys. The impression was so strong, though, that when people ask me what you're both like in person, I always answer that you're like a couple of samurai.

NASU: Takeuchi is the samurai... I'm more like the village geisha.... Uh, no. More like the totally useless young lord of the castle.

OTA: No, no, you're both like noble samurai! Well, that's the impression I got. Especially Mr. Takeuchi—he was like a swordsman from the end of the Tokugawa era. He gave off this intense aura.... It was like he wouldn't care if you said something rude to him, but if you insulted Mr. Nasu, then he'd slice you in two there and then.

NASU: It feels more like he's projecting a "Keep away" kind of aura these days. Like he's been through a lot and doesn't trust people easily.

TAKEUCHI: Hmm. I guess I'm just not the hungry wolf I used to be. [*laughs*]

OTA: But it's because I got that impression of you that I was able to understand how your artwork got across to the readers. I said something incredibly rude at that first meeting, actually. I told you that you weren't a very skilled artist. . . . Do you remember?

TAKEUCHI: Nope. [*laughs*]

OTA: But I also said that your drawings were really good. There are more skilled artists than stars in the sky, but not many who can draw great pictures. I remember getting a strong feeling that, out of all the people in the world, the drawings by the artist called Takashi Takeuchi were ultimately drawn for one person alone—Kinoku Nasu. That's why they have such a heroic soul to them. I'm always amazed at how brilliantly the finished product turns out whenever the two of you team up.

TAKEUCHI: I'd like to think that's the case. I don't really understand it myself.

OTA: I figured that *The Garden of Sinners* self-published book had sold tens of thousands of copies and was already probably a sellout item across town, but I still really wanted it for a Kodansha hardback. I do remember telling you that I didn't think sales figures for it would be that high.

NASU: We didn't think it could outsell the version we'd published, either.

OTA: It took a whole year to get your permission to publish it.

NASU: Because we were just about to start making *Fate / Stay Night* at the time. It was just when we were making the move from fan publisher to professional company. We were being really cautious about things. But one day Takeuchi gave me a nudge, so I asked you if you were still interested in doing it, and you said, "Of course!" You'd always been in constant contact, and when you said that you wanted to put the book out as a collectors' edition, it was like a dream come true. Takeuchi and I had thought that *The Garden of Sinners* fan-published book had used up all the sales it was going to get, so we were against the idea of publishing it for real. We thought it wouldn't benefit us at all. But we were really happy that the editor of Kodansha was willing to deal so sincerely with a couple of know-it-all kids like us for a year.

OTA: You two were so busy with *Fate / Stay Night*, and here I was every month coming over and saying "How about this?" I completely didn't get it, did I . . . ? [*nervous laugh*] Oh yes, I remember. . . . I didn't really leave you much choice in the end. I didn't want the whole thing to just fizzle out, so I conspired to enlist the help of one of Mr. Nasu's gods—a certain Mr. Kiyoshi Kasai—and set up a visit to his house. He was a hard fellow to say no to then, wasn't he? I mean . . . five minutes after we arrived, he said, "Well, let's go to the hot springs," and thirty minutes later, we're all sitting in a hot spring like best buddies and he's saying, "So then, Nasu, you're going to publish *The Garden of Sinners* with Ota here, hmm?" [*laughs*]

NASU: We were thinking, "So this is what he was up to. These must be the sneaky backdoor tactics a pro uses." [*laughs*] Though it was less a backdoor thing and more a full frontal attack. There was no way we could say no.

OTA: Well, it was all because I wanted to give you a totally perfect debut. I don't think I'll rack my brains and exert my meager strength so hard ever again with a new author. You'd both become big figures out in the world while I was trying to persuade you to let Kodansha publish it as a hardback, but you were still kind enough to choose me despite your superstar status, and that was something I really wanted to put all my effort into paying you back for.

NASU: We were both shocked by your collectors' edition. We were like "Look at this incredible box he's put together!" when we saw the sample you'd brought along. "Somebody stop this guy! There's no need to go so overboard!" [*laughs*]

OTA: And it sold out in just two hours. Bookstore owners still hate me now, you know. It was pretty rough on them.

NASU: Yeah, that was all your fault, too! [*laughs*] I guess only people who managed to grab a copy will know what I'm talking about, but it was an insane and totally over-the-top design.... I'm really sorry for the people who couldn't buy one, but I hope those who did will treasure it like gold dust.

OTA: It may have had important links to TYPE-MOON's other works, but to think that a novel-only product—something that didn't come out in any other media—would become one of the bestselling Kodansha novels of all time. Mr. Takeuchi's exclusive original drawings and illustrations were really good, too. I remember being totally convinced that it would sell as soon as I saw the cover for volume one.

NASU: I thought the same thing. "This will sell." But if I'd known how *well*, I'd have worked over the contents a few more times! [*laughs*]

OTA: I heard all kinds of malicious talk, saying how of course it was going to do well, since TYPE-MOON was the "in thing" at the moment, but the fad would die off and suddenly sales would grind to a halt. But it's still a top seller in the novel world today. It's already a must-have book among otaku, and it's attained a timeless-classic status. It's just been a novel up until now, never crossing over into any other kind of media, so what do you think about the whole seven chapters being adapted into a full seven-part movie version?

TAKEUCHI: I still can't believe it. I always thought that *The Garden of Sinners* would have to be made more easily accessible for the masses if it was turned into a movie, or have parts changed to get it on TV, etcetera, but since I didn't want anything changing in any way, then I figured the only way it would work would be as a super-small-scale OVA or something... that we'd have to aim it only at a few dedicated people who love the original with a passion. This movie adaptation is taking exactly the opposite mind-set, and though I was pretty worried when I first heard, I think in the end both approaches have the same goal in mind. In order to preserve the integrity of the work, I'd have kept the scale small, but I guess these guys have decided on going for a massive scale instead. I was quite shocked by their approach, but now I've been gradually won over.

OTA: What about Mr. Nasu?

NASU: Well, I laughed so hard it hurt. [*laughs*] I didn't think anything could shock me at this point, but I'd never experienced that kind of blow before.... I remember that I asked you to repeat it after you told me. I couldn't believe it. It was a kind of a joke until I heard that ufotable were in charge of production; then I sat up and listened. The whole thing was like a dream, and I got a bit carried away.

OTA: I'm always impressed when I see how much effort the two of you are putting into the anime, actually.

TAKEUCHI: From a massive distance, though.

NASU: Judging from my experiences with anime adaptations so far, I can't say whether it's better to completely hand the whole thing over to the people making it or get slightly involved with the process myself. So I didn't know whether to announce that I'm going for absolute involvement and joining Ufo completely or standing back and not going in very often but giving my full assistance when I do. This time we've gone for the second option.

OTA: Mr. Takeuchi had Mr. Toushi's designs worked over from scratch, and Mr. Nasu is spending his whole day at scriptwriting meetings once a fortnight. Ufo seems to be really kind and accommodating.

TAKEUCHI: I'm just happy that the Ufo staff never tell us something can't be done.

NASU: You just have to speak your wish and it's granted. It's a pretty great power to be wielding.

TAKEUCHI: I've noticed recently that neither of us can just say "*Do it!*" But, still, I'm really happy about all they do for us. I feel totally welcome on the production committee. Even when they've had to put their foot down with us, they've never lost their temper and said "That's just the way it is, dammit." The whole committee listens to what we have to say and takes it into consideration before making a decision.

OTA: Well, even if they're a production committee, it's still a company with a product to make. None of them are turning up at the meetings just because it's work. Passion and sincerity are essential for a discussion, and there isn't a person on the committee who doesn't have both. That's why it's going so well.

TAKEUCHI: Actually, I'll tell you what I've been glad about recently. The starting idea: "Seven chapters—seven movies. That's how *The Garden of Sinners* should be!" That way the plot flows perfectly, and nothing ends up confusing or incoherent. I think it's great that the whole committee was able to naturally take to this concept. It really is the best way to adapt the book to film.

NASU: It's already too late to cut it down into just two or three parts. Usually with anime, the length is absolutely set in stone, so you end up having to cut the story down, but this time everyone is like "How are we going to extend the last five minutes to wrap it up?" [*laughs*] A normal anime would just cut bits out without question. It's kind of amazing when you think about it.

TAKEUCHI: What Nasu and I are asking for is more than 100 percent... more like 101 percent or 102 percent. The fact that we're actually getting it this time is such a great feeling... something like that. I think it's going so well because everyone involved has such a desire for improvement. Not settling for standard quality is what's making everyone give that 101 to 102 percent.

NASU: Even if the different directors get it wrong from chapter to chapter, the staff have got the groundwork down right so it shouldn't be too jumbled. Though nobody knows what's gonna happen with chapter 5! [*laughs*] I really hope it just follows the storyboard exactly.

OTA: Let's just have faith that every part will be a masterpiece of anime. When I saw the finished movie of chapter 1, I really felt like it was well worth the eighteen hundred–yen admittance, even though it's only fifty minutes long.

TAKEUCHI: I guess people don't mind handing over cash for a quality product.

NASU: But if kids in the countryside want to come and see it, it'll cost them five thousand yen just for the train fare. And they might come all the way to find the cinema is full and they can't get in. If they do, I'll just give them Mr. Ota's home address. [*laughs*] But I'd like people to come and see all seven if they can. Mr. Ota's planning to try out making a different pamphlet for each of the movies and selling them, so that people can look at them after all seven parts have finished and remember how they were *there* for this *Garden of Sinners* movie festival. Afterward, you'll have seven pamphlets to show for it, and you can look back and think "Ah, that was a good time." That's the hope that we're putting into them.

OTA: They're taking a huge amount of time and money to put together, after all. They have foil front covers, and all the text will take at least thirty minutes to read. They really are some fantastic pamphlets.

TAKEUCHI: Well, it's all very well if you live in and around Tokyo, but what about the people who live in Hokkaido? [*laughs*]

OTA: I guess they'll just have to run away from home.... But all joking aside, studio morale and the committee's mood are on the rise, and the original novel is now a Kodansha trade paperback. Mr. Nasu, what do you think about the fact that famous authors are providing commentaries for the Kodansha paperback editions of *The Garden of Sinners*? Yukito Ayatsuji is doing volume one, Hideyuki Kikuchi volume two, and Kiyoshi Kasai volume three.

NASU: Well, put it this way: When I die and they read my will, there'll be a sentence after the part where I thank Takeuchi and my parents, and it'll read "Thank you, Mr. Ota, for convincing those three!" Having your childhood heroes comment on your work is an incredible honor for an author. But this is almost too much of a reward for me to take. [*laughs*] Mr. Ayatsuji, Mr. Kikuchi, and Mr. Kasai have all interpreted the books in totally different ways. Hopefully, it'll confirm just how many different ways there are of looking at my work. I feel just a little bit proud of myself for writing all these stories now.... Having these three look at my work in this way... I felt like my heart was going to explode. But it wouldn't have happened if not for Kodansha and you, Mr. Ota. I don't think another editor would have been able to get them or would even have come up with the idea in the first place.

OTA: I just thought that, since Kodansha was finally doing *The Garden of Sinners* in paperback, I wouldn't be able to show my face again if it didn't have that extra something that distinguished it from a Dengeki Bunko or Sneaker Bunko book. As someone flying the Kodansha banner, I'd just end up being criticized as exploiting you if we turned out the same book that anyone could have printed. It wasn't a triumph just for me alone but for all of Kodansha.

NASU: Contentwise, I don't think there's a single page that wasn't retouched for the paperback version. It's embarrassing.... There's so much I didn't put in the first time around. Damn. I want people to read only the paperback now and leave the hardback well alone!

OTA: What are you saying? [*nervous laugh*]
Well, finally, do the two of you have any closing statements?

NASU: I'd like to make a machine to go to committee meetings instead of Takeuchi. The poor guy gets in to work at ten in the morning, is in the meeting until whenever it ends, then has his own work to get done. By the time it's all finished, it's past midnight before he gets home.

TAKEUCHI: If I had to say one thing, it would be that I want Nasu to just write about the things he enjoys writing about. Nowadays, I get the feeling he's on some kind of life-and-death mission... like there's this sword hanging over his head making him feel like he's got to write a fantastic work that everyone will hail as a thing of unparalleled splendor.... I want him to write stories not as Kinoku Nasu the major writer. His comedy name shows the fun side of him, and I want him to write about fun things that he enjoys.

NASU: But I can't just write crap, though, can I?

TAKEUCHI: That's true, but just remember that you don't have to feel pressured into producing a masterpiece of historical significance every time you write.

OTA: I'm sure I'm speaking for all the fans when I say that as long as the two of you just stay yourselves, then I'm sure everything will work out fine!

Faust is having an American release in the summer of 2008 and will feature chapter 1 of *The Garden of Sinners: A View from Above*. In fact, this interview is going to be appearing there, too. Could I ask what the two of you think about it?

TAKEUCHI: I'm looking forward to seeing how it'll be received in America. When it was written, *The Garden of Sinners* was packed full of things that Kinoku Nasu is nuts for, and they're definitely very "Japanese," so it has to be said that it's kind of a favorite dish full of stuff that the two of us really love. After it was finished, we made things with the mind-set "Maybe everyone else likes the same stuff as us," and in hindsight, I think we guessed right. But will that apply to the rest of the world, though? I can't wait to see if a foreign country finds the same things interesting as we do.

NASU: I'm a little scared, actually. If it's totally lost on overseas readers, I might end up thinking "Oh well . . . heh heh heh . . . Guess I'd better stay cooped up in Japan farming the rice fields after all." [*laughs*]

TAKEUCHI: And that's fine, too, you know?

NASU: We crammed all of our favorite things into a story and put it out there in the world, along with our feeling of unshakable pride. . . . Now it's crossed the language barrier, so let's see how far it goes. There's a genuine pleasure just in that alone. At the same time, though, if it's accepted somewhere, it's sure to be hated somewhere else. I mean, we're talking about the country that made *Team America*, after all! [*laughs*] It's amazing how broad-minded people must be to accept that level of black humor and for it to be accepted as entertainment. People can be incredibly tolerant. It's known as a melting pot of races and cultures, after all.

TAKEUCHI: It is, isn't it? It'll be fun if English-speaking readers look at *The Garden of Sinners* and say something like "It was interesting, but I'd have done it this way instead...." And isn't the Japanese author Haruki Murakami being ranked as the literary successor to such American writers as Fitzgerald and Salinger? So maybe—in, say, ten or twenty years' time—people will be talking about how Kinoku Nasu's literary successor was an American writer. I, for one, hope that's the case.

▲▽▲▽

FROM JAPAN TO THE WORLD, FROM THE WORLD TO JAPAN

Yukari Shiina

Translated by Paul Johnson

The popularity of manga in the United States has given rise to any number of debates about its place in American comics culture. America has its own powerful comics tradition, ranging from newspaper strips and superhero comics to indie comics and literary graphic novels, but manga has proven to have unstoppable commercial and cultural influence. Now American readers are asking themselves questions such as "Why is manga so popular?" "What effect will this have on the American comics scene?" "Are young creators who are now working in the manga style truly creating manga, or something else?"

Yukari Shiina's essay shows that the Japanese comics scene has its own similar debates. Japan has been resistant to the introduction of comics from other world traditions, but Shiina argues passionately that this may be changing. Shiina, a translator and columnist, is the manager of the *Eigo de! America Manga* blog (the website address is http://d.hatena.ne.jp/ceena), and the founder of an agency whose goal is to introduce comic artists from all over the world to Japan and set them up for publication. She has become a key player in bringing world comics into Japan.

▲▼▲▼▲

My job is to introduce foreign comics to Japanese manga readers. In short, I'm an agent: I show non-Japanese comics to Japanese publishers, in an attempt to help them find a way to Japanese publication; I also work on such competitions as *Kodansha Morning*'s International Manga Competition.

But whenever I explain the kind of work I do, I'm frequently asked the same question: "Why are you so interested in bringing foreign comics to Japan?" While they don't actually say it out loud, the people who ask this question seem to be thinking, "Japan is already overflowing with manga. Why do we need to go out of our way to publish foreign comics?" and "Foreign comics have never sold here in the past, so surely you're just wasting your time?" In other words, they're thinking, to borrow an old phrase, "Can you sell ice to an Eskimo?"

It's certainly true that foreign comics and manga aren't exactly popular in Japan. Yes, there are Japanese fans of foreign comics. And *Persepolis*, by Marjane Satrapi, recently sold more copies here than anyone could ever have expected. What's more, even though it's still unusual, some foreign comic artists do have their works serialized in Japanese magazines and the like. But, at the end of the day, these are definitely exceptions to the rule. Kodansha published some works by foreign authors in the 1990s, but the endeavor didn't exactly meet with resounding success. Even publication of "mainstream" American superhero comics dropped off at the start of the nineties in Japan, and only a few companies are putting them out now, albeit sporadically. So people certainly have a point when they ask, "Why should we go out of our way to read foreign comics?"

But this doesn't in any way mean that foreign comics will never sell in Japan. The reason I believe this is because there are countless artists out there in the world with supreme talent who can draw incredibly interesting manga and comics. There are plenty of reasons why things haven't worked out before: The works brought over to Japan weren't to Japanese readers' tastes, the timing was not right, and so on. . . . But the fact is, few works imported in the past have met with success. But the situation will without a doubt change. Japanese manga has become popular throughout the world, and the number of people drawing their own manga has skyrocketed. And when I say *manga* here, I mean "drawn in the style of Japanese manga."

North America, too, has seen a lot of this type of manga published in the last few years. Of course, this kind of Japanese-style but foreign-drawn manga is nothing new for the States. There have been artists there proclaiming their love for Japanese manga and bringing out their own Japanese-style comics ever since the 1980s. But it's only recently that this phenomenon has grown from a series of individuals working alone into organized groups—like a movement, in fact.

It isn't just North America where Japanese manga is read, though, and it's thanks to the huge global expansion that manga culture is now shared throughout the world and the number of people drawing it has increased so much. The scale of Japan's manga market, and the sheer number of working manga artists in Japan, means that it's still the major world power in manga—the main source of the superpopular manga titles that are being enjoyed worldwide. As the number of non-Japanese manga artists keeps increasing throughout the globe, however, as time passes, we'll see more and more fascinating manga coming from outside Japan.

For a culture to develop, it's imperative that a country doesn't just import cultural products from abroad but that its own native artists step up and create lots of popular domestic titles of their own. When a new culture takes root, its growth is decisively dependent on that country's producing its own cultural products. For instance, as the number of native manga artists in North America increases, the American market for manga should also expand. And that, in turn, will lead to ever more interesting manga being created and published.

Since the 1980s, when Japanese manga first became commercially available in America, it's taken twenty years for manga to become truly popular. From the 1980s to the 1990s, it was still just a niche market for devoted fans, and it took until the millennium for it to be sold in major stores. Even now, it's doubtful whether manga has been accepted into mainstream culture in North America, but, even so, titles such as *Naruto, Bleach,* and *Fruit Basket* were apparently popular enough to top the *USA Today* bestseller list, and manga enjoys a stable and sustained popularity. Whether its popularity will continue to increase, decline, or merely stabilize depends in part on how North American manga artists develop.

The popularity of Japanese manga in North America still took two decades to take root, even when boosted by the popular anime and social craze that was Pokémon. But American manga may well find itself becoming established in Japan much faster than that. When you consider the fact that Japanese manga was accepted in America, a country where books are read left to right, with the Japanese-style right-to-left format and sound effects left intact (depending on the company), then the fact that Japanese people are already familiar (in theory, at least) with American culture—through Hollywood movies and popular Western TV shows—means that the foundation has already been laid for Japanese readers' accepting Western manga.

I have so far been using the term *manga* to refer to Western manga drawn in the Japanese style, but I accept that its label will become a subject for discussion as the number of artists drawing Western manga in North America increases. It doesn't happen so often today, but for a time, there was much debate online about the question "What do you call non-Japanese manga?"

The whole war of words that went on surrounding some American fans' declaration that "It's only manga if it's Japanese. Anything else isn't manga" is, in fact, a phenomenon with which Japan is already familiar. When jazz crossed over to Japanese shores and was being played by Japanese musicians, or when Japanese sci-fi novels, created under the influence of foreign sci-fi works, started being published, some people said, "What the Japanese are playing isn't jazz at all," and "Japanese sci-fi can't really be called sci-fi." Because of this, even Japanese people will understand the American debate about what to call non-Japanese manga, but, for convenience's sake, I shall continue to refer to it here simply as *manga*.

On a side note, as I'm sure you're aware, the Japanese word *manga* simply means "comics" and has nothing to do with a comic's country of origin. The English word *comic* is even used in Japan to refer to Japanese manga itself. If you were to ask a Japanese manga reader for his or her opinion on a specific manga's country of origin, a popular view would most probably be that "it doesn't matter where it's from, as long as it's interesting to read."

What is "interesting," exactly, changes from person to person, but Japanese people are as a rule very familiar with manga and love reading it. There are a great many people who want to read interesting manga no matter where it comes from. Just as Japanese manga is now a marketable product in America, it's not that much of a stretch to imagine seeing the names of foreign manga artists up there next to Japanese manga artists even on the streets of Japan—popular and shelved next to Japanese artists as a normal, everyday sight.

So far, I've talked about Western comics created in the Japanese manga style, but personally I also wonder if it's possible for distinctly un-Japanese-style foreign comics and graphic novels to become widely accepted in Japan. I think that by accepting distinctly non-Japanese manga that was drawn overseas, Japanese readers would open themselves up to a diverse range of manga, and, as a result, the chances of their accepting completely non-manga-style foreign comics would increase.

I lived in America in 2001 and personally witnessed the manga corner in my local small-town bookstore getting bigger and bigger every time I went in. Public exposure to Japanese manga had been steadily increasing since the 1980s, and various conditions came into alignment to bring about a sudden dramatic change. Who's to say that the foreign comics corner in Japanese bookshops won't enjoy such a sudden transformation?

Actually, I feel that the Japanese manga publishing houses are showing more interest in foreign manga, especially recently. The latest volume of the original Japanese *Faust* features *MegaTokyo* translated into Japanese, and a special volume is planned for release under the Kodansha label (I'm the one translating it, incidentally). *Kodansha Morning*'s International Manga Competition, too, exhibits works of foreign manga artists with publication in mind and not only the grand prize winners. The editor of *Morning 2,* where the winning entries are shown, has stated, "Not all the manga artists serialized in *Morning 2* have to be Japanese, as long as their work is interesting to read." I can't give much away at this point, but projects are being proposed to Japanese publishing houses that involve not only Asian manga artists but

European ones, too. I know of several in the works, and they're just the few that I'm involved with.

Just as Japanese manga has inspired huge numbers of people all over the world to draw in the manga style, there are plenty of reasons why foreign manga could have a major influence on Japanese artists and bring about a great change in the manga that they draw. I don't doubt the infinite possibilities to be found in manga and see only a bright future ahead for it. And if foreign works find publication in Japan and mix things up even more, I believe it will only stimulate the further growth and development of manga in Japan. I believe that the best possible future is for manga titles from North America, Japan, and the whole world to influence current manga and spur it on to evolve further.

We can already see this kind of mutual influence happening in other realms of pop culture. For instance, in the world of sci-fi movies, we'd never have had director Mamoru Oshii's *Ghost in the Shell* without *Blade Runner,* and we wouldn't have had *The Matrix* without *Ghost in the Shell.* Naturally, a mutual influence is already happening in the world of manga, but I think we'll see it expand from here on in. The same goes for novels, too.

As a huge fan of *Faust* myself, I'm incredibly happy to see it getting a North American release. Mr. Ishin Nishio and Mr. Kiniko Nasu are extremely popular writers who continue to turn out new entertainment novels in Japan today. Maybe, with their works now being published in America, they'll inspire new kinds of American novels to be written in the future. And then, perhaps, we'll one day see those new stories appearing on the pages of the original Japanese *Faust* for Japanese readers to enjoy. It makes me excited just thinking about it.

A cultural exchange between North America and Japan is definitely happening in the world of novels and manga, and I predict that these two countries, separated by the vastness of the Pacific Ocean, are going to really see that world igniting on both their shores. The change might not happen tomorrow, but it will happen. So whatever you do, be sure not to take your eyes off the Japanese and American manga scenes.

F

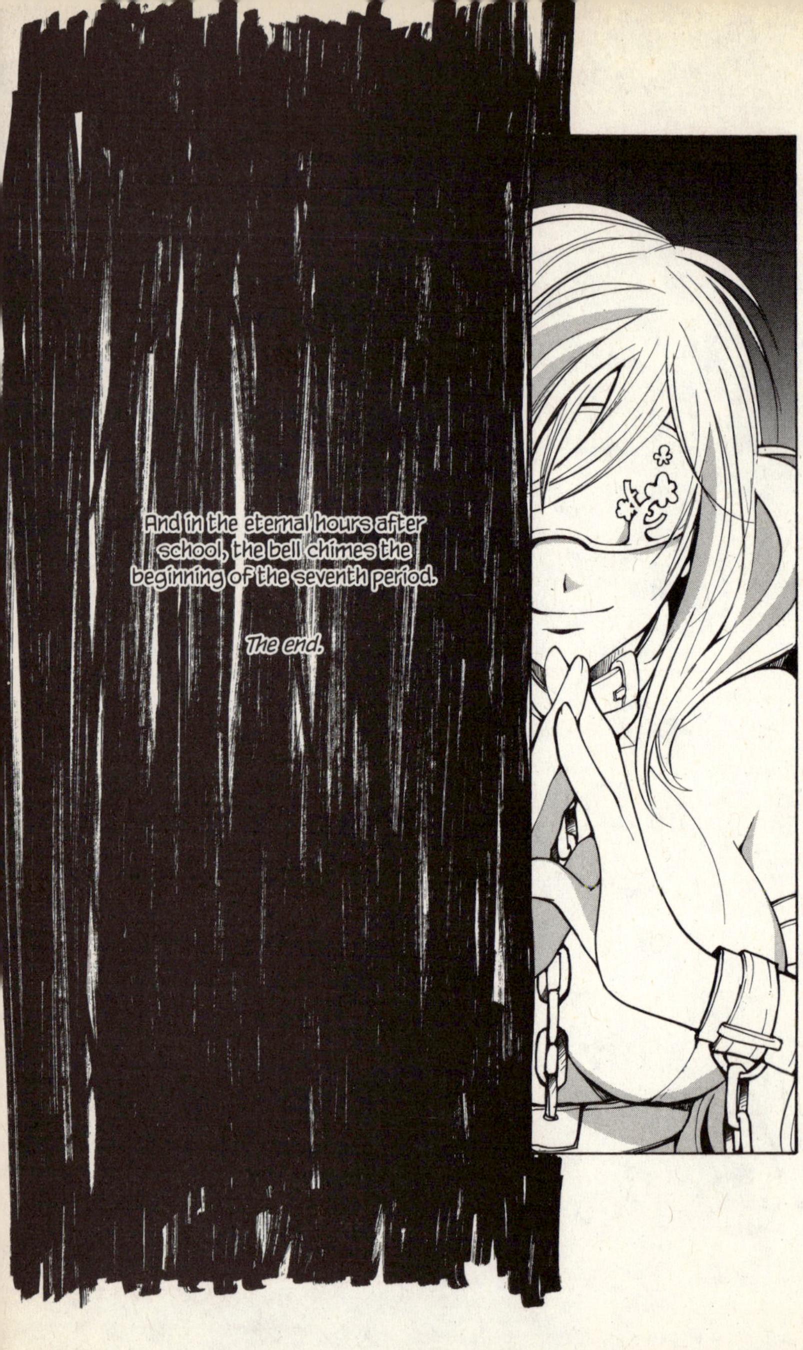
And in the eternal hours after school, the bell chimes the beginning of the seventh period.
The end.

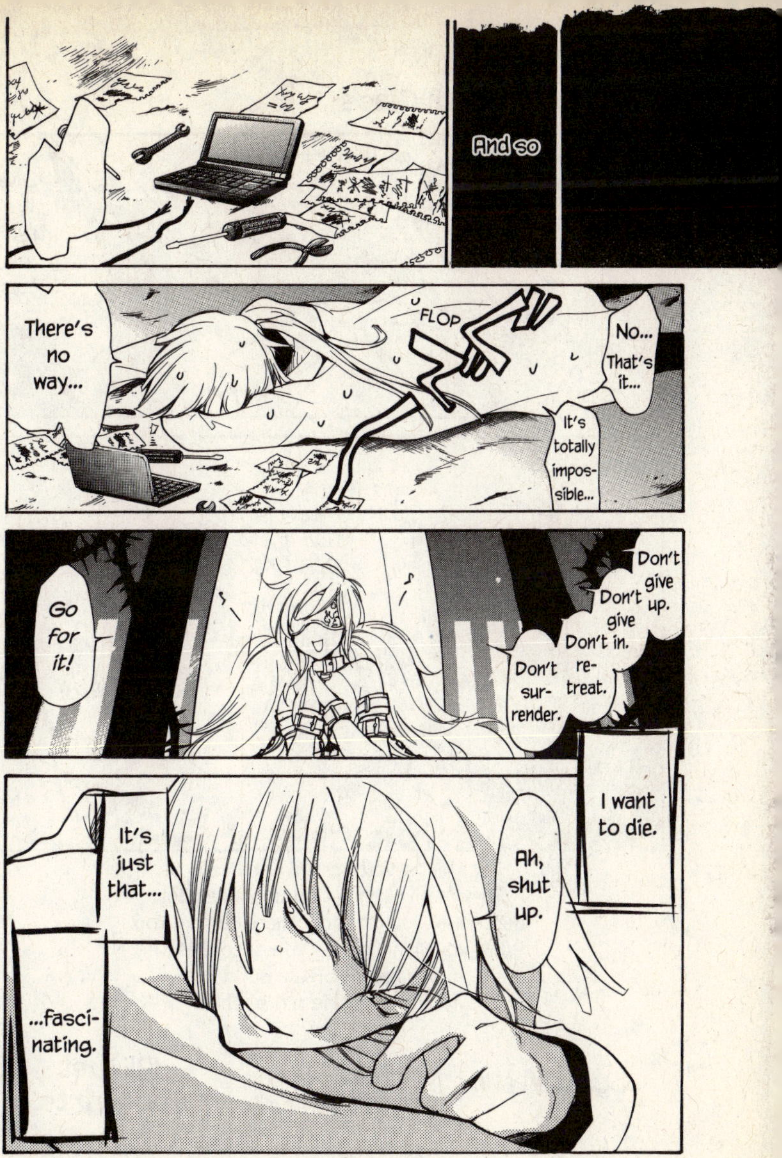

And so
No... That's it...
It's totally impos-sible...
FLOP
There's no way...
Don't give up.
Don't give in.
Don't re-treat.
Don't sur-render.
Go for it!
I want to die.
Ah, shut up.
It's just that...
...fasci-nating.

After School: 7th Class

Give it a try, if you can.
...No...
Maybe you *shouldn't* do it if you can....
RATTLE
...Huh?
It's a *conso-lation match.*

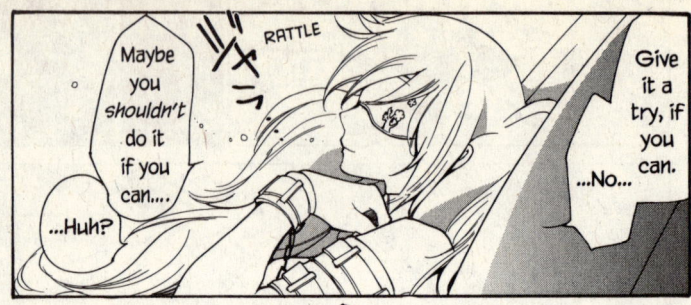

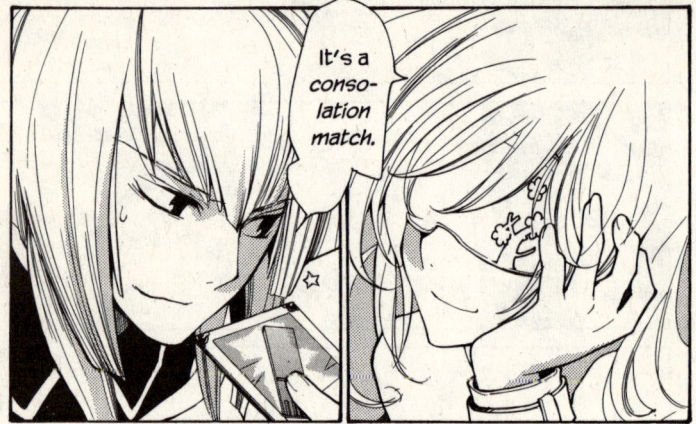

The things you worked frantically at.
They're all already things of the past.
The things you can do, others can do, too.
What you think makes you special is just
the reality of the world.
My dream is this girl's reality.

Completely.

Everything, like grasping at air.

All just footprints.

I can totally feel all motivation draining away.

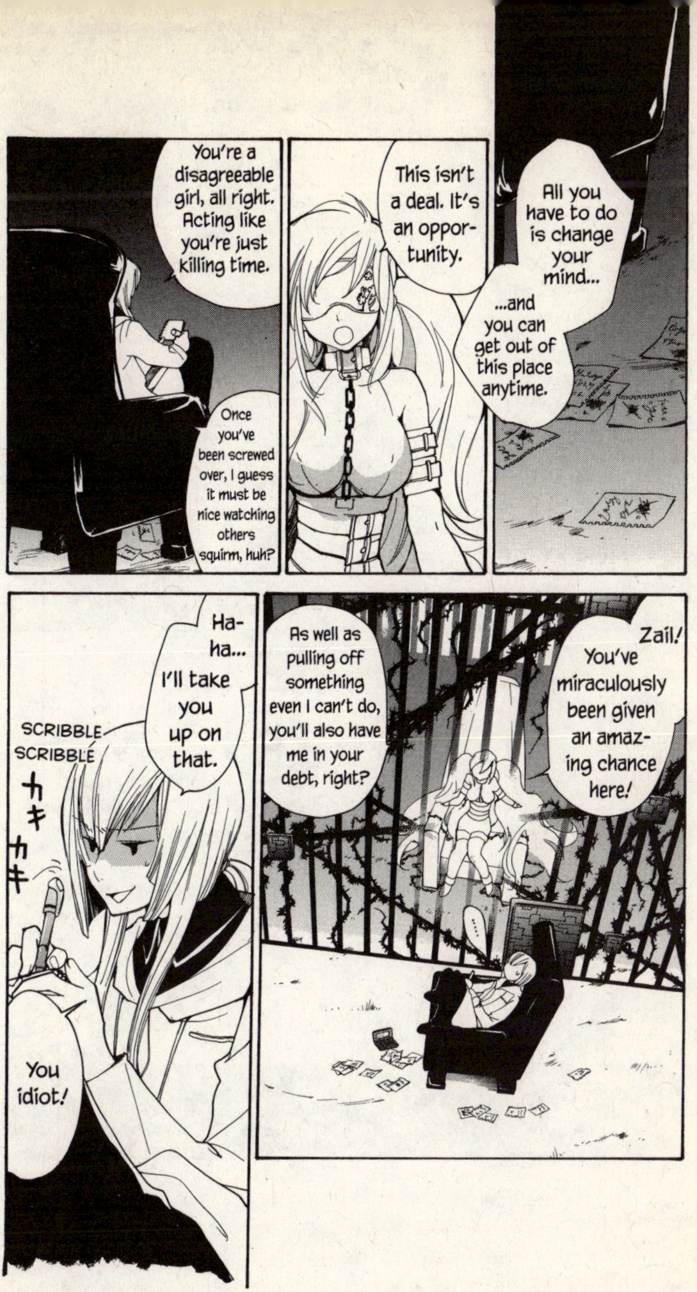
All you have to do is change your mind...
...and you can get out of this place anytime.
This isn't a deal. It's an opportunity.
You're a disagreeable girl, all right. Acting like you're just killing time.
Once you've been screwed over, I guess it must be nice watching others squirm, huh?
Zail! You've miraculously been given an amazing chance here!
As well as pulling off something even I can't do, you'll also have me in your debt, right?
Ha-ha... I'll take you up on that.
SCRIBBLE SCRIBBLE
カキ カキ
You idiot!

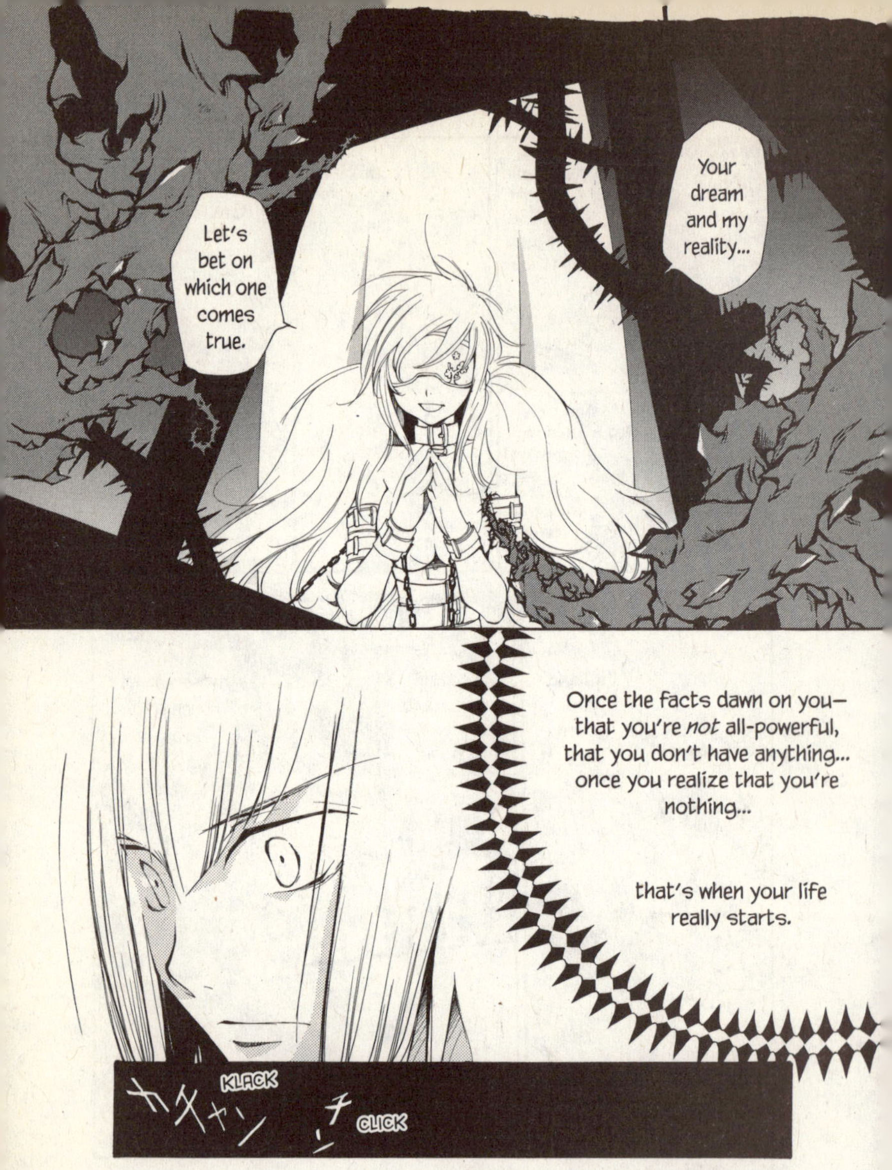

Your dream and my reality...
Let's bet on which one comes true.
Once the facts dawn on you— that you're *not* all-powerful, that you don't have anything... once you realize that you're nothing...
that's when your life really starts.
KLACK
CLICK

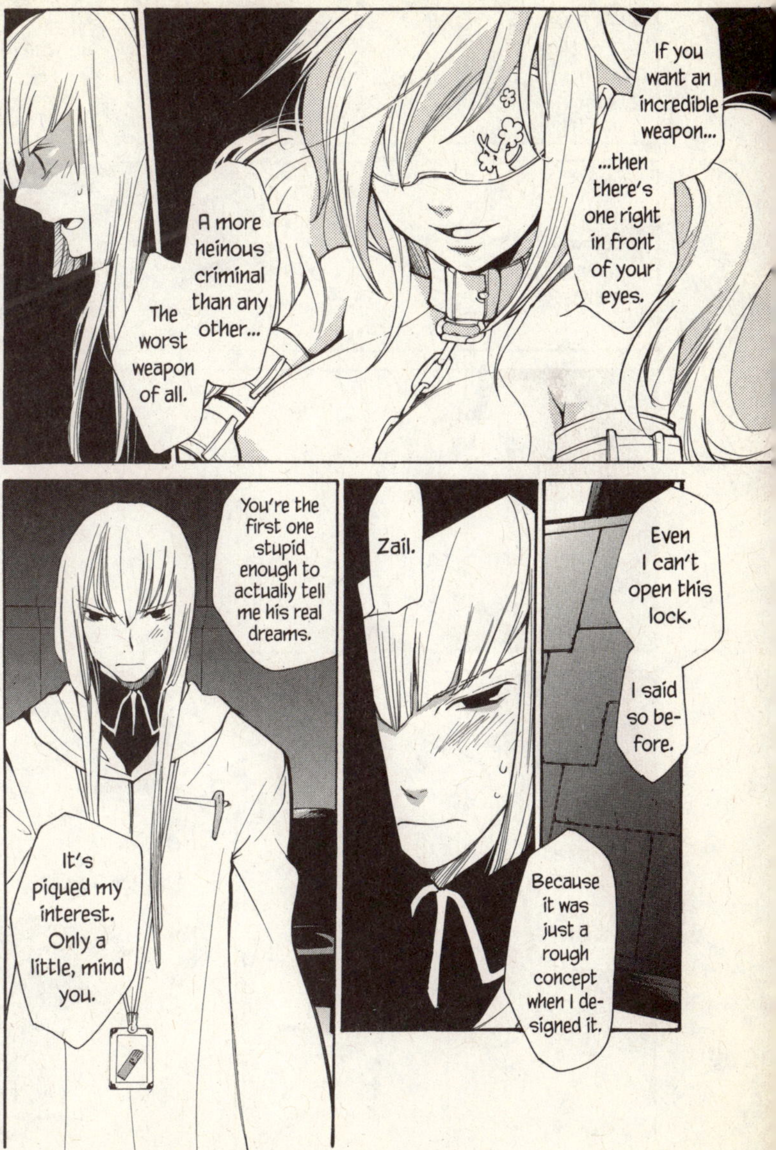
If you want an incredible weapon...
...then there's one right in front of your eyes.
A more heinous criminal than any other...
The worst weapon of all.
Even I can't open this lock.
I said so be-fore.
Because it was just a rough concept when I de-signed it.
Zail.
You're the first one stupid enough to actually tell me his real dreams.
It's piqued my interest. Only a little, mind you.

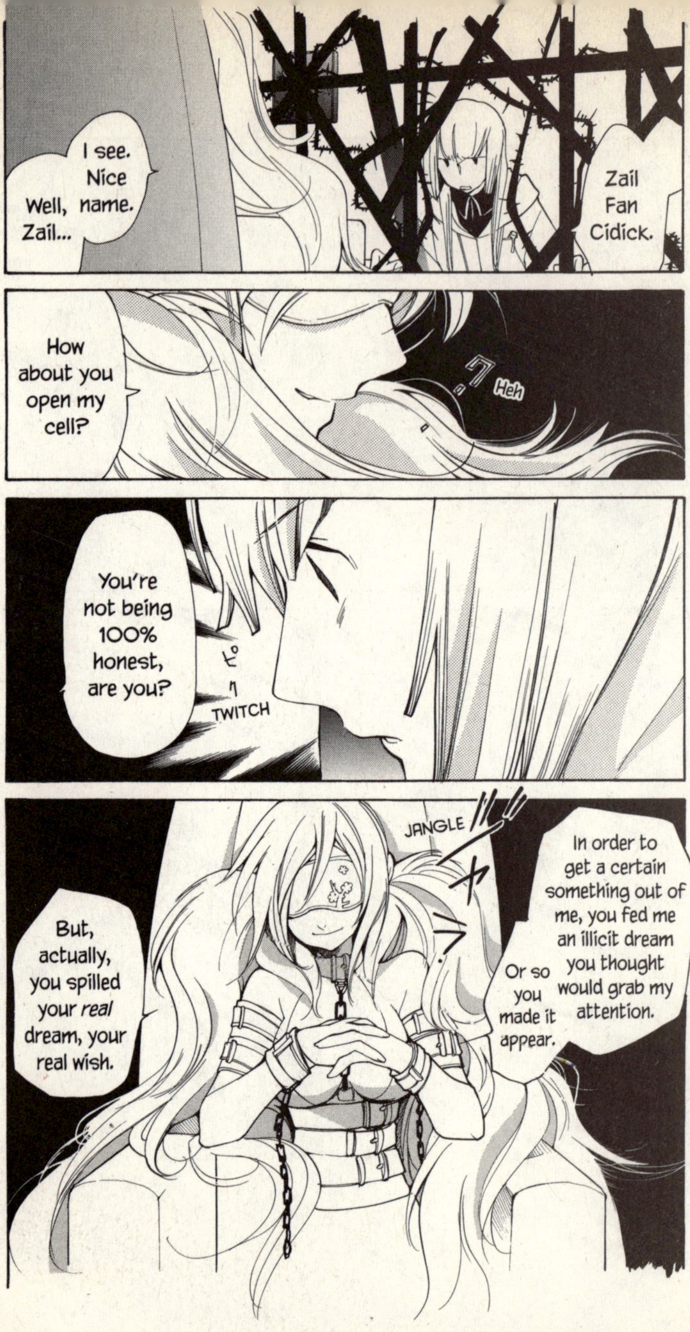
Zail Fan Cidick.
I see. Nice name.
Well, Zail...
How about you open my cell?
?
Heh
You're not being 100% honest, are you?
TWITCH
JANGLE
In order to get a certain something out of me, you fed me an illicit dream you thought would grab my attention.
Or so you made it appear.
But, actually, you spilled your *real* dream, your real wish.

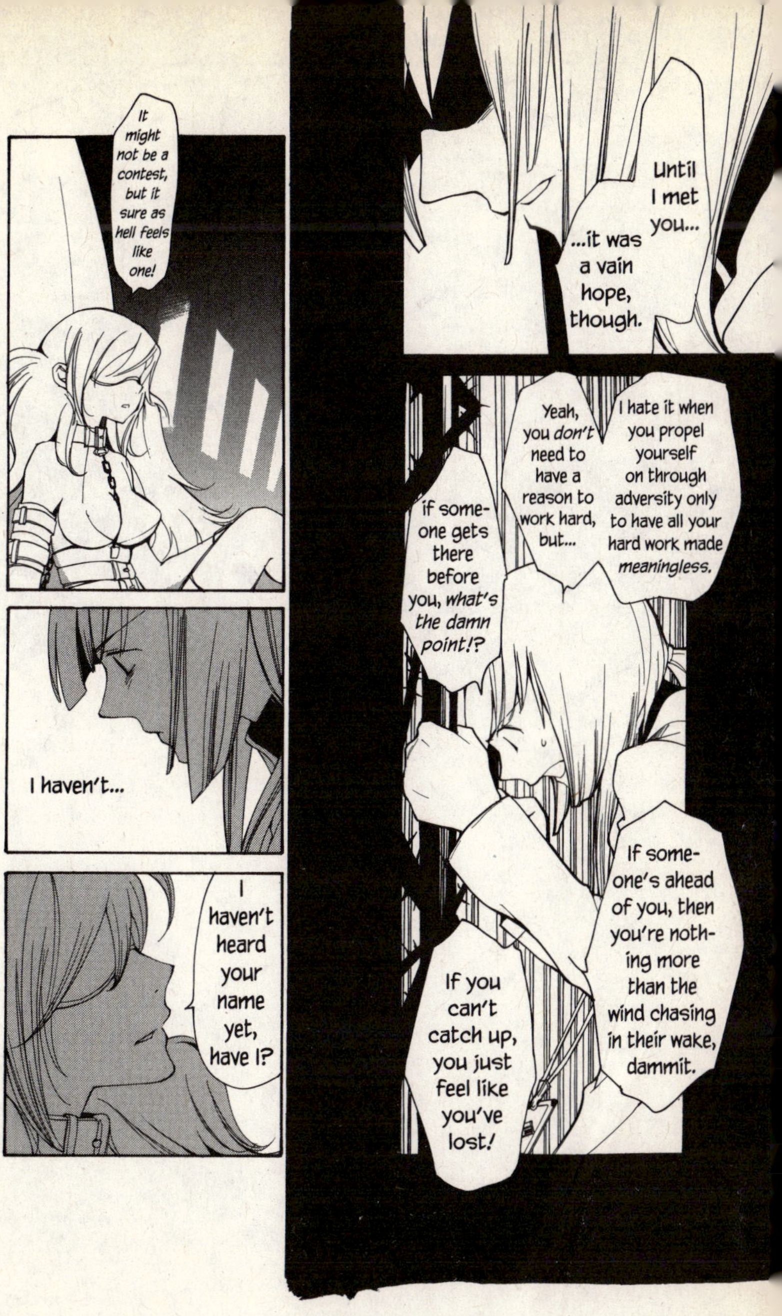
Until I met you...
...it was a vain hope, though.
I hate it when you propel yourself on through adversity only to have all your hard work made *meaningless.*
Yeah, you *don't* need to have a reason to work hard, but...
if some-one gets there before you, *what's the damn point!?*
If some-one's ahead of you, then you're noth-ing more than the wind chasing in their wake, dammit.
If you can't catch up, you just feel like you've lost*!*
It might not be a contest, but it sure as hell feels like one!
I haven't...
I haven't heard your name yet, have I?

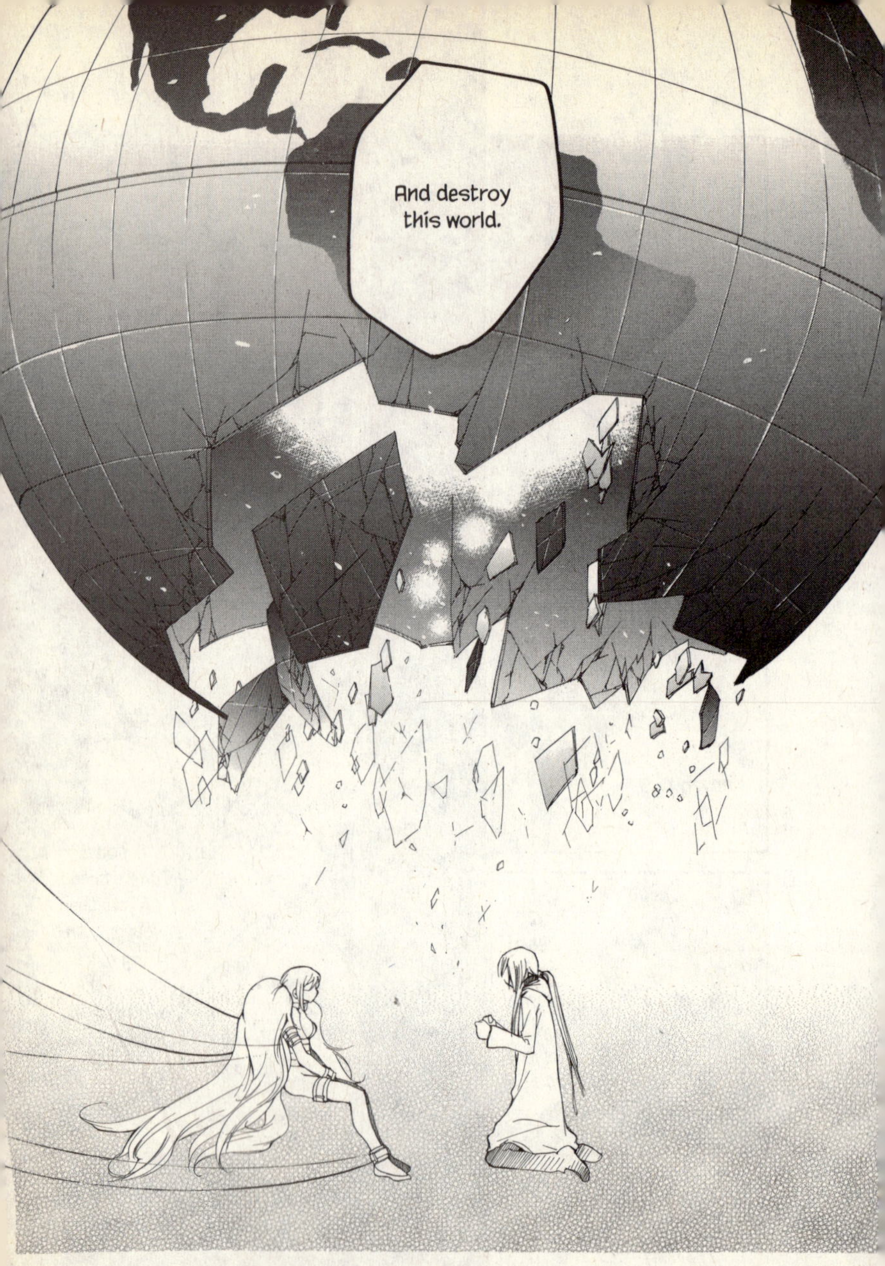
And destroy this world.

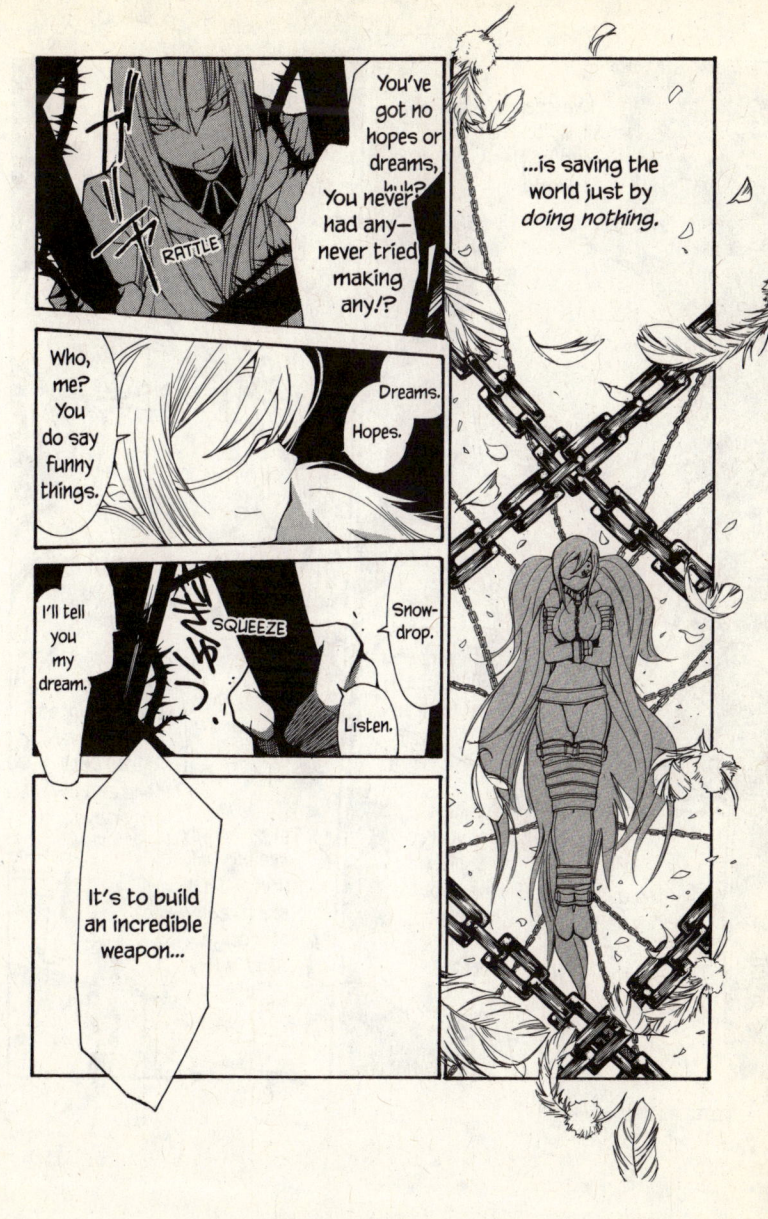

"You've got no hopes or dreams. You never had any— never tried making any!?"

RATTLE

"...is saving the world just by *doing nothing*."

"Who, me? You do say funny things."

"Dreams. Hopes."

SQUEEZE

"I'll tell you my dream."

"Snowdrop. Listen."

"It's to build an incredible weapon..."

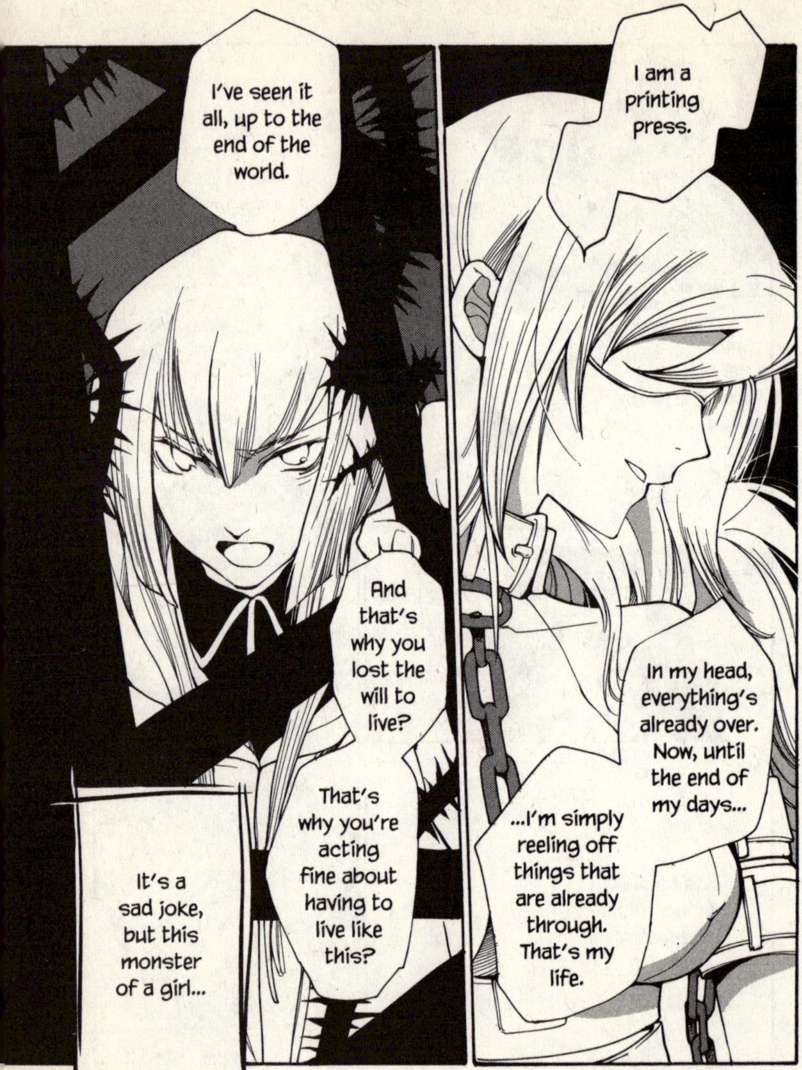
I am a printing press.
In my head, everything's already over. Now, until the end of my days...
...I'm simply reeling off things that are already through. That's my life.
I've seen it all, up to the end of the world.
And that's why you lost the will to live?
That's why you're acting fine about having to live like this?
It's a sad joke, but this monster of a girl...

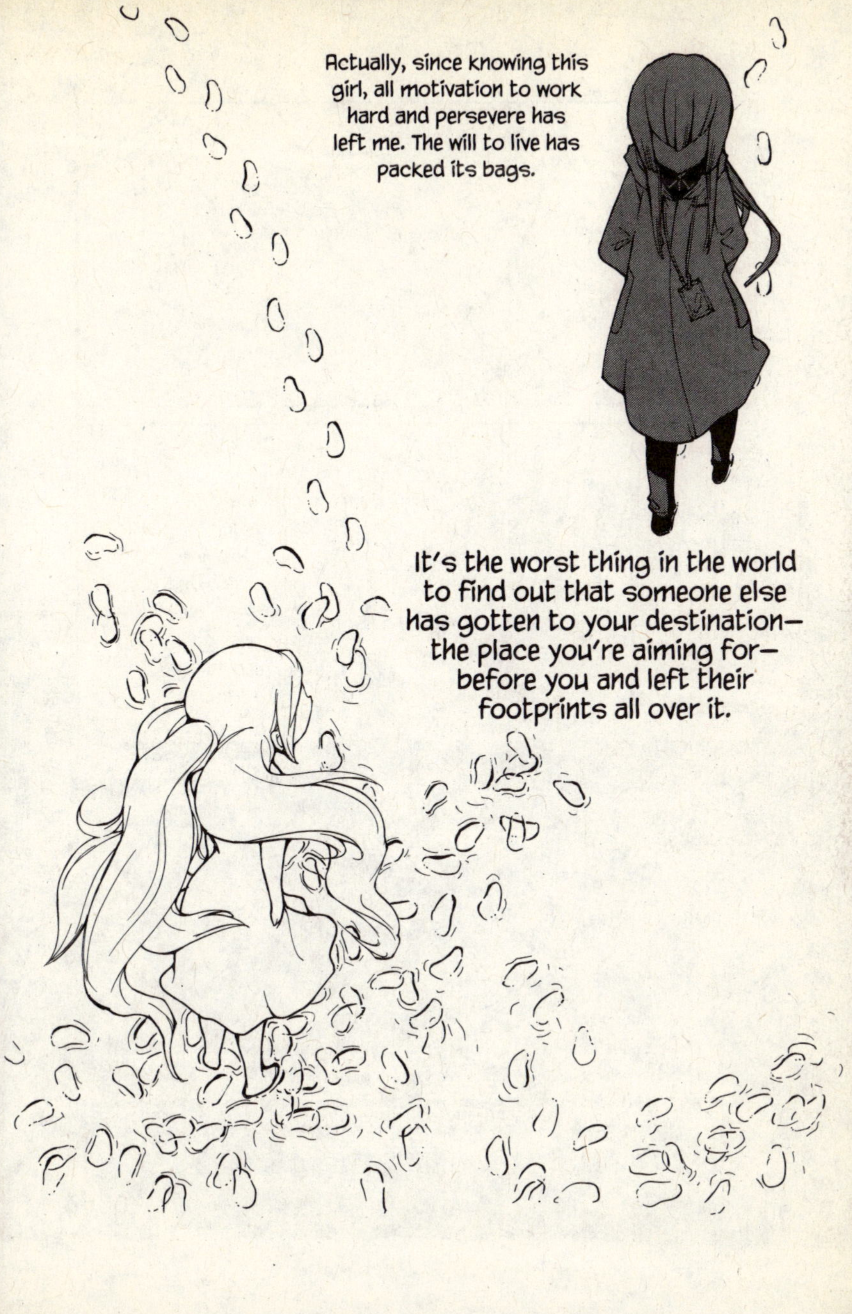
Actually, since knowing this girl, all motivation to work hard and persevere has left me. The will to live has packed its bags.
It's the worst thing in the world to find out that someone else has gotten to your destination—the place you're aiming for—before you and left their footprints all over it.

We totally agree.

Completely.

Still, even that kind of example means nothing to this girl.

...You say that, but... when you reach the goal line only to find someone *else* got there before you...

Being a genius makes you almighty.

You feel *omnipotent*.

Which means you're almost like a *god*.

All-powerful.

In the same way people argue that there must be a god, natural prodigies must exist in the world, too. Though thinking something might be nice if it existed and actually *wanting* it to exist are two deceptively different things.

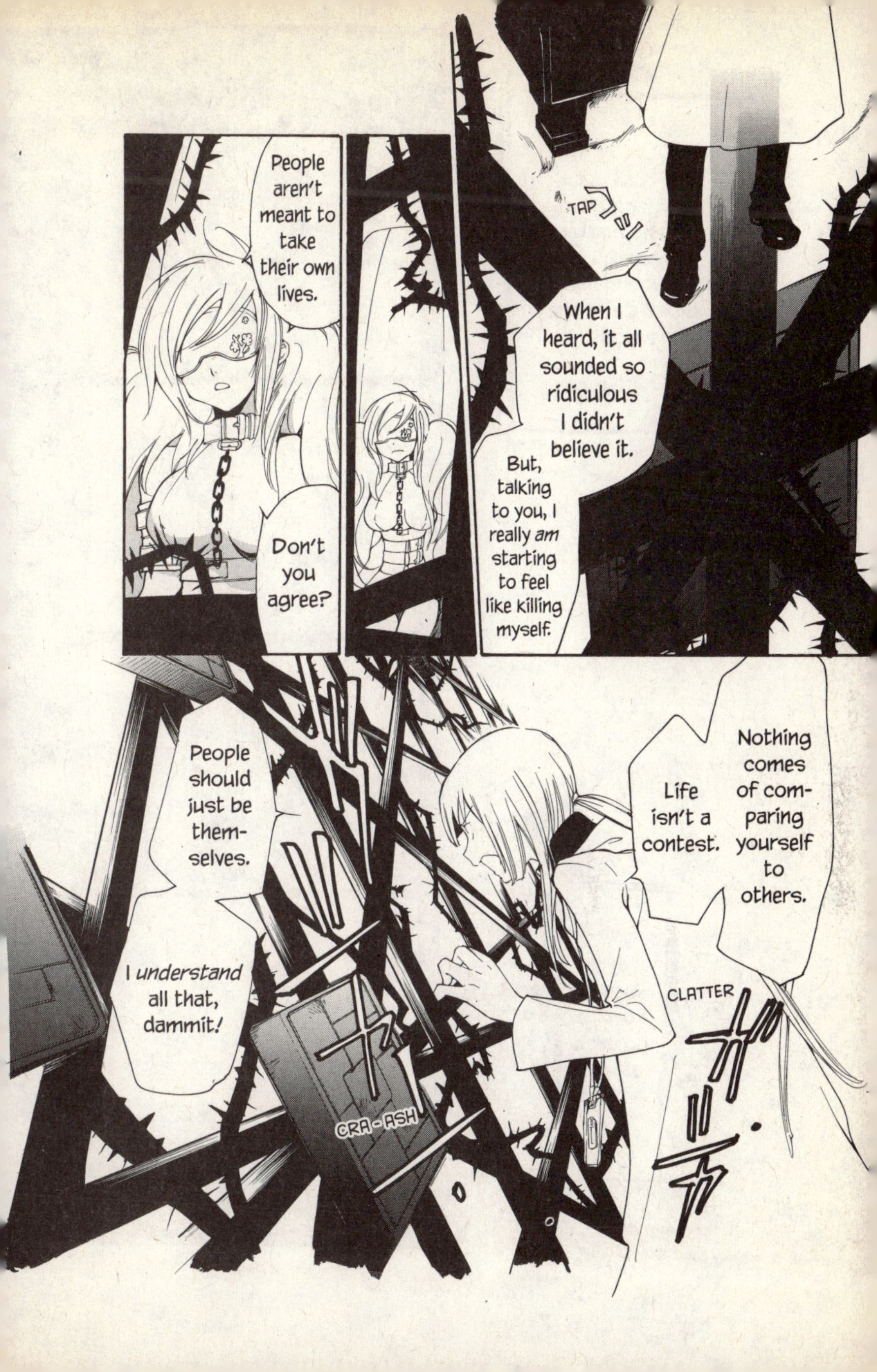
TAP
When I heard, it all sounded so ridiculous I didn't believe it.
But, talking to you, I really *am* starting to feel like killing myself.
People aren't meant to take their own lives.
Don't you agree?
Nothing comes of comparing yourself to others.
Life isn't a contest.
People should just be themselves.
I *understand* all that, dammit!
CLATTER
CRA-ASH

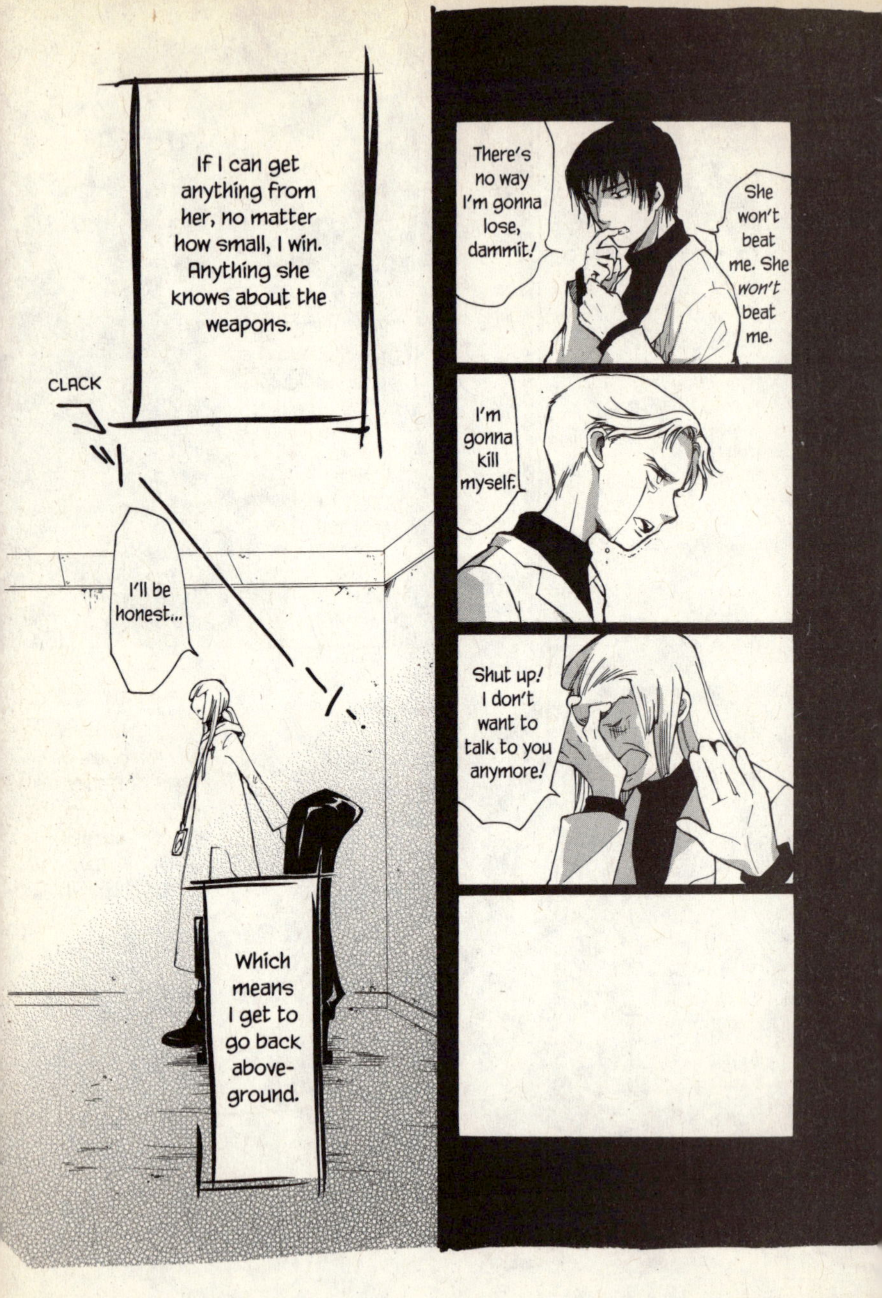

There's no way I'm gonna lose, dammit!
She won't beat me. She *won't* beat me.
I'm gonna kill myself.
Shut up! I don't want to talk to you anymore!
If I can get anything from her, no matter how small, I win. Anything she knows about the weapons.
CLACK
I'll be honest...
Which means I get to go back above-ground.

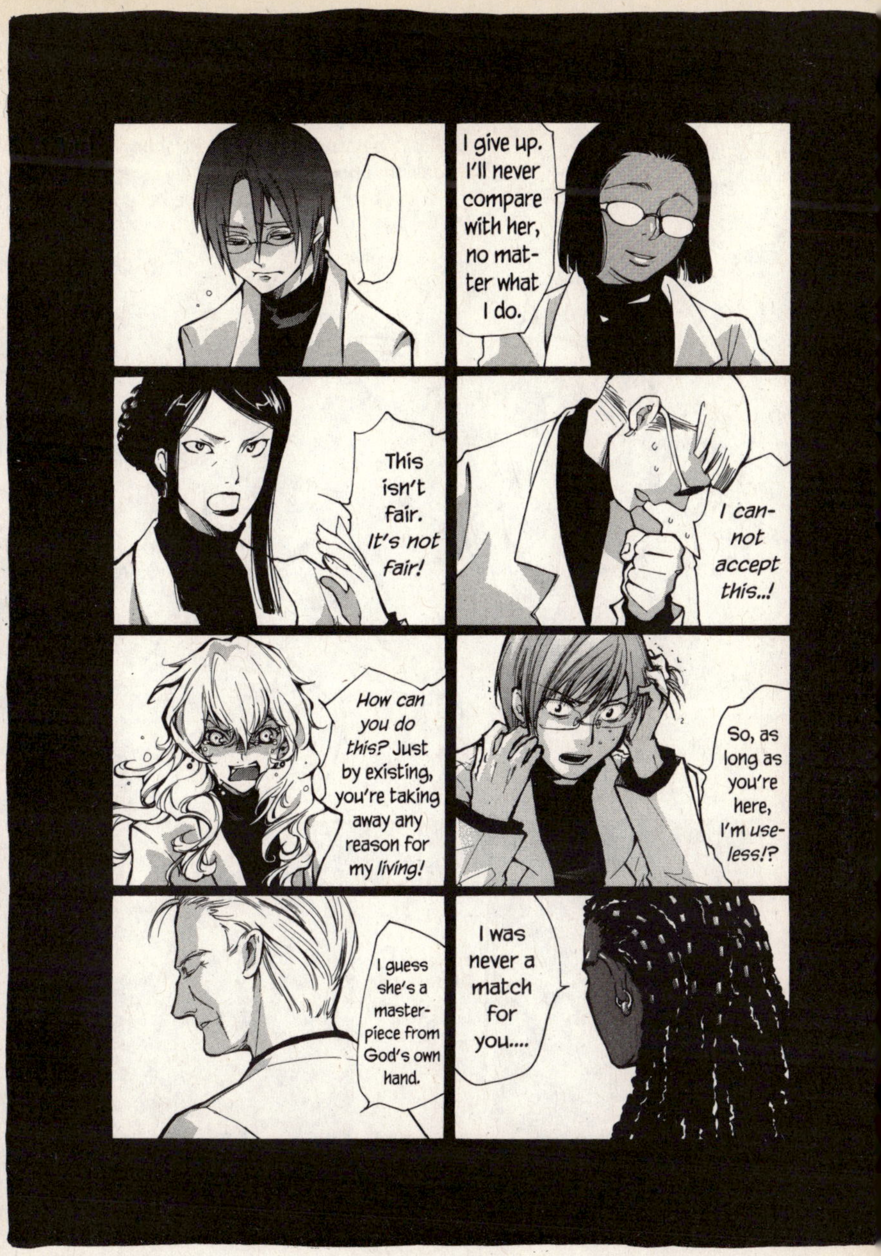
I give up. I'll never compare with her, no matter what I do.
I cannot accept this..!
This isn't fair. It's not fair!
So, as long as you're here, I'm useless!?
How can you do this? Just by existing, you're taking away any reason for my living!
I was never a match for you....
I guess she's a masterpiece from God's own hand.

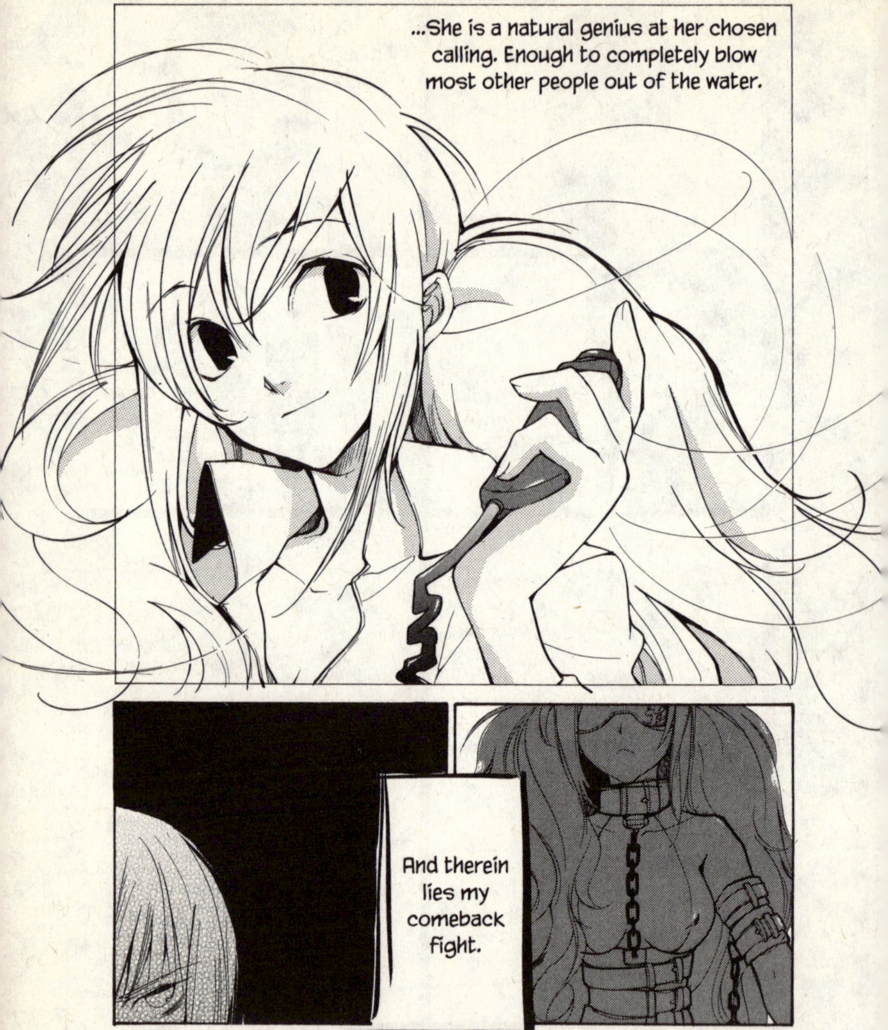
...She is a natural genius at her chosen calling. Enough to completely blow most other people out of the water.
And therein lies my comeback fight.

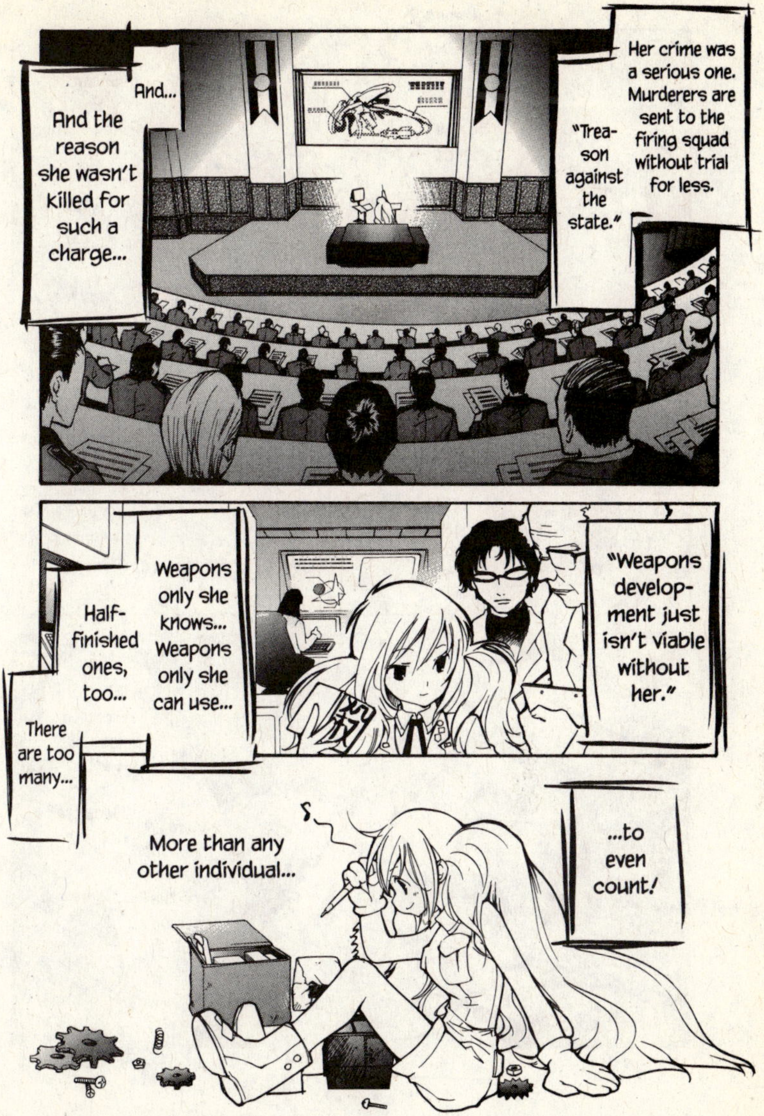
Her crime was a serious one. Murderers are sent to the firing squad without trial for less.
"Treason against the state."
And...
And the reason she wasn't killed for such a charge...
"Weapons development just isn't viable without her."
Weapons only she knows... Weapons only she can use...
Half-finished ones, too...
There are too many...
More than any other individual...
...to even count!

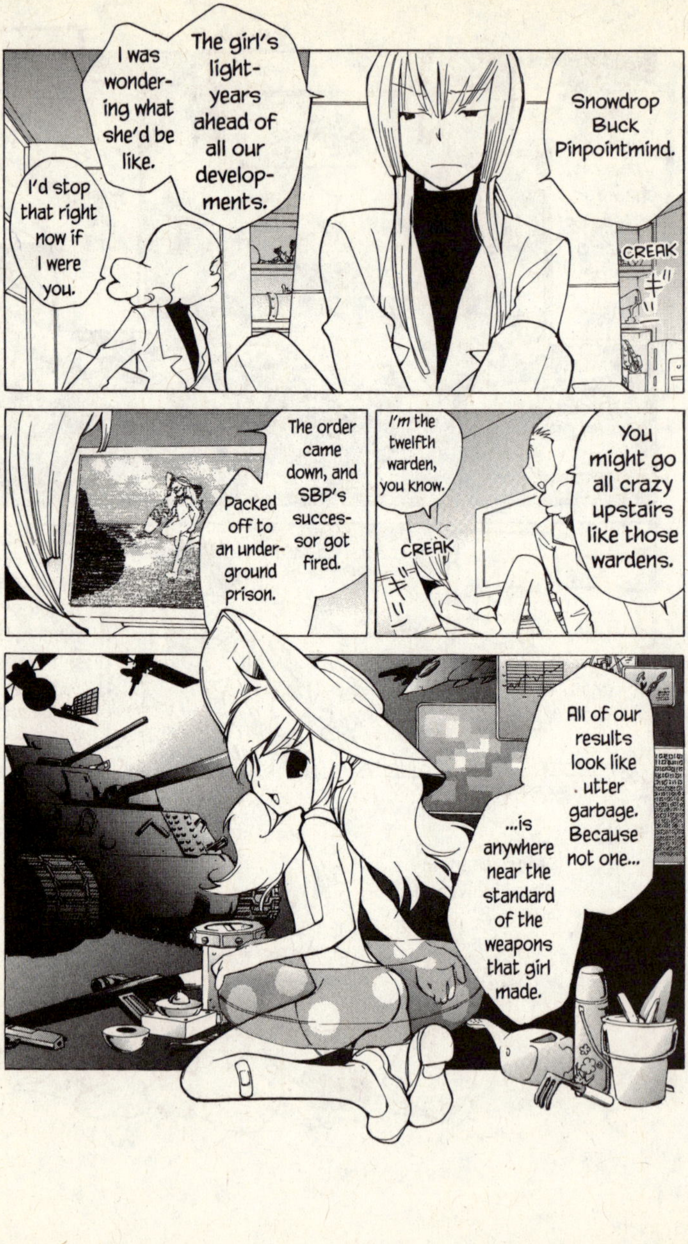

Snowdrop Buck Pinpointmind.
The girl's light-years ahead of all our developments.
I was wondering what she'd be like.
I'd stop that right now if I were you.
CREAK
You might go all crazy upstairs like those wardens.
I'm the twelfth warden, you know.
CREAK
The order came down, and SBP's successor got fired.
Packed off to an underground prison.
All of our results look like utter garbage. Because not one...
...is anywhere near the standard of the weapons that girl made.

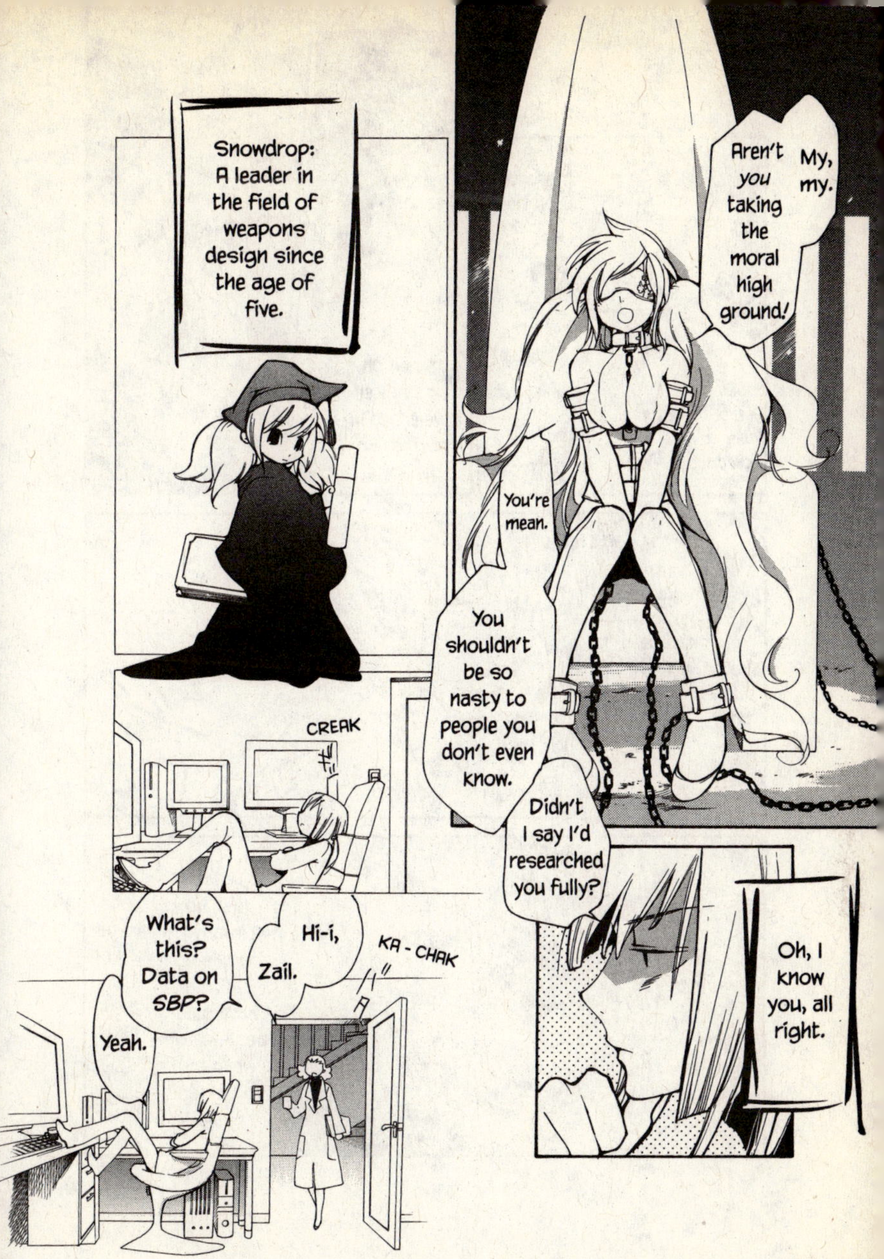

My, my.
Aren't *you* taking the moral high ground!
You're mean.
You shouldn't be so nasty to people you don't even know.
Didn't I say I'd researched you fully?
Oh, I know you, all right.
Snowdrop: A leader in the field of weapons design since the age of five.
CREAK
KA - CHAK
Hi-i, Zail.
What's this? Data on *SBP*?
Yeah.

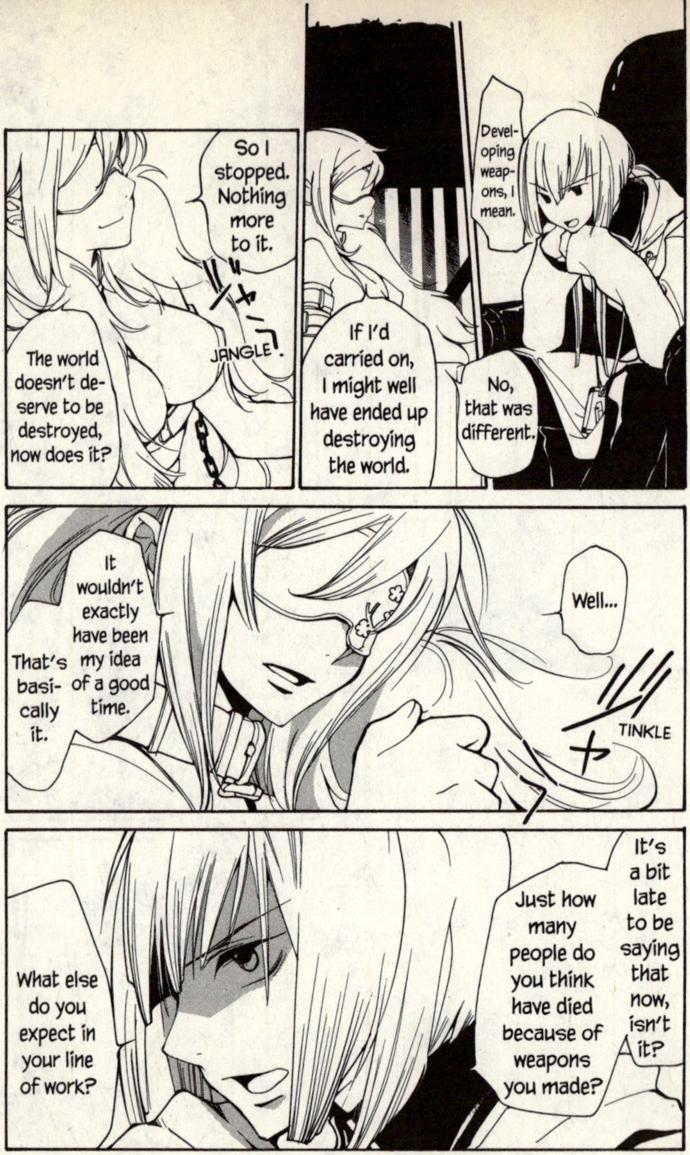
Devel-oping weap-ons, I mean.
No, that was different.
If I'd carried on, I might well have ended up destroying the world.
So I stopped. Nothing more to it.
JANGLE
The world doesn't deserve to be destroyed, now does it?
Well...
TINKLE
It wouldn't exactly have been my idea of a good time.
That's basi-cally it.
It's a bit late to be saying that now, isn't it?
Just how many people do you think have died because of weapons you made?
What else do you expect in your line of work?

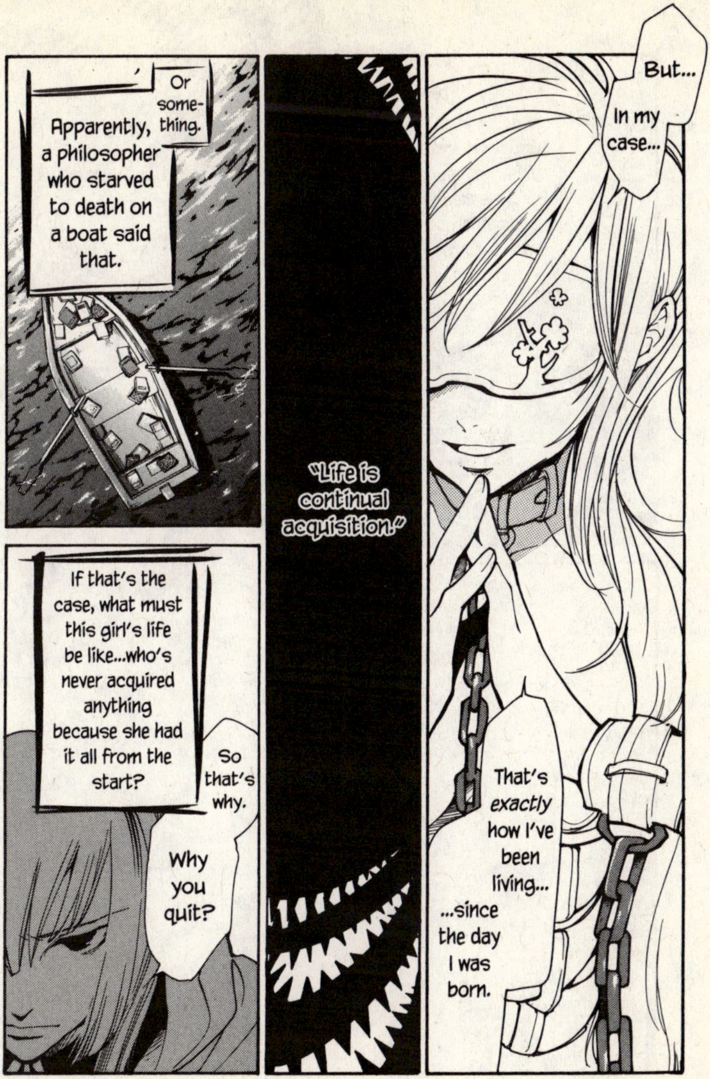

"Life is continual acquisition."
Apparently, a philosopher who starved to death on a boat said that.
Or something.
If that's the case, what must this girl's life be like...who's never acquired anything because she had it all from the start?
So that's why.
Why you quit?
But...
In my case...
That's *exactly* how I've been living...
...since the day I was born.

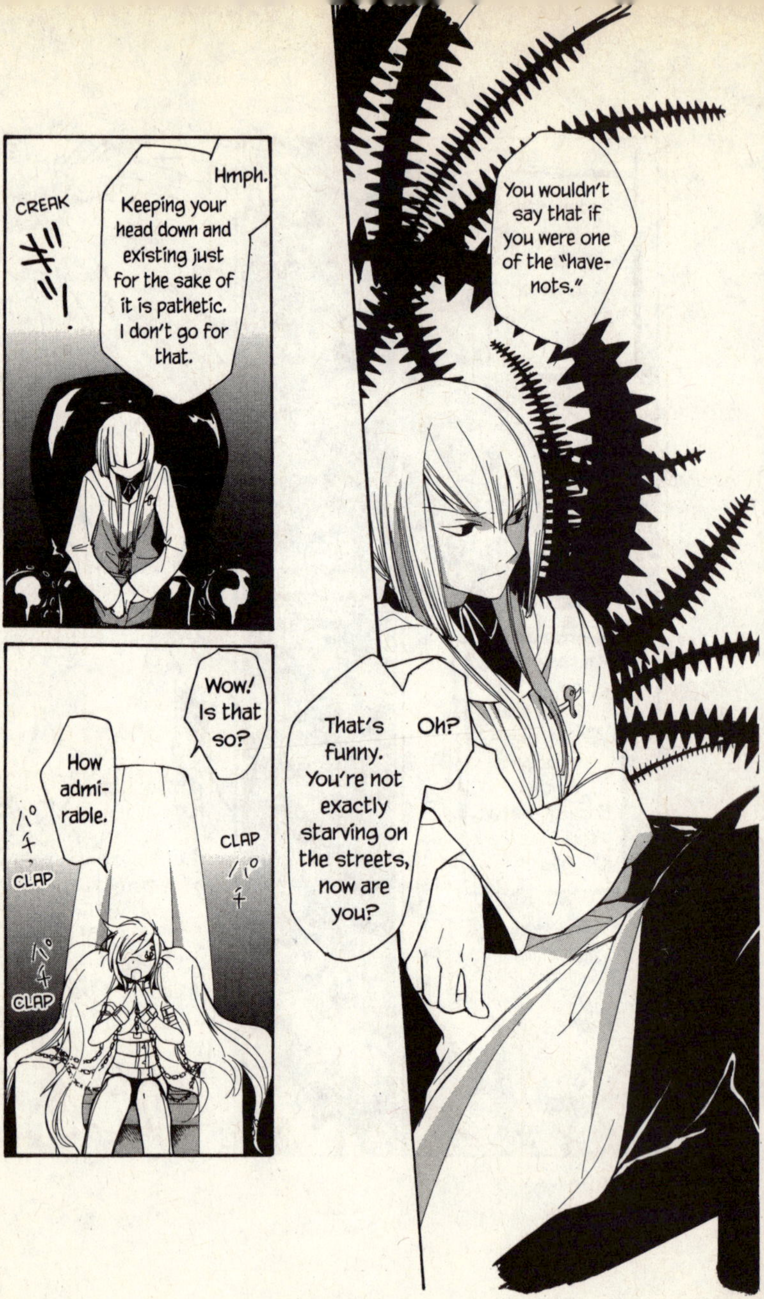
CREAK
Hmph.
Keeping your head down and existing just for the sake of it is pathetic. I don't go for that.
You wouldn't say that if you were one of the "have-nots."
Oh?
That's funny. You're not exactly starving on the streets, now are you?
Wow! Is that so?
How admirable.
CLAP
CLAP
CLAP

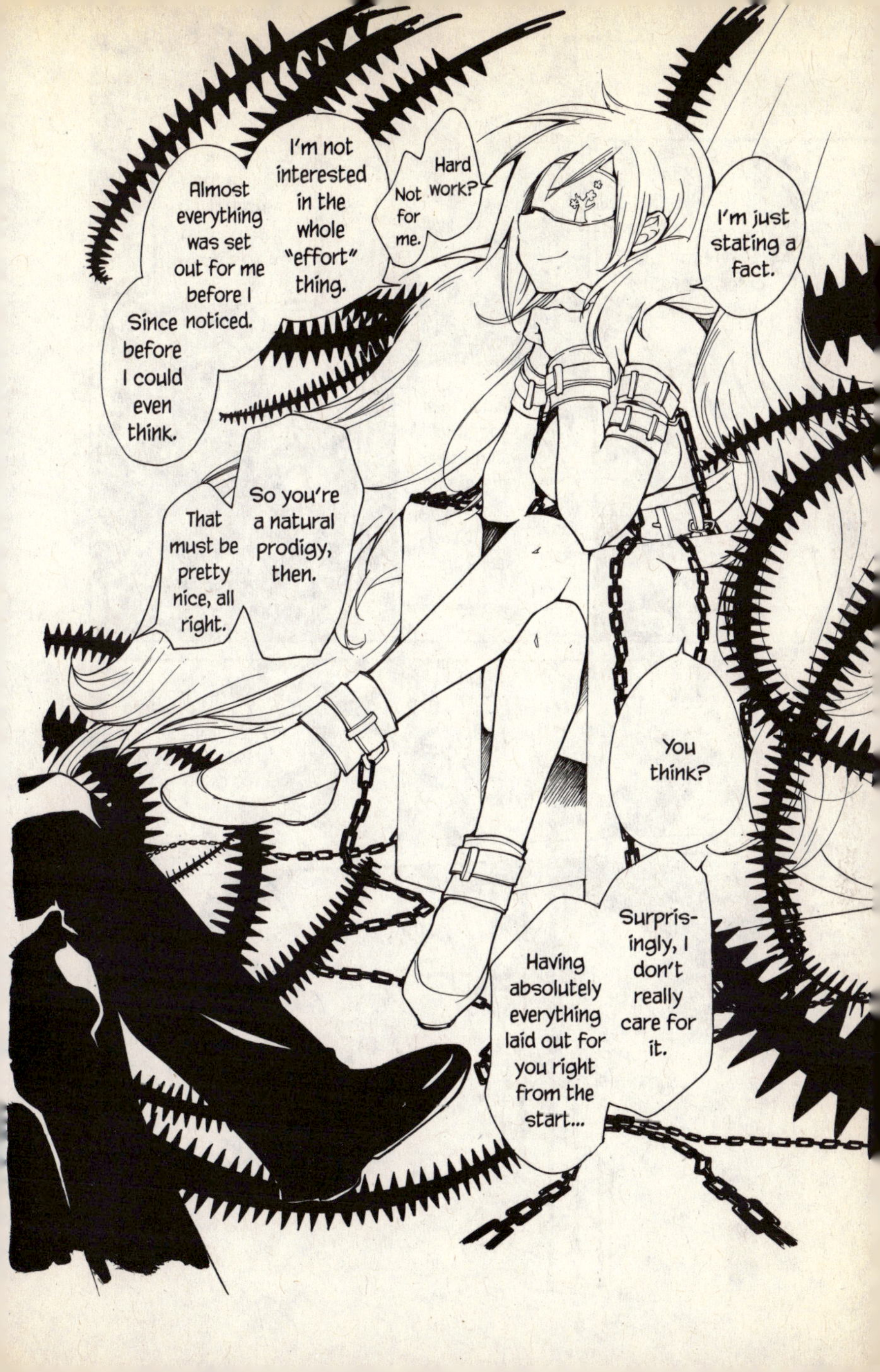
I'm just stating a fact.
Hard work?
Not for me.
I'm not interested in the whole "effort" thing.
Almost everything was set out for me before I noticed.
Since before I could even think.
So you're a natural prodigy, then.
That must be pretty nice, all right.
You think?
Surpris-ingly, I don't really care for it.
Having absolutely everything laid out for you right from the start...

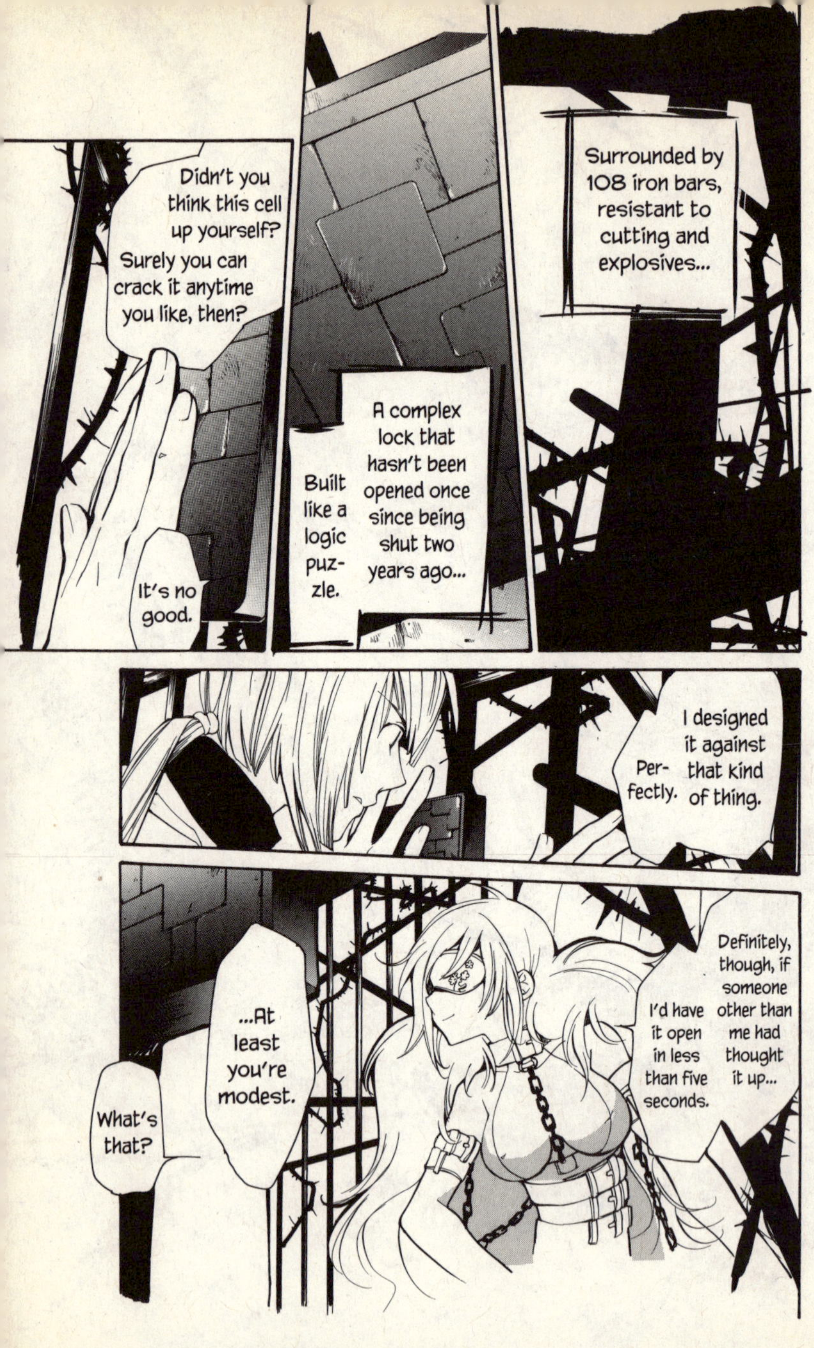
Surrounded by 108 iron bars, resistant to cutting and explosives...
A complex lock that hasn't been opened once since being shut two years ago...
Built like a logic puz-zle.
Didn't you think this cell up yourself?
Surely you can crack it anytime you like, then?
It's no good.
I designed it against that kind of thing.
Per-fectly.
Definitely, though, if someone other than me had thought it up...
I'd have it open in less than five seconds.
...At least you're modest.
What's that?

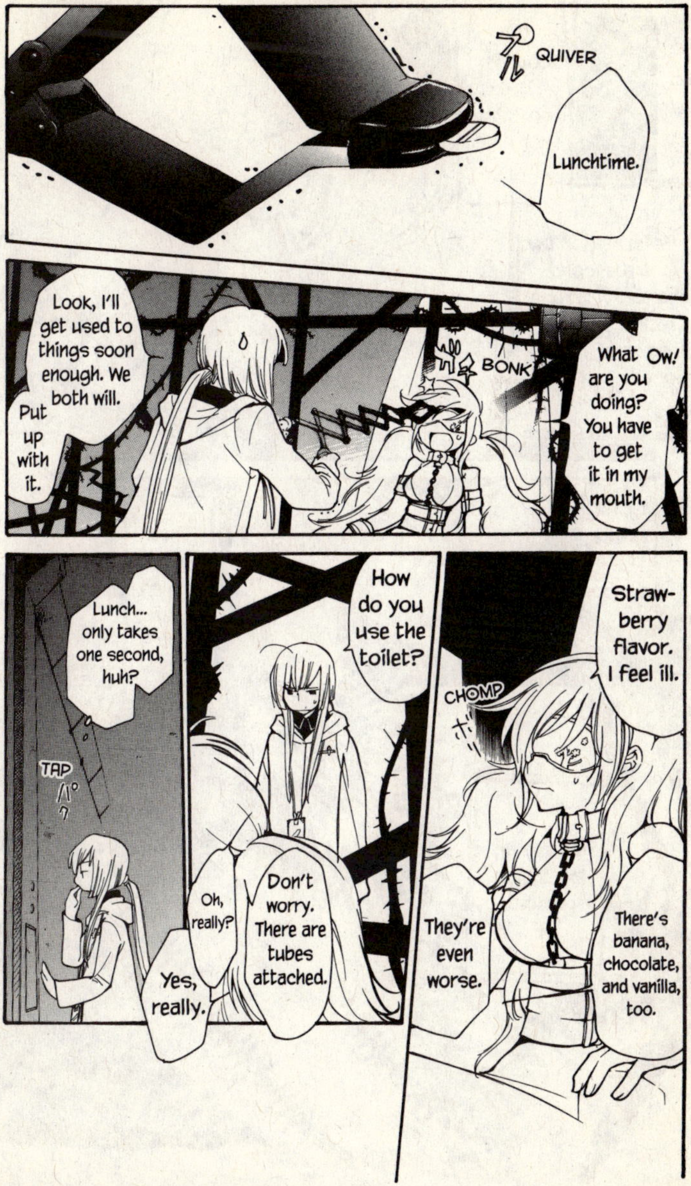
QUIVER
Lunchtime.
What are you doing? You have to get it in my mouth.
Ow!
BONK
Look, I'll get used to things soon enough. We both will.
Put up with it.
Strawberry flavor. I feel ill.
CHOMP
There's banana, chocolate, and vanilla, too.
They're even worse.
How do you use the toilet?
Don't worry. There are tubes attached.
Oh, really?
Yes, really.
Lunch... only takes one second, huh?
TAP

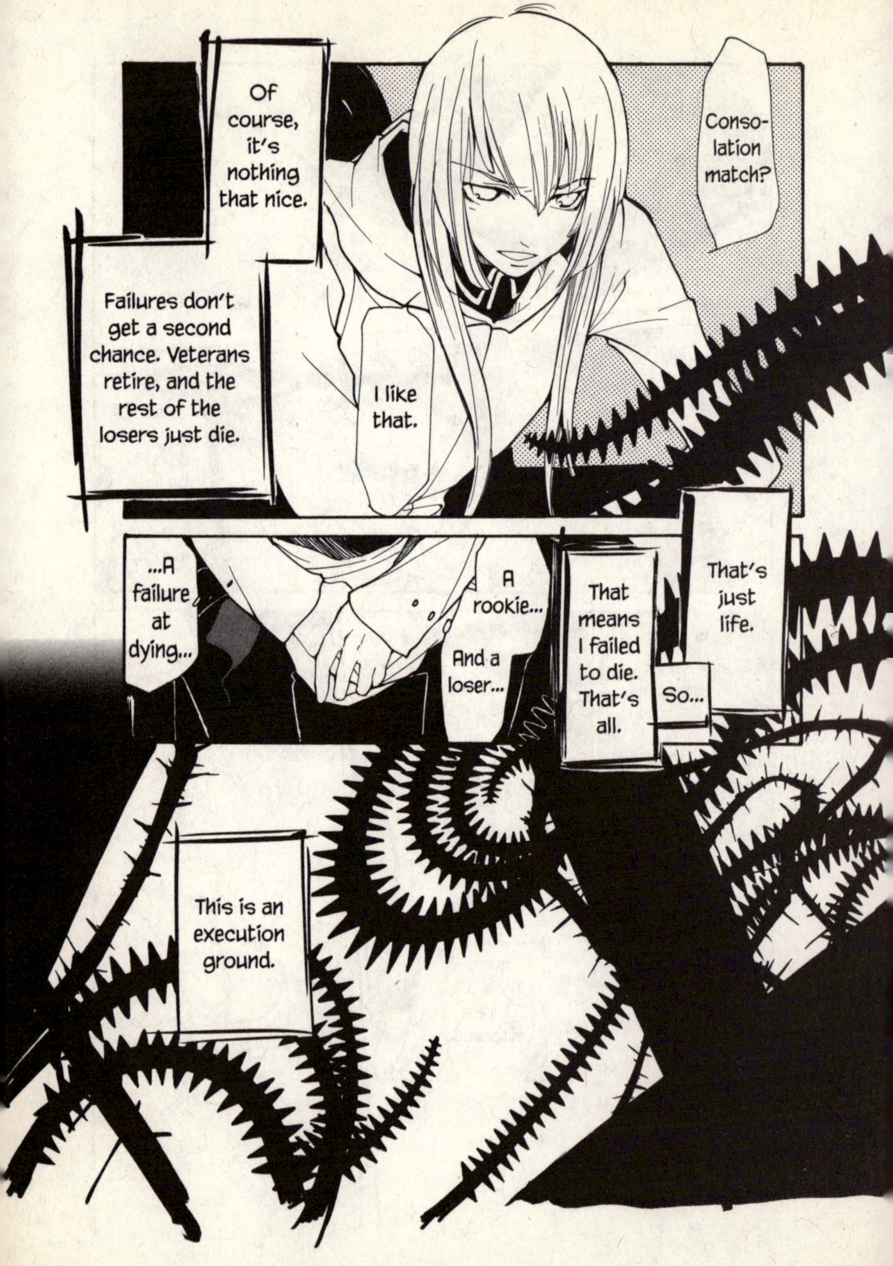
Conso-lation match?
Of course, it's nothing that nice.
Failures don't get a second chance. Veterans retire, and the rest of the losers just die.
I like that.
That's just life.
So...
That means I failed to die. That's all.
A rookie...
And a loser...
...A failure at dying...
This is an execution ground.

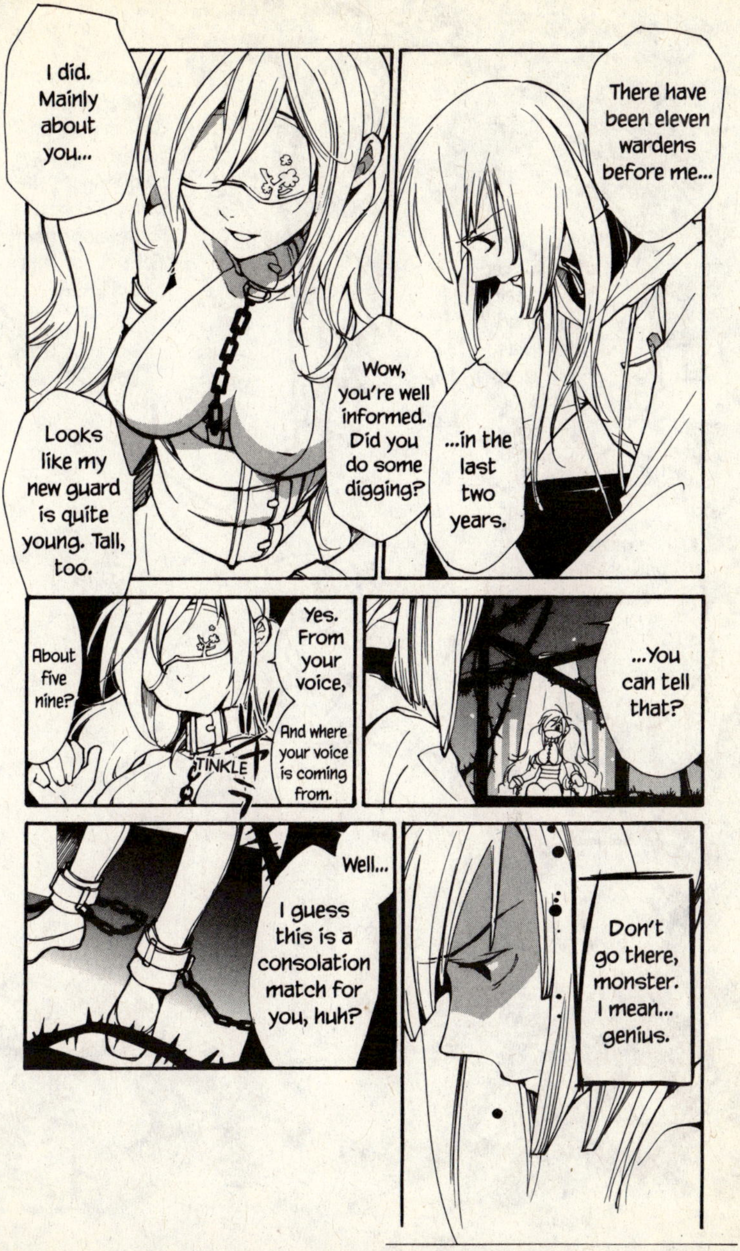
There have been eleven wardens before me...
...in the last two years.
Wow, you're well informed. Did you do some digging?
I did. Mainly about you...
Looks like my new guard is quite young. Tall, too.
...You can tell that?
Yes. From your voice,
And where your voice is coming from.
TINKLE
About five nine?
Well...
I guess this is a consolation match for you, huh?
Don't go there, monster. I mean... genius.

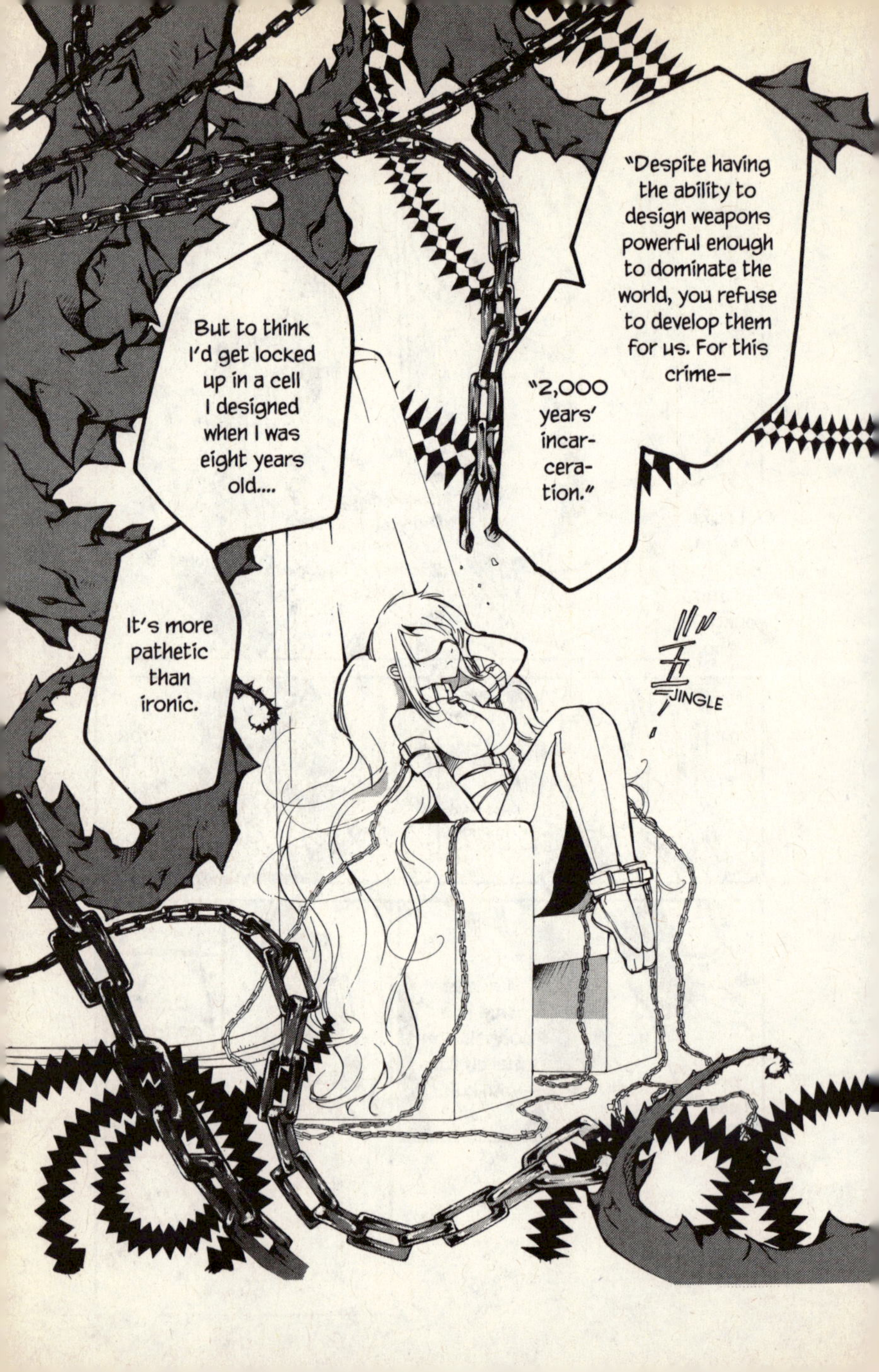
"Despite having the ability to design weapons powerful enough to dominate the world, you refuse to develop them for us. For this crime—
"2,000 years' incarceration."
But to think I'd get locked up in a cell I designed when I was eight years old....
It's more pathetic than ironic.
JINGLE

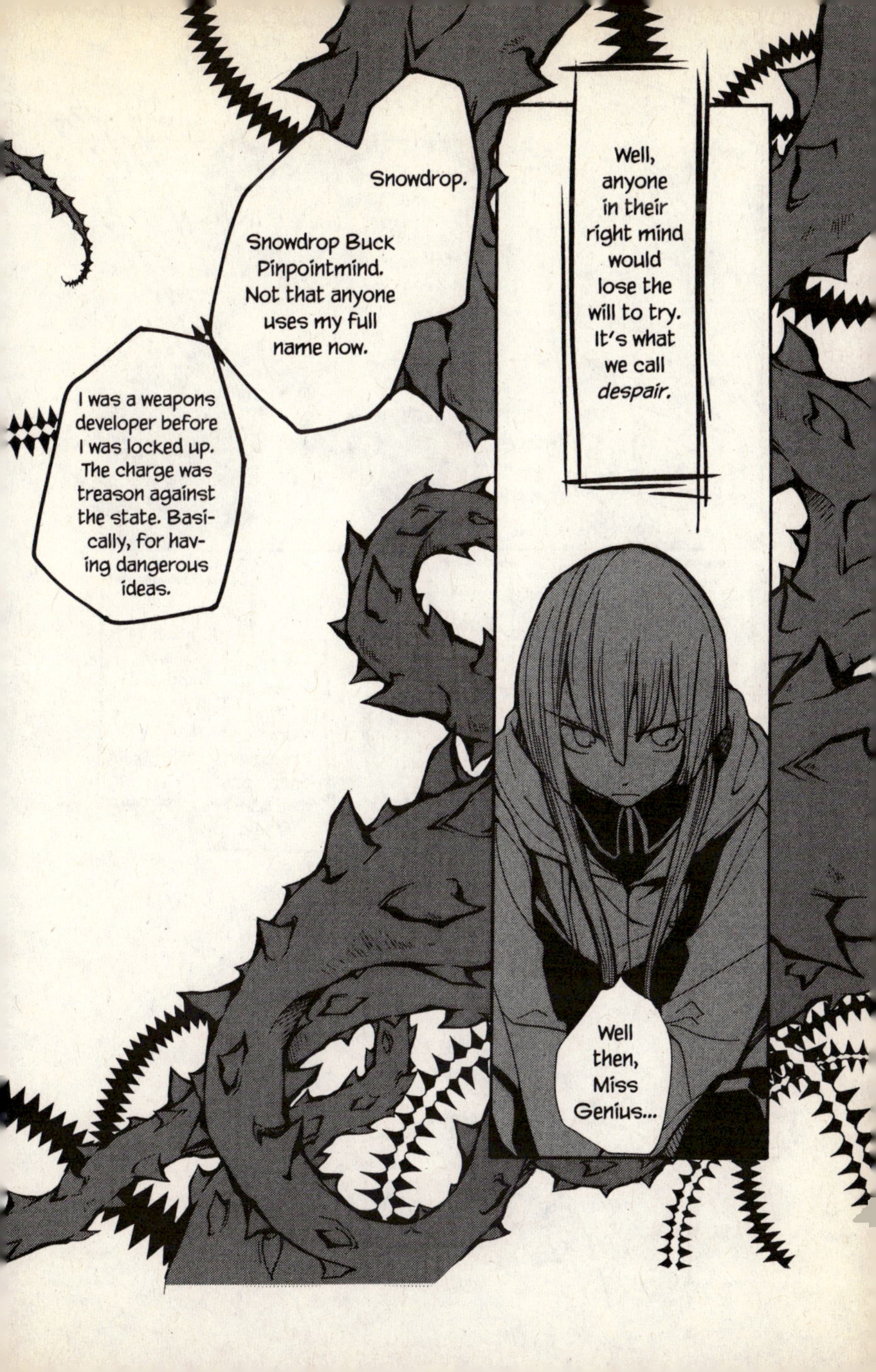
Well, anyone in their right mind would lose the will to try. It's what we call *despair.*
Snowdrop.
Snowdrop Buck Pinpointmind. Not that anyone uses my full name now.
I was a weapons developer before I was locked up. The charge was treason against the state. Basically, for having dangerous ideas.
Well then, Miss Genius...

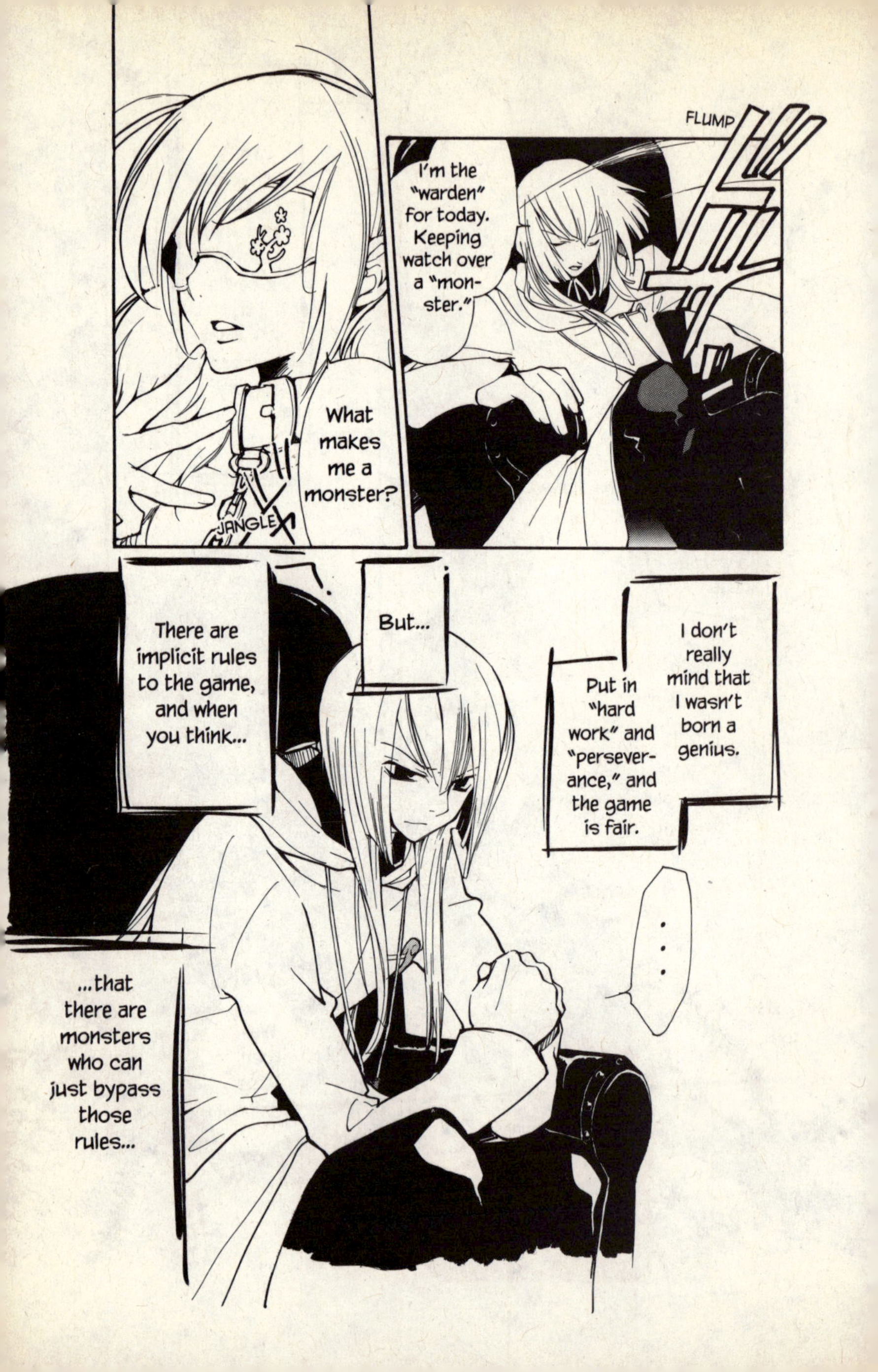
FLUMP
I'm the "warden" for today. Keeping watch over a "monster."
What makes me a monster?
JANGLE
I don't really mind that I wasn't born a genius.
Put in "hard work" and "perseverance," and the game is fair.
But...
There are implicit rules to the game, and when you think...
...
...that there are monsters who can just bypass those rules...

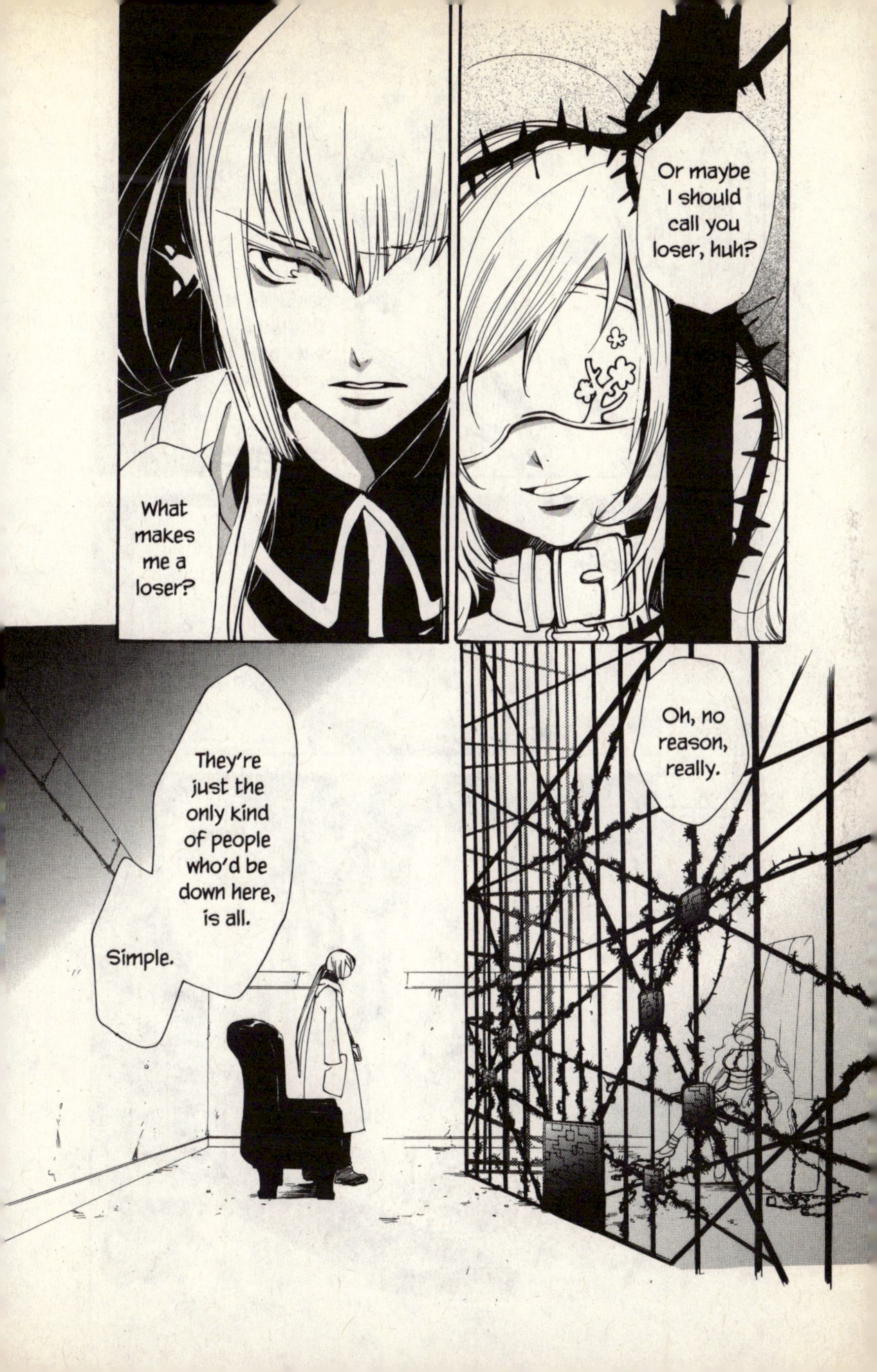
Or maybe I should call you loser, huh?
What makes me a loser?
Oh, no reason, really.
They're just the only kind of people who'd be down here, is all.
Simple.

There are geniuses in this world, and I'm not one of them.

So the problem isn't with me. It's an external issue.

Or whatever.

Of course, I'm no idiot, either. I figured out that I was no genius long ago.

Aren't you even going to say hello?

...Rookie?

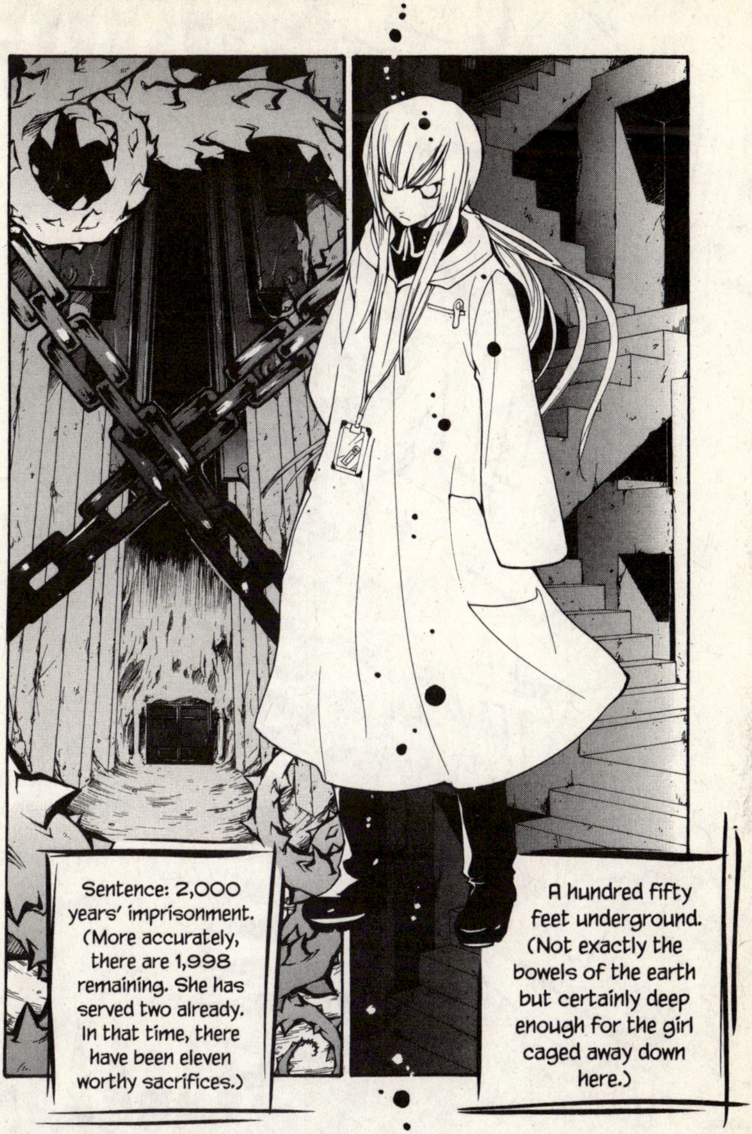
Sentence: 2,000 years' imprisonment. (More accurately, there are 1,998 remaining. She has served two already. In that time, there have been eleven worthy sacrifices.)
A hundred fifty feet underground. (Not exactly the bowels of the earth but certainly deep enough for the girl caged away down here.)

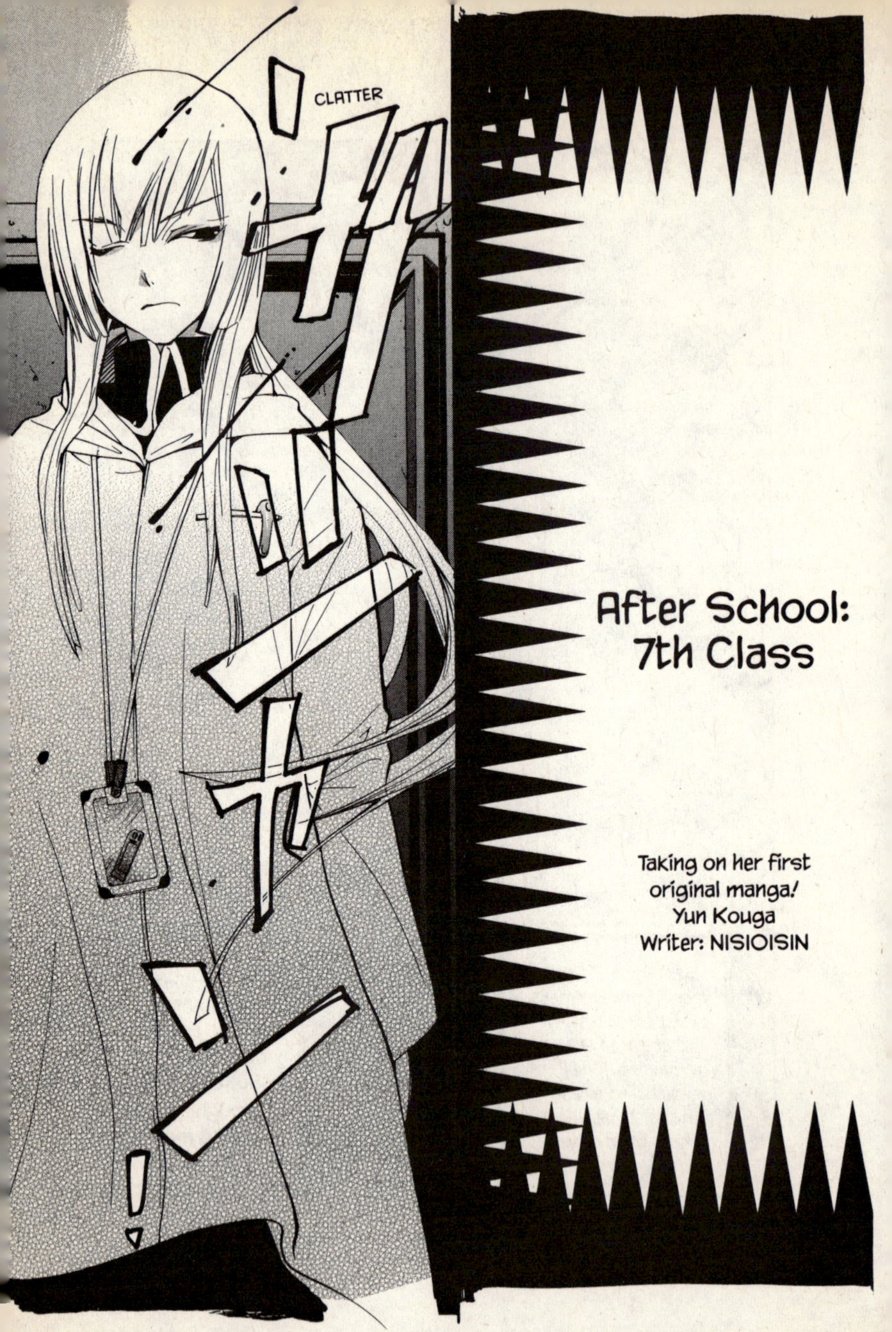
CLATTER

After School: 7th Class

Taking on her first
original manga!
Yun Kouga
Writer: NISIOISIN

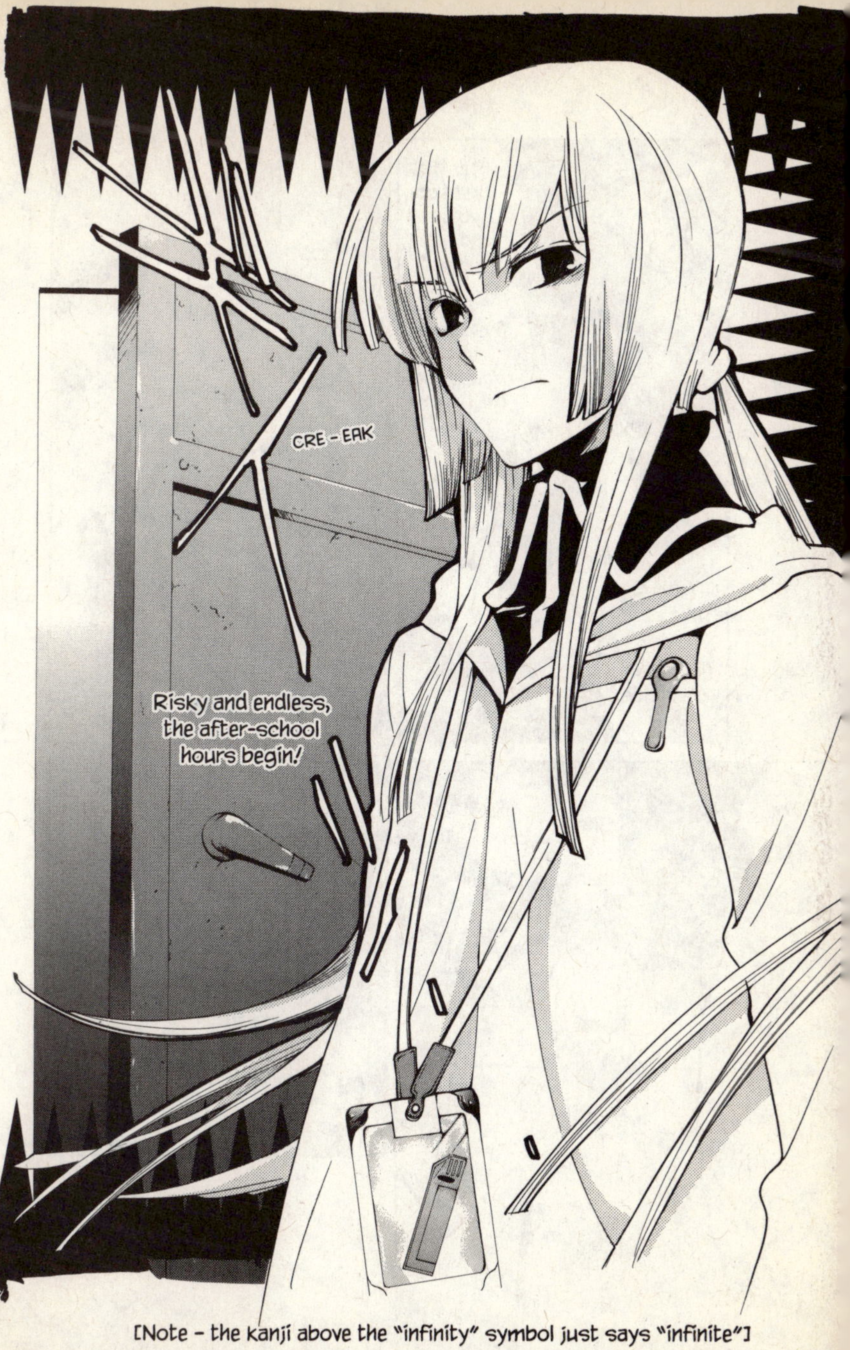
CRE - EAK
Risky and endless, the after-school hours begin!

[Note - the kanji above the "infinity" symbol just says "infinite"]

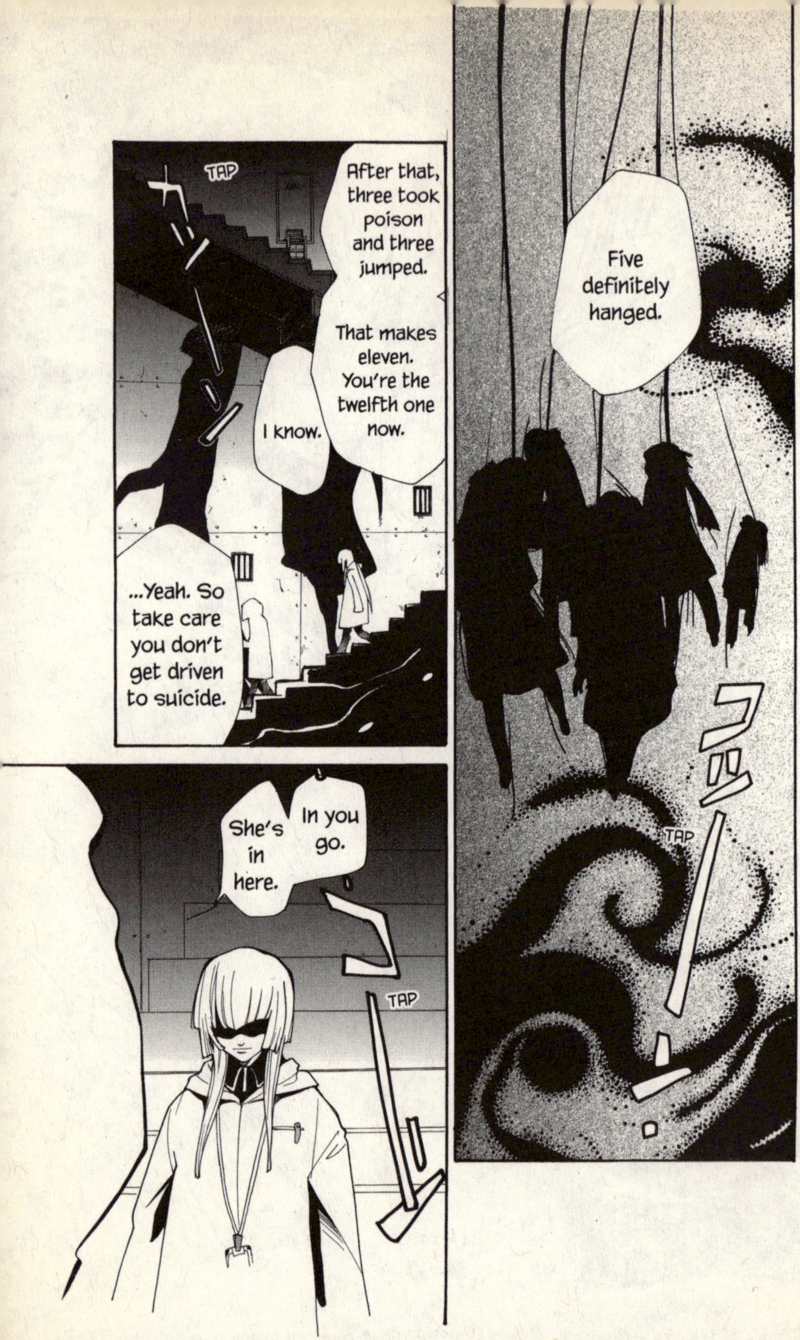
Five definitely hanged.
TAP
After that, three took poison and three jumped.
That makes eleven. You're the twelfth one now.
I know.
...Yeah. So take care you don't get driven to suicide.
TAP
In you go.
She's in here.
TAP

▲▼▲▼

AFTER SCHOOL: 7th CLASS

Art by Yun Kouga

NISIOISIN

Translated by Paul Johnson

NISIOISIN has come to dominate the Japanese literary world—this prolific bestselling novelist is one of Japan's most popular writers. In this story, he provides the story for a manga piece, in collaboration with one of Japan's most prominent manga creators: Yun Kouga.

Kouga's name is already seared into the minds of America's manga fans, thanks to her massively popular series Loveless, one of the top-selling manga in the United States. Like Ken Akamatsu and CLAMP, Yun Kouga is one of the many popular manga creators who arose out of Japan's Comiket (Comic Market, Japan's biggest comics convention) and doujinishi (fan fiction, self-published manga, novels, and other works) culture. Since then, Loveless, currently being serialized in *Comic Zero-Sum,* has cemented her reputation as a major talent. Adding to her accomplishments, she is the character designer for the latest installment in the mega-blockbuster Gundam franchise, *Mobile Suit Gundam 00,* a major honor for a manga artist.

▲▼▲▼

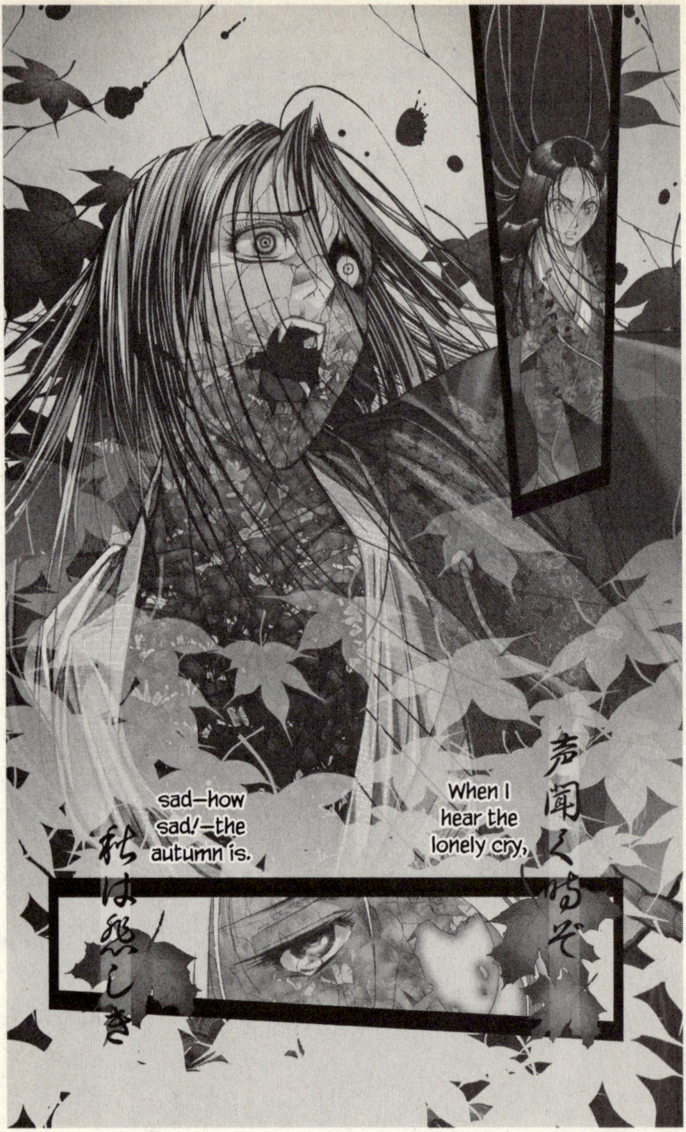
声聞く時ぞ
When I hear the lonely cry,
秋は悲しき
sad—how sad!—the autumn is.

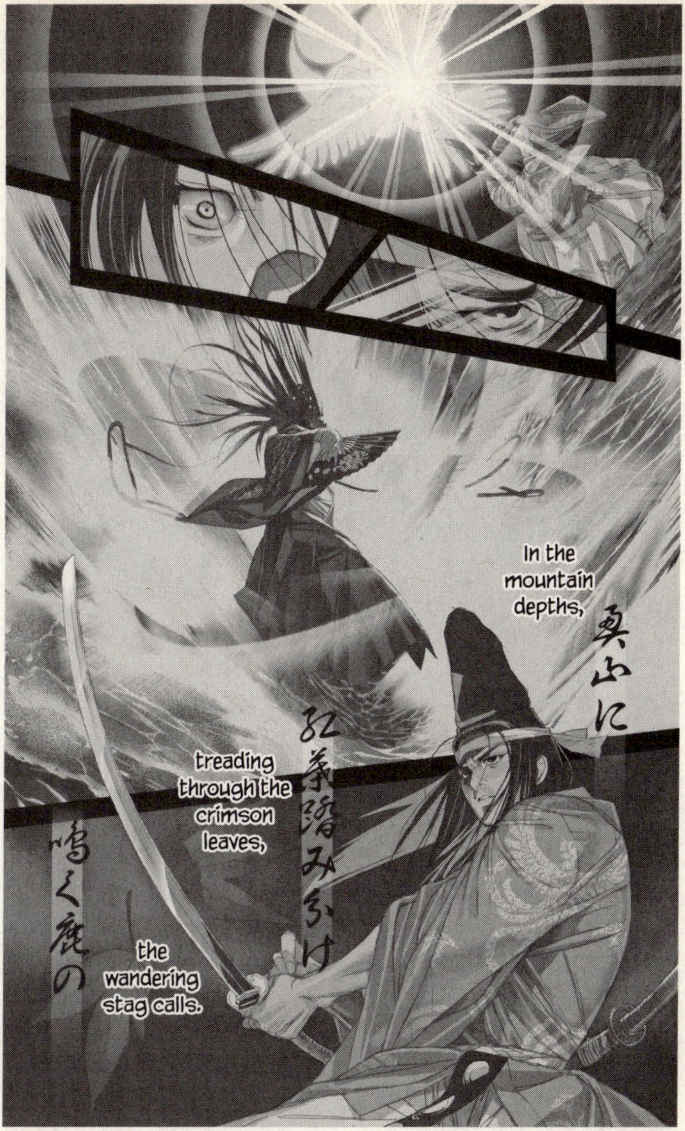
In the mountain depths,
奥山に
treading through the crimson leaves,
紅葉踏みわけ
the wandering stag calls.
鳴く鹿の

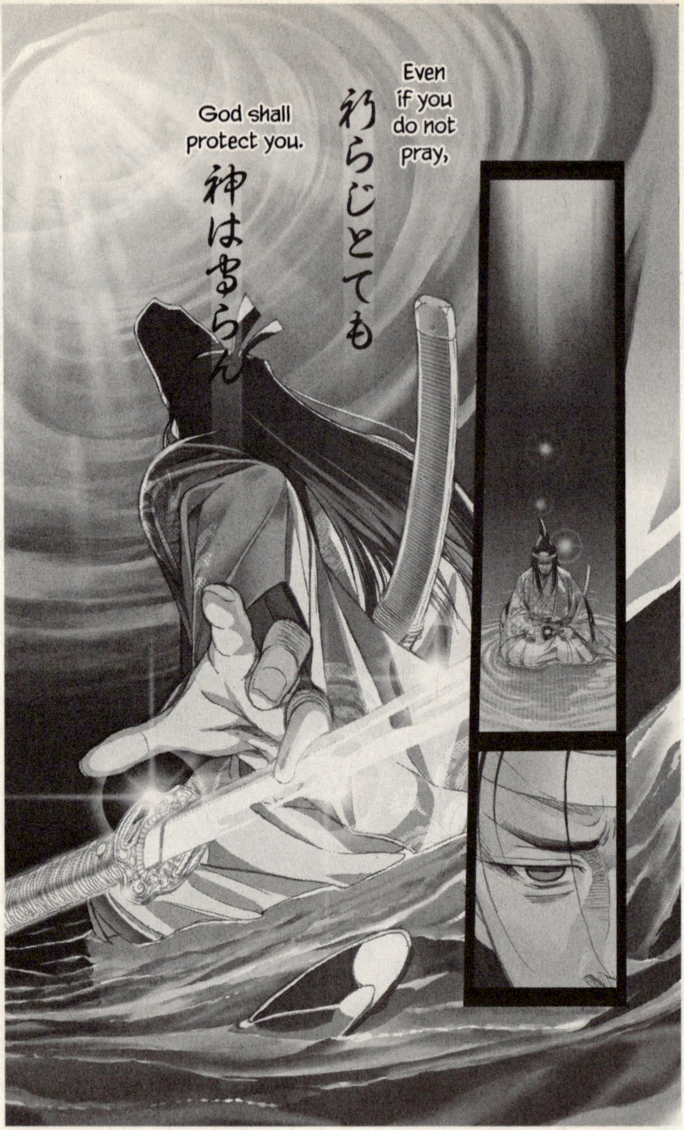
Even if you do not pray,
祈らじとても
God shall protect you.
神は守らん

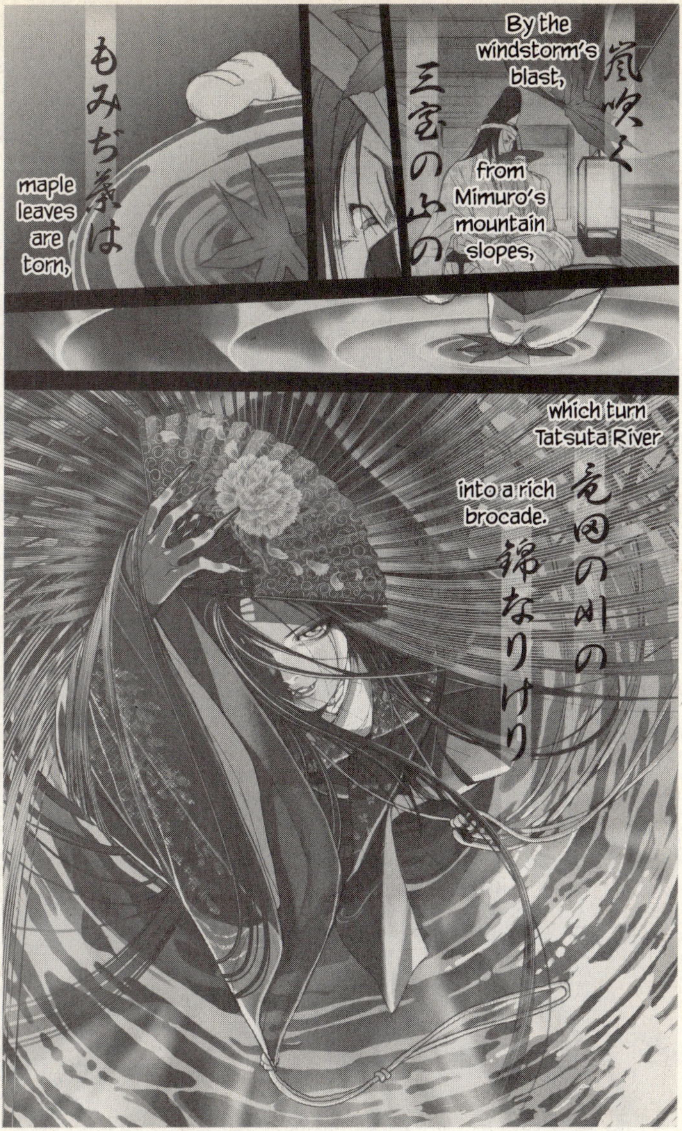
嵐吹く
By the windstorm's blast,
三室の山の
from Mimuro's mountain slopes,
もみぢ葉は
maple leaves are torn,
竜田の川の
which turn Tatsuta River
錦なりけり
into a rich brocade.

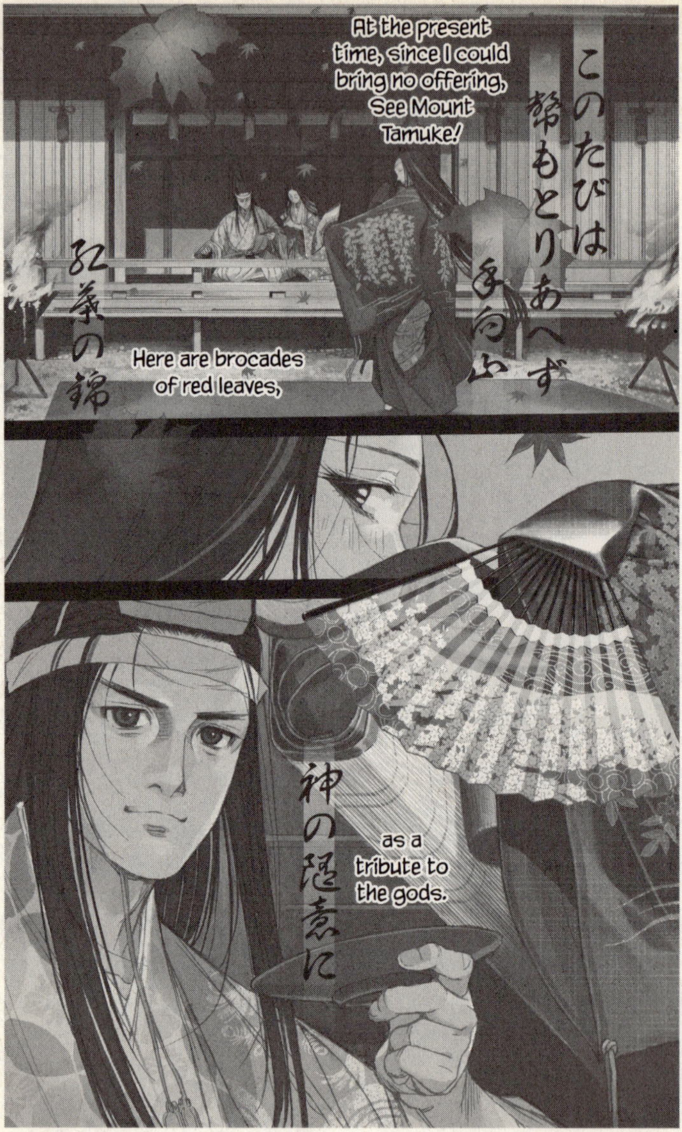
このたびは
幣もとりあへず
手向山
At the present time, since I could bring no offering, See Mount Tamuke!
紅葉の錦
Here are brocades of red leaves,
神の随意に
as a tribute to the gods.

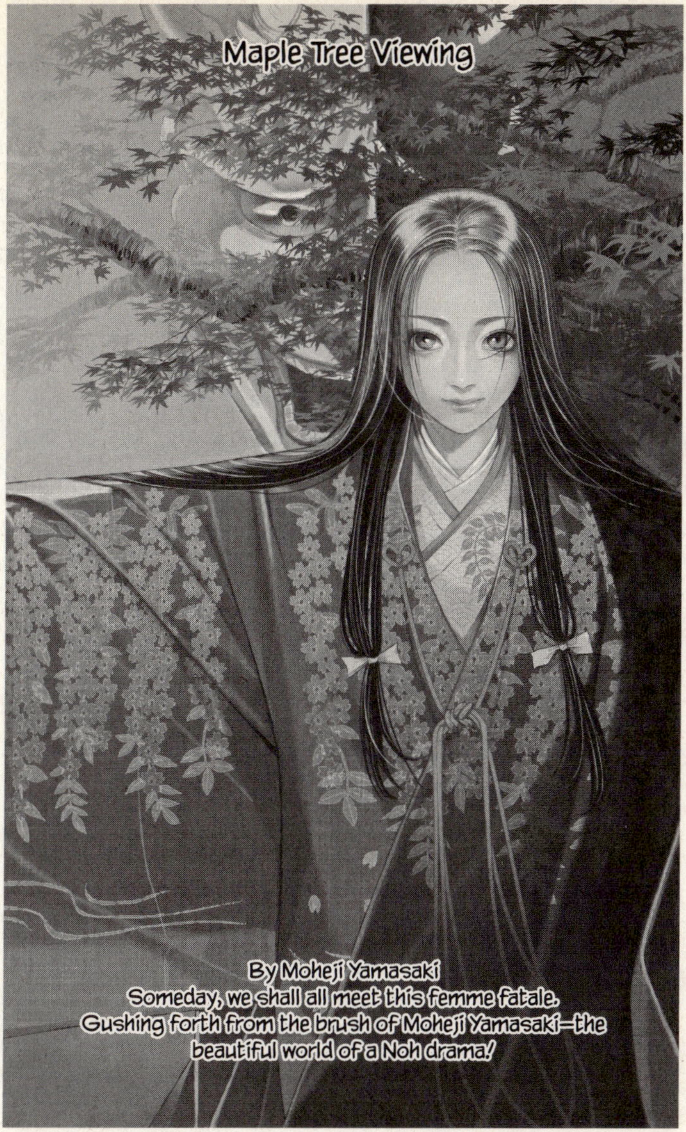
Maple Tree Viewing
By Moheji Yamasaki
Someday, we shall all meet this femme fatale.
Gushing forth from the brush of Moheji Yamasaki—the
beautiful world of a Noh drama!

▲▼▲▼

MAPLE TREE VIEWING

Moheji Yamasaki

Translated by Paul Johnson

M*aple Tree Viewing* is a fascinating mix of the new and the old. Artist Moheji Yamasaki's superbly contemporary style has made him a popular manga creator. But this piece is identified in the subtitle as a "Noh play, filled with color." Noh is a highly stylized and ritualized form of Japanese drama, with more than six hundred years of history. It is the foundation of the Japanese theatrical tradition, and while it has supernatural elements, vampires are a particularly modern addition to this manga drama! The blend of the classic and the modern is also shown in the accompanying text. This story, unlike most manga, contains no dialogue; instead, the text is drawn from classic Japanese poetry.

Moheji Yamasaki's most well-known work in Japan is his manga *The Adventures of Boy Detective Kyousuke Kouhaku: The High School Years* (based on Kaoru Hayamine's original novel series). He has established his reputation through a colorful fine art style.

▲▼▲▼

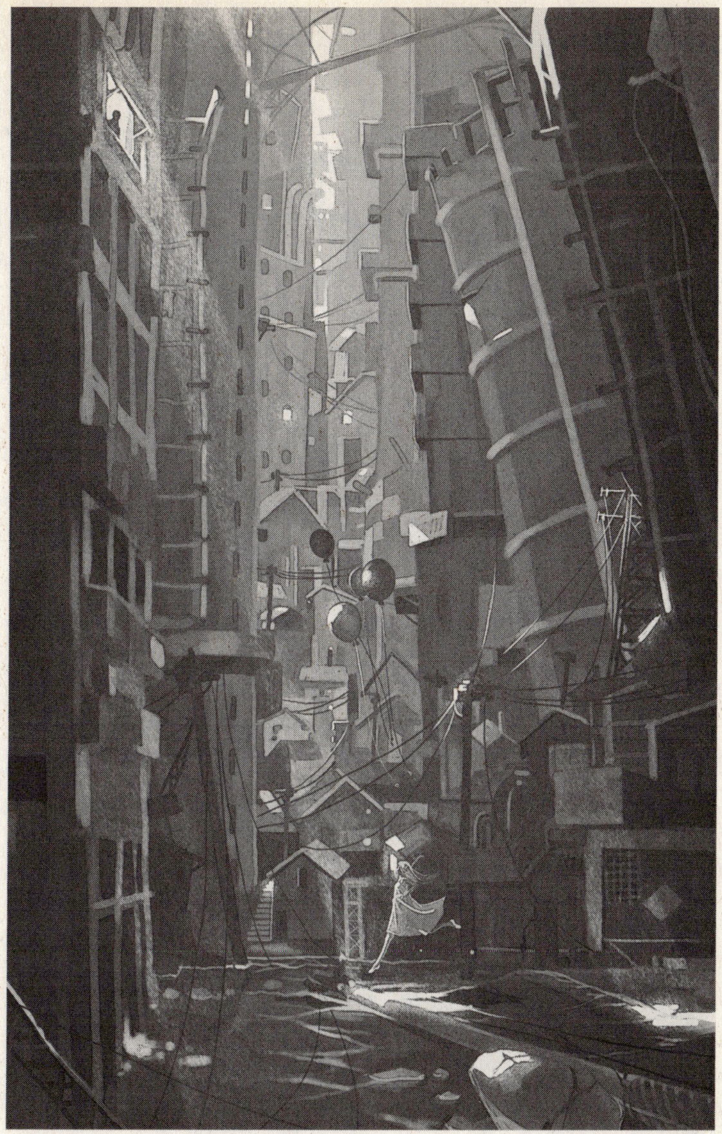

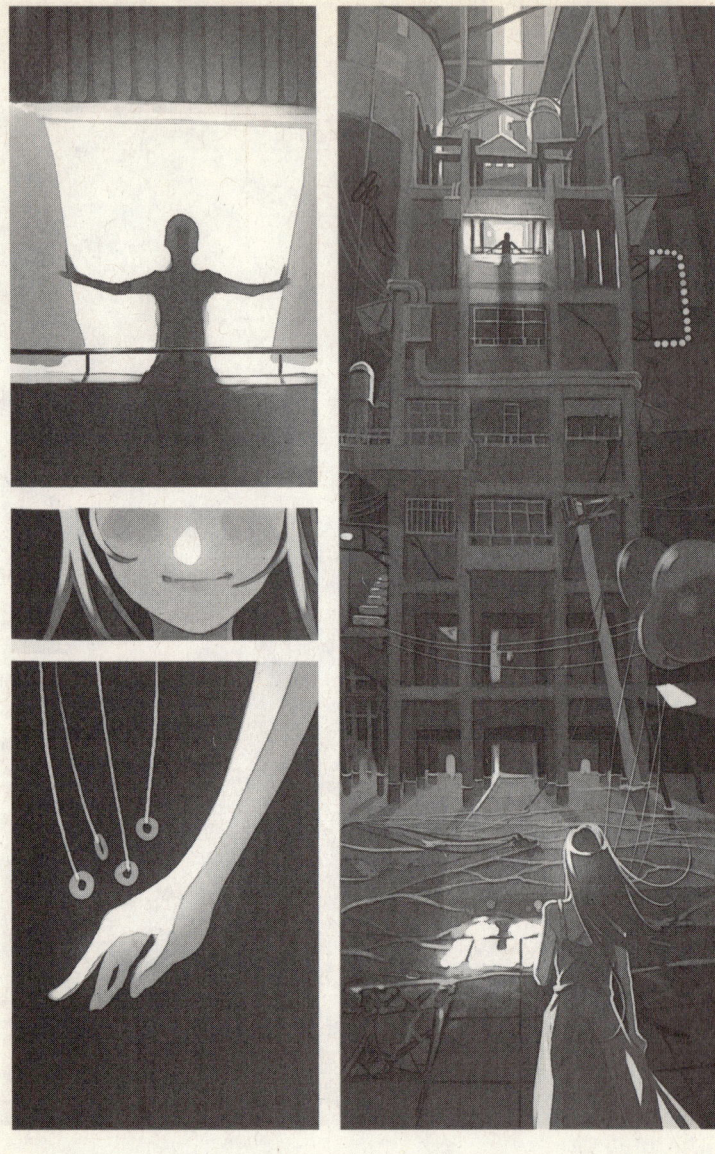

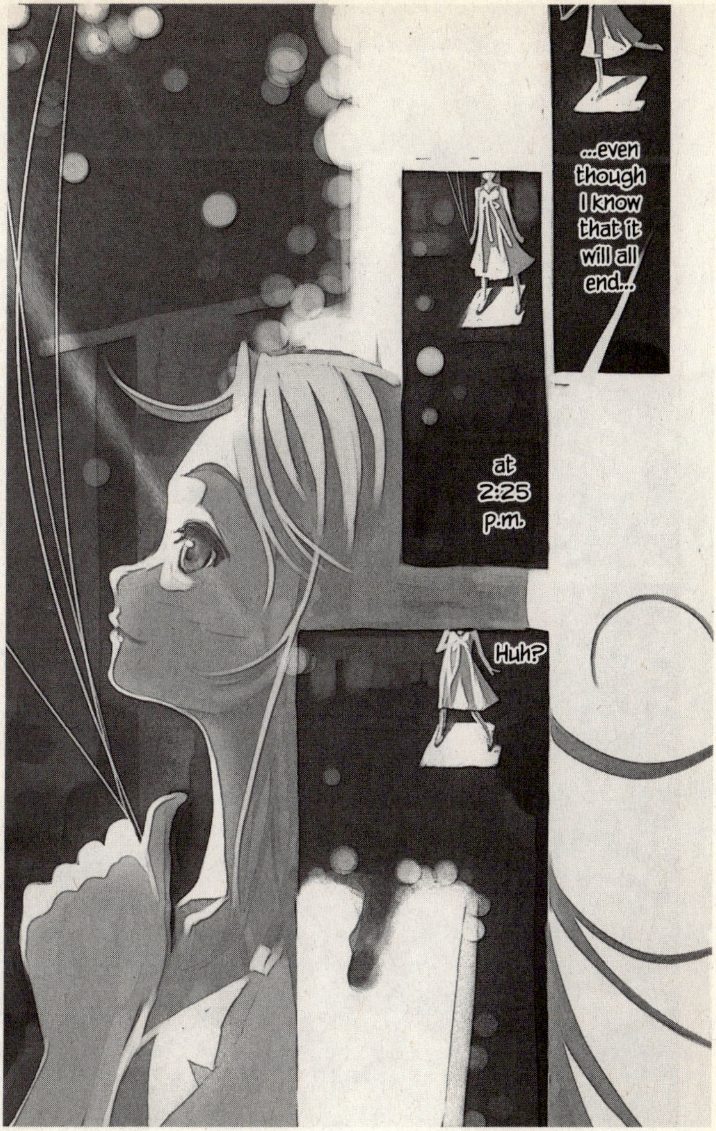
...even though I know that it will all end...
at 2:25 p.m.
Huh?

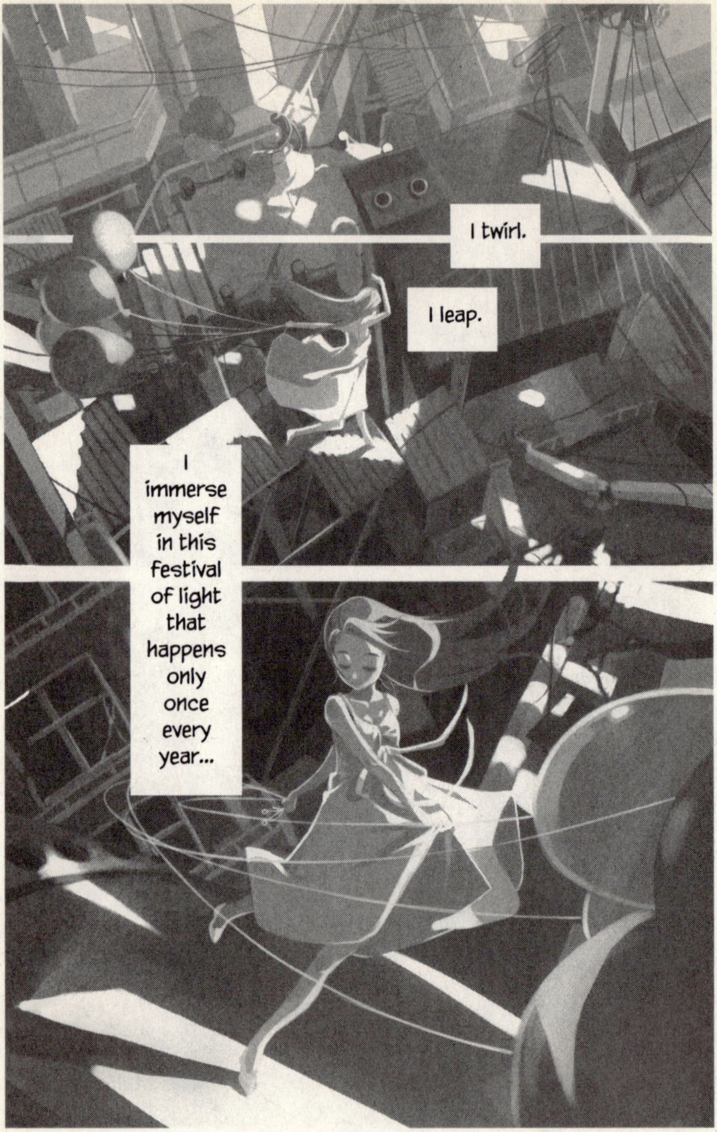
I twirl.
I leap.
I immerse myself in this festival of light that happens only once every year...

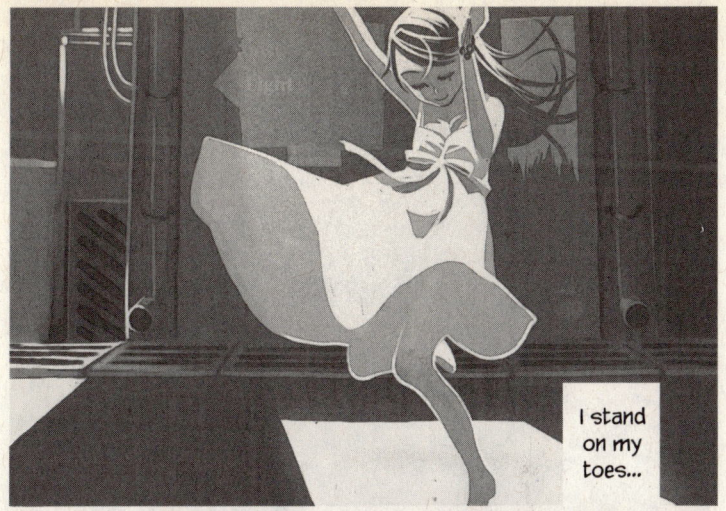

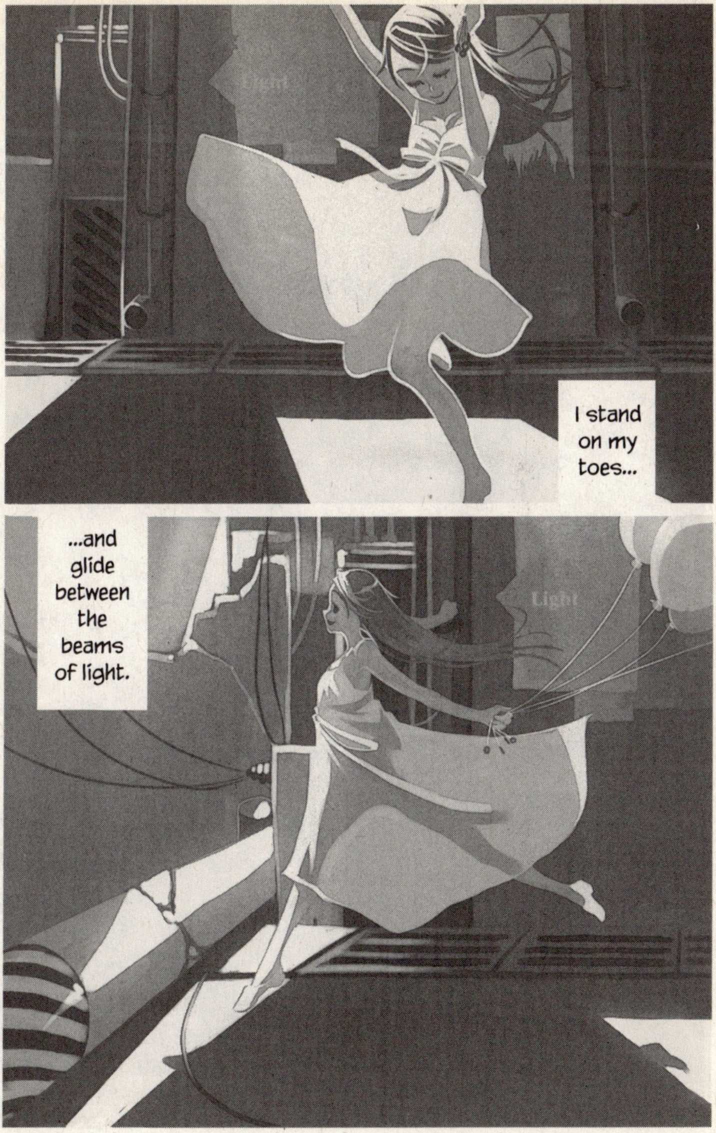
I stand on my toes...
...and glide between the beams of light.

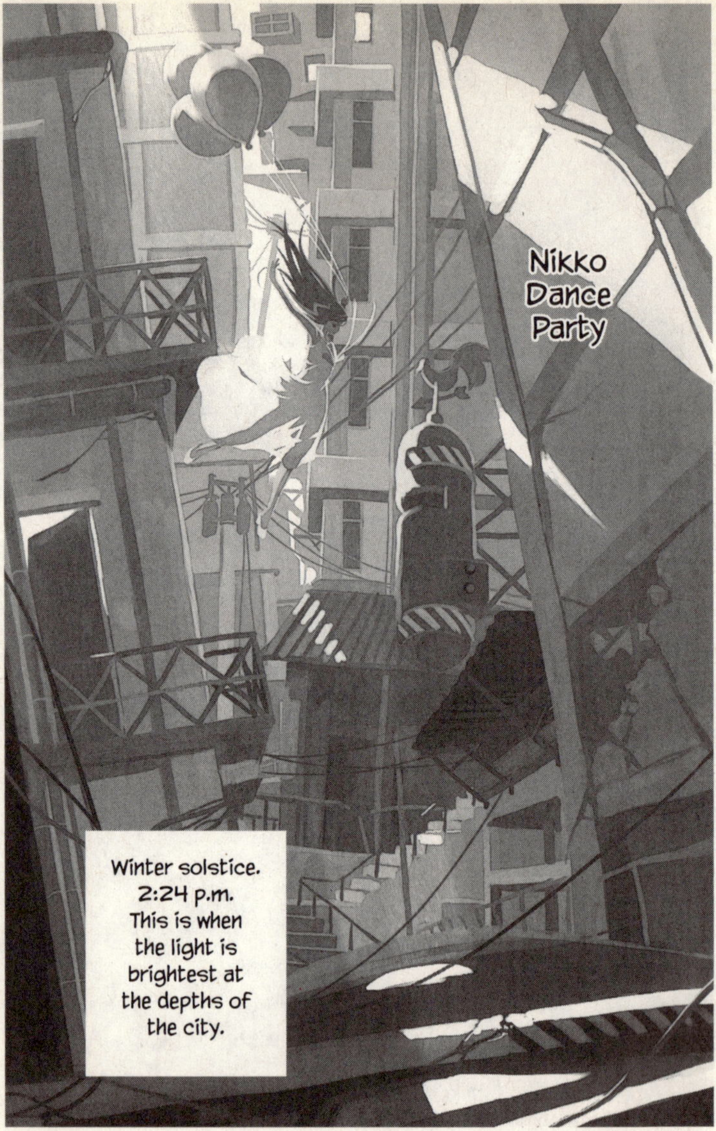
Nikko Dance Party
Winter solstice. 2:24 p.m. This is when the light is brightest at the depths of the city.

▲▽▲▽

NIKKO DANCE PARTY

VOFAN

Translated by Nancy Tsai

While *Faust* features the best and the brightest talents from Japan, *Faust*'s tireless editor, Katsushi Ota, is open to talents from abroad. VOFAN is one of the international stars he discovered for *Faust*. Born in 1980, VOFAN is Taiwanese. He has produced cover art for the Taiwanese edition of *Famitsu* magazine, and his illustrated stories are being published in *Monthly Challenger*. He has earned praise for his beautiful use of lighting, and has been called the "magician of light." He is in charge of art direction for NISIOISIN's new work *Bakemonogatari* and has a great many fans in Japan. His art book, *Colorful Dream* (published by Max Power in Taiwan), is scheduled for publication in Japan.

▲▽▲▽▽

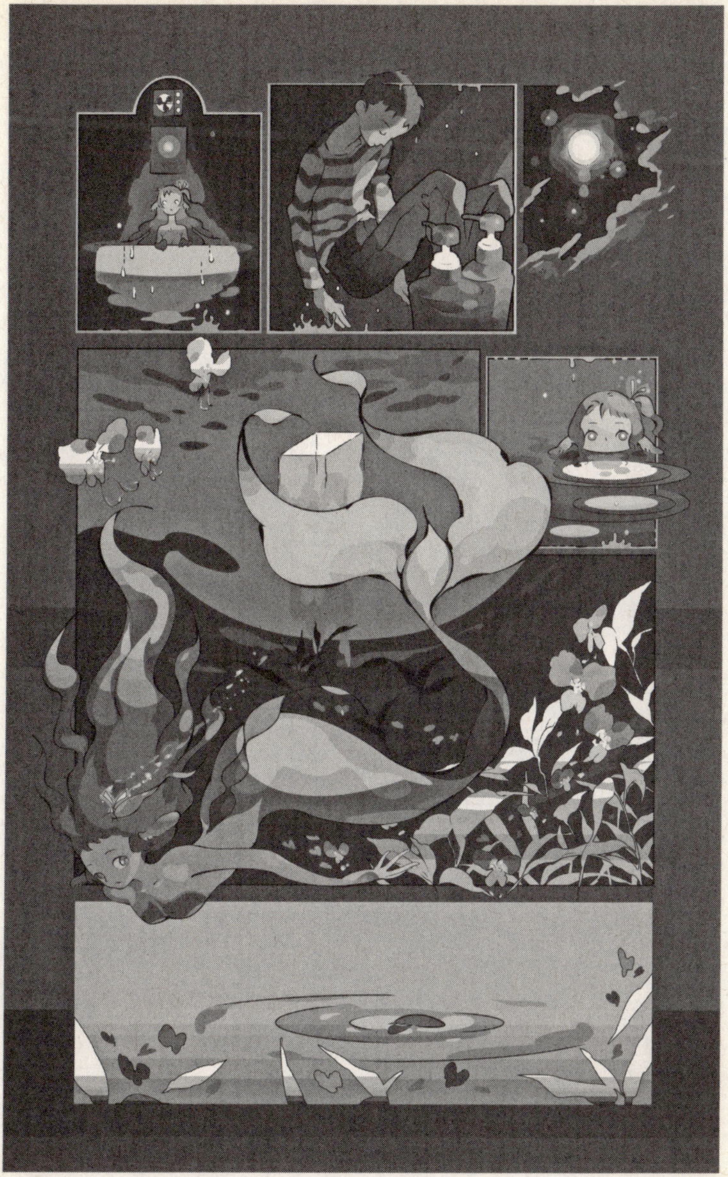

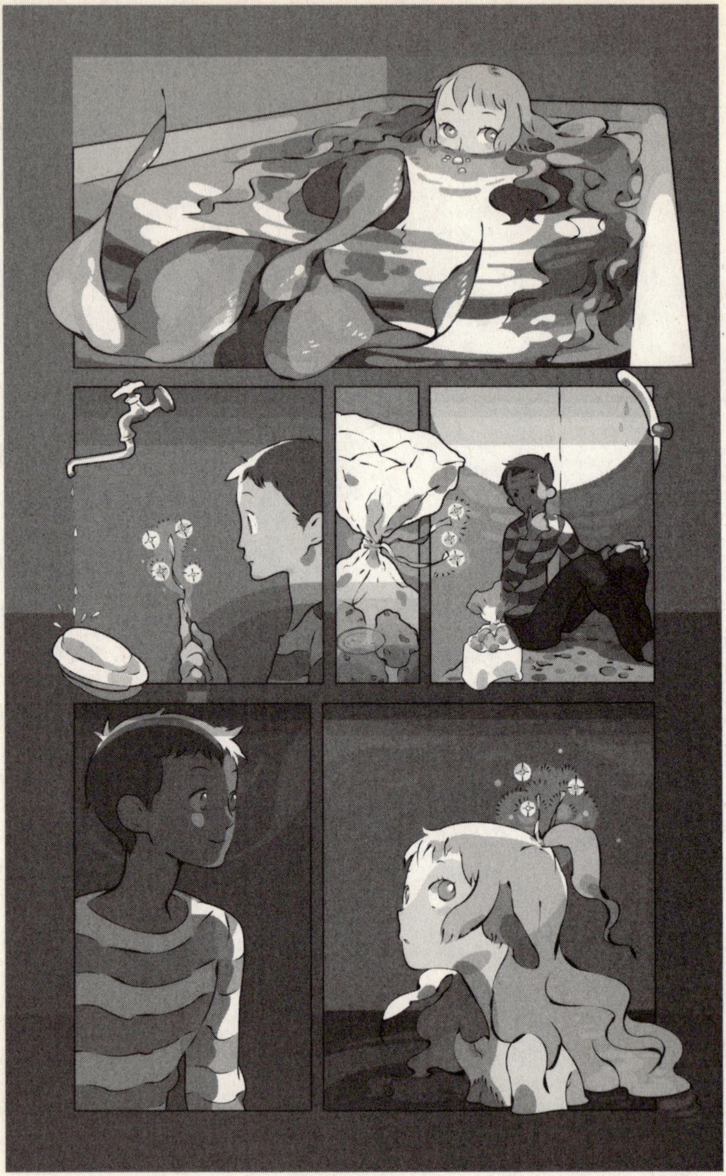

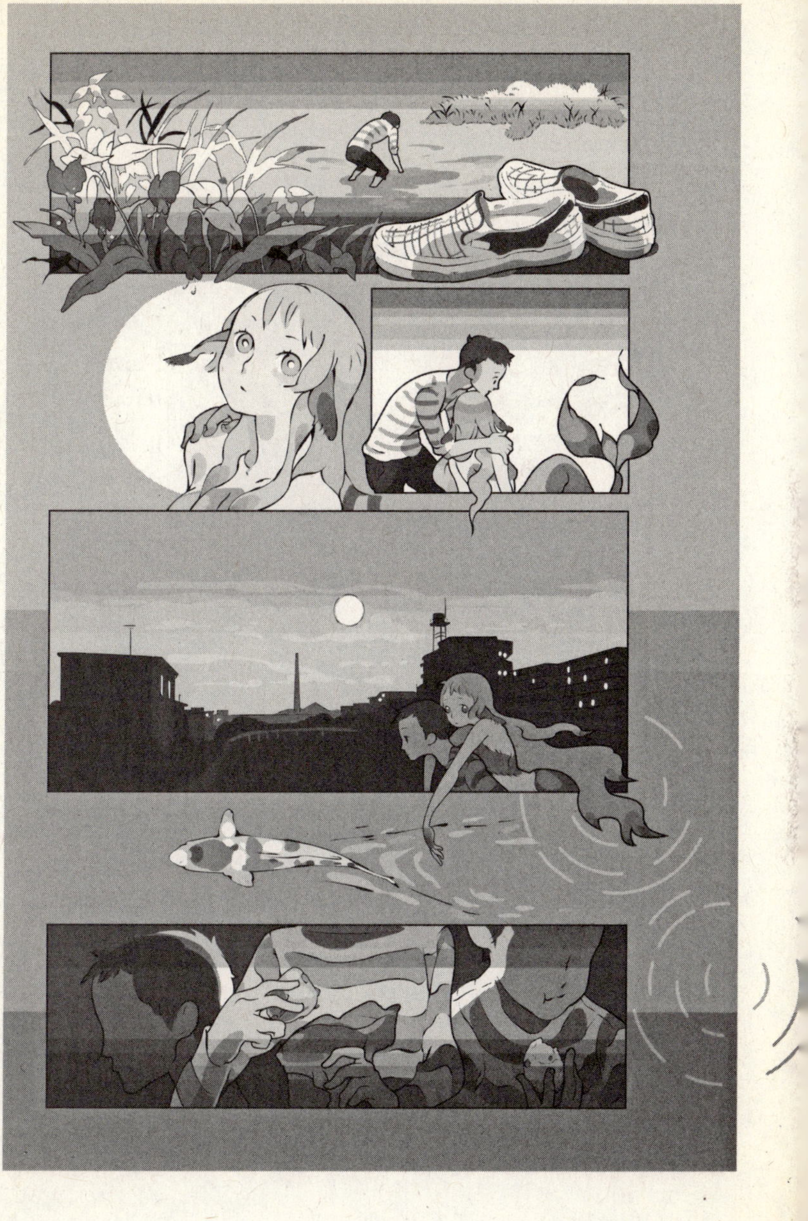

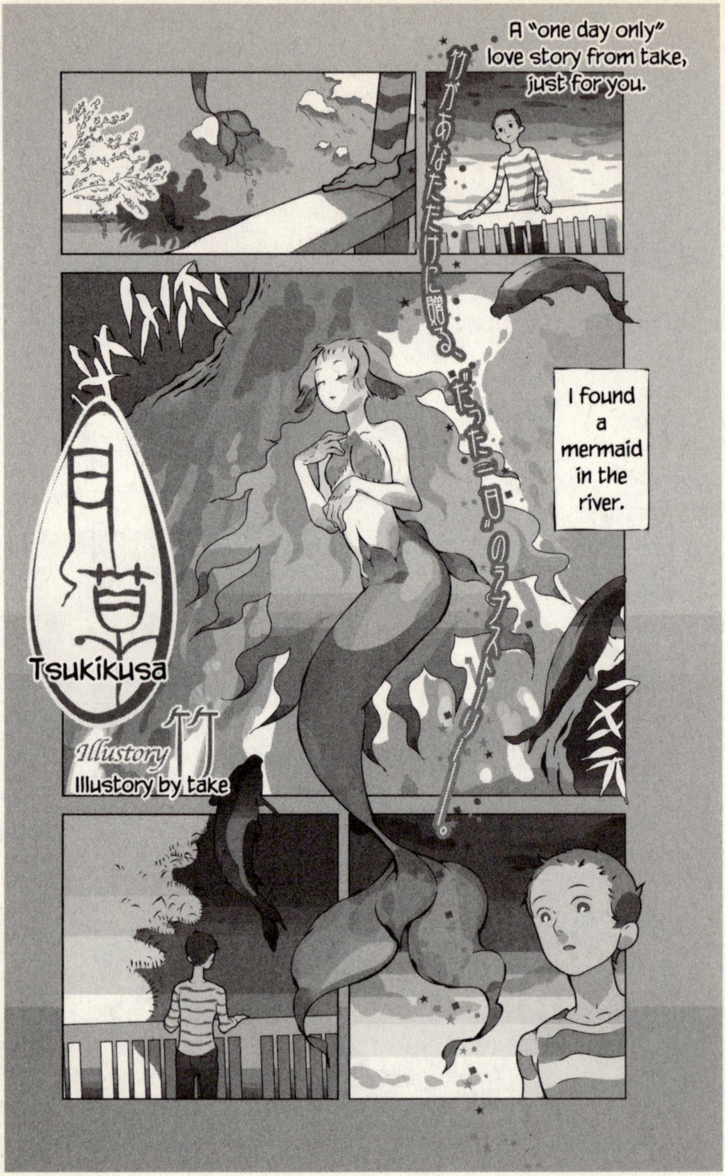
A "one day only" love story from take, just for you.
竹があなただけに贈る、"たった一日"のラブストーリー！。
I found a mermaid in the river.
月草
Tsukikusa
Illustory 竹
Illustory by take

▲▽▲▽

TSUKIKUSA

take

Translated by Paul Johnson

F*aust*'s Japanese version always features a mix of manga and prose fiction, of which *Tsukikusa* is a great example.

Tsukikusa is by a popular illustrator very closely identified with *Faust*, and one of *Faust*'s most popular authors, NISIOISIN. Born in 1983, take made a brilliant debut with his gorgeous, ultramodern illustrations for NISIOISIN's Zaregoto series. Just as that novel cemented NISIOISIN's reputation as one of the leading lights of Japanese pop culture, take's illustrations for these bestselling novels made him a star in his own right. His first-class character designs captured the readers' hearts in one fell swoop, and he is now ranked as one of the top young illustrators in Japan. This brilliantly talented illustrator loves cats and manga genius Osamu Tezuka. The cover illustration, specially commissioned for the United States edition of *Faust*, was also provided by take.

▲▽▲▽▽

CONTENTS
▲▼▲▼▲

MANGA AND ILLUSTRATED STORIES

Tsukikusa   420
   take

Nikko Dance Party   414
   VOFAN

Maple Tree Viewing   406
   Moheji Yamasaki

After School: 7th Class   398
   Art by Yun Kouga *story by NISIOISIN*

A NOTE ON READING THIS VOLUME

▲▼▲▼▲

Faust collects the best in cutting-edge Japanese fiction—whether the author's chosen medium is prose or manga.

Japanese books customarily read from right to left. Of necessity, the prose fiction and essays must be laid out left to right and can be found on the other side of this volume. However, the manga selections in this volume present a different challenge—to preserve the artist's original vision for his or her artwork. Therefore, in order to respect the creators' vision, the manga selections are presented on the following pages, in their original right-to-left orientation. Please turn the book over to read the prose selections.

山川に
風のかけたる
しがらみは

流れもあへぬ
紅葉なりけり

In a mountain stream, there is a wattled barrier built by the busy wind. Yet it's only maple leaves, powerless to flow away.

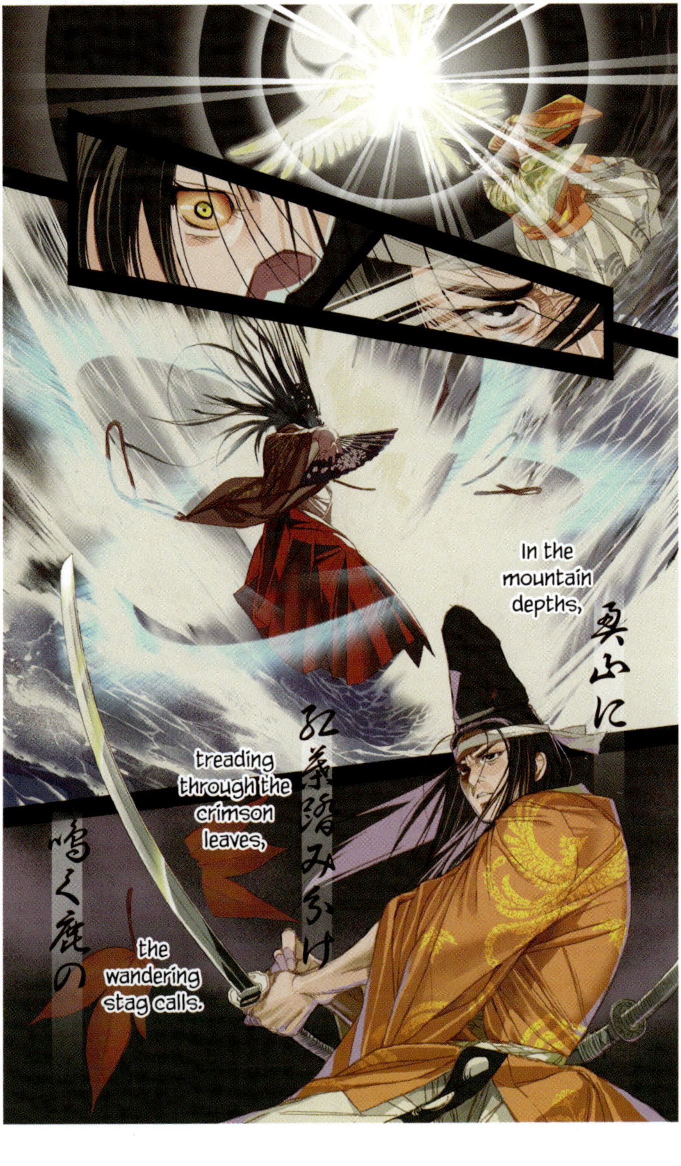
奥山に
In the mountain depths,
紅葉踏みわけ
treading through the crimson leaves,
鳴く鹿の
the wandering stag calls.

▲▼▲▼▲
MAPLE TREE VIEWING
Moheji Yamasaki
Translated by Paul Johnson

Maple Tree Viewing is a fascinating mix of the new and the old. Artist Moheji Yamasaki's superbly contemporary style has made him a popular manga creator. But this piece is identified in the subtitle as a "Noh play, filled with color." Noh is a highly stylized and ritualized form of Japanese drama, with more than six hundred years of history. It is the foundation of the Japanese theatrical tradition, and while it has supernatural elements, vampires are a particularly modern addition to this manga drama! The blend of the classic and the modern is also shown in the accompanying text. This story, unlike most manga, contains no dialogue; instead, the text is drawn from classic Japanese poetry.

Moheji Yamasaki's most well-known work in Japan is his manga *The Adventures of Boy Detective Kyousuke Kouhaku: The High School Years* (based on Kaoru Hayamine's original novel series). He has established his reputation through a colorful fine art style.

▲▼▲▼▲

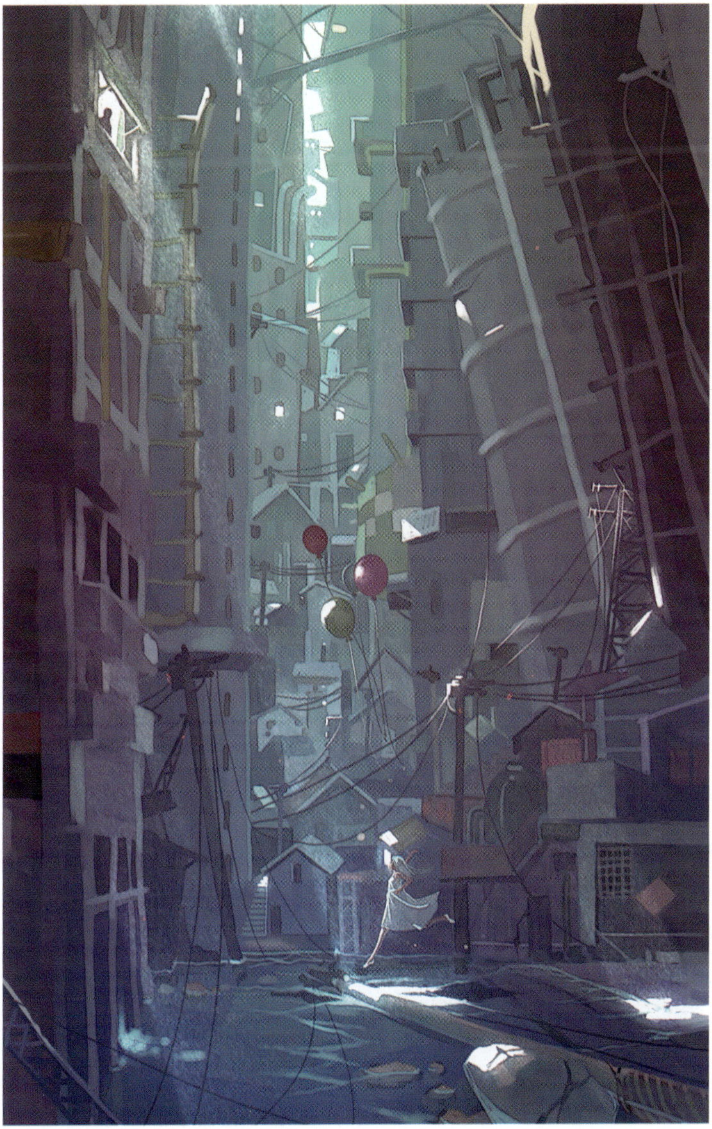

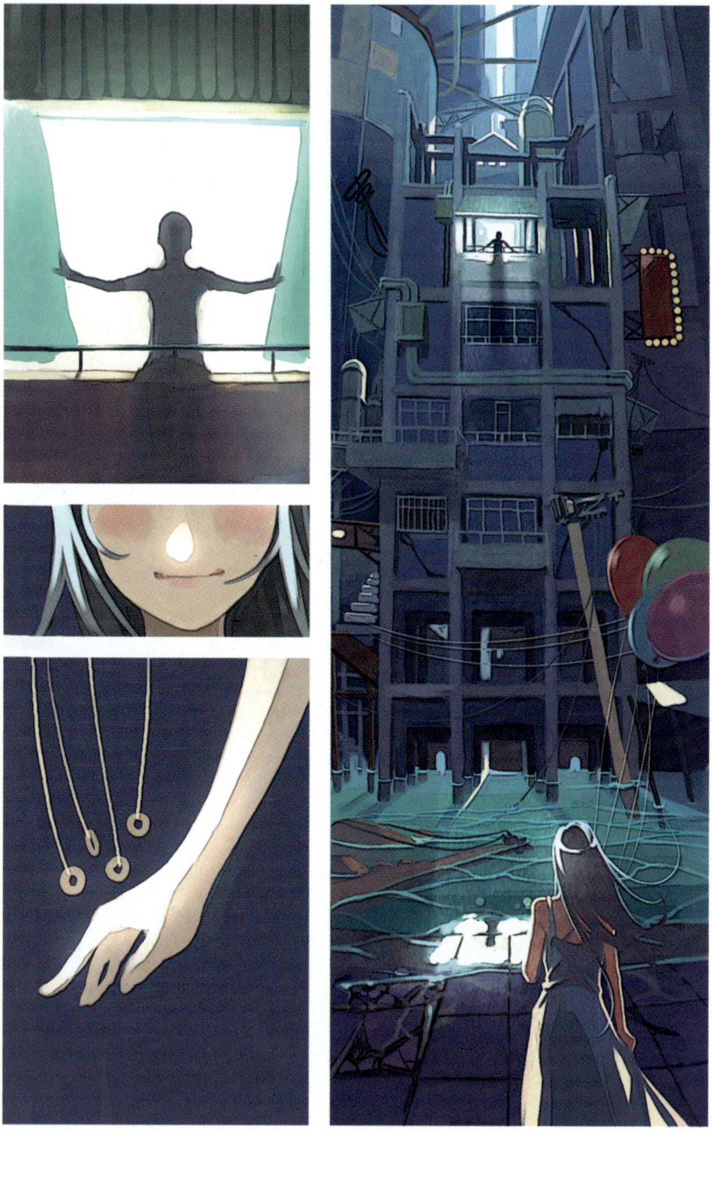

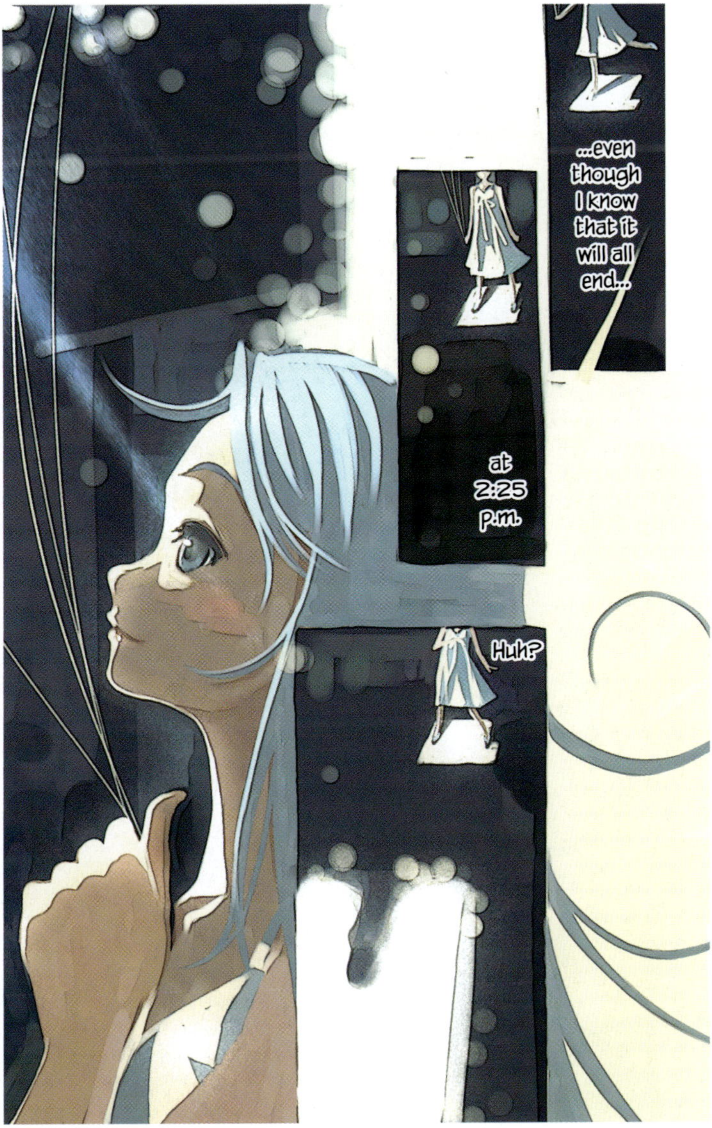
...even though I know that it will all end...
at 2:25 p.m.
Huh?

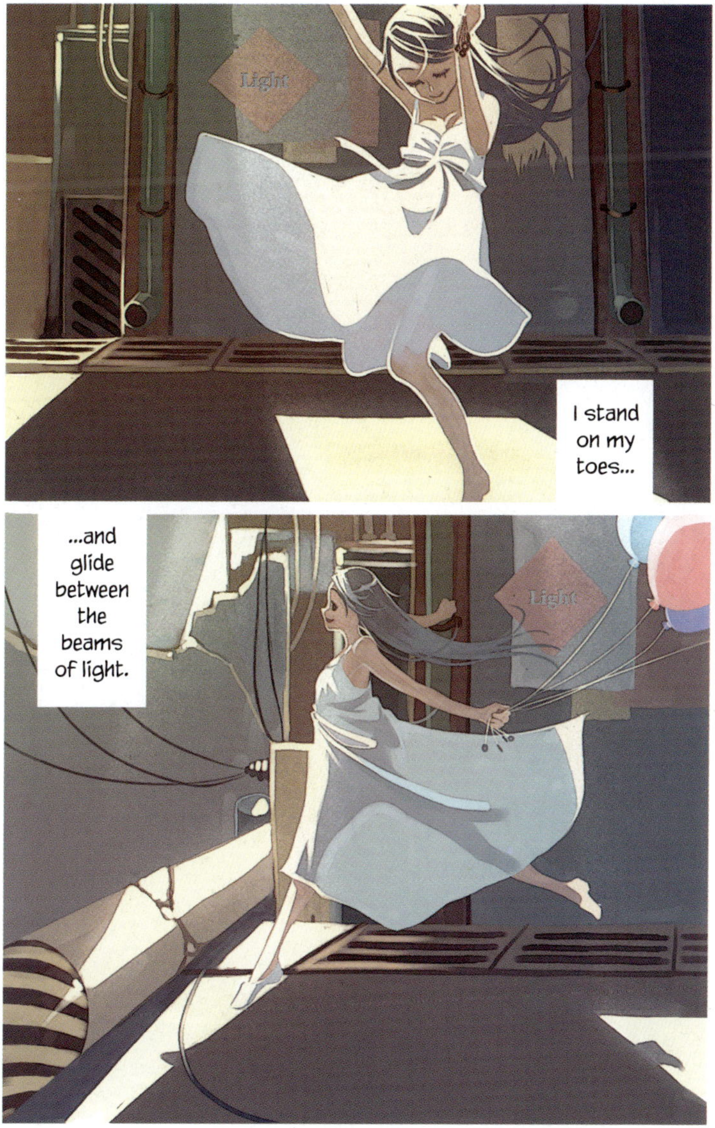
Light
I stand on my toes...
...and glide between the beams of light.
Light

F

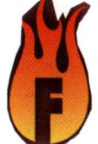

▲▼▲▼

NIKKO DANCE PARTY

VOFAN

Translated by Nancy Tsai

While *Faust* features the best and the brightest talents from Japan, *Faust*'s tireless editor, Katsushi Ota, is open to talents from abroad. VOFAN is one of the international stars he discovered for *Faust*. Born in 1980, VOFAN is Taiwanese. He has produced cover art for the Taiwanese edition of *Famitsu* magazine, and his illustrated stories are being published in *Monthly Challenger*. He has earned praise for his beautiful use of lighting, and has been called the "magician of light." He is in charge of art direction for NISIOISIN's new work *Bakemonogatari* and has a great many fans in Japan. His art book, *Colorful Dream* (published by Max Power in Taiwan), is scheduled for publication in Japan.

▲▼▲▼▲▼

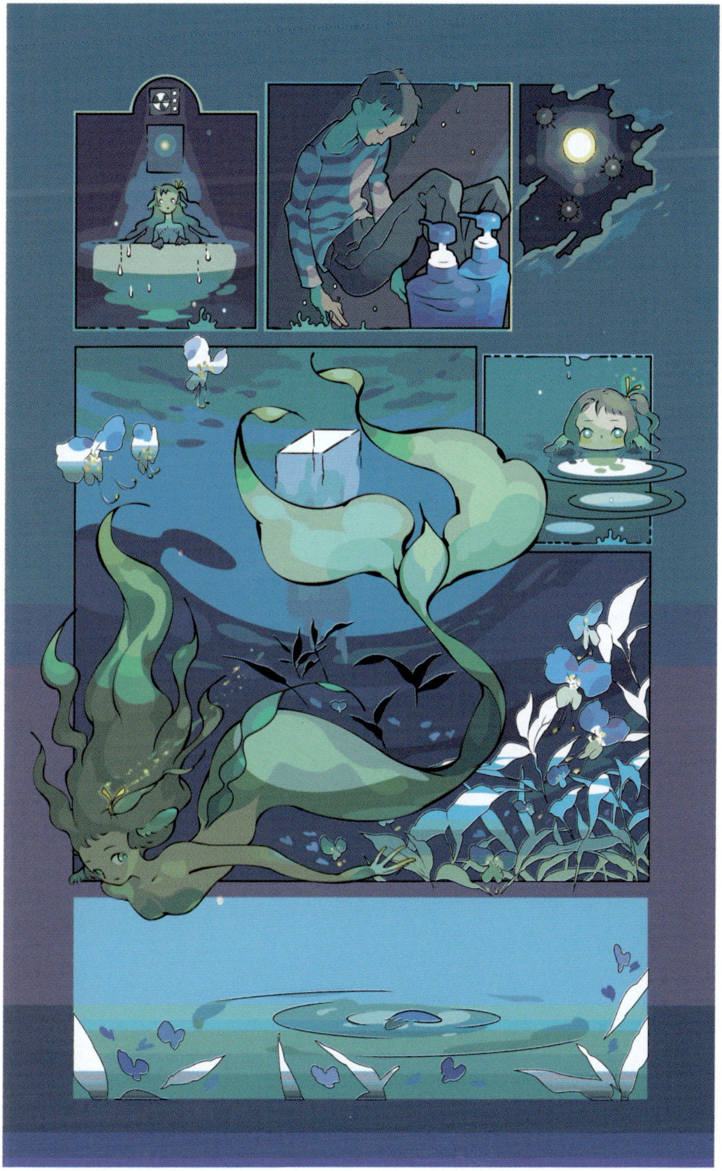

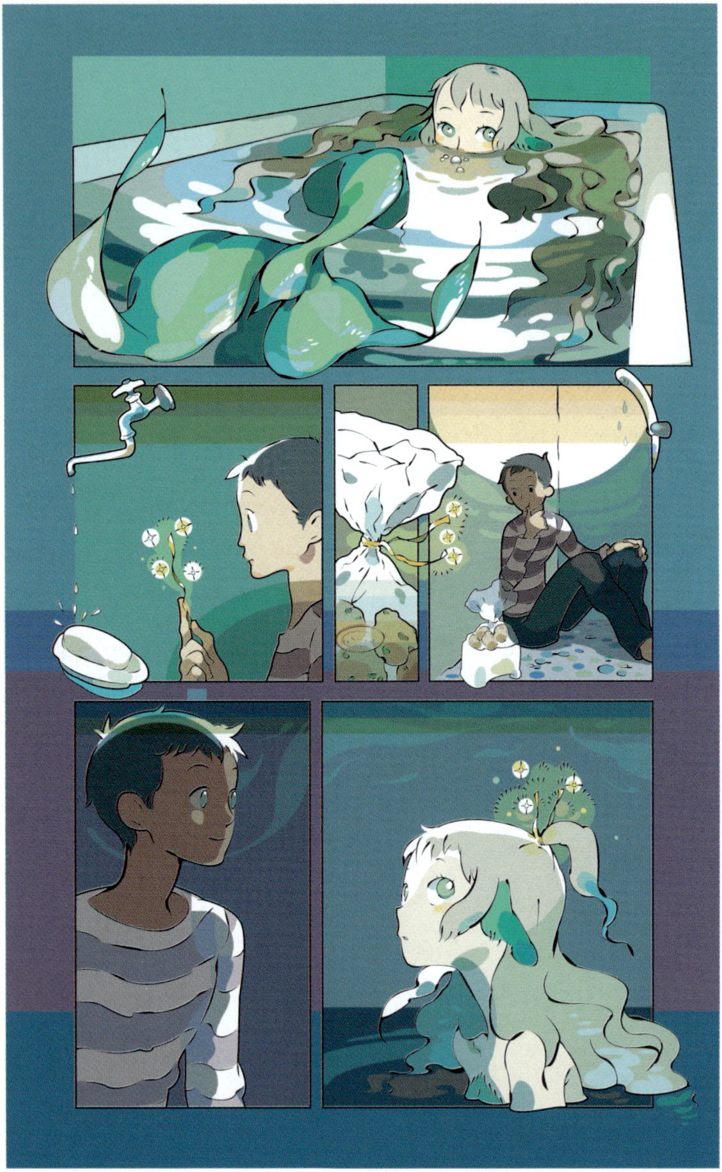

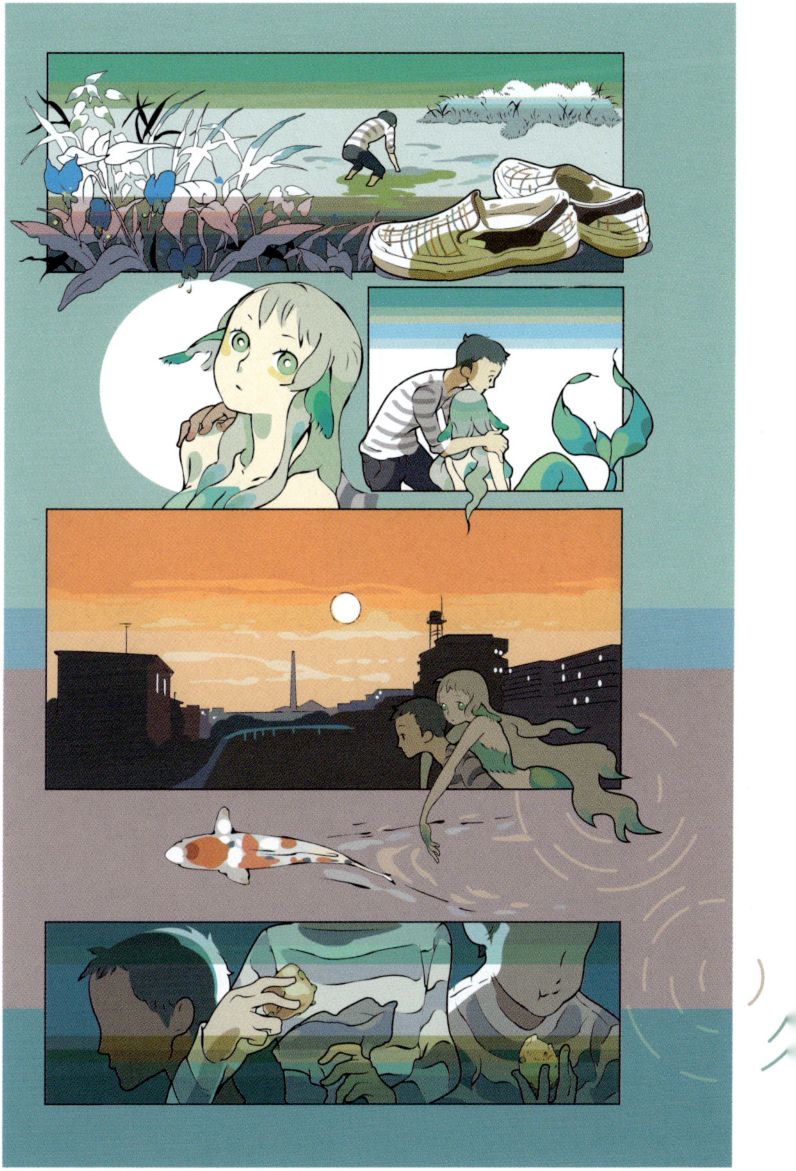

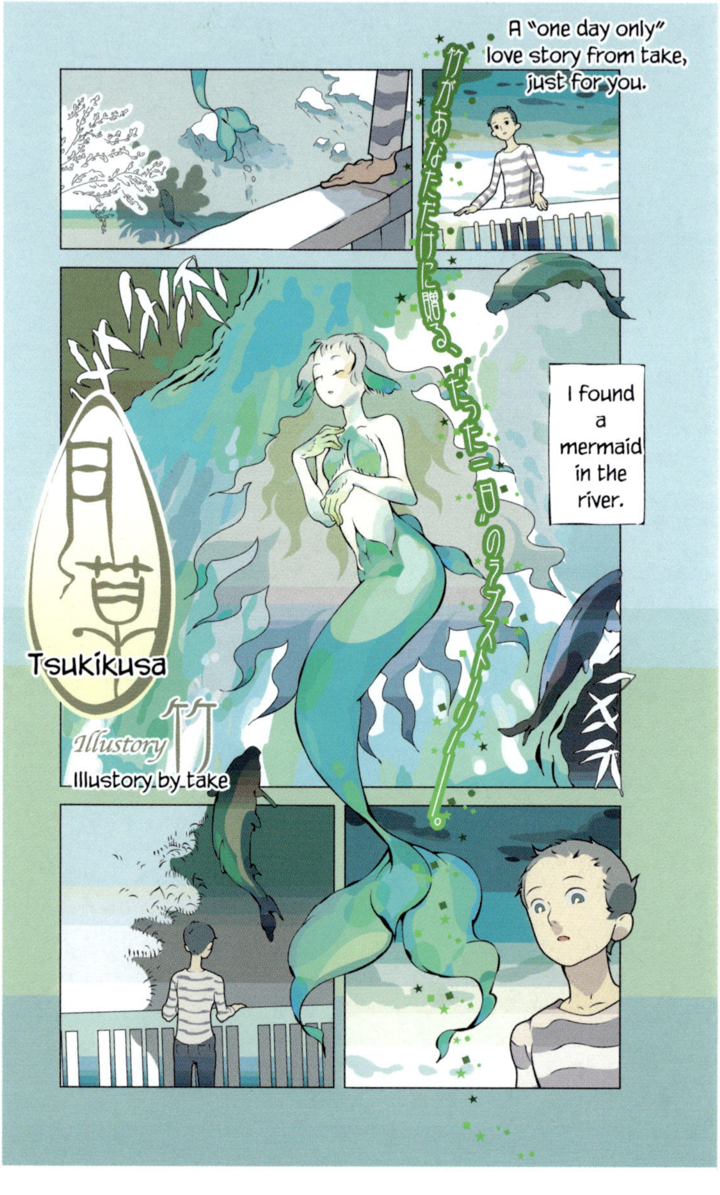
A "one day only" love story from take, just for you.
竹があなただけに贈る、たった一日のラブストーリー。
I found a mermaid in the river.
月草
Tsukikusa
Illustory 竹
Illustory by take

F

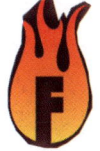

▲▼▲▼▲

TSUKIKUSA

take

Translated by Paul Johnson

Faust's Japanese version always features a mix of manga and prose fiction, of which *Tsukikusa* is a great example. *Tsukikusa* is by a popular illustrator very closely identified with *Faust,* and one of *Faust*'s most popular authors, NISIOISIN. Born in 1983, take made a brilliant debut with his gorgeous, ultramodern illustrations for NISIOISIN's Zaregoto series. Just as that novel cemented NISIOISIN's reputation as one of the leading lights of Japanese pop culture, take's illustrations for these bestselling novels made him a star in his own right. His first-class character designs captured the readers' hearts in one fell swoop, and he is now ranked as one of the top young illustrators in Japan. This brilliantly talented illustrator loves cats and manga genius Osamu Tezuka. The cover illustration, specially commissioned for the United States edition of *Faust,* was also provided by take.

▲▼▲▼▼

CONTENTS

▲▼▲▼▲

MANGA AND *ILLUSTRATED STORIES*

Tsukikusa take	420
Nikko Dance Party VOFAN	414
Maple Tree Viewing Moheji Yamasaki	406
After School: 7th Class Art by Yun Kouga *story by NISIOISIN*	398

A NOTE ON READING THIS VOLUME

▲▼▲▼▲

Faust collects the best in cutting-edge Japanese fiction—whether the author's chosen medium is prose or manga.

Japanese books customarily read from right to left. Of necessity, the prose fiction and essays must be laid out left to right and can be found on the other side of this volume. However, the manga selections in this volume present a different challenge—to preserve the artist's original vision for his or her artwork. Therefore, in order to respect the creators' vision, the manga selections are presented on the following pages, in their original right-to-left orientation. Please turn the book over to read the prose selections.